I0648105

ALL-STAR ZEPPELIN ADVENTURE STORIES

ALL-STAR STORIES • SEATTLE, WASHINGTON, USA
WHEATLAND PRESS • WILSONVILLE, OREGON, USA

"SO YOU NEED ME TO STOP THE NAZIS FROM BUILDING A DEATH RAY?"

The General's brow creased. "I suppose you could put it that way, yes. The device will be so massive that only an airship can transport it effectively to inland targets. And they intend to begin construction on the weapon system in a matter of days."

"You can count on me, General," said Hugh. "Those Nazis won't know what hit 'em."

"Subtlety, Betcha," the General said. "This can't make the news. Best if the Nazis never know you were there. We don't want anyone launching a war just yet. The last thing we need right now is another international incident."

"I'm not afraid of the Nazis, sir—they're a cowardly lot. I'll do my darnedest to make sure that America won't fall under Hitler's tyrannical heel."

"And I don't mean subtle like that weapons cache you blew up in Czechoslovakia last fall—"

"We're wasting time, General," said Hugh. "I'd love to stay and chat, but the Nazis won't wait."

"All right, then," said the General. "Oh, I almost forgot. Sally couldn't come to see you off, but she asked me to give you this." He handed Hugh a rubbery chew toy. "For the ferret."

Hugh took the toy and saluted the General.

"God bless America."

—Jed Hartman, "The Last of the Zeppelins"

ALL-STAR
ZEPPELIN
ADVENTURE STORIES

edited by

David Moles & Jay Lake

ALL ✪ STAR STORIES

SEATTLE, WASHINGTON, USA

🌾 Wheatland Press

WILSONVILLE, OREGON, USA

Anthology and front matter copyright ©2004 by David Moles and Joseph E. Lake, Jr.

"The Voice of the Hurricane" ©2004 by Paul Berger.
"The Last of the Zeppelins" ©2004 by Jedediah Hartman.
"The Eckener Alternative" ©2004 by James L. Cambias.
"Instead of a Loving Heart" ©2004 by Jeremy Tolbert.
"This is the Highest Step in the World" ©2004 by Carrie Vaughn.
"The Sky's the Limit" ©2004 by Lawrence M. Schoen.
"A Perilous Warm Embrace" ©2004 by Michael Manis.
"Sky Light" ©2004 by David Brin. First part originally published as "2020 VISION: Journalism the Day After Tomorrow" in *Online Journalism Review*, March 2004. Reprinted by permission of the author.
"Negation Elimination" ©2004 by Robert Burke Richardson.
"Why a Duck" ©2004 by Leslie What.
"Matriarch" ©2004 by Forrest Aguirre.
"Aerophilia" ©2004 by Tobias S. Buckell.
"The Jewels of Lemuria" ©2004 by Richard A. Lupoff.
"Counting Zeppelins" ©2004 by Eric T. Marin.
"Love in the Balance" ©2004 by David D. Levine.
"Where and When" ©2004 by James Van Pelt.
"Seven Dragons Mountains" ©2004 by Sarah B.E. Kindred.
"Silk" ©2004 by Lee Battersby.
"Biographical Notes to 'A Discourse on the Nature of Causality, with Air-Planes' by Benjamin Rosenbaum" ©2004 by Benjamin Rosenbaum.
"You *Could* Go Home Again" ©1993 by Howard Waldrop. Originally published as a limited edition by Cheap Street Publishers, October 1993. Reprinted by permission of the author.

All rights reserved. No part of this publication may be reproduced or transmitted in any form or by any means, electronic or mechanical, including photocopy, recording, or any information storage and retrieval system, without permission in writing from both the copyright owner and the publisher. Requests for permission to make copies of any part of the work should be mailed to the following address: All-Star Stories, 3518 Fremont Ave. N. #524, Seattle, WA 98103.

These are works of fiction. Names, characters, places and incidents either are the products of the authors' imaginations or are used ficticiously, and any resemblance to actual persons, living or dead, business establishments, events, or locales is entirely coincidental.

Library of Congress Cataloging-in-Publication data is available on request.
ISBN 0-9720547-7-4

Cover painting and jacket design by Lara Wells
Interior design by David Moles

DAVID'S DEDICATION

*To my grandfathers, pilots both: Marine Capt. Francis W. Moles,
U.S.M.C. Reserve, and Capt. David W. Henderson, U.S.N.—men
who, in a different world, might have flown zeppelins*

JAY'S DEDICATION

*To my grandfathers: Floyd Ival Bryant, who didn't live long enough
to know me at all; Charles Lawrence Kessler, who might have
understood and would have been proud; Dr. Lloyd Euel Lake, who
haunts my words with his fierce, iron love, but will never know why.*

As well as all the people who keep me flying every day.

And most of all to TL, who does know why.

PREFACE

DAVID

SUMMER, THE LAST YEAR OF THE COLD WAR. A second-class compartment of a west-bound express, somewhere east of the Wall. The Gypsy guitarist who shared our compartment for the first leg of the journey is gone now, removed by the guards some time in the night, when we crossed the Byelorussian frontier.

A day and a half ago, in Moscow, we bought some cheese *piroshki* and some small, pale apples from a street vendor. Since then—being less than tempted by the dining car's greasy fare—I have eaten almost nothing, and this may go some way toward explaining my fevered scribbling, the disorder of my thoughts.

The paper in front of me is full of formulas: the equations of ellipses and ellipsoids, collections of scratched-out integrals and derivatives, Boyle's Law.

Let $v=4\pi r_1 r_2 r_3$ be the volume of the airship. Let $28(0.78) + 32(0.22) \approx 29g/mol$ be the molecular weight of air. Let $4g/mol$ be the molecular weight of helium . . . .

My shoes are full of black-market rubles.

My head is full of zeppelins.

Once, and not that long ago, zeppelins were the future. The end of the Victorian era saw the fabulous and solitary flying machine imagined in Verne's 1866 *Robur le conquerant* give way to the crowded commercial skies of Rudyard Kipling's 1905 "With the Night Mail," filled with airships of every description, from passenger liners, to tramp freighters, to tethered navigation beacons, to the swift, faithful, steadfast Night Mail of the title.* In the early days of Dr. Eckener's dream machine, the future Kipling imagined did not seem at all far-fetched, and it became the model for countless others. It remained a plausible future, or at any rate a possible one, all through the first half of the twentieth century, before it was finally overtaken by events—made obsolete in the real world by the DC-3 and the Boeing 377 and the Lockheed Constellation, and in the collective unconscious by the Space Age.

So why do zeppelins still capture the imagination today?

The real zeppelins of the past, the *Graf Zeppelin* and the *Hindenburg*, England's *R.101*, capture our imagination the way trains do, and ocean liners, and flying boats: they evoke for us a vision of a time (it seems to us, now) when travel was more civilized, when journeys were measured not in hours spent in a holding pattern over Cleveland but in days spent dancing to the music of the ship's band, when men wore hats and women wore dresses, when in-flight meals were *haute cuisine* served on bone china, when one might find half the cast of an Agatha Christie novel as one's chance-met table companions.

This vision has its dark side, of course. A ticket for one of those voyages would have been more expensive, in today's terms, than a first-class intercontinental ticket on Virgin Atlantic; and that very exclusivity is part of what makes the spacious, elegant cabin of a zeppelin compare so well to the cramped and pedestrian confines

*You can find "With the Night Mail" on line, in various places. Another Kipling airship story set in the same future, "As Easy as A.B.C.," is collected in Tom Shippey's *Oxford Book of Science Fiction Stories*.

of a modern airline seat. We can only hope that we may be forgiven the occasional anti-democratic fantasy.

Then there are the unbuilt zeppelins of the futures we never had. Kipling, like the mid-century pioneers of genre SF (who taught a generation to look forward—in vain—to moon colonies and flying cars and robot servants), wrote "With the Night Mail" in what must have been, for him, a time of great optimism. The British Empire was at the height of its power, Europe was at peace, scientific progress seemed sure to make the twentieth century an age of wonders. But the twentieth century we got—one of immense technological and social advancement, true, but also one of incalculable horror and suffering—is not the one we were promised, and the twenty-first isn't looking so good, either. A generation may be growing up now, at last, that has never had to live with the fear—no—the *certainty* of nuclear annihilation; but we now have a menu of new fears to choose from, not least the ever-more-likely-looking prospect that the twenty-first century will just be more of what the twentieth was for so many: war, poverty, oppression, brutality, and more war.

At a time when the future looks dark, it's natural to turn back to a time when it looked brighter, whether to ask "What went wrong?" or merely to lose ourselves, for a little while, in the dreams of what now seems a more innocent age. From here, the view of Kipling's tranquil, airship-filled skies (there are no wars in his future, and no government other than that provided by the light and reluctant hand of the postal service) looks very inviting.*

*Michael Moorcock skewered this nostalgia very deftly in his three Oswald Bastable novels, particularly the first, *The Warlord of the Air*— a classic zeppelin story if there ever was one—which shows us first a Kipling utopia and then its dark underside, an alternate twentieth century that in the end is revealed as a mirror of our own.

Nevertheless, that's a lot of weight for one lighter-than-air symbol to carry.

Not all of the stories in this book are as peaceful as "With the Night Mail," or as relaxing as a transcontinental voyage on Howard Waldrop's U.S.I.A.S. *Ticonderoga*. It seems that when you offer most authors a zeppelin, their first impulse is to crash it, set fire to it, or blow it up. (Or, in one extreme case, set upon it an undersea monster that would not look out of place in a Toho film.) These are, after all, zeppelin *adventure* stories. But there are also any number of adventures one can have aboard a zeppelin that leave the zeppelin intact, and our authors have provided plenty of those as well. We did allow certain liberties to be taken: there is a hot-air balloon story; there is a high-altitude helium balloon story; there is even a tethered barrage balloon story. There are talking zeppelins, living zeppelins, zeppelins dead and embalmed, giant zeppelins, miniature zeppelins, real zeppelins, dream zeppelins, zeppelins of the future, zeppelins of the past—zeppelins of the imagination.

So raise the gangplank, let fall the cables and the ballast. Open the throttles on those twenty-cylinder Maybachs and bring the nose up. The skies of the future may no longer belong to zeppelins, but the skies of the imagination are open, and always will be. ✪

JAY

MY FIRST MENTAL IMAGE OF A ZEPPELIN is from the iconic Led Zeppelin album cover. I was a small child when that was released, but it permeated my consciousness early on. Later zeppelin favorites include Moorcock's *The Warlord of the Air*, all the conveyances of Barsoom, and—in more recent years—*Sky Galleons of Mars* and

Crimson Skies played on tabletops long into the night at the Western Oregon Wargamers clubhouse in southeast Portland.

Real zeppelins? Pshaw. Terrible, clumsy things. Dangerous and slow. Emblems of gilded age capitalism and Junker hierarchy running amok across our cloud-raddled skies. Until you see one, of course. And there are no zeppelins, not any more—though there are changes on that front, too, as of the summer of 2004—but we still have airships. So you scoff and you scorn until you see one, then you stop your car or get off your bike and tilt your head back and stare into that same cloud-raddled sky with your mouth open like any kid with a spring cold, breath rattling until your lips go gummy.

It is the fascination of the large.

c-17s and 747s go by too fast. Buildings don't go anywhere at all. Aircraft carriers are so big as to be unreal. In fact, the only thing that compares to an airship in sheer wonderment is the Spruce Goose, now in permanent retirement here in Oregon, far from any water she could ever lumber across again.

Howard Hughes' defense boondoogle has a lot in common with those airships of old. Sheer improbability. Bloody-minded individualism of Randian proportions.

And largeness.

If you don't have a zeppelin to visit, come to Oregon and check out the Spruce Goose in McMinnville. Then head on down to Tillamook and visit the air museum, conveniently located in an old Navy blimp hangar. You'll appreciate large all over again.

Large, romantic objects beget large, romantic fiction. Not every story in this book is so big on the outside. Some are quite small, packed tightly into dreams and fancies. But others splash across the canvas of pulp and adventure and even, almost, into planetary romance. And they all live large, hearts of gas within

doped fabric, while smart-suited minions race along perilous catwalks on unknown, static-free missions. Come motor the skies at
your ease with these authors and their worlds, and marvel at what
will never be. ✪

ACKNOWLEDGMENTS

The editors would like to thank the following people: Deborah
Layne of Wheatland Press, our publisher, not only for making
this book possible but for making its creation, at every step of
the process, much easier and more pleasant than it might have
been. Greg van Eekhout, for bravely volunteering to come up to
Portland and help us sort through the hundreds of submissions
we received, and for nobly forgoing the chance to write his own
zeppelin story. Lara Wells, for painting us a fantastic cover despite
David's meddling. Jed Hartman, for bringing to our attention
Howard Waldrop's "You *Could* Go Home Again." Sen Nagata,
for, once upon a time, introducing David to the films of Hayao
Miyazaki. David's father, Wayne Moles, for providing the radio-
controlled blimp we flew at Norwescon 27. Darrel Schweitzer,
for persistently invoking at TorCon 3 the name of the all-but-
apocryphal *Spicy Zeppelin Stories*, sparking in our heads the light
of an idea we were never quite able to extinguish.

And, finally, we would like to thank everyone who sent us a
story. ✪

CONTENTS

VOICE OF THE HURRICANE

BY PAUL BERGER

WHEN A HERD OF ZEPPELINS comes over the horizon, you can kiss your farm goodbye.

Imagine a swarm of lackadaisical locusts—better yet, imagine a throng of elephants in the sky over your fields, arrogant, untouchable and rapacious, scooping up crops, silos, topsoil, outhouses, and lifting them through five hundred feet of empty sky into loose, slow-chewing maws.

Now make each of those elephants fifty times bigger. That's what you've got when the zeppelins find you.

It is the great zeppelin herds—leaving blackened trails a mile wide across the plains—that have kept the white man from settling the Midwest for so long. The Sioux have their tricks for trapping them of course, and in a good year a tribe might get one or even two, and then there will be zeppelin-hide clothes and impermeable gas bladder teepees and smoked zep steaks for them all well into the next hunting season.

But one or two a year won't make a difference, any more than one or two drops siphoned out of the Mississippi would change its course. Ask the owners of a Kansas clipper smoking cigars in some Chicago club what their business is, and they'll tell you, Why of course, it's feeding the unquenchable hunger of city folks back east for the hydrogen to lift their airships. You must remember the owners are one thing, and the crews of those clippers are another; we're no businessmen, or else we'd be sleeping at sea level and eating hot meals three times a day. We do what we do because God has blessed our nation, and civilization must spread from one side of this great continent to the other.

We hunt the zeppelins.

Every groundworm gets a sky-daddy to teach him the ropes and the knots, and how to keep his feet on the catwalks when she's headed two points into the wind and her nose is leaping like a stuck pronghorn. I was burdened with my first worm three days out of St. Louis. Penrose must have padded his age with a year or two when he claimed to be eighteen, but then, half of us on board had started our careers the same way. Like all clipper-men, he was built light and wiry, but there was a weariness and a wariness in his green eyes, and he had an old man's tendency to let his shoulders stoop. He listened and learned well enough, so I did not torment him more than necessary.

"The main thing you must know," I declaimed, bringing him up top and settling him on the broad round back of the *Kingfisher*, "is this: If God wanted to be a bird, He would be a zeppelin. There is nothing between earth and heaven that will command your respect and awe such as that which we go to hunt. This good ship, as grand as she is, is but a pale ghost of a living, breathing zeppelin, and if you've never seen one—"

"Oh, I have," he said with gravity. "I most certainly have seen one."

"A Yankee like you? I wasn't aware they made it out as far as

Boston."

"No, my family left Massachusetts a few years back when the government parceled out Nebraska Territory. We tried our luck with a farmstead."

Not too many farm boys became clipper-men. Unless . . . . "And how'd your luck turn out?"

He shrugged. "In three years, they came three times. Sometimes they even skipped our neighbors' places. It was like they knew just how to find us, and knew just when we were about to harvest. After the last time, we had nothing left."

He stood and walked to starboard as far as he dared, where the smooth curve of the *Kingfisher*'s back became a sheer drop. Beyond that were the flat bare plains, hundreds of feet below us, visible for a hundred miles out all around.

"I just wanted you to know," he said, looking off. "You know— in case I'm cursed."

"That's thinking like a lubber," I answered. "Up here, a man who can bring zeppelins is the best sort of luck."

The Denver shipyards can put anything into the air, from your aunt's bathtub to the ironclad dreadnoughts that bombarded Richmond. To hunt zeppelins though, to match their speed and move in the wind as they do—and to come within striking range—nothing beats another zeppelin. That's why a Kansas clipper is the corpse of a bull zep.

Pull out the entrails with their knotted, five-chambered stomach that converts vegetable matter to precious hydrogen, and most of what's left in a zeppelin is the gas bladders and a light, flexible skeleton. Cure the hide and varnish it, mount two broad wooden screws and the clockwork motors to turn them, install the helm in the cavity that formerly held the beast's great, unblinking eye, and you've got yourself the start of one fine zep hunter. Just don't expect the accommodations to be anything to write home about, unless you are fascinated by bamboo scaffolding lashed between ribs and vertebrae, or the prospect of giving up your pipe and the hope of ever seeing a cooked meal—every material on board a clipper falls somewhere along the spectrum between flammable and explosively combustible, and a spark would be suicide.

The *Kingfisher* cruised north through Kansas territory, pursuing the spring migration as the zeppelins moved up from Mexico. Our course was the unmistakable black road the herd ahead of us had carved through the grass. Morale was high. We knew the cows would be heavy with calves and moving slowly, and we expected to engage them at any time.

I do my shifts below-aft with everyone else winding the motors, but once the hunt is on, I become royalty. I'm the port-side harpooner. I take a one-fifteenth share of the hydrogen from every zeppelin I fasten to, and only the Captain and the owners take more.

We spotted the herd at the horizon, like a line of clouds over a patch of shadow. They grazed as they went, uncurling finger-tipped proboscises as long as their bodies to wrench up tracts of sod and deposit them in their mouths. The dusty haze of their detritus filled the air beneath them. Anyone standing in their way would have welcomed an Old Testament plague by comparison.

I took my station on the open balcony just aft of the pilot house. I had drilled the boy on preparing my gear in every free moment we had, and now he spread tubs of coiled rope at my feet and placed my rack of barbed harpoons within reach. We waited as we closed the gap to the herd. We could hear the long, booming bleats of the stragglers as they called to one another.

The Captain stared forward like a pointer and selected a cow that lagged behind the main body of the herd. "She'll do," he announced. "Wind's in the east, and we'll take the weather gage on her. Port harpoon gets the first shot."

Whittaker, my counterpart across the deck, spat tobacco over the side, and I stepped up to my ballista. Penrose helped me work the crank that spanned it. I tested harpoons until I found one with an edge that shaved the hair from my forearm, and fitted it to the string. Penrose lifted the rope-end from the closest tub, and I attached it to the shaft just behind the barb. The boy stood behind my left shoulder, awaiting instructions.

The Captain directed the helm to put the *Kingfisher* a few degrees into the wind, and when we were nearly parallel to the cow, ordered the motors engaged to their lowest gears. The wind turned us, and we drifted west. Ahead of us now, the cow fanned herself with her tasseled fins and chewed a cud the size of a haystack. I swiveled the ballista until I could sight her over the harpoon shaft.

If there were nothing more to a harpooner than a good shot with a big crossbow, any fool could do it. But only a few men in a thousand can watch a zeppelin and the weather and know which way each will turn. I waited.

The Captain stepped to my right shoulder. "Aim low, damn you," he growled. A harpoon that struck a zeppelin too high could punch through its flank as if it were a pumpkin and destroy a gas bag.

The cow stirred and made a slow turn in the *Kingfisher*'s direction. We could see the dark, multi-faceted eye below her bow, looking out and down and around, like an igloo made of black ice. We drifted closer.

"Now!" said the Captain.

There had been something about the way that eye had scanned us that suggested interest. I waited.

She was well within range now, but she was making the shot easier for me every minute. I wondered how close she'd come.

"Shoot!" demanded the Captain, but the harpooner takes no orders when the hunt is on.

"Five degrees starboard," the Captain called to the helmsman.

"Belay that," I said. No one moved.

With a swish of her tail the zeppelin slowed, so that our bows approached as gently as a kiss. If I struck her at this range, her throes would smash the *Kingfisher* to kindling.

The cow uncurled her proboscis, and with an audible intake of air, reached over and sniffed our bow. Finding nothing, or the hint of something, she slid along the curve of the hull to our port side, rubbing against it like a cat and snuffling as she went. No zeppelin had been known to approach an airship this way. Was there some familiar scent of the old bull left beneath the sealant and paint? The crew held their breath.

She stopped when she reached the harpooner's platform, and rolled to let her glittering eye pass over us. Each facet was tall enough to reflect my entire body as she passed. She let the snaky tip of her trunk caress the length of our hull for a thoughtful moment, then snorted and broke away. Her breath smelled like yeast and grass pulp and dust. She swung backwards and pointed her bow towards the herd, and as she turned to go I pulled the trigger.

The harpoon struck true, just behind the eye, where the latticework of springy bones that protect the brain provides the best purchase for the barbs. The zeppelin convulsed and bellowed, and at the same moment Penrose screamed in triumph behind me.

The rope was already whistling out of the tub as she ran.

"Tie it off!" shouted the Captain, and someone twisted the rope around a post that was anchored deep in the *Kingfisher*'s frame. It pulled taut as steel, and the Kansas clipper lurched. Now the whole crew cheered.

The cow dumped her ballast in a torrent of liquid waste to leap upward, and charged for the safety of the herd. We'd have more control, and better luck keeping her out of it, with another line or two in her.

"Again!" I demanded, but Penrose was no longer behind me. With a string of oaths, I struggled to crank the ballista on my own, then slotted a second harpoon and released it. It fastened low but well back, in a softer, fleshier spot.

The cow roared in pain—a sound like an ox in a cathedral—and dove into the herd.

Zeppelins stampede when they are startled. We watched as a wave of panic spread through the herd from the point where the cow entered out to the furthest edges, and then back inward again, intensified. They thrashed and bellowed and struck and tumbled over one another, and the hollow booms of the countless impacts were the sound of rolling thunder, and the rushing noise as their thousands of fins buffeted the air was the voice of a hurricane. The air was crazy with whipping currents and vortexes.

A creature that is lighter than air cannot tow heavy loads, and the *Kingfisher* massed as much as the zeppelin that struggled to escape it. The herd curved west and charged downwind, and our cow fell far to the rear again. We unfurled our sky anchors to increase the drag, and let her run that way for hours. For us in the clipper, every minute was like shooting rapids in a Conestoga, as the cow dove and twisted to shake the barbs free. The Captain and

I leaned out over the railing and grinned into the gale.

Her struggles became punctuated by gasping pauses, and finally she rolled in place, exhausted.

"Haul in—haul in!" cried the Captain, and the capstan clicked as we were drawn closer to her heart.

"She's yours if you want her," he told me, and offered me the long killing lance. I took it.

Dead zeps don't fall if you've killed them right; the greater danger is that they'll drift off higher than you can follow, and not come down until they're over the Atlantic somewhere. We extended booms and tackle and secured the cow to the clipper, her head to our stern. The *Kingfisher* then became a floating slaughterhouse as we rushed to strip away her body with saws and flensing knives. It's always a massive job, and the crew swarmed over the carcass like ants dismantling a barn. Scavengers followed below us on the ground and in the air as we rained down the gore and offal. By the next afternoon, we were left with a spine running across the tops of thirteen gas bags in a neat row like peas, small ones at either end and the biggest in the middle. The oldest zeppelins can carry more than twenty bladders. Sometimes we can still find one.

Penrose appeared next to me while my watch was over the side on the cutting stages, sealing the bladders with pitch. It was the first I had seen of him since I had struck the zeppelin, and I cursed myself for forgetting his absence during the frantic activity that followed.

"Thought maybe we lost you during the ride, boy," I said. "Where were you?"

"Cable tier, I think." The cable tier, where we stowed the ropes and chains, was the darkest, most airless part of the ship. With forty men sharing the limited floor space on board, it was also the place where you were most likely to be alone. "I don't rightly remember." He surveyed our butcher-work. "It hardly looks like a zep at all now. Hard to believe you fellows did all this since this morning."

"We didn't. Son, you've been gone a day and a half. You sure you all right?"

"Well, everything was spinning when I woke up, but I'm tip-top now and ready to work."

"In that case, each one of these gas-bags has to be marked with the owners' name and registration number so that there'll be no mistaking it from far off. Why don't you tie onto a monkey rope and step out there with paint and a brush?"

A good clipper-man can claim at least one trapeze artist or mountain goat in his ancestry, and the boy made an admirable effort at nonchalance as he ran out along the spine, five hundred fifty feet up in a stiff cross breeze.

He was done tagging the first six and was out in the middle of the row when there was a report like a shot, and I looked up to see the spine crack under his feet and the vertebrae scatter out into space. Just bad luck—it'll split under a man's weight sometimes, though usually it won't. The gas-bags bobbed, and the boy hit the end of his line and thumped against the *Kingfisher*'s hull. Any bladder that hadn't been secured directly to the airship yet—and that was half of them—slipped free. We stood there and watched our profit sail off into the vault of heaven like toy balloons lost at a fairground.

We hauled the boy in, and the Captain stormed round to lay our ears back. He decided Penrose must be some sort of fool and was all for tossing him over the side again, this time without the safety line. In the boy's defense, we proved he had kept his head all along by presenting the paint can and brush he had refused to drop even as he crashed against the side.

At last the Captain grudgingly assented that it might have been an act of God and fumed off chewing his beard, but Penrose whispered to me, "Looks like I am cursed, after all."

When we had done preparing the remaining bladders, we fixed a long anchor chain to each, and lowered a team to plant the ends in the soil of the Plains. After our hunt, we would report the locations of all the bladders we had left behind, and they would be collected by a team out of Fort Smith or Jefferson City, lashed into rafts and floated east. We watched the ground team go with envy, because when they had finished their task, they would build a fire and grill steaks and drink hot coffee before we winched them back up.

Alone in a broad sky dotted overhead with cumulus clouds, the *Kingfisher* stowed her booms and stages, and cast back and forth to pick up the spoor of the herd we had lost. In the mid-morning, the crew spotted a gray bulbous shape far to the north of us, drifting above the line of the horizon. The Captain sent a young man with good eyes and a Swiss telescope up to the crow's nest, a platform mounted high over the airship's back. The lookout called down that it was another clipper, cutting into a zeppelin. We made our name and number with signal flags on a line running from the crow's nest down to the stern.

The distant airship saw us, and signaled in response: JEROBOAM, OUT OF ST. LOUIS 2 MONTHS. RETURNING TO PORT TO RESUPPLY. Back when we served under Grant, I had brawled with some of the *Jeroboam*'s crew; they were good men.

—OUT OF ST. L. 11 DAYS, the *Kingfisher* responded.

—TOOK 117 BLADDERS THIS TRIP. LAST A 13-BAGGER.

The Captain ordered the signal DITTO. I wondered if they'd

seen the bladders we let slip.

The *Jeroboam* sent LARGE HERD 1 DAY W OF HERE HEADED NW.

That was basic courtesy after such a good run, but the Captain nodded and tapped his fingers against his thighs. The *Kingfisher* signaled MANY THANKS BROTHER.

—HAPPY HUNTING.

—HOT MEAL WARM BED, we sent back.

And we went our separate ways, never having come closer than five miles.

The Captain was determined to make up for the hydrogen we had lost in Penrose's mishap, and so the motors needed constant winding as we sped west-northwest on the highest gear. We back-tracked along the trail of the *Jeroboam*'s gas bladders, which stood up from the Plains like marker buoys or clusters of toadstools. She had indeed had a good run.

As morning dawned the next day, we saw the herd spread out in front of us, the zeppelins catching the light even before the mountains behind them. They were meandering northwards and grazing, tearing up the prairie and turning it into hydrogen. All the plain in their wake looked like it had been harrowed for planting—it was probably the largest herd that would gather this season.

The clipper bore down on a cow well behind the main mass, her calf close at her flank.

"To hell with that. No more damn stragglers," said the Captain. "I want something big. Increase altitude another two hundred feet and take us right into the herd."

The helm changed course and we soon began to slip silently past zeppelins on either side.

"Harpoons! Strike me a fat old grandfather of a bull that will make us all rich. Take your shot when you see it," he ordered. Whittaker and I would be competing for this kill. "And get that damn clumsy boy out of the way. I don't want him fouling this."

I sent Penrose up the companionway to the crow's nest, which was as far from the action as one could get. He gave me a jaunty nod as he went, but it was cruel to make him sit out the hunt, and harsher still to do it in front of the whole crew that way. Whittaker embraced his ballista, and I stepped back to mine.

Only the largest zeppelins could reach the ground from this height, and there was plenty of maneuvering room between them. The mass of the smaller beasts below us, however, made a floor that we could not have descended through. That was no concern—they would all scatter soon enough. I sighted the eye of a big bull over the top of my harpoon shaft and waited while we shortened the distance. He presented his majestic flank to us, and I saw he had to be at least a twenty-bagger, maybe twenty-three. It would be a long ride before that one tired.

The bull turned to face the *Kingfisher* and drove closer with a sweep of his tail fins. My finger stroked the trigger, but then, out of the corner of my eye, just around the hull of the airship, I saw another zeppelin approach from the stern. This one was nearly on us.

"Belay there! Hold your harpoon!" I shouted.

"Damn you, I've got a clear shot on this side!" Whittaker called back.

"They're too close! Look around you!"

Just as the cow had the other day, bulls drew towards the clipper from all sides, like carp converging on a crust of bread. If startled, any one of them could have destroyed the ship. They reached over and snuffled along the length of the *Kingfisher*'s hull, obstructing her headway. One bumped her bow with enough force to jolt us all.

"Full stop, damn you," the Captain ordered. Aft, the flywheels were disengaged from the propellers. We were dead in the air. More zeppelins cruised in, blotting out any sight of the blue sky. There was nowhere to turn.

"Goddammit, goddammit, goddammit," the Captain hissed, his beard between his teeth. "Has the world gone topsy-turvy?" He withdrew a key from under his shirt and opened the steel lock-box at the rear of the pilot house. Inside were a stack of gold coins and a flare pistol. He pulled out the pistol and loaded it. A flare would send the zeppelins running, but if it struck one inside the herd, the entire sky would erupt in a conflagration from horizon to horizon.

The bulls closest to us jostled to sniff along the *Kingfisher*'s back.

Up top, Penrose screamed the way he had when I struck the cow. I ran up the ladder and out along the open deck.

The boy stood in the crow's nest, his arms straight out from his sides, his head lolling. A half-dozen bull zeppelins wedged their bows together around him, forming a wheel of spokes the diameter of the sky, with Penrose at its hub. The only breeze came from their breath; otherwise, it was as still in this space as the bottom of a well. The hide of each bull was a piebald pattern of blue and gray, and the ends of their fins trailed off in floating pennants. The air seemed to buzz as something within the drum-tight skin of their bows reverberated. Their eyes were directed at the boy, and his reflection surrounded us in a hundred black mirrors.

I scrambled up to the crow's nest. The vibration shook my innards below my belly and grated against the inside of my skull.

"What are you doing, boy?" I said. There was no response. "Come on, let's get you below."

"They're trying to talk to me," he said, and he sounded sick or drunk. "It feels like they're putting pictures inside my brain. Only the pictures don't come from human eyes—they're all shattered, like—and it's hard to make sense of them."

The zeppelins made high arches with their trunks in order to hold their tips near us. They waved them as the boy spoke, as if they were tasting his words.

"It's just buzzing," I insisted. "They don't talk. They're mindless beasts. I've cut up enough of them to know."

"No, I don't think they're stupid. They're just so . . . strange that we don't realize it. I see broad, windy skies, and a hard journey ending over lots of rich grass growing in the sun . . . . I think they're saying they're very happy they've found me. I think they've been looking for someone like me for a long time."

"Why, so they can eat your farm for the fourth time? Let's go down, boy. This buzzing is making you feverish in your head." I grabbed his elbow.

"What the hell is going on up here?" the Captain demanded, clambering up the ratlines and onto the platform with us. The flare pistol was tucked into his belt.

"I see me flying with them, and it's not like sailing in a clipper at all," said Penrose. "It's more like swimming along with a great big fish. And they don't understand legs. They wonder what it's like to have legs."

"Boy, I want you down below before you do something to get these bulls vexed," the Captain ordered.

"Thunderstorm," muttered Penrose.

"Stow that foolishness. This is the wrong damn time for pranks, boy."

The wall of bull zeppelin bodies surged tighter.

"They know what a Kansas clipper is for, now that they've seen you up close," the boy warned him, "and they're not going to abide it."

"What, they've held a caucus and decided they would rather we didn't hunt them any more?"

"I don't think they know anything about hunting. What they're planning looks more like war."

The Captain laughed, and the *Kingfisher*'s hull suddenly rocked and shrieked under the bulls' pressure.

"Well boy, before they think about war, they'd better have a good plan for dealing with this." He brandished the flare pistol in Penrose's face.

The buzzing swelled and then cut off. In a single languid motion like a flower unfolding, the zeppelins around us backed clear in all directions, and turned away. The last to flee reached out its proboscis with the ease of a man tossing a horseshoe, and snatched up Penrose from between us. In his dreamy state, the boy didn't even struggle. The Captain aimed the flare pistol.

"Don't! That will kill him for sure," I said. I had already seen the bull curl his long trunk into a basket shape—much like the crow's nest—around the boy, and sweep him up to eye level. It was a gesture of taking someone into confidence, like putting an arm around a shoulder, as if the bull wanted to consult him about certain plans.

In response to some unseen signal, the entire herd aligned itself and shot away, fleeing northeast in a coordinated burst of speed. It was utterly unlike the stampede we had seen, and there was no hope of our clockwork motors keeping pace with them. Penrose was whisked beyond our reach forever, and soon we could not even tell which bull carried him. Who would have thought you could ride a zeppelin? The clipper was tossed in their wash.

It took less than three minutes for the sky to clear.

"Well, we've lost a fool who was no good, and this damn stretch of sky is hunted out," the Captain said as the last to go streaked past us.

"Maybe so." I didn't quite know what to think of the boy, but I was still port-side harpooner, and all this changed none of the important things, except—"Now you'll be able to tell a good one about the one that got away, if you can make sense of it."

"Why bother?" he answered. "We're headed south from here. Time's a-wasting, and there are plenty of other zeppelins to kill." ✪

THE LAST OF THE ZEPPELINS

BY JED HARTMAN

For Ed C. and Alex W.

HUGH BETCHA PARACHUTED OUT of the cloudy night sky to land hard on the flat roof of Building X-9 of the Luftschiffbau Zeppelin airship works. As soon as he was down, he shrugged out of his parachute harness and let fall the heavy oversized duffel bag that was attached to the harness.

He kicked open the flimsy door that led to the stairwell, and charged down the stairs three at a time. Halfway down, a door screeched open a level below him, and loud footsteps clattered up the stairs toward him. Hugh grabbed the iron railing and swung over it and down into the stairway underneath, planting his boots solidly in the face of the uniformed Nazi guard there. The man smashed against the wall; Hugh landed on his feet, and two quick punches knocked out the guard. Hugh yanked the man's gun from its holster and tossed it over the railing into the dark stairwell, then continued down the steps.

He moved more cautiously as he descended past the ground floor and into the underground levels. Sounds of industry echoed from elsewhere in the building: the clank and rumble of heavy machinery, orders barked in guttural German, marching feet and rolling wheels. In these dark days the factory's army of technicians and workers never slept.

Hugh eased open the door from the stairwell into the sub-basement. A concrete hallway led off to either side. Voices and footsteps were approaching from around a corner.

Hugh held the door open a crack, just enough to see through. He put a hand in the pocket of his leather flight jacket. "Keep still, Scraps," he whispered; he felt the little ferret in his pocket sniffing inquisitively at his fingers. "Let's just wait here a minute till these Nazis go past, then we can search for those plans. They've got to be somewhere around here."

On the night Hugh had been given his orders, at a secret Corporation airfield near New York City, the weather had been cloudy and dark. Thunderheads had been gathering on the horizon.

Hugh strode onto the landing strip. General Bore—a wiry man in his sixties, gray-haired but hale—stood waiting, near the Corporation-owned passenger plane that had dropped Hugh off on many previous missions.

"Thanks for coming on such short notice, Betcha," said the General. "We've received information that the Germans are developing a new class of zeppelin code-named *drachenflieger*—'dragon-flyer.' The new zeppelin will serve as an aerial platform for a powerful new weapon, a system that can shoot devastating beams of energy and lay waste to entire cities."

"So you need me to stop the Nazis from building a death ray?"

The General's brow creased. "I suppose you could put it that way, yes. The device will be so massive that only an airship can transport it effectively to inland targets. The blueprints are at the Luftschiffbau Zeppelin airship works in Friedrichshafen. They've completed a prototype *drachenflieger*—the *LZ-132*, christened the

Hitler. Smaller, faster, and more maneuverable than its big brother the *Graf Zeppelin II*, but built along the same lines. The technical details are in your briefing packet. And they intend to begin construction on the weapon system in a matter of days."

"You can count on me, General," said Hugh. "Those Nazis won't know what hit 'em."

"Subtlety, Betcha," the General said. "This can't make the news. Best if the Nazis never know you were there. We don't want anyone launching a war just yet. The last thing we need right now is another international incident."

"I'm not afraid of the Nazis, sir—they're a cowardly lot. I'll do my darnedest to make sure that America won't fall under Hitler's tyrannical heel."

"And I don't mean subtle like that weapons cache you blew up in Czechoslovakia last fall—"

"We're wasting time, General," said Hugh. "I'd love to stay and chat, but the Nazis won't wait."

"All right, then," said the General. "Oh, I almost forgot. Sally couldn't come to see you off, but she asked me to give you this." He handed Hugh a rubbery chew toy. "For the ferret."

Hugh took the toy and saluted the General. "God bless America," he said.

Hard-heeled German footsteps rang out, nearing Hugh's hiding place behind the stairwell door. A voice, cultured and smooth as mother-of-pearl, gave rapid-fire orders in German.

Hugh knew that voice: Baron von Sturmdrang, evil mastermind behind many of Hitler's recent political maneuvers. The last time Hugh had seen von Sturmdrang had been the day Hugh had shot down the Baron's single-engine Messerschmitt 109 in a dogfight in the skies over Madrid two years before, but he should have known the Berlin Fox was too wily to fall in any ordinary battle.

Von Sturmdrang's tall, gaunt figure strode into view, waving a long roll of blueprint paper, a black cloak billowing behind him. He was followed by a dozen other men in military uniforms. Hugh had one glimpse of the Baron's chiseled features as he passed by the door: the pencil-thin mustache, the high cheekbones, the jagged scar won during the Baron's days as an *Oberkanone*, a Top Gun, back in the Great War, not long before Hugh was born.

The Baron was still speaking to his subordinates. Hugh's German wasn't good enough to follow it all, but he caught the phrase *verdammt Göring*, the name LZ-132, the word *Luftüberlegenheit*—"air superiority"—the word *London*, and the word *Todesstrahl*—"death ray."

The Baron and his men trooped through a nondescript office door at the end of the hall.

"Those blueprints must be the plans!" Hugh whispered to Scraps. "Now all we have to do is steal them." The ferret squirmed in his pocket.

A few minutes later, the Germans came out of the office again, without the blueprints. An *oberleutnant* carefully locked the door and slid the brass key into his pocket, and the group departed.

Hugh released his hold on his diminutive pet for a moment—and Scraps leapt from his pocket and skittered across the corridor. "Scraps!" Hugh hissed. "This is no time for games!" The black-masked ferret glanced back at Hugh and then disappeared through a wide crack in the base of the wall. Hugh rolled his eyes and shrugged; he knew from long experience that the ferret could take care of himself.

After another minute of waiting, to be sure the coast was clear, Hugh went to the office door. He tested the handle; locked, of course. He considered simply shooting the handle off, but decided that it wasn't worth risking the noise. Sighing, he slid a set of lockpicks from his pocket and knelt in front of the door. Just then, a chirp and a metallic clatter came from the floor nearby. Startled, Hugh looked down; it was Scraps, looking very pleased with himself, and in front of him, a brass key.

"Sometimes I almost think you're smarter than I am," said Hugh. "Good work, boy!" He fed Scraps a ferret treat from his pocket, then opened the door. Scraps rushed past him into the room.

The office was a model of German neatness and efficiency. The desks were clear, the filing cabinets locked. By the time Hugh finished trying the desk drawers—all either locked or empty— Scraps was standing atop the frame of a large painting hanging on the wall, darting back and forth excitedly, sniffing at everything in sight. The painting rocked to one side, and Hugh caught a glimpse of the metal behind it.

It was but the work of a moment for Hugh to lift the painting out of the way, crack the safe, and retrieve the plans. It didn't take much longer for the duo to make their way (Scraps now safely back in Hugh's pocket) back through corridors and stairways to the roof, where the heavy duffel bag still lay. The bag held a special collapsible autogiro, hand-built by the Corporation's engineers.

Hugh assembled the lightweight machine quickly and unerringly despite the velvety darkness. He was just tightening the last bolt when a voice cried out, *"Anschlag!"* Hugh looked up and was almost blinded by a bright flashlight beam. He dove to one side and rolled as the crack of a gunshot shattered the night's quiet. He came up firing his trusty Colt .45 automatic. The man with the flashlight staggered back off the edge of the roof, his falling scream ending in a crash. Lights began to flick on all over the compound.

Hugh slipped the roll of blueprints into the waterproof duffel and seated himself in the autogiro's small open cockpit, checking to be sure that Scraps was safe in his pocket. The engine roared to life and the craft sped across the flat roof and took to the air.

It wasn't until hours later, as he flew over a forest somewhere in northern France, that Hugh was sure he was being followed.

It began with a steady thrum in the distance, drawing ever closer; then the clouds parted and, looking back, Hugh saw a sleek dark shape silhouetted against the moon. "It's the *132*," he told Scraps. "They must have had it ready to fly already—there's no way they could get it moving this quickly otherwise. Good thing the death ray isn't built yet." The ferret chirped noncommittally in response.

Hugh knew the numbers all too well. If the Corporation's intelligence was accurate, the *Hitler* carried fifty tons of fuel, and could travel for nine thousand miles at ninety miles an hour. Hugh could outrun it for a little while in his autogiro, but running the autogiro at maximum speed would quickly deplete even the special fuel provided by the Corporation.

Hugh zigzagged low over the trees, looking for a place to hide. Searchlights stabbed out from the airship. One swept across him, and quickly returned; he was pinned in its bright beam.

Hugh dove for the trees as the zeppelin's machine guns clattered into action. He swerved and plunged into a small clearing, then sped along just above the ground, the autogiro's stubby wings barely slipping through the gaps between trees. Bullets tore through the forest canopy all around.

A train whistle sounded from not far off. Hugh darted between trees and found himself in a long narrow break in the woods, the train tracks below him glinting in the moonlight. He spared a glance upward; the zeppelin hovered nearby, searchlights still sweeping the forest. One light swung toward him.

The train whistle came again, much closer. Hugh jerked his head around and saw a train engine steaming down the track toward him, a scant few dozen feet away. Hugh desperately pulled up, and the engine's plume of black smoke engulfed him moments before the searchlight would have found him.

Hugh hovered in the smoke plume, coughing and spitting and wiping furiously at his goggles. Below him, he dimly saw a half-empty coal car approaching. He cut the autogiro's engine and plummeted into the open-topped car, landing in the coal with a crunch.

Above him, the zeppelin's searchlights swept across the smoke trail and were gone.

There was no sign of the zeppelin for the remainder of the journey to the coast. Hugh and Scraps crossed the Channel in the hold of a small freighter, and made their way to an R.A.F. base outside Ipswich, where Hugh's old friend Captain Stephen Upperlip kept a watch on the skies for Nazis and other undesirables.

"I'll come right to the point, Captain: I need a plane," said Hugh, as the two shook hands on the airstrip.

"That's what I like about you Americans," said the Captain. "You come right to the point. 'How are you? How are things in Old Blighty? How did you escape from certain death at the hands of Friedrich Blitzkrieg back in '35?' No, none of that for you; it's just 'I need a plane.'"

"It's vital to stopping the rise of the Nazis."

"And that's another thing: You're always helpful. Yes, when the R.A.F. needs a hand fighting off Nazis, you're always right there to lend aid, assistance, and succour. You would never hang back, three thousand miles away, and let your old friends the British prepare to save the world alone; no, you're right there in the thick of things, helping with the war effort."

"It would mean a lot to Scraps and me."

"Scraps!" The Captain bent down to pet the furry beast as it poked its nose out of Hugh's jacket pocket and snuffled at him. "How are you, old fellow? I think I have a bit of a ferret treat somewhere about me—ah, yes, here you go." Scraps squeaked gratefully and nibbled on the food.

"Well," said the Captain, straightening up. "When you put it that way, I suppose we can spare a plane, for old times' sake. Not a big plane, mind you. The only one we can let go is a Percival Vega Gull one-seater. Not much to look at, but she was modified with extra fuel tanks a few years back."

"That's all right, Captain. Scraps and I will manage. Before I go, may I send a telegram?"

"Be my guest. Talk to Leftenant Beasy over in the communications shed."

"Thank you, Captain."

"Good luck, Betcha. And good luck to you as well, Scraps."

"We make our own luck, Captain."


```
FROM: HUGH BETCHA
TO: GENERAL GARRULOUS BORE
HAVE ACQUIRED PLANS STOP RENDEZVOUS CORPORATION
TRANSPORT NEWFOUNDLAND USUAL LOCATION STOP GOD
BLESS AMERICA STOP


FROM: GENERAL GARRULOUS BORE
TO: HUGH BETCHA
GOOD WORK BETCHA STOP SEE YOU SOON STOP SALLY
SENDS LOVE STOP WORLD COUNTING ON YOU STOP
REMEMBER SUBTLETY STOP
```

The Atlantic crossing was nearly twenty-four hours of frozen hell, an endless rush through frigid air over bottomless water that stretched to the horizon in all directions. The only good side was that there was still no sign of any pursuit. "We must have lost them, Scraps," said Hugh. Scraps didn't respond; he was busy sulking in Hugh's pocket.

As they neared Newfoundland, Hugh tapped the fuel gauge worriedly. "It's going to be close," he said.

A dark strip of land grew on the horizon.

The engine began to sputter as they flew over the choppy waves that beat steadily against the rocks.

Hugh fought the plane into an emergency landing. The wheels crumpled as they hit stone. He was hurled against the windshield, face-first.

The last thing he heard as he lost consciousness was the oily voice of Baron von Sturmdrang. "So. If it isn't our old friend Hugh Betcha. Guards—*schnell!*"

Hugh awoke with a headache the size of Manhattan.

He was apparently in some kind of a warehouse. Darkness stretched all around; shadowy crates stood stacked nearby. The harsh tang of gasoline suffused the air.

"Excellent. Mr. Betcha returns to us." The Baron stood nearby, smoking a cigarette in a long holder, looking out a window into the moonlight.

"What are you going to do to me, Baron?"

Von Sturmdrang turned, quirking an eyebrow. His cruel scar was livid in the moonlight. "I? I am not going to do anything to you, Betcha. Why should I? I have the plans safely back in my possession." He took a puff of his cigarette and exhaled a perfect smoke ring.

"No hard feelings, then? So why am I tied up and"—Hugh shifted his arms behind him—"handcuffed to this chair?" He sniffed the air, coughed, and realized why his clothes were wet. "And soaked in gasoline?"

Von Sturmdrang laughed a suave and cultured laugh. "I personally bear you no ill will, Betcha. But the Fatherland cannot allow one of your ability to live, as long as you oppose us. The high explosives that my men have planted in this warehouse will, no doubt, leave very little of you, if you have not yet burned to death by the time they go off. Goodbye, Betcha." He turned and strode away. As he reached the door, he turned again and said, "You have been a most ... stimulating opponent these last few years. Even more so than your father was. I find that I shall miss you." He considered his cigarette, then took it from its holder between thumb and forefinger and threw it to the ground as if tossing a dart.

Then his hand shot forward and up, palm down. "*Sieg heil,* Betcha!" He laughed again, and was gone.

A thin line of flame sputtered to life—a fuse, eating its way across the floor toward the boxes.

Hugh struggled with his bonds, but the Baron's men had tied him too tightly.

There was a hiss from across the room; Hugh looked up to see the fuse's flame split in two. The fuse continued toward the boxes; the new flame was igniting a line of gasoline that ran across the floor to where he sat.

He jerked in the chair and succeeded in shifting it a few inches. It still had one leg in the puddle of gasoline on the floor. He jumped the chair sideways again. The smell of gas filled his nostrils.

There was a muffled *chirrup* near his feet.

"Scraps!"

The ferret poked inquisitively at Hugh's leg, which was still bound tightly to the wooden chair. There was a gleam of metal at the end of his snout.

"Scraps, up here. What's that in your mouth, boy?"

The ferret obligingly climbed up Hugh's leg, stretched, and curled up in Hugh's lap.

The puddle of gasoline caught fire at all once, a small explosion. Hugh's right trouser leg began to burn.

"Is that a key?" Hugh asked desperately. "Is it the key to the handcuffs? Come on, Scraps, bring the key around to my hands. Behind my back."

Scraps whuffled to himself and attempted to burrow into Hugh's crotch, wrinkling his nose at the gasoline smell. The chair leg was on fire now, and Hugh's right ankle was in agony.

"Scraps," he said through gritted teeth. "Look, there are ferret treats in my pocket, but I can't give them to you till I get untied, okay? Now be a good ferret and—"

But at the mention of treats, the intrepid animal had begun clambering along the ropes, around to the back of the chair. Hugh opened his hand, and a bit of metal poked into it, along with a whiskered nose.

"Good boy, Scraps!" Hugh twisted and tugged. The key fit; the handcuffs clattered to the floor. Hugh grabbed his knife from the concealed sheath at his left ankle. He sliced the remaining rope and threw himself away from the flaming chair. Hugh's trousers were aflame; he slapped at them, biting his lip to keep from crying out.

But there was no time to put the fire out. The door was ten yards away, past the tall stacks of explosive-filled boxes, and the bright sizzle of the fuse was a bare inch from the first box. Hugh stuffed

Scraps into his jacket pocket and, ignoring his burning clothing, whirled and leapt through the window, arms bent over his head for protection. Glass shattered all around him as the explosives went off with a mighty boom, hurling Hugh across the clearing outside the warehouse. Hugh hit the boughs of a spruce tree hard, then plunged through the branches to the ground, followed by a cascade of flaming needles. He beat at his flaming clothing and rolled in the dirt until the fire was out.

Across the clearing, the warehouse roof collapsed. Flames shot fifty feet into the air.

Scraps hissed. "It's all right, boy," panted Hugh. "Here. Have a ferret treat."

There was no sign of the zeppelin or the Baron.

A Corporation car sat at the appointed meeting place; the driver they'd sent—a retired O.S.S. man named Jeeves—lay on the ground nearby, a dozen bullets in his back.

"You deserved better than this, old fellow," said Hugh. "But don't worry, they'll pay—for this and for all their other crimes." He observed a moment of silence. "Come on, Scraps, we'd better go."

He stepped into the car and they were off.

Amalgamated Technologies Corporation's main offices occupied the house and grounds of an old mansion outside of Trenton, New Jersey.

The sky was darkening into twilight when Hugh strode across the quiet lawn that surrounded the deceptively peaceful building. General Bore came out to meet him.

"Betcha! Welcome back," said the General. And then: "Where's Jeeves?"

"I'm sorry, sir," said Hugh. "They got him. And they got the plans."

"Hugh!" yelled a feminine voice, and a petite blonde form launched herself at him. It was Sally Firth, the general's step-daughter.

Hugh caught her up in his arms. "Sally!" he said. "Gosh, am I glad to see you."

"Oh, Hugh!" Sally said, holding him close. And then, pulling away for a moment, nose wrinkling at the remaining gasoline smell: "Looks like you had a rough time." She licked her finger and dabbed at the blood and soot on his face.

"I'll gladly bear any hurt in the service of my country," Hugh said.

"Never mind that, Betcha," said the General. "Where are the plans?"

"The Baron took them back, sir. I assume he's returning to Germany with them. I'll have to follow him."

"Scraps!" said Sally, laughing. The ferret was investigating the dark space at the back of her neck, under her shoulder-length hair, snuffling down the back of her blouse. Sally retrieved him and petted him. "Have you been taking good care of our boy? Yes, you have! Who's a good ferret?" She slipped a hand into Hugh's jacket pocket and came out with a ferret treat, which Scraps happily set to work devouring.

"You won't have to follow the Baron far," said the General.

"Sir?"

"Too many people saw the *Hitler* on this side of the Atlantic for the Krauts to keep it quiet—it would look like spying, or worse yet, invasion. Germany has declared it to be an official goodwill visit from the Baron, so the zeppelin has made a brief stop in Washington to meet with officials and take on fuel and supplies.

The Baron talked with Mr. Ickes and the Munitions Control Board one more time about buying helium from America—"

"But of course the big boys said nothing doing," interjected Hugh.

The General nodded. "So the Baron and the zeppelin are heading back to Germany tonight—by way of New York."

"Perfect!" said Hugh. "I'll take an autogiro and recover the plans."

"I thought you might," said the General.

"Oh, Hugh," said Sally. "Be careful."

The General said, "And subtle. Don't forget subtle."

"Piece of cake, sir. I'll be back in a few hours."

As they walked around the mansion to the well-appointed hangar and landing strip out back, the General said, "Betcha, why are you so eager to get back into the fray?"

"Just doing my duty, sir," said Hugh. "I love zeppelins and America too much to see the Germans get the upper hand. I owe it to my father's memory."

"What a fine zeppelin pilot that man was," the General mused. "Such a pity he decided to take passage on the *Hindenburg* that fateful day.... I remember the time that your father and I had the Baron on the run, over Liechtenstein, back in—But never mind. He'd have been proud of you, Betcha."

"I hope so, sir."

It began to rain as Hugh took off in a Corporation autogiro, and by the time he reached the coast, storm clouds had blotted out the moon and stars.

A single lighthouse stood near the end of Sandy Hook, at the northeasternmost tip of New Jersey's Atlantic highlands. The lights of Brooklyn and Staten Island glittered from a few miles across the water to the north, barely visible through the rain. The lighthouse beam swept out over the water and the land, piercing the growing storm.

In its light, Hugh could see the great zeppelin approaching from the south. The huge black swastikas on its tail fins stood out in stark relief against the blackness of the night. Hugh gunned his engine, and the autogiro leapt forward.

Hugh reached the zeppelin just as it overflew the lighthouse. He set down gently on the zeppelin's upper surface, lit only by a bright flash of lightning, and leapt from the autogiro onto the airship's rain-slick skin.

After checking to be sure Scraps was safe in his pocket, Hugh punched a grappling hook through the airship's skin, hooked it around a duralumin strut, and walked himself backward down the zeppelin's starboard side, paying out his long rope as he went. As the slope steepened, he began to rappel, kicking out, dropping, swinging back in, kicking out again. When he reached the zeppelin's widest point, he kicked off with all his might and let the rope slide fast through his gloved fingers in a barely controlled fall. Lightning flashed, and the rumble of thunder merged with the engines' throaty roar as Hugh swung back in and crashed through the broad starboard window of the control gondola in a shower of glass and rain.

"Der Amerikaner!" came a shout, and guns began blazing. Hugh drew his Colt and fired back, ducking behind a control panel. A stray bullet hit the overhead light, and the cabin was plunged into darkness except for a few small lights on the instrument panel. Wind and rain gusted through the broken window.

Hugh had apparently kicked the pilot in the head during his entrance; the man lay on the ground in a growing pool of blood, and nobody was at the wheel. Hugh spared a glance behind him,

out through the still-intact front window; the zeppelin was headed directly for Brooklyn, and downtown Manhattan beyond. Another gunshot rang out, and a bullet whined past Hugh's head;
he ducked past the wheel, rolled, came up shooting. There was a
scream, and the enemy fire stopped.

Scraps darted from his pocket. "Scraps, no!" Hugh whispered,
but the ferret was gone.

Hugh crawled toward the bridge door, staying low, looking for
enemies. He could hear muffled shouts to the aft.

In the passageway leading to the cabins, the lights were still on.
Hugh shot them out, one by one, then reloaded. The passageway
was empty. Hugh remembered the plans for the *Graf II* he'd admired on an earlier trip to Germany, and hoped this zeppelin had
a similar enough layout. The first passenger cabin was probably
the Baron's. Hugh ran toward it.

Someone shot at him from further along the passageway. Hugh
returned fire, and with his left hand tried the door to the cabin.
It was locked.

There was no time to pick the lock. Hugh backed across the
narrow passageway and then threw himself against the door. It
burst open.

A flash of lightning from outside the low windows illuminated
the Baron's cabin as Hugh stumbled in. The cabin was trim and
clean and very small, with a wash basin, a little collapsible writing-desk, and a neatly made bed. There on the writing-desk lay
the roll of blueprints.

Hugh grabbed the roll, folded it, and stuffed it halfway
down the back of his trousers. He heard careful footsteps approaching from down the passageway. He stole a glance out the
window: they were over open water. There was only one place to
go.

He fired a clip of special armor-piercing bullets into the ceiling in a circular pattern, then used the little writing-desk to smash a hole. He boosted himself up into the space above the cabin just as gunfire tore through the room. He had come up next to a catwalk, with the giant silk gas cells and the spidery infrastructure of the zeppelin's interior looming in the darkness above him, a dark maze of wires and girders. The air inside the zeppelin's body was as cold as the outside air had been. His breath steaming, Hugh ran along the catwalk toward the nose of the zeppelin.

Behind him, he heard shouts, confusion, more gunfire. Then silence. He leapt behind one of the gas cells and stood, heart pounding, listening.

"I know you're in here, Betcha," came the Baron's silky voice.

Hugh fired blindly toward the voice.

A soft laugh in the darkness. "So that is the way you want to play it, eh? Be careful you do not ignite the hydrogen cells. This would be safer if your Mr. Ickes had given us the helium we asked for."

"America will never succumb to your demands, Nazi!"

The Baron said, "It will go easier on both you and the girl if you give up voluntarily."

And then a female voice, sounding more tired than scared: "Don't listen to him, Hugh."

Hugh stood uncertainly for a moment. Then he said, "Sally? What are you doing here?"

The Baron said, "Come out with your hands in the air and nobody will get hurt."

Hugh peered around the curve of the gas cell. He could dimly see a pair of silhouettes on a catwalk not far away.

Sally said, "I thought you might need some help, so I took an autogiro and—"

"Silence!" the Baron interrupted. And then, conversationally: "I think the girl will look less pretty with a hole in her head, no?"

"He's bluffing, Hugh," said Sally.

Hugh cried, "Let Sally go, you monster!"

"Betcha. You know it doesn't work that way. Throw your gun away and then come out."

Hugh weighed the heavy Colt in his hand, and then threw it into the darkness. It clattered off into the distance below them.

He took a deep breath and stepped out from behind the gas cell.

The Baron's gun flashed in the darkness. A bullet whined past Hugh's head, and the gas cell beside him tore open. With a soft *whump*, the escaping hydrogen caught fire, a small jet of light and heat from just behind Hugh.

Hugh hurled himself away from the cell as Sally let loose a wordless shout. There was a thud of flesh on flesh, and the Baron screamed a falsetto scream and tumbled from the catwalk. "Take that, you son of a bitch," said Sally. Before Hugh could reprimand her for her language, or take her to task for following him into danger, she said, "I'm heading for the backup control room. I'm gonna bring this thing down—you get the plans and get out of here."

She was gone before he could tell her he already had the plans.

Another gunshot came from below, where the Baron had fallen.

Hugh leapt for a girder above his head and pulled himself up. The flash and crash of gunfire followed him. He climbed a ladder, ran along another catwalk, up some steps, along another catwalk. The Baron's mocking voice and gun were never far behind. Another gas cell ignited, and another—now half a dozen growing jets of flame glowed in the vast space. *What a waste,* Hugh thought.

This magnificent machine, dying, all because of that Nazi rat. He ran between two gas cells toward the outer shell of the zeppelin—and tripped, sprawling forward and over the edge of the catwalk. He grabbed at a girder and caught it with one hand, swinging from it for a moment, and then pulled himself slowly up to kneel and then stand on it.

The Baron stood gasping for breath a few yards away, pointing a deadly-looking Mauser pistol directly at Hugh's head. His black cloak hung from his shoulders.

"Betcha, it is imperative that you listen to me," the Baron panted. "There is more going on than you know. Your Corporation—"

A ball of fur dropped onto the Baron's face, hissing and spitting and clawing at the Baron's scar. The Baron screamed and fired wildly into the air. Hugh leapt to another girder and ran.

He made his way silently past more gas cells, and finally dropped through a trapdoor and into a passageway. He was back in the control gondola, at the entrance to the main control room. He opened the door.

The Baron stood there, waiting for him, face bleeding. There was no sign of the Mauser, or of the ferret.

The pilot still lay on the floor; the wheel was still unmanned. The storm raged outside the windows. Below were trees; judging by the airship's earlier course and the city lights dimly visible in the distance, this had to be Central Park. A dark tower loomed ahead and below: Belvedere Castle, the miniature castle near the middle of the park.

"Did I ever tell you I knew your father, Betcha?" said the Baron.

"You were defeated by my father, you mean."

"He was a great man, and a great zeppelin pilot. Such a pity about his death. He and I were very close, you know. Yes, very close indeed." The Baron smiled and licked his lips.

"Don't talk about my father, you scum!"

"There are those who say that the destruction of the *Hinden-burg* was not an accident. There are powerful forces arrayed against those of us who love the zeppelin, Betcha. Your father knew—"

"I told you not to talk about my father!" Hugh launched himself at the Baron, and his momentum carried them through the port-side window with a crash. Grappling amid a thousand twinkling shards of glass, the two fell into the storm-wracked sky—

—and landed hard on stone a few feet down. The zeppelin had just cleared the top of Belvedere Castle. The airship slid by over-head, blotting out the clouds and the rain.

Hugh gathered himself to his feet, nursing his left shoulder. The Baron had rolled away and had regained his footing at the edge of the parapet; he stood arms akimbo, cloak trailing behind him in what little moonlight filtered through the clouds. Thun-der rolled. Hugh took one unsteady step toward the other man, and then another, then threw himself forward with a roundhouse swing.

"This," he gasped as his punch connected, "is for the red." The Baron staggered back. "This is for the white!" Hugh said, his voice gaining strength, and he landed an uppercut that snapped the Baron's head back. "And this," Hugh yelled, "is for the blue!" And with one final mighty blow he knocked the Baron flat.

Hugh stumbled over to a corner, holding himself up against the low stone rail by sheer force of will. He bent over, hands on knees, gasping for breath. A gust of wind and rain made him lurch off-balance—just as the Baron leapt for him, a long jagged knife flashing in his hand with reflected lightning.

Hugh threw himself to the side, and the Baron went over the rail.

Hugh grabbed for the man as he went by, but only succeeded in catching his foot. It took all of Hugh's waning strength to hold on. The Baron was flailing, dangling from Hugh's hands over the long drop below. "Hang on, Baron," said Hugh. "I'll help you up—"

The Baron twisted, lunging upward, slashing at Hugh with his knife—and his foot came out of his boot.

"I'll be back, Betchaaaaaaaa!" he screamed as he fell. There was a sickening thud as he hit the rocks below; then he rolled off them and into the icy waters of the shallow lake at the castle's foot.

Hugh stood silently for a moment, but saw no movement. "In that case, Baron," he said at last, "you'll need your boot." And he dropped the boot into the lake.

From Hugh's left came a gigantic rending noise. He turned. The zeppelin, in flames, was grinding its way into the trees at the water's northern edge.

"Scraps!" he yelled. He ran to the castle's stairs, and leapt down them three at a time. As he hit the bottom, a huge ball of red and orange flame leapt from the trees as several gas cells exploded at once. The heat and light washed over him. "Scraps!" he yelled again. And then, "Sally! Oh my gosh." And then, "Oh, that poor zeppelin."

He ran through the rain and mud around the pond's shore, toward the site of the explosion. There was no way anyone could have survived.

But the thrum of an autogiro's engine made itself heard over the rumbling thunder, and in a moment Sally was leaping from the aircraft and into his arms, a sopping wet Scraps scolding them both from her shoulder.

In the midst of their joyful reunion, Hugh heard another engine sound, a growing rumble in the sky like approaching thunder. He looked up and saw a sleek black DC-3 airliner touching down in a perfect short landing on the new Great Lawn to the north. As it grew closer, Hugh saw that it wasn't quite like any DC-3 he'd seen before: the fuselage and fairings were more streamlined, the engines smaller, the wings longer. It taxied to a stop not far beyond the edge of the burning copse of trees.

Hugh looked around for a weapon or a hiding place—but it was only the General who stepped out of the plane's passenger door and jumped to the ground. Rain slid off the man's gray fedora and trenchcoat.

Hugh and Sally—the latter still carrying a complaining Scraps—walked to meet the General near the still-burning remains of the zeppelin.

"Good work, Betcha," said the General. He looked at Sally, an eyebrow raised under the brim of his hat. "The plans?"

Sally nodded in Hugh's direction.

"Here you go, General—safe and sound!" Hugh pulled the battered blueprints from under his jacket. "Now *we* can build the death ray! With these plans, we can create a zeppelin fighting force the likes of which the world has never seen! America will become the greatest air power in the world! We can knock out those Nazi rats' military capabilities before they even know what's coming!"

The General took the plans, unrolled them, glanced over them, and rolled them up again. "Good," he said, and tossed them deep into the zeppelin's burning wreckage.

"General!" cried Hugh. "What are you doing?"

The General looked at him sadly. "I'm sorry, Betcha, but none of that is going to happen. The age of the zeppelin is over."

Hugh gaped at him in shock.

"It's the airplane's turn," the General continued. "Your mission was to keep the death ray out of the Nazis' hands; you did a fine job. But the world doesn't need death rays any more than it needs zeppelins. This 'death ray' of yours is too horrific a weapon to unleash on the world regardless of who owns it. Anyway, we don't have an airplane that can carry a device like that—and airplanes are the future."

"What are you talking about?" Hugh managed. He started to move past the General, toward the wreckage. Maybe if he dove through the flames, the rain would protect him long enough to rescue the plans, and then—

The General pulled out a pistol, a shiny new black Luger of a model Hugh didn't recognize, and aimed it at Hugh. "I'm afraid I'll have to ask you to let them burn, son," he said quietly.

"But, but—" Hugh stammered. He looked at Sally; she was watching him sadly. Scraps was nowhere to be seen.

"Betcha," said the General. "The Corporation has longer-range plans than this upcoming war. We envision a day when huge airplanes cross the skies, carrying hundreds of people. The war won't last long—a half-dozen years at the most—and when it ends, we'll be in a perfect position to take advantage of the new global economy."

"But Germany has to be stopped!"

"Germany isn't the enemy, Betcha. Men like Minister Göring are forward thinkers who recognize what's coming—now that the energy weapon is gone, you won't see the German zeppelin program continue under Göring's leadership. The enemy are the men who can't see that the world is changing, men who don't recognize the new age that's dawning. Men like the Baron. Men like your father."

"Leave my father out of this!"

The General held up a placatory hand. "It doesn't matter.

What matters is that the airlines see what's coming, and are preparing for it. The Corporation sees it too; we'll be launching a new business after the war, a world-wide network of airlines. We'll have a place for a man like you; we'll need a lot of pilots. What do you say?"

Hugh drew himself up to his full height. "I would die first."

"Just like your father," said the General. "Well, have it your way." He cocked his pistol.

"This can't be happening," muttered Hugh. "You must—you must be under the Baron's control! That's it—he must have had some kind of mind control device, and—look, General, I'm sorry about this, but you'll thank me later." He leaped at the General.

The General fired. Hugh felt the sharp pain of a bullet tear through his right bicep; it threw him off-balance, and he and the General went down in a heap together. Hugh scrabbled for the gun and knocked it away, but the old man's fist slammed into his jaw.

Hugh rolled away, came up in a crouch. The General got to his knees, shaking his head as if to clear it. Hugh darted forward and punched the General one-two in the gut, clenching his teeth against the agony in his right arm.

The General went down. Hugh bent, grabbed the man's collar in his left hand, and lifted, holding the General up off the ground one-handed. The General's head lolled back, and a thin line of blood trailed from the corner of his mouth, but his eyes were open. "Betcha . . . ," he managed.

Hugh cocked his right fist back for the knockout blow, ignoring the pain.

"Hugh," said a voice.

Sally's voice, from behind him.

"Hugh. Please don't."

Hugh half-turned, still holding the General off the ground.

Sally stood, chin high, in the rain nearby. A flash of lightning lit up the blonde hair framing her face. She said, "Let him go, Hugh. There's nothing to be gained from this. Nobody will believe you."

"Are you on his side?" Hugh said.

"Of course I am. I'm going to fly for one of the new airlines. He's right, Hugh. Zeppelins have had their turn. It's time to let go."

"I can't accept that."

Sally turned slightly so Hugh could see what she cradled in her arms: Scraps. The firelight danced red on Sally's face. She stroked the ferret gently, letting her fingers curl tightly around the little animal's neck. She said, "Do you want your ferret to live?"

"Sally!" cried Hugh.

Sally said, "We can all still walk out of this. You go your way, we'll go ours."

A sudden roar made both of them turn. The last of the zeppelin's gas cells went up in a magnificent gout of flame.

Hugh closed his eyes and took a breath. After a moment, he lowered the General gently to his feet.

Sally moved to take her father's arm. She let the ferret jump to the ground; Scraps ran to Hugh, who picked him up.

Sally and the General walked off toward the airliner, the General limping. Neither of them looked back.

Hugh watched them climb into the plane, then turned to watch the last remnants of the zeppelin sputter and spark in the rain.

At last, Hugh said, "Never mind, Scraps." He patted the ferret and winced at the pain in his arm. Then he turned away from the flames. "We'll come up with something to do. I hear there's a war on the way; America will need defending." And as the last of the zeppelins burned behind him, Hugh Betcha strode off, whistling, to face a gray and uncertain dawn. ✪

Thanks to Arthur, Mary Anne, Chris, Rick, and Don (for a little of Hugh's dialogue).

THE ECKENER ALTERNATIVE

BY JAMES L. CAMBIAS

THE *HINDENBURG* SWUNG GENTLY on the mast at Lakehurst as the sky over New Jersey turned to purple twilight. All the passengers, the reporters, the newsreel men were gone. A couple of sailors stood guard beneath the big ship to enforce the no-smoking rule.

John Cavalli waited until the watchman below had turned away, then slid down the stern rope to the ground. He hunkered down next to the big rolling anchor weight for a couple of minutes, then hurried off into the darkness beyond the floodlights.

Once he was clear, Cavalli stopped to peel off the Russian Army arctic commando suit he'd been wearing ever since the zeppelin had lifted off from Frankfurt-am-Main. It had kept him warm as he hid among the gas cells with his IR goggles and fire extinguisher, but now in the warmth of a spring evening it was stifling.

He hit the RETURN button on his wristband and disappeared.

"You can't make big changes," said the instructor the first day of Temporal Studies class. He was a very laid-back physicist recruited

43

from California in the 2020s. "That's the most important rule. The folks we work for are the result of a particular set of historical events. Change history too much and their probability level drops below 50 percent. If that happens, all this"—his gesture encompassed the Time Center—"goes away and we're out of a job. If we even exist anymore."

A student in the row ahead of Cavalli raised his hand. "What about making little changes?"

"Little changes are fine. We make little changes all the time. Most of them are things like making long-term investments, buying up art treasures for safekeeping, keeping species from going extinct, that kind of thing. You're going to learn all about gauging the effect of changes, avoiding heterodynes and chaotic points, and when it's okay to step on butterflies."

Cavalli was listening, but in the margin of his notebook he was doodling airships.

The timegate stage was dark and the control room was empty, just as he'd left it. The Coke can was still on the console. Was it maybe a little further to the left than he remembered? He stepped off the stage and took a drink. Still tasted the same. It would take a pretty big timeshift to change the flavor of Coca-Cola.

Cavalli locked the door behind him with his purloined master key—the Time Center used mechanical locks because they were a bit more resistant to minor time-shifts—and headed for the library. He found a book about zeppelins he didn't remember and skimmed the pages. *Hindenburg* served safely until 1939; scrapped when World War Two broke out. No postwar zeppelins. The usual "return of the airship" speculations.

Damn. It hadn't worked. He had hoped erasing the vivid image of the *Hindenburg* fire would have been enough to keep passenger airships alive, but the war still marked the end of their era.

"So why don't we stop things like the Holocaust or the firebombing of Dresden?" It was a relatively quiet dorm room party with half a dozen trainees blowing off steam after the first written exam. Cavalli didn't see who asked the question, but he sounded drunk.

Anna Kyle, the third-year trainee, answered. "Too big. The models predict major shifts in the 21st Century if there's no Holocaust. You lose the Cold War and the whole Jihad era. We just stay away from World War Two if we can help it. Rescue a few things from museums before they get flattened, take some videos for historians, that's all."

"Why not stop the whole war?"

"Kill Hitler in 1918? Everybody from the 20th and 21st wants to do that, or maybe kidnap him as an infant and leave him with a nice family of Buddhists in Tibet. The answer is, forget it. Removing the biggest conflict in human history makes the bosses go poof, not to mention just about everyone else born after 1950 or so. Frankly, we don't know what history would look like if you change something that big."

Cavalli was waiting outside the Houses of Parliament when Lord Thomson came out, trailing a crowd of aides and hangers-on. The monocle in Cavalli's eye displayed a targeting circle and he swung the umbrella up until the bright circle was centered on the side of the Air Minister's neck. He squeezed the handle and the umbrella fired off a smart dart loaded with pneumonia bacilli. Thomson was pretty healthy; he'd get over it in a few months. Plenty of time for the Cardington team to get the *R.101* really airworthy.

There was a candy bar next to his Coke when he returned. He didn't remember getting one from the snack bar. It was a Heath bar, his favorite brand. He ate it on the way to the library.

The British Imperial Airship Service had a rocky start, but by 1935 there were direct routes to Canada, India, South Africa, and Australia. Plans to extend the service to New Zealand were put on hold in 1936 and abandoned when war broke out. The airships served as fleet scouts for the Royal Navy during the first years of the war. The Japanese shot down *R.100* and *R.103*, and *R.101* was scrapped in 1940. *R.102* was used to evacuate some key people from Singapore as the Japanese approached, made an epic flight home to England via Africa and the Azores, and spent the rest of the war in a hangar at Cardington before being donated to the Royal Air Museum. In his room he watched a movie on videodisk about the last flight of *R.102*, with Michael York as the heroic captain.

At lunch one day Anna asked the Big Question. "So if you could change one thing, what would it be?"

The other trainees gave the usual answers—save Jesus, kill Hitler, stop Cortez, save Lincoln, give machineguns to Lee. Cavalli shrugged. "Find some way to save the airships, I guess."

A couple of people who knew him just rolled their eyes, but Anna looked curious. "How come?"

"I just think they're cool."

He clung to the fabric covering of the *Akron* as she cruised out over the New Jersey coast. It was a lot harder to stow away aboard a Navy airship than a passenger craft. His first two attempts had ended in quick aborts when he ran into sailors inspecting the gas cells, so finally he moved the focus to a point just above the ship and hoped nobody was watching.

Keeping a careful hold he pulled out the radio handset and began tapping out the Morse code message he had written on the sleeve of his commando suit. It had all the proper authentications and ordered the *Akron* to return to base at once. By the time they straightened out the "hoax" the line squall would be long past.

The Coke was in a bottle when he stepped off the stage. He finished it as he leafed through a big glossy coffee-table book about Navy airships in World War Two. There was an exciting picture of *Akron* going down amid a swarm of Zeroes at the Battle of the Coral Sea, and some photos of *Macon* on U-boat patrol over the Atlantic. The last page of the book was a fund-raising appeal from the U.S.S. *Macon* Association, hoping to finish the restoration project and get her airborne again in time for the 50th anniversary of Pearl Harbor. The book noted in passing that the luxury passenger airship never recovered after 1945.

Cavalli started going to bed as soon as classes ended, sleeping through dinner and waking after midnight to use the projector. He made up the lost meals at breakfast.

In 1917 he disabled the radio of the zeppelin *L-59* long enough for the ship to miss the recall message and reach its destination in German East Africa. As a result during the 1930s the *Graf Zeppelin* made a couple of voyages to Cape Town, but inevitably the war ended all that. Cavalli did get a nice Art Deco poster showing a zeppelin over the pyramids to put on his dorm room wall.

He tried going back to San Francisco in 1864 and giving Frederick Marriott a couple of uncut diamonds and a printout of suggestions to improve his *Avitor* airship. The result was that in the 1930s America purchased four big Navy airships instead of only two. The three that survived Pearl Harbor were scrapped.

He gave the German Navy's airship commandant Peter Strasser a bad case of pneumonia in 1915, so that zeppelins were used as reconnaissance platforms and fleet scouts rather than strategic bombers. More ships and skilled airshipmen survived the war and the *Graf Zeppelin* was filled with American helium. All nine passenger airships were scrapped in 1939.

He stood among the sand dunes on the North Carolina coast with the dart gun umbrella in his hand, but went home again.

He did manage to ride from Rio to Friedrichshafen aboard the *Graf Zeppelin,* and even exchanged a few pleasantries with Hugo Eckener. Dr. Eckener was convinced the airship could maintain its position despite the growing competition from airplanes. He gestured around the comfortable lounge. "Who would not trade a cramped seat in a noisy box for this?" Cavalli agreed.

Anna tapped on the door of his dorm room. "I know what you've been doing after hours. The projector keeps a record of every time it's used."

"I don't know what you're talking about."

"Good reaction. But I checked the times and places. Friedrichshafen, Lakehurst, San Diego. The London trip had me puzzled until I found out the Air Minister came down with pneumonia the next day."

"He insisted on going to India early and the *R.101* crashed."

"Give me one good reason why I shouldn't tell Temporal Integrity about you."

"I've been careful. I haven't made any major changes. None of these are butterfly points."

"Glad to hear that they're certified safe by a first-year trainee."

"Look, I'm not hurting anyone. It's just a little side project. A hobby."

"John, it's not going to work. Airships had their day from 1900 to World War Two. The war changed everything too much—they couldn't survive as military craft and they couldn't make money as passenger liners. Airplanes just got too good."

"I thought of maybe stopping the Wright Brothers."

"What?!"

"—but I changed my mind. Too big a butterfly." He looked at her. "I still don't understand something. Why don't we do more? Why don't we change things? We've got the power."

"Major changes would erase us."

"So what? It would be a better world for everyone else. Maybe time travel would get invented sooner."

"You can't know it would be better. Stop World War Two and you could cause something worse. Maybe a nuclear war."

"Better the devil we know, eh?" He looked at her. "I take it you want my master key, too?"

"If you don't give it up I have to call in Temporal Integrity."

He sighed and dug in a pocket. "Here. I got it from Dr. Stirling's office when he made me help move his plants."

She took the key and turned to go.

"Now be sure you don't try any history editing yourself," he said.

He wasn't sure how long he had. She might try to use the key herself, or Dr. Stirling might, and then they'd realize it was just the key to his dorm room. No time for much preparation. He checked a date in the library, let himself into the supply room, and hid in an unused classroom until dinnertime.

The stage was just warming up when somebody started pounding on the door. Cavalli leaped onto the platform just as the frosted glass smashed and a Temporal Integrity agent reached inside to undo the deadbolt. The last thing he saw of Time Center was Anna's face. She was shouting something, but it was drowned out by the hum of the field projector.

He hoped he'd been clever, setting the controls for Berlin in early 1932. Maybe the TI agents would assume he was going for Hitler, and concentrate on guarding his apartment and Nazi Party headquarters. But Cavalli spent as little time in Berlin as possible; an hour after arriving he was having dinner aboard the express to Munich. At midnight he got a room in a cheap but tidy hotel in Friedrichshafen.

"Doctor Eckener?"

This particular morning Hugo Eckener looked tired and a little irritable. Running an airship line in the depths of the Depression would do that. "Yes, good morning. My secretary says you have come from America with a business proposal?"

"Actually, no. I just told her that to get in here."

Eckener scowled. "I do not have time for sight-seers."

"Oh, no. It's about politics. The Central Party and the Social Democrats have invited you to run for President."

"Ah, a reporter. And a very good one, too. That was all discussed in strictest confidence. I am afraid I can say nothing."

"You must accept the offer."

"I cannot. Hindenburg is a hero. He is the only thing keeping Germany from falling into anarchy right now."

"But he's going to give the Chancellorship to Hitler!"

"That little fraud? Impossible. The President is not a fool."

"The Nazis are the biggest party, and they're in favor of rearming Germany. Field-Marshal Hindenburg approves of that."

"This is all speculation. Besides, my zeppelins keep me too busy to enter politics."

Cavalli hesitated for a split second, then reached into his pocket and pulled out his computer. "Watch this," he said, and called up the encyclopedia entry on Hitler. Eckener raised his eyebrows when he saw the little glowing screen in the young stranger's hand, but then he began to actually watch the newsreel shots and read the text.

"Another war?"

"Worse than the first. By the end of it, Germany was in ruins, thirty million people were dead—and zeppelins were gone forever."

"How—" Eckener stopped and composed himself. "Never mind. You have travelled in time, like the man in Mr. Wells' story, or possibly you are an angel, like the one sent to Lot. But I am afraid it is still impossible. Even if I ran, the Nazis would oppose me. They know I loathe them."

Cavalli took out the package he'd stolen from Mission Supply, and poured a heap of diamonds onto the table. "These are worth about ten million pounds," he said. "You can blanket the country with ads, rent stadiums for campaign rallies, and hire guards to keep the Brownshirts away."

Eckener picked up one diamond and scratched a vase with it, then quickly put it down again, as if it was hot to the touch. He was silent for a while. "I do not think I am qualified to be President of Germany," he said at last.

"You're an economist by training, and you've kept the Zeppelin company going through war and revolution and economic collapse. You're a national hero. And from everything I've read about you, you seem like a decent man. Germany needs a decent man now, Dr. Eckener. The world needs one."

Eckener looked at him out of those pouchy basset-hound eyes.

"Who are you? Why are you doing this?"

Cavalli was about to give him another spiel about the need to stop Hitler, but then he stopped and shrugged. "I guess I just like zeppelins," he said. "I figure with you as President there will be lots of zeppelins."

Nine months later Cavalli was in the lounge of the *Graf Zeppelin* over the Atlantic. The window was open and he was holding his shift bracelet. If he hit RETURN now what would happen? Would he snap forward to Time Center or whatever occupied the site in the no-Hitler future? Would he just pop out of existence?

He watched it fall to the blue water below, then went to the bar to refresh his drink. The zeppelin droned on into the unknown. ✪

INSTEAD OF A LOVING HEART

BY JEREMIAH TOLBERT

I HATE IT HERE. It's too cold for my motors, and it never stops snowing. Dr. Octavio says that the weather is conducive to his experiments. I'm still not certain that he isn't working to replace me. He tells me impatiently that he isn't, but I live in constant fear of it. I have nightmares that he will withhold the fuel that is my sustenance, that my parts will run down slowly until they can no longer nourish my brain, while the rest of me turns to red dust. No oil can would bring me back.

It is a terrible sort of death; one that I could sit back and watch unfold in gruesome detail. I want to go quickly, when the time comes.

We are somewhere among the tallest mountains of the world. When we arrived, I was locked away in a cargo hold, so I don't know exactly where. Our home is a small, drafty castle with a separate laboratory. Dr. Octavio had the locals construct the lab before he tested the new death ray on their village. There's very little left there. In my little bit of spare time, I try to bury the bodies and collect anything useful to the doctor's experiment.

My primary duties consist of keeping the castle's furnace running and clearing the never-ending snow from the path between the buildings. Sometimes it falls too fast for my slow treads and shovel-attachment to keep up with and I find myself half-buried in the snow. It is horrible on my gears when this happens, but I use heavy-weight oil now and it helps.

It is one of the few benefits of my metal frame that I appreciate. Life in this contraption is like being wrapped in swaddling clothes. I wonder if I would feel anything if my casing caught on fire? I need to ask the doctor when he isn't in one of his moods.

I am plowing fresh snow from the path when the wind begins to blow harder than usual. I swivel my cameras and spot Lucinda's zeppelin landing on the rocky field behind the castle. It is the perfect transportation for a jewel thief of her skill; painted black, with stylized diamonds on the sides. She calls it the *Kingfisher* because it can hover above her prey. It is faster and more agile than the blimp that was her previous method of transportation.

I feel a twinge of happiness that she has caught up with us, even though it will send the doctor into a fit of anger. Before the S.O.E. destroyed our previous laboratory, they argued and she left without telling me goodbye. Dr. Octavio grumbled the next day about money. Often, Lucinda became stingy and demanded "unreasonable results"—so says the doctor.

Dr. Octavio assembled this new fortress on a very tight budget. We have no automated machine-gun turrets, or shock troops. We do not even have rabid Yetis to protect the compound. There is only me and my flamethrower attachment against whatever is out there. The death ray broke down from the cold.

I roll up the path as fast as my treads let me. Lucinda climbs out of the *Kingfisher*'s gondola wrapped in a scarlet cloak, her trademark color. Her raven hair is braided into a ponytail that flails in the wind like a dangerous snake. When she sees me, she smiles. I examine myself for a reaction. I cannot find one.

I have no heart, like the tin woodsman from the Baum books I read as a child. Only he was lucky enough to lose his body a piece at a time.

"Zed! What are you doing out in the cold?" she says. She uses the name Octavio gave me, z-03. I try not to imagine what life was like for my predecessors.

"I must keep the path clear of snow for the doctor," I answer in my monotone, mechanical voice. I hate it nearly as much as the loss of my hands; I once prided myself on my ability to tell jokes. Now even the funniest punch line would fall flat. "I saw you land. Come into the castle where it is warm."

She shakes her head. "I need to see Father immediately."

"He left me with orders that he is not to be disturbed."

Her smile fades. I cannot disobey Dr. Octavio's orders, she knows this. My body inflicts unbearable pain when I do.

"Fine, then. Lead the way."

I plow a path around the castle to the servants' entrance into the kitchen and allow Lucinda inside while I swap my shovel attachment for my manipulators. They have pressure sensors.

Inside the kitchen, I put a kettle on the stove while Lucinda warms herself beside the radiator. "The tea will be ready in a few minutes," I say.

She doesn't answer, and I turn to see what has captured her attention. She has uncovered my easel and is looking at the latest of my failures. "Hmm? That'll be fine, Zed." She takes a seat at the small table in the corner. I recover the painting and roll to be opposite her. She reaches out and holds one of my manipulators in her hand. SIX PSI. SIX PSI.

"What's his mind like these days?" she asks. She looks at me when she speaks, unlike the doctor.

"It's fine," Dr. Octavio says, voice full of irritation, from the doorway. I hadn't noticed the gust of cold air. How could I? "What are you doing in here?" He points at me. "You're *my* servant, not hers. Get out there. I nearly broke my back on the ice, you useless heap of scrap!"

When I see the doctor, I see him in his youthful prime. He has designed me that way. Where his aged voice comes from, I see a stretched-out man with fidgeting hands and fevered blue eyes. I know that he must be decrepit by now. I do not know exactly how old he is, but he rants about the American Civil War as if he had been there.

Lucinda gives me an apologetic look, and I roll outside, but stop on the opposite side of the door. I extend my microphone and maximize the gain.

"I saw the village—or what was left of it, anyway!" Lucinda says. "So you're a mass murderer now? What did those people ever do to you?"

"They knew too much!" Dr. Octavio says, raising his voice to match hers. "The S.O.E. found me too easily last time! No one must know we are here. But you needn't worry," he grumbles, sounding like a child with a broken toy. "The death ray failed to function afterwards."

"Thank God for small miracles," she says. "I want to inspect the weapon, to be sure that you're not lying again, *father*." It is quiet for a moment, and I fear that I might have made a sound. No one comes to the door. Finally, Lucinda continues. "What are you working on now?"

"I don't have to tell you that!" Dr. Octavio nearly shrieks. "It's not a weapon, if that's what you want to know."

"It had better not be. The Germans are looking for weapons,

and if I find out you have been dealing with them, you will learn the true meaning of poverty." If I could shudder, I would at the tone of Lucinda's voice. When dealing with the subject of money, she can become as cold as this mountaintop.

They argue about money for an hour, and then the subject turns to Lucinda's latest heists, so I hurry away to the path. Sometime in the night, Lucinda departs.

I still sleep, much to the doctor's dismay. Sleep is a requirement of the mind as well as the body. Mostly I have nightmares, but sometimes I have a real dream. I dream that I still have hands that can paint, that can sculpt, that can play the piano. In the dream I have six arms, and I do all at once. When I drift awake, there are only the manipulators, reporting pressure. ZERO PSI. ZERO PSI.

My internal clock tells me that it is six A.M. and I must wake the doctor. I take the crude elevator that he has rigged to allow me access to all the floors. His bedroom chamber is dark and baroque, full of intricately carved furniture. The set was a gift from Lucinda last Christmas, and somehow he managed to retrieve it from our previous fortress in the South Pacific.

"Dr. Octavio, it is a new day," I say tonelessly. He groans and rolls out of the bed, apparently a well-muscled man in his mid-twenties. Well-endowed. He shuffles into the bathroom and waves me away. "Go clean something, Zed."

I obey.

Once Lucinda asked Dr. Octavio why he chose me, an unknown painter, to be the brain of his servant-machine. His reply is burned into my mind.

"Because he is an artist. Art serves no purpose but to distract. How does it improve the lives of men? Science is ultimately the true path of all men, even artists like him. Unfortunately, he is stubborn."

Dr. Octavio kidnapped me from my Paris studio, removed the brain from my body, and implanted it in a machine, to prove a philosophical point to no one in particular.

That is how the man's mind works.

"Zed, I need your assistance in the laboratory," he says to me from the doorway. His words hang in the air amidst the fog of his breath. How long has it been since he last asked me to assist him?

I turn from my shoveling and join him inside the laboratory. I wait for my lenses to clear. When they do, I witness his latest experiment.

Rows and rows of vacuum tubes connected with haphazard wiring line the walls, connected to more arcane machinery that I have no words to describe. Some of the machinery resembles parts of me, especially a manipulating arm that resembles mine, but significantly more advanced. I feel a deep pang of greed at the sight of it. The emotion surprises me, and I relish the sensation.

"What is your bidding, Dr. Octavio?" I ask.

He motions towards the arm. "I need you to interface with this. Come over here."

Dr. Octavio attaches me to the arm, and I flex it, checking the wiring. It seems good. It relays seven decimal pressures to my brain, far more sensitive than my own manipulators. "What would you like me to do with it?"

He shrugs, his attention already returning to a workbench crisscrossed with wiring. "I don't care. Give it a through testing for range of motion and dexterity."

"Can I retrieve a few things?" I ask.

"Fine, but don't be long. I have other tasks to attend to," he barks.

I collect my easel and paints from the kitchen and bring them to the laboratory. Dr. Octavio impatiently hooks me to the arm again, and I take up my brush.

An hour later, I want to weep. I haven't achieved this level of technique since Paris. I call for the doctor to inspect my work.

He picks up the canvas and examines it. He walks to the furnace and throws it inside. "The quality of the arm is sufficient. You may go."

It is spring when Lucinda returns. The snow has turned into freezing rain, and I've been using my flamethrower to clear ice from the path for a week. I clean the path before sunrise because I cannot sleep. After the Doctor caught me using the arm late one night, he has kept the lab padlocked. He shattered the sculpture with a sledgehammer.

Lucinda's zeppelin lands quietly and I watch as she leads several grey-uniformed men to the laboratory. They make short work of the lock, and I hear them breaking things inside the laboratory. Several minutes later, they leave with armfuls of equipment. Lucinda walks down the path to me.

"I'm sorry to do this to you, Zed," she says. Her face is bruised. "I owe money to some people." She stares at the castle for a moment, and then curses. "I'm sorry I'm leaving you here with him. One day I'll come back for you."

"Will you be all right?" I ask.

She forces a smile, and I almost believe her when she says yes.

"There's a war breaking out in Europe. The Germans have taken Poland. It will be a good time for someone in my profession." The men come out of the gondola and shout down at us in German.

They have guns. Lucinda walks back, slipping only a little. She waves at me from the cockpit when the *Kingfisher* takes off.

"Failed projects," Dr. Octavio says when he inspects the damage. "All junk. They have damaged my masterpiece, but it will only take a week to get back up to speed." He grins and rubs his hands together. He enjoys a good setback. It gives him an opportunity to refine work that his manic brain would not otherwise allow.

"What is this project?" I ask.

"Why should I tell you?" He says and squints at me. "I'm not going to let you use the arm again. You'll waste its potential on worthless doodles."

"Will it replace me?" I ask.

The doctor muses for a moment. "I think that in the end, it will replace all of us."

"What is it?"

He grins again. "My greatest invention. A machine that will be smarter than myself. A thinking machine, capable of creating machines more intelligent than itself."

"How can you create a machine that is smarter than yourself? Isn't that a . . . paradox?" I ask.

Dr. Octavio laughs. "No, it is not, but that is a good question. To create a mind smarter than my own, I only have to improve upon my design and give it a desire to further improve upon itself. By eliminating the flaws in my own mind, it will be superior. Then from its heightened perspective, it will analyze itself and continue to improve, all much faster at thinking than even the human adding machine." He taps his head. "It will be the Supreme Intellect, my ultimate achievement, and the ultimate achievement of science!"

"So the arm is for creating?" I ask, fear growing in me. I can sense my brain sending signals to a non-existent body. Run. Do something. The body does not obey these primitive signals.

"It will create others in its own image. I suspect humanity will become extinct in a century at the most." He says. "I have more vacuum tubes being air-dropped this afternoon. Go wait for them, and bring them straight to me when they arrive."

I obey.

There is no doubt in my mind that these machines will have no use for me. They will create themselves to be capable of serving all their needs. They won't need assistants. Nor will they need artists.

I roll down the unused road to the old village, keeping an eye on the sky for the airdrop. I maximize the gain on my microphone, listening for a hiss like snakes.

I awake from my nightmares to the sound of explosions. The castle shudders beneath me. Outside, it is raining in the darkness. There are British voices inside the castle. Dr. Octavio calls for me above it all using the radio commander. "Come quickly! Kill all who stand in your way!"

I attach my flamethrower as quickly as my manipulators allow and then I roll out into the hallway. British commandos spill through a break in the wall. They ignite like cheap wax candles and flail around uselessly. I press past them towards the elevator.

Dr. Octavio has fallen silent, and I suspect he has been captured. When I arrive at the highest floor of the castle, a commando opens fire with a machine gun. Bullets ricochet from my armor-plating and kill him.

Colonel Allen Stone of the S.O.E. stands over the doctor. He looms with his broad frame and thick arms, arms that I have wrestled before, years ago on the island. Dr. Octavio is handcuffed to a chair. "Tell us where the super-weapon is, Octavio!"

"What super-weapon?" The doctor asks. His eyes search around him wildly. Blood trickles from a cut in his upper lip. He sees me. "Zed, tell them. I have no weapons!"

I roll from the shadows. Stone and his men train their weapons on me. I can barely make the words. "It is in the . . . laboratory . . . ." My mechanical voice shuts down.

As my body shuts itself down, the world speeds up.

Dr. Octavio lurches forward in his chair roaring. One of the commandos spins and pulls the trigger. The gunshot deafens me, overriding all sound from my microphone. "Destroy everything down there," Stone says on his radio. My microphone shuts down.

Then the cameras. I am in darkness.

It starts as a buzzing sound. Someone is speaking. My cameras come back on line and focus sluggishly.

"He can hear me now?" Stone asks the balding technician in a white parka. The technician nods and backs away. We are outside in the snow.

"Stone," I say.

"Good. It's time to leave," Stone says, cigar clenched between his teeth. His zeppelin looms overhead. The laboratory billows smoke below us. Nothing will have escaped the fire.

"I must wait for someone," I say.

He looks away uncomfortably. "That wouldn't be Octavio's daughter, would it? Infamous jewel thief Lucinda Octavio, aka 'The Scarlet Ghost?'"

"Yes," I say. I feel something familiar rising from the depths of my reptilian brain. Fear? I have almost missed it.

"I guess you have no way of knowing, living out here . . . ."

I stare at him. If he doesn't say something soon, I will set him ablaze with the remaining fuel in my thrower.

"She's been captured by the Nazis." He pauses, considering his words. He stares at me with a perplexed expression, one I recognize as the result of searching me for outward signs of emotion. Lucinda has given me that look many, many times. I feel sorry for him. "Seems she tried to steal from Hitler himself. They've been trumpeting it in their papers and on the radio. Truth is we've been afraid she would lead them to Octavio. That's why we moved so quickly when you radioed us."

I pretend that I feel nothing. I have no heart.

"Come with us and you'll make a difference. British Intelligence has a lot of questions for your girl. We're going to go after her, and we might be able to use your help. What do you say, Zed?"

"My name is not Zed," I say.

"What the bloody hell should I call you then?"

I can barely remember my old name. It's time for a new one, I decide, to separate me from both my pasts.

"Tin Man."

Stone shrugs. He walks up the ramp into the gondola hanging a few feet above the ground. I turn my cameras to watch the smoke from the laboratory for a few more minutes, until I can be sure that I will never doubt the destruction of Octavio's masterpiece.

It begins to snow, and I roll up the ramp to join Stone. My thermometer shows that it is warm inside. I've finally come out of the cold. But to what end?

Even though I cannot feel the warmth, I am glad for it. ✪

THIS IS THE HIGHEST STEP IN THE WORLD
BY CARRIE VAUGHN

North of Tularosa, New Mexico. August 16, 1960. 0525.

WEARING THE PRESSURE SUIT, the oxygen supply, instrument pack and other equipment strapped to his back, Joe weighed over three hundred pounds. He moved ponderously. His breath fogged the inside of the plastic face shield of his helmet. The canned air smelled metallic and dry.

Clambering into the four-and-a-half-foot-wide gondola was an effort. His ground crew eased him to his perch. Compared to the fully contained and sealed gondolas of earlier projects, the Excelsior III gondola seemed flimsy: half a steel shell with a cutaway door, completely open.

Someone had painted a sign on the lower edge of the doorway: "This is the highest step in the world."

Don't fly too high. Your wings might melt.

Bullshit.

High above the gondola, a helium-filled polyethylene balloon strained into the pre-dawn sky, a silver teardrop reflecting floodlights. Joe's breath caught and his stomach churned. On paper, this mission looked like suicide.

His crew progressed to the end of a thousand-item checklist.

"Ready, Captain?" Daniel's voice was muffled through Joe's protective gear. Through the barrier of the helmet, the world seemed strangely silent, distant.

Joe gave him a thumbs-up. Please, God, make this one good.

A messenger ran from the meteorologist's van, legs and arms pumping. "The mission is cancelled! Storm's coming, abort!"

At the same time a pop sounded, a tiny explosion that meant the balloon's restraint lines had released.

Free at last, the balloon bucked and lurched up, hauling Joe with it.

100,000 feet above Tularosa. 0705.

At high altitude, the helium expanded in the low atmospheric pressure. The balloon transformed from a long teardrop shape to a sphere, three hundred feet high. Three million cubic feet of helium strained in all directions.

Joe couldn't move his right hand.

At about forty thousand feet, where the weight of the atmosphere began to thin until it was almost a memory, he discovered that the right glove of his suit had failed to pressurize.

The partial-pressure suit he wore was lined with tubes, bladders that filled with pressurized oxygen and compressed against his body, replacing the atmosphere and countering the physiological problems that accompanied travel in extreme altitudes: pooling blood, bursting vessels, and the like. He'd felt the suit's comforting squeeze press against his body as he left safe altitude, except in his hand. The seal must have broken.

He should have radioed the ground as soon as he realized what was happening. They'd abort the flight, he'd have to come home, and they'd be right. He knew what would happen. His hand would swell as his blood pooled, the pressure inside his body straining to burst into the low atmosphere, like the helium in the balloon. Circulation would cease, and his hand would freeze. It was already stiffening painfully.

But it wouldn't *kill* him.

Your wings might melt.

He should have radioed and aborted the flight, vented helium and sunk bank to earth. But this had to be the best flight yet. Excelsiors I and II hadn't flown past 80,000 feet. Except for the problem with his glove, everything was going smoothly, by the book. He couldn't let a little discomfort ruin that. He'd already talked to the ground crew about the storm, and they'd decided that completing the mission was worth the risk. There was a good chance the storm would pass to the north, and Joe would probably be back on the ground before it posed a threat. He'd convinced them that the mission was important enough to take the risk.

He wouldn't let down his team. If they were willing to risk a storm, he could risk an injured hand. He could take a little pain. If he couldn't move that hand, he'd make do. When ground control asked how he was doing, he said fine, and tried to keep the strain out of his voice.

The altimeter pointed at 102,800, some twenty miles above the surface of the Earth.

Now the real fun began.

Dangling from the balloon, the gondola twisted, panning his view one way and the other. The horizon curved. He was high enough to see the shape of the planet. Clouds had gathered. Far to the west, roiling cumulus banks swelled, the hint of another thunderstorm. He hoped he didn't have to worry about it.

He disconnected the radio. From now on, it was just him and the tape recorder. Slowly, methodically, Joe stood. He was cold, his joints were stiff, his suit awkward. His right hand was useless. He inched toward the doorway of the gondola. The clouds below looked very far away, featureless batting rather than the fluffy cotton balls he saw at lower altitude. They looked solid.

He inched a little farther, lugging his equipment with him: oxygen, a box of instruments that would record his next few moments. And his parachute.

His beating heart echoed inside his helmet. He moved slowly, in time with that rhythm. Toes edged over the rim of the gondola.

Twenty miles to fall.

"Lord, take care of me now."

He stepped out.

He felt no wind. The fabric of his suit didn't ripple with passing air. No Newtonian forces of gravity and inertia grabbed him and wreaked havoc with him. His body turned lazily, floating with apparent weightlessness.

Damn. I'm too high. I'm not falling. This can't be right!

He turned his head in time to see the immense silver globe of his balloon hurl away at terrifying speed, as if a hand had reached out and yanked it away from him. In moments it was only a flash against the blue-black sky of near space.

The sky was dark and the sun was shining, searingly bright.

Ninety-five thousand feet to fall.

He could no longer hear his heart.

95,000 feet above the New Mexico desert. 0710.

New Air Force jets had the capability to climb to higher altitudes than ever before. As pilots traveled to the upper atmosphere with greater frequency—and as the first astronauts began traveling into space—there was a chance they'd have to bail out. Joe wanted to prove that a pilot could eject at extreme altitude and survive the fall back to earth.

Parachuting out of a high-altitude balloon was cheaper than bailing out of a jet airplane and letting it crash.

Sixteen seconds after stepping from the gondola, Joe's stabilizing chute deployed successfully on an automatic timer. This was a small chute that wouldn't slow him, but would stabilize his descent. Without it, he ran the risk of entering a flat spin that would knock him unconscious and churn his internal organs to a pulp. They'd learned that from the test dummies.

The main chute wouldn't deploy until around 18,000 feet. Any sooner and his descent would be too slow and he'd freeze or asphyxiate before he reached the ground. Also, at this altitude he was falling too fast, close to seven hundred miles per hour. The force of a chute deploying would break him in half.

He had to survive four minutes of free-fall, approaching the speed of sound without the benefit of aircraft.

Pilots had once held the staunch belief that the sound barrier couldn't be broken. Strange things happened when they tried: they met massive turbulence, planes shook themselves apart. But the sound barrier *had* been broken. It had taken work, but they'd done it.

And here he was just *falling* through it. No sonic boom, no wind. Just him and the cloud layer coming closer. His mind froze, thinking of it.

Don't think. Do. People would get into space yet. Colonies on the moon before the end of the century. His grandchildren would look back on this stunt and think it was quaint, the way he thought the Wright Flyer was quaint. This was just a step. The highest step, but only so far.

He was falling, straight and true as an arrow. "Perfect stability!" he said for the benefit of the tape recorder documenting the jump. It was marvelous! He could move his arms, he could breathe, he could look around.

A light flashed, and he flinched. Something skittered across the face plate of his helmet. Little objects danced in the wind, reflecting sunlight. Feathers. A handful of long white feathers fluttered around him.

He was falling through the feathers, and the feathers were coming off the wings of a boy who was falling with Joe.

He must have been about fifteen, thin and still baby-faced. He wore a short tunic belted around his waist and leather sandals laced up his calves. The fabric of the tunic and his shoulder-length hair rippled and tossed in the wind. *It's an angel—*

The wings were artificial, bound to his arms and shoulders with leather straps. They were disintegrating, feathers whipping off in clumps. He flapped his arms, trying to steady himself, but he tumbled, legs flailing, wings bent back. They no longer had the right shape to give him enough lift for a proper glide.

Joe had to be seeing things. The boy shouldn't even be alive. He was practically naked, no pressure suit, no oxygen. He should have been frozen solid and purple with broken blood vessels.

Joe fell toward him, and for a moment they fell together. The boy looked over and met his gaze, even through the barrier of his helmet. His young face was gaunt with terror. He reached for Joe, clawing the air, but he spun away, buffeted, his wings ripping apart and slapping him. His mouth was open, but Joe didn't hear his scream. Joe plummeted away.

Too high! This is too high!

Joe's arms and legs flailed, and for a moment he thought he might enter the dreaded flat spin, despite the stabilizing chute.

The boy was falling to his death, and so was he. If only there was a way to go back to the balloon, if he could just slow down, the speed of sound was too fast for a lone human body to fly, oh God he was too high—

No. No, he wasn't. He'd planned this jump. His team of engineers and technicians, the best in the Air Force, who he trusted with his life, had planned this jump. This was the first step. Only the first step. It wouldn't even be the highest step for long. Humanity was destined to go in to space, destined to travel even higher, even farther.

The boy had flown too high, but Joe hadn't. Here was the proof: the boy didn't have a parachute. Joe did.

The boy was a hallucination born of fear.

Forty thousand feet.

40,000 feet above the New Mexico desert. 0718.

He thought it best not to mention the hallucination on the voice recorder.

The compression exerted by his suit eased up and disappeared. He returned to livable atmosphere. Thick air cushioned him and slowed his descent to a sane speed. His right hand was still ice-cold.

The thunderheads blew north. Joe wouldn't be falling through any storms today. The cloud layer still waited for him. He could finally see them as something more than flattened sheets of cotton. They looked solid, unyielding beneath his feet. Unconsciously, he tensed in anticipation of impact.

He passed through them, then out of them.

At 18,000 feet, the trigger in his main chute snapped, and a canopy of red and white striped silk burst forth and flowered around him. As air caught the chute, it billowed and spread. Joe jerked against the harness, his descent arrested. The chute would lower him gently the rest of the way to the ground. All he had to do was enjoy the ride. His wings hadn't melted, not this time.

"Thank you, God, thank you."

He cracked open his faceplate to take a breath of cool, succulent air. The earth had become recognizable: hills, dry riverbeds, the expanse of the New Mexico desert beneath him. The horizon was flat again. He heard the beat of a helicopter racing to the point where he'd touch down, west of Tularosa.

The balloon had taken an hour and a half to carry him over a hundred thousand feet up. He'd taken thirteen and a half minutes to fall the same distance back to earth.

It wasn't his best landing. He rolled, the parachute fell around him, and he chose to just lie there and let his crew come find him. They did, tumbling out of the helicopter. A half a dozen of them clustered around him, shoving aside chute cords and silk and pawing at his helmet. He waved a hand to let them know he was alive. Feeling—intense pins and needles—started to come back to his right hand. Maybe he wouldn't lose it after all.

Breathlessly, he told them how happy he was to see them.

He sat up as they pulled off his helmet. Looking down, his brow furrowed.

"Joe, what's the matter?"

With his still-gloved hand, he awkwardly tugged at something caught in one of the lacings on his pressure suit. He held it up, bright in the sunlight: a white feather, sticky with what looked like melted wax. ✪

As of 2004, Joseph Kittinger, Jr.'s record for the highest altitude parachute jump still stands.

THE SKY'S THE LIMIT

BY LAWRENCE M. SCHOEN

I AM SITTING WITH TWO PROMINENT CITIZENS in a booth of a Philadelphia restaurant where they serve a piece of prime rib as big as your head and I tell you this is not a thing I normally do, not just because I am rarely of an inclination to visit this city of brotherly love, but also as the price of this dinner represents the better part of my rent back in New York. But this is not concerning me as one of my dining companions, Joey Morlock, is also my host and his potatoes will be paying for my beef. Most nobody knows the reason, but Joey Morlock is called this on account of his peculiar reading habits in which he is having no time at all for the hard news or the racing form or the society page. Joey does not peruse the newspaper at all, saving his eyes, which look big as peaches behind his thick-as-soda-bottle-bottoms eyeglasses, solely for the reading of scientific romances.

I do not judge a man by the stories he favors, though personally I can find no use for tall tales of time machines or trips to the moon and guys know that I lose my patience with Joey on more than one occasion as he wants not just to read these stories but to talk of them too. His eyes pop open wide and glaze over like some bum who is sleeping one off in an alley and snaps up wide awake from some nightmare born of bad hootch. When this happens to Joey Morlock there is no stopping him and whosoever has the misfortune of being nearby can either rush for the exit or groan and endure the latest synopsis. But most times Joey is aces, a sport and a generous friend to have around. He is also the luckiest man I know in all forms of wagering and propositions, and I know more than a few. I am knowing Joey Morlock to wander up to Belmont on a whim with just a few dibs and leave there at the end of the day holding fifty large, and this is not an unusual circumstance for the guy. He is in fact so lucky that he is barred from most establishments and he is usually at a loss to find a track or crap game or card house that will let him in more than twice.

So when I hear word from Beans McAllister of a special card game that is forming in Philly, one in which there is to be no limit on the wagering, I immediately think of Joey Morlock and make mention of this development to him. Joey is delighted at this news and he insists I join him in Philadelphia as his guest, but this is also to his advantage as I can then introduce him to Beans and gain his admission to this friendly game whereat he plans to leave with as many potatoes as he can carry out. Joey is also kind enough to stake me to a seat at the game, which is entertaining for me but no loss to him as he will take all those potatoes back too, hand by hand. So knowing this now you should find no surprise that the third guy chowing down on the prime rib with Joey Morlock and me is none other than Beans McAllister who is making the acquaintance of Joey Morlock and enjoying a pricey bit of beef on his nickel.

Beans clearly favors the grub, but he looks on edge, nervous like, and the way he hunches over reminds me of a dog who gets beat six out of seven days as a pup and now is always flinching when you make to pet him. Not that I want to pet Beans, not even close. He is a little guy in a suit that looks like he slept in it under a bridge. But that is not why I do not want to be sitting with him; I am not the kind of guy who looks down on a joe because he does not know how to dress. No, I do not much want to be sitting with him because he is an accountant for a group of Philadelphia lawyers and I like bean counters only slightly less than I like shysters, and when I look over at Joey Morlock I can see he is of the same opinion. But Beans knows people in this town, and he knows where the game is, and I have explained this to Joey Morlock before we come to the restaurant so for the sake of the game he stakes Beans to the best meal of his bean counting life, confident that this will lead to many potatoes in the end. All through dinner Joey Morlock talks, but he does not talk of games or bets or propositions for fear of putting Beans more on edge and instead yammers like a doll at the cosmetics counter of Wanna-makers, on and on about giant bugs and invisible men. Finally, as Beans wipes his plate with the last bit of bread Joey switches over to the business at hand.

"Beans, our friend here tells me you can get me into a game," says Joey Morlock and he glances my way and I nod. "We are talking high stakes, right?"

"Highest you have ever been in," says Beans McAllister, and he laughs and gives me an elbow in the side, which I do not much appreciate on account I have just filled myself to bursting with some of the city's finest prime rib.

The look on Joey Morlock's face must be telling Beans that we do not get the joke because right then he leans over the table, giving me a closer look at his rumpled lapels and says to us both. "You ever been on an airship before?"

I give him a laugh back and say, "Oh sure, we come down from New York in one of them zeppelins. We had to leave it across the river in Jersey on account of high winds."

"No, really," says Beans. "You know what an airship is?"

"I have seen one," I says. "About eighteen years ago the Brits landed one in New York."

And just like that Joey Morlock's eyes pop wide and glaze over like they do when he is talking about them books he likes to read so much. He reaches out to grab my hand and begins pumping it like I just mentioned I went to school with the kid brother he ain't seen since the war. "You saw the *R.34* dirigible," he says, but his voice is soft as a hush and almost reverent and does not sound the way you expect to hear him talk. "I have only seen the American Navy airships, and only two of them, the *Shenandoah* and the *Macon*."

I have no idea what he is talking about so I just smile and retrieve my hand and pretend to take a sip from my water glass. Beans McAllister breaks into a grin but does not look like he knows what all is going on any more than me. I am still trying to understand why Beans asked about airships at all, and then it clicks and I roll my eyes because sometimes I can be dumber than a mortician's daughter.

"Your card game is on an airship," I says, and even I am not sure if I am asking a question.

"Yup," says Beans McAllister. "The game is on an airship. Only it ain't my game. It is Manhole McGovern's game."

When he says that name I can feel the ice water running in my veins and almost count the time it takes for my heart to freeze. I do not want to say even one bad word about Mr. Manhole McGovern. I do not want to say even one because I most firmly believe that am I to do so there is a very good chance that somehow, someday, Manhole will know and the very next day I will wake up that morning to find I am dead in my sleep of the night before. This is the kind of fellow Manhole McGovern is, and I know this only by reputation for he lives in Philly and I live in New York and if he ever decides to move to New York that is when I decide to move away, pausing only to tell my seven best friends to likewise move, and sparing no more time to warn anyone else. I have heard stories that Manhole McGovern is usually very methodical and precise in all he does, but that he has a temper like a volcano and when he is losing it even delights in inflicting pain in great quantities just to hear the effect it creates. This is not a natural way for a man to be, even such a man as rubs other fellows out, but this is what I hear from everyone about Manhole McGovern and now maybe you understand why I am saying these things and not saying them too. This is not a man I want to cross, and this is not a man I want to beat at cards, no matter how many potatoes may be involved.

I turn in the booth to explain all this to Joey Morlock and I am thinking if we hurry we can still catch the late train out of Union station back to New York when I stop dead. For if I am of the opinion that Joey Morlock's eyes are aglaze before then he is even worse off now and I know I am lost.

"An airship," he says. "I have always wanted to ride on an airship. What a tremendously perfect idea."

Perfect. This is what I think to myself. Perfect that I am going to play cards with Manhole McGovern flying in the sky. Perfect because if I start winning it will be easy for him to shove me out a door or a window. And I will not be able to hold onto the door or window because Manhole McGovern will first take the time to break each of the joints in each of my fingers before aiming me to the outside. Perfect.

*   *   *

So it is the next morning that Beans McAllister and Joey Morlock and I are standing on the air field and we are looking at an airship which I must tell you is at once both an amazing thing to behold and also very silly looking. I think of fat fat birds when I look at it, and I feel my stomach begin to go queasy. Now to be fair, part of this may be from the scrapple which I eat with breakfast not an hour before, but scrapple is what they eat in Philadelphia and so I give it a try and hope I am not to be regretting it later, but which I am now. Joey Morlock does not appear to share my discomfort, for he is gazing upon the airship and he has that look in his eyes again. You will believe me I am sure when I tell you I am weary to death of seeing this look of his.

"Who owns it?" says Joey Morlock, for he explains to me over breakfast that the navy is ever making only three airships and each of these crash one by one, a fact which though interesting does not fill me with confidence in the mode of travel.

"It is the property of a private concern," says Beans McAllister, and then he gives us a wink.

"How is it that Manhole McGovern can hold his card game there?" I says.

"He has a controlling interest in the private concern," says Beans.

"How controlling?" I says.

"Completely controlling. It being a gift from his cousins," says Beans and he smirks in a way that tells me he is doing some book work for Manhole McGovern on the side, which goes to explain how a guy like him has the inside word on a high stakes game like the one we are about to join. This, and because it is well known to me that Manhole acquires 'cousins' the way other men acquire neck ties, though no doubt he squeezes the cousins for far more potatoes than a new tie costs.

A car arrives and when the passenger door opens a doll steps out and time seems to stop like in one of those scientific romances that Joey Morlock talks about. This is no ordinary Judy, believe me, and I am not such a one as tends to lose his head over a doll. But this is the kind of doll whose kisser launches ships, and lots of ships, several hundred at least, though not usually of the lighter than air variety. I am still staring at this doll when I hear Joey Morlock asking who she is, which impresses me because myself I cannot put two words together to ask a question.

"That is Miss Caroline Carrock," says Beans, and even coming from this guy the name sounds like music. "But you can put your peepers back in your heads the both of you as she is Manhole's girl and I am advising you not to forget this distinction."

Manhole and his doll come over to us then and Beans McAl-lister makes with the introductions. While we are doing this, an-other car arrives, carrying the three other players in our little game but Joey and I barely notice them for we are still staring at the doll who is now on Manhole's arm and strolling with him across the airfield. We follow after, aiming for what looks like a tiny house which attaches to the bottom of the airship. Beans rushes on ahead, scurrying just behind Manhole and the doll, and the other three players are behind him. Joey Morlock and I are bringing up the rear, which is when he leans into me and says right in my ear, "I think I am in love."

Well this makes me stop in my tracks and I haul him to a stop too because there is something which I need to say and which he needs to hear. "Joey," says I, "you are the luckiest guy I know, and you have always been straight with me. On account of this I will return the favor and remind you of what you should already know. Namely, that a if a palooka is lucky enough to be lucky, he is lucky in cards or he is lucky with love, but no guy can be so lucky as to be lucky with both. Any guy who has a sweet-looking Judy like Miss Caroline Carrock on his arm is lucky in love, and you my chum are already known to be of the card-lucky persuasion."

I am saying all of this with my most sincere tone, but if Joey Morlock really hears any of it then I am a baboon smoking a Havana cigar. Instead he gives me this moon calf smile, sighs, and says, "I guess it is my lucky day."

This is when I am sure that the sinking feeling in my stomach is due to more than just Philadelphia scrapple. I am about to be in a card game with Manhole McGovern, staked by a pal who is hearing chirping bluebirds for a Judy who does not know he is alive, in an airship that I fully expect will crash if its owner does not throw me out an open door first after breaking my fingers. What can possibly happen to make this a worse day?

Understand, that while I know quite a bit about one Mr. Manhole McGovern, I do not know these things from direct observation, but have built up my knowledge from first hand accounts of a number of prominent citizens. Nor do any of these tales venture into the area of what games of chance Mr. Manhole McGovern favors. I know only that we are in a fancy room that does not look like what I am expecting to find under an airship but is instead bigger than any two rooms at a boarding house but more opulent and regal like. There is a fancy brass door at one end of the room that is our entrance, and another fancy brass door at the other end which leads to the second and less ritzy room. I come to know this because Joey Morlock is asking to see everything in the airship and Manhole McGovern very graciously obliges him, and looks to be taking an instant liking to Joey because he is getting to show off his fancy airship. In this way we learn that the other room is where the crew what pilots the airship sits and they are all decent guys who also like answering Joey Morlock's questions until finally Manhole McGovern pulls us all back into the main room. I am not such a guy as knows much about decor, but the room is pretty swell and reminds me of a posh hotel back in New York with all its dark polished wood and fancy upholstery with shiny brass buttons everywhere. Both long walls are overflowing with windows, the lead glass kind that must be murder to replace, and as he leads us back across the room I can see the air field on either side, and I am thinking that it is wholly unnatural for a pair of rooms to leave the ground and fly around, even for something as important as a high stakes poker game. We pass a tiny bar with three stools nudging up against one of the windows, and I am wishing for a drink to settle my insides but Manhole hustles us past the bar, closer to the first door that soon will lead to open air, where I spy two dolls what are just setting up chairs and a collapsible card table with lush green felt and no small amount of polish on the wood.

From these facts even Beans McAllister's mother can determine that we are here to play cards, and this woman is dead for some years may she rest in peace. I will go further though and say that even this posthumous mother of an accountant knows we are not present for just any game of cards, but specifically those variants which men of character know as poker. It does not enter into my mind even once that we will play canasta nor gin rummy nor bridge, though I confess in some circles they are recognizing me as being no slouch at this last game.

But no, we are here to play poker, and when Joey Morlock and I sit down it is poker I expect us to play. I am no stranger to high stakes games, and I know there are rules of the house and I am expecting there are rules of the airship too. This should be no problem I think, as high stakes games are simple and direct, and maybe there will be some slight quirks that are new to me but little other surprises. I am expecting draw poker and stud poker and maybe a hand or two of seven-toed Pete or the occasional wild card, just to keep it interesting. And in this I soon find I am mistaken. Manhole McGovern does not play traditional poker and he makes this clear to us. It is not enough for him that a Pair beats a high card, or a Full House beats a Flush which beats a Straight, or any of the usual objects of play in poker. For I discover as he explains the rules of the house that Manhole McGovern plays with a complexity of shades and special hands that I have only heard tell of here and there, by ones and twos for flair, but never all together in a single game.

This is not a problem though as Manhole takes from the inside pocket of his coat a small book which any of us can see is a copy of Hoyle and the final word on the rules of the game. I will confess that I am never reading this book, learning all I know about cards and dice and horses from friends and other acquaintances, and I say this to Manhole, hoping he will not take it the wrong way. But Manhole is patient and it is only when he is reviewing all these special hands for the third time, pointing out each special hand in his book, that I detect a growl in his voice as he distinguishes a Big Tiger from a Flush, a Little Dog from a Straight, a Skeet from a Blaze, and a Skip Straight from a Round-The-Corner Straight. I am making notes to myself to keep them all clear and I fear I am not doing so well and I ask if I can borrow his book, just to review while we play at cards and he is most agreeable on this point. I offer to share the book with Joey Morlock, but he merely nods and winks, and looks like he knows all these things which have never come up in any game of poker in which I have the pleasure to participate before. He knows them, but from his wink he is telling everyone that they are not for him, or so I think his wink means, but it is only a wink and so there is no telling for certain.

Or maybe it is just that he is remembering the most basic rule of poker, which as any card player will tell you is that in the showdown 'the cards speak for themselves' even if you do not know what your hand is worth. When I think of this I find it very encouraging and decide I will not worry so much about looking up every hand in Hoyle over and again and this is when I return Manhole's book to him. Also because beating Manhole at cards is a foolish proposition; no matter how much I might win here and now I am losing some time soon after the game is complete.

We begin to play, and there are six of us around the table. Manhole introduces two upstanding citizens from the great city of Chicago, and though he gives their names as Little Douglas and Cinnamon Bob, I am recognizing them as members of the mob and know that back in Chicago they go by Rob Roy and the Cologne Kid. Any doubt that might be in my noggin does not linger as in the closeness of the room it is clear how the Cologne Kid gets his name, and it is not cinnamon that I am smelling. The third fellow I also recognize and he recognizes me right back as we have sat with some of the same people in the same restaurants back on Broadway and I only nod when Manhole introduces him as the Duke of Paris. I know him by another name, but it is not a name I will be using here. It is a private game and I am thinking perhaps it is a game that afterwards no one will say ever happened because Manhole introduces Joey Morlock and me as H.G. and Arturo the Hungarian. I am thinking he must have some funny sense of humor with the way he is making up names, but it is his game that we are crashing so I do not make my comments out loud but keep them inside of my head where they will not offend or do me harm. Also in the room with us are Beans McAllister who does not have the potatoes of his own to play, and Miss Caroline Carrock who at the start is still hanging on Manhole but soon moves to a chair behind him and against the window as the game commences. The couple of dolls turn out to be bar hostesses and at Manhole's nod they go about making sure everyone has plenty to drink. Once all the introducing is over Manhole has one of the hostesses pass word to the crew flying the airship and soon after I get this feeling in my stomach like riding a Ferris wheel at the world's fair and we leave terra firma behind and venture into the sky. From my chair I can turn my head to look out the windows on either side, but there is nothing much to look at but the empty blue sky. I do not mind telling you that I am feeling a bit of apprehension, but also admiration as well for Mr. Manhole McGovern discovers a sure way for his card game to avoid a raid by the cops and this is most definitely a good thing as many a high stakes card game has seen shady cops bust in and take away all the potatoes for themselves.

And then it is time to play. It is dealer's choice and I win the first deal so start us with draw poker and that first hand sets the theme for me. I am losing, and with hands which I should rightfully win, but Manhole beats my Straight with a Little Tiger in one hand and in another he smokes my two pairs of aces and fives with a pair of kings and queens and a jack which gives him five face cards which according to Hoyle is a Blaze and he is laughing and taking my potatoes.

Joey Morlock is sitting to my left and when the deal comes to him again he deals a round of stud poker and I am hoping I will do better but it is not to happen. I come up with just a single pair but Manhole beats me playing a four flush, and he does this again and again as we play, one special hand after another taking not only my potatoes but also those belonging to the two citizens of the windy city and my longtime acquaintance from Broadway. But this is okay I say to myself, this is just jake, because I am learning the Dogs and Tigers, Big and Little, and I have almost got it straight and we are going to be playing for some time so though I do not expect to win as I previously mention, I hope to not lose too shamefully.

But as the cards go around and around I realize that my education in poker is not yet done, not when Manhole McGovern has dealer's choice. Again he reaches into his coat and opens the pages of his book and begins reading to us about other kinds of poker and as he is our host and it is his airship we have little choice but to play them. From just Stud Poker we move to Mexican Stud. And then Shotgun. And then Baseball. And then Double-Barreled Shotgun and Midnight Baseball. We play Cincinnati and Anaconda and Cold Hands and Double Dip and several more games which are poker but not the poker I know and love, and the names of which I can not remember because I can barely remember the rules of each and all of Manhole's special hands too, and I am regretting the drinks I take from the hostesses all unknowingly.

And it is not just me who is having trouble but also the guys from Chicago and the Duke of Paris and I am thinking that maybe if I really go by the moniker of Arturo the Hungarian these games might make more sense to me. I am finding no surprise that Manhole knows these games as his copy of Hoyle shows the wear of many careful readings, but Joey Morlock knows them too, and he is matching Manhole McGovern play for play, game after game, until hours go by and the rest of us surrender our potatoes to one or the other and just sit back in awe for never before do two fellows play the game of poker with such verve and style. And it is especially curious because when Manhole wins it is usually with one of the special hands that are making my head swim, but when Joey wins it is always with a regular hand and never a Big Tiger or a Skip Straight, not once, nor ever with a wild card of a winking Jack or a King with a deathwish, but only with regular solid hands. I feel like I am watching the giants of the game and all the time when I look out the window at the empty air I am thinking that if either Joey Morlock or I ever hope to see New York again that he needs to start losing soon. But if this thought crosses Joey Morlock's mind it does not stick there but trickles out his ear for he is winning more often than he is losing and bit by bit he is taking all of Manhole McGovern's potatoes.

By this time the boys from Chicago are dozing in their seats and the hostesses are taking away many empty glasses from them. The Duke of Paris is on my right hand side and is giving me significant types of looks which I read to mean that he is thinking what I am thinking but even the both of us thinking it cannot make Joey Morlock think it.

For most of the game Miss Caroline Carrock is sitting in her chair with her nose in a book, a fact which surprises me some because in my experience your brainier dolls are not such sweet Judys but this is a day for exceptions. During the last hour or so though she is peeking over her pages at Joey Morlock, and usually just after the showdown when he is raking in potatoes that are previously someone else's. I notice this. The Duke of Paris notices this. We notice each other noticing this. Manhole McGovern cannot notice this because Miss Caroline Carrock is sitting behind him and he is not the kind of card player to turn around even if he hears his mother calling fire which is not something you want to hear when you are playing poker onboard an airship. Whether Joey Morlock notices I cannot say though I remember the look he gives her before on the airfield and him saying he is in love. Right now though he looks only to be in love with the cards and the cards are in love with him because he is slowly taking all of Manhole McGovern's potatoes.

It is at this time I believe that the Duke of Paris and I are thinking two things. First, that it is going to end badly for Joey Morlock because Manhole McGovern is surely packing a shooter and will be reclaiming all his potatoes before we are done. And second, that an airship is not the best of places to be in when you are looking to make a quick exit to avoid sharing the lead that is about to be aiming itself at your fellow card player, especially lead from a guy as thorough about such things as I am knowing Manhole McGovern to be.

They are down to playing two card Hurricane and Manhole has put in the last of his potatoes, and the pot is the largest it has been all day. He has nothing left to bet, which is a shame because Joey Morlock does the ungentlemanly thing and raises.

"I find I am short at the moment," says Manhole. "But surely you will take my marker so that we may play out this hand."

"Do not be taking offense at this," says Joey Morlock and I am sweating off all the booze I ever drink in my life and going suddenly sober when I hear this because it is likely Manhole is going to take offense and the lead will begin to fly. "Do not be taking offense at this, but I am not from this city of Philadelphia and so cannot accept your marker in good conscience for I do not know when I might come this way again as I am visiting only to enjoy a quiet game of poker which I am doing, and thank you for inviting me."

"If you will not take my marker, then I cannot see your raise."

"If you cannot see my raise, then you must fold and the hand is over and I win. Unless . . . is there something else you have of value here?"

Manhole begins to frown and by now even Beans McAllister realizes what the Duke of Paris and I long since know, and is looking for a place to hide but there is none. But this is when we get ourselves a reprieve.

"I will wager you this airship," says Manhole McGovern, and everyone sighs with relief that the lead is not yet flying, except for the boys from Chicago who are snoring, and Miss Caroline Carrock who by now is no longer even pretending to read her book but is watching Joey Morlock with keen interest and a funny look in her eye. And I am thinking that maybe we will not all die today because at the offer of the airship Joey Morlock's eyes glaze over again and I know he is picturing himself as a character in one of his scientific romances and surely this distraction will make him lose.

"I accept the wager," says Joey, all breathy like.

"Hah!" says Manhole McGovern and he lays down his cards showing a pair of Kings. Now in Hurricane this is a very difficult hand to beat and so it is not surprising to anyone that Manhole is reaching for all the potatoes in the pot to pull them back to his side of the table.

"I do not think so," says Joey Morlock as he turns his cards over revealing a pair of bullets, intending no irony I am sure. He gently disengages Manhole's hands from the pot and rakes the potatoes back to his side leaving nothing at all on the other except Manhole McGovern who is staring down at his pair of kings with astonishment.

"I do not believe I lost," says Manhole.

"It is a very near thing," says Joey, which is a pretty sympathetic thing to say, considering, but will not keep us all from being thoroughly dead if Manhole McGovern is even one tenth the bad sport I hear him to be.

"One more hand!"

"I would, and gladly," says Joey Morlock, "only you do not have anything left to bet."

I notice that Miss Caroline Carrock is looking Joey Morlock's way and her eyes are getting all moist with interest because surely she has never seen anyone take all of Manhole McGovern's potatoes from him in a poker game and for some reason she finds this very attractive.

"One hand," Manhole says again, but Joey shakes his head. Well, this is apparently too much for Manhole and he finally does what the rest of us have been expecting him to do which is to pull a heater from his pocket and aim the business end at Joey Morlock's chest across the table.

Joey is sitting there, his eyes still glazing because now he has his very own airship and maybe does not yet see he is about to own nothing but a funeral plot and maybe a nice new headstone if Manhole McGovern is feeling generous. Or maybe not, because he only shrugs and says, "If you shoot me, you still will not beat me at cards."

This just makes Manhole even madder and he is pounding the card table with the heater now and it is a miracle he does not accidentally spray lead around the room. Instead, he begins to shout. "One. More. Hand."

"What will you bet?"

Which is when Manhole McGovern jumps up from his chair, grabs hold of the arm of Miss Caroline Carrock and hauls her over to the card table and says, "I will bet you my doll here."

"What is the game?" says Joey Morlock.

"Simple poker, no draw, nothing wild. Just five cards down, winner take all."

Joey Morlock just nods and reaches for the deck of cards and starts shuffling. Manhole McGovern puts his heater away then cuts the deck, all the while keeping one hand tight on Miss Caroline Carrock's arm and it is clear to all of us that this is one Judy who does not like being a wager in a not-so-friendly game of cards, but at the same time she is making eyes at Joey Morlock as if to say it is not such a bad thing if he wins her. Joey does not even notice though. He deals out the cards but when he is done he does not pick his up. Manhole turns his cards over and I am breathing the proverbial sigh of relief, which echoes from the Duke of Paris and Beans McAllister, for we are looking at a Straight Flush and thinking we are all going to live to see another day.

"What do you have?" says Manhole, but Joey still does not pick up his cards and he does not turn them over. Instead, he stands up and walks across the room and stands by the door where we come in in and he lays his hand upon the fancy brass handle.

"What do you have?" says Manhole again, and he is getting up from his chair and bellowing at Joey Morlock. "What do you have?" He reaches across the table and flips over Joey's cards and stares at them. I stare too. So does the Duke of Paris and even Beans McAllister. From where I am sitting, it appears that Joey has a Flush, which is a fine hand to have, though it cannot beat a Straight Flush. But Manhole McGovern must see something different because his face begins to change color, going from red to purple to umber and he is turning and yelling and charging at Joey across the room. And this is when Joey Morlock opens the door and steps lightly to the side. Manhole is moving fast, but the room is not so big and he is moving not so fast that he cannot stop himself from racing out the door. But Joey is standing there with one hand still on the handle and he reaches out with his other hand and grabs hold of Manhole McGovern's lapel and gives such a yank as pulls him forward another couple steps. Now this is unfortunate but still not tragic, as Manhole McGovern's feet are inside the room and all is fine. Except Joey puts his foot out, right where Manhole's foot is about to be, and Manhole trips and stumbles forward another couple steps which is about one step too many and he is gone, out the door, out of the room, and out of the airship, at which point Joey Morlock closes the door again and steps back to the card table.

Beans McAllister is in shock and cannot speak. The Duke of Paris is likewise in shock and cannot speak. The hostesses are feeling the most shock and they are cowering by the other door. Miss Caroline Carrock does not say word one, but I do not believe she is in shock because she rushes to Joey Morlock's side and slips her arm through his and I am thinking she has been wanting and waiting for something to happen to Manhole McGovern for a very long while. I go to Joey and before I can ask him what is transpiring he catches my eye and points to his hand still face up on the card table. I look at it again. It is still just a flush to my eyes, the nine, seven, five, trey, and deuce of hearts. Clearly there is something here I do not comprehend and it shows on my face and the Duke of Paris comes up and points out what I am missing.

"It is one of Manhole's special hands," he says. "It is a Skeet Flush, a nine and five and deuce with two cards in between, which always beats a straight flush."

While we are looking at the cards Joey Morlock is looking at Miss Caroline Carrock and it does not surprise me that he has that glazy look in his eyes again and she is staring at him with the same kind of look. He takes her by the hand and leads her to the other door which he opens and I hear him telling the crew to land the airship as soon as is convenient.

"Excuse me," I says, reluctant to break into my friend's bit of paradise as he seems to have the girl and the airship and all the potatoes, but one thing is still gnawing at me and I know I will not have any peace if I do not get an answer. "You got up and never once do you look at your cards. How is it you know it is the winning hand?"

But Joey Morlock does not answer as he is too busy gazing out the window with his arm around his new doll, and this reminds me again that he is the luckiest guy I know. Instead the Duke of Paris comes up to me and gives out with an explanation which makes no sense to me.

"He knows because of the cards," says the Duke of Paris. "The cards tell him so."

"Tell him?" I says. "How can the cards tell him? Cards do not talk. They do not whisper. They do not so much as yammer or jaw."

"That is not altogether true," says Joey Morlock without turning away from the window. "Any card player will tell you, the cards speak for themselves." ✪

A PERILOUS WARM EMBRACE

BY MICHAEL MANIS

AT NIGHT GEORGE SWEPT and watched the monkeys. When the zoo closed down, things were different. The birds were livelier in their cages, and the cats, who did nothing but sleep during the day, played with gusto. The noises came with the moon. Different kinds of sounds, contrasting with the usual cries of children reluctant to walk on the hottest days. George smiled at night, because those were the sounds of the wild: the cats roaring, the birds chirping. It was something fresh in a world of categorized monotony.

But the monkeys were something else.

George leaned against his broom and peered into the open-sky habitat built a few years before. His favorites were the gorillas. They reminded him of teddy bears, the way the little ones attached themselves to their mother's breast. Always hugging. Very late at night, when George was supposed to be home, the gorillas would weave together masses of leaves. The zookeepers said it was jungle instinct to make their beds out of foliage. George could never make a bed like that, but he could sweep and he wondered if they admired his cleaning as much as he admired their weaving.

George was happy when he watched the gorillas.

And then there were the chimps. The vets said they were stronger than three men and could rip his arm out of his socket without thinking twice. George did not think about the chimps that way, because they were always smiling and dancing for the tourists. They seemed happy in the same way the gorillas seemed content. Sometimes George would wave and the chimps would wave back.

But all that was during the day; at night they were not the same.

The gorillas sat close together when the zoo closed, and every so often one of them would look up at George. It creeped him out. The chimps gathered and the two groups mingled near the middle of the habitat. The monkeys were not lively like the rest of the animals at night. George wondered why and his curiosity kept the sidewalks around the monkey cages cleaner than any others in the zoo.

George would ask about the monkey gathering, and because the zookeepers were nice, they would tell him the apes were curious about each other, that's all. He figured that made sense. George wouldn't watch the monkeys if it weren't his own curiosity. But he felt unsettled while staring at the simian gathering. It went beyond curiosity into the realm of something profoundly social. George took out a box of matches, lighting his cigarette. One gorilla stared up at the flame. The others followed suit.

George took a step back. It was time to talk to Dr. Andrew about the monkeys, even though he was mean and once called George a retard because he laughed when a monkey ran away with Dr. Andrew's lab coat. George did not like being called a retard, and just thinking about it made him want to smoke more. He dropped the spent cigarette into a trash can. Sweeping, George listened to the primal serenade of bird and cat.

"They never did find that lab coat," George mumbled to himself.

George came to work early the next evening.

It was not long before the zoo closed down. He relieved the janitors on duty. George's uniform was brown; his mom thought it was ugly, but he liked to put it on anyway. George checked the to-do list left for him by the morning crew. It was full of the usual stuff, emptying garbage and the like, but at the bottom was something about helping feed the monkeys. George laughed; he knew the monkeys must have broken the feeding machine again. Those chimps had long arms. Sometimes they could reach inside and pull at the wires. Then George thought how dangerous that could be, and he stopped laughing.

He grabbed his broom, but before he started working, he jogged across the grounds to Dr. Andrew's office. For some reason Dr. Andrew always locked the door. George had to knock twice before he let him in.

"What is it, George?" Dr. Andrew asked.

George took a few steps forward, hesitating because the doctor looked busy.

"I want to talk about the monkeys," George said.

Dr. Andrew dropped his pen and looked up. "Yes?"

"I've been noticing, at night. The monkeys come together all weird. The gorillas and—"

"Apes George," Dr. Andrew interrupted. "How many times do I have to tell you, monkeys have tails, apes do not."

"I'm sorry." George smiled. "I mean the apes, they get together at night. I can see them. The chimps and the gorillas stand by each other for a long time. I don't think that's normal."

"Right. Um, look George, apes are social creatures. Gorillas are very curious and like to be around their own kind. That's why they gather. It's normal."

"But with the chimps?"

"It's getting late George, don't you have to get to work?"

"Yeah, but . . . ."

"Then you better do it, right?" Dr. Andrew asked.

George nodded.

The doctor picked up his pen and set to writing. George couldn't help but notice Dr. Andrew had a new lab coat . . . .

Sweeping, George felt a zookeeper tap him on the shoulder.

"Hey, George, we need you to help us with feeding," the zookeeper said.

George lowered his eyes. "I'm sorry, Charlie. Sometimes I forget things."

"It's okay. Come on."

He followed the zookeeper past bird cages to the door labeled *Employees Only* in big black letters. Charlie opened the door and George passed first, following along the edge of the tunnel to a cart filled with a menagerie of fruits and vegetables. George opened the gate to the habitat. Piece by piece they took the food, placing it in the feeding areas. When it was time to leave, the monkeys understood they could eat; they did not seem to mind the wait. George picked up a bundle of carrots. He approached the large, plastic platform the animals played on and spread the carrots out on top of it. The platform was loose and he made a mental note to tell Charlie.

An obtuse shadow cut across manicured grass.

George turned; from under the platform square shoulders emerged. Black fur encircled a pair of eyes and there was a smell when the gorilla made eye contact. Neither moved until the zookeeper noticed, and the black mass waddled forward. George took a step back.

"Charlie," George whispered.

"It's okay," the zookeeper said. "Keep calm, she's just a little curious, that's all."

"I don't know about that."

The gorilla picked up a carrot, smelling before dropping it and taking a few more steps. George could not move, and when he felt the gorilla's breath on his face, something in his stomach told him to run.

His legs did not comply.

He felt Charlie behind him, taking slow steps forward. The drone of the zookeeper's voice amounted to nothing while George focused on the leathery mass of fingers probing his uniform like an empty banana peel. She grunted, gesturing toward his tiny side pocket.

"Is—"

"Don't talk to her," the zookeeper interrupted.

The gorilla looked down at him.

"Do you want what's in there?" George asked, pulling at the matchbook in his pocket. He held it between two fingers.

"Stay still, George!" the zookeeper snapped.

The gorilla smiled, grabbed the match book and leapt back toward the group. Charlie cursed; he pulled George around by the shoulder.

"What'd you give it?" Charlie asked.

"She wanted my matchbook."

"Jesus George." He shook his head. "They'll have our asses for this."

The zookeeper pulled George into the tunnel. When they shut the gate, the monkeys started eating. Never had George seen something so large breathe just like he breathed. He peered down at his hands and noticed stagnant hairs littering his uniform. George smelled like the gorilla—a musty kind of odor reminiscent of an old dog. Silent, he watched the monkeys eat while Charlie called someone on the phone.

George wondered if the monkeys watched him too.

Dr. Andrew's office seemed very dark that evening.

He'd finished with Charlie, and George was invited in. He sat down at the desk. The doctor did not make eye contact.

"They didn't find the match book," Dr. Andrew said.

"We tried to find it," George mumbled.

"Yes, but you didn't. George, I know you may have trouble understanding this, but those matches can be very dangerous to an ape."

"Don't call me a retard," George said.

"I didn't call you a retard."

"That's what you mean, though, isn't it?"

Dr. Andrew smiled.

"No," he said. "That's not what I mean at all. I won't try to explain it to you, George. But Charlie told me everything I need to know. I'm afraid . . . ."

"Those monkeys or apes or whatever, they're not right. I told you they're not right—stealing things!"

"George, I told you, apes are curious. From what I heard, she didn't steal anything, you gave it to her."

"I'm not a retard," he mumbled.

"No one is saying you are. But this environment is a little complicated for you. I promise I'll write you a letter if you need one—"

"Don't do this."

"But we can't keep you here anymore."

And that was that.

George had three days to turn in his keys and clean out his locker. He did not stay around to talk to Charlie. Walking to the parking lot, he imagined different insults he could have said to Dr. Andrew. But the ones he found funny Dr. Andrew wouldn't get, and by the time George had another chance to say them, he wouldn't remember.

George still smelled like the gorilla; he was reminded of her breath against his face and he smiled.

He found his car and drove home. He did not shower that night.

Two nights and a holiday rolled over the calendar.

There was a skeleton crew at the zoo, and the parking lot was nearly empty so George took a spot near the front. He wore his uniform, but he didn't know why. He wanted to say goodbye to everybody—even Dr. Andrew and Charlie, but they were already gone when George came to their offices.

Oh well.

He strolled through the zoo, listening to the reverberation of crickets against the cloudless sky. The sound of his footsteps echoed so perfectly, he stopped himself. There was no purr of playful cats. No coo of excited birds. It did not feel wild to George. There was tension, yes, but not wild tension.

Everything was anticipatory.

George stood in the center square of the zoo. There were cages all around him; the ones for the smaller mammals, and he liked to think of them as dukes. The minor nobles lining the path like a red carpet to that open space in the distance where the kings awaited their tribute. It was romantic, and he followed that red carpet—the beaten path.

The dukes seemed to bow when he passed.

The sidewalks around the habitat were very clean. George was proud of his work. He stopped to admire it more to delay the inevitable than to congratulate himself. He did not want to leave the monkeys forever, because they wouldn't understand. George listened to the night sounds some more.

Then, even the crickets stopped.

It came in intervals over the wall of the habitat. First the curvature of the eggshell balloon, woven together by the permission of foliage in accordance with the incredible dexterity of simian hands. A white lab coat was sewn onto the nose of the inflated thing, a hub of strength. It could have been lined with bark, but George was not sure. There were ropes dangling from all directions: a favorite plaything of gorilla and chimp alike. The thing rose like a turtle walks, revealing a plastic platform attached by clever knots. Gorillas gathered round a pit of flame. The hottest air drifted skyward, proving wings obsolete. Chimps stood in line next to piles of fruit; they rotated in unison a log connected to an arrangement of rods and protrusions. It spun and spun, and George could not take his eyes away.

Up . . . everything was up.

The balloon was heavenly against the backdrop of stars. George did not know whether to run or yell or stand, but George did not know many things. So he watched the monkeys gather like the nights before. George smelled them, and the construct hovered just above the habitat.

The monkeys smelled him too.

A gorilla found the end of the platform. George locked eyes with her and grinned when she displayed his matchbook between thumb and forefinger. George's body decided to free up. He took hesitant steps forward. The gorilla did not recoil. Did not judge. And George was not a retard.

Simian strength can be a terrible thing. It can crush a man or tear even the most difficult fruit to insignificance. But its embrace is something perilously warm, and George knew the reason those little gorillas never let their mothers go. It was cold so high in the sky. Stars twinkled like the city below. The moon came out to play. It was all so wild to him, the breath of those monkeys against his face, that he did not miss the usual sounds of his own habitat. George rubbed his forehead against the arm of the gorilla but did not want to fall asleep. She ran her palm over his face. He saw row after row of teeth below giant eyes.

George's own eyes closed.

They were all silhouettes against the moon.

And everything was open sky. ✪

SKY LIGHT

BY DAVID BRIN

TROLLING FOR NEWS AT STREET LEVEL is getting harder all the time, Tor thought. *I'm glad I won't have to do it for a living any more.*

Not since one of the big ratings clubs gave her a Big Nod, boosting her credibility level all the way to National. One benefit of achieving professional status—in any field, not just the news biz—was getting to rise above all the hungry amateurs and semi-pros out there, scratching to be noticed.

The way she used to. But no more of that.

Well, not as much. From now on it would be office towers and arranged enterviews. Politicians. Celebrighties. Enovators. Luminatis. All sorts of nelites, no flashpans or sugar-coated surrogates.

Still, with her bags already stowed aboard the liner that would take her to a new life at MediaCorp Central, Tor underwent a sudden hanker—to go walking along the sidewalks and urb-ways, down by the waterfront, or under some of the bright bridges spanning the new ethnic neighborhoods of Sandiego—the Big S.

Call it strolling ... or S-trolling ... for something worthy of the news. A story fresh in her pocket to show the ace *tellers* when she arrived at MCX. Or at least for some distraction, to avoid chewing the active elements off her manicure while waiting for the embarkation whistle to blow—a throaty moan beckoning passengers to board the *Spirit of Chula Vista*.

Typically for an autumn morning, there had been another micro-monsoon just hours before dawn. It coalesced out of the swirling Catalina Vortex then drove ashore in a brief howl of horizontal rain. Now pavements glistened and pedestrians stepped gingerly over bits of debris. Some sea weed. An unlucky fish or two that had been sucked into the funnel at sea, then haplessly dropped here. Light stuff, mostly. None of the boats or rocks or surfers that gloomy commentators used to predict, back when the phenomenon began a decade ago, when it seemed the very sky was falling.

Some guys will say anything for ratings, she thought. People were always getting excited, overplaying bummer-effects of global warming without mentioning the good stuff.

Tor sniffed, relishing the up-side of a micro-monsoon. A fresh breeze. Washed clean of any pollutants from Old Town, it felt almost electric.

Other folk seemed affected the same way. Her specs, tuned to track bio signs, emphasized the flush tones of people who were in good spirit, for the most part. Smiling street vendors stepped out from their stalls, murmuring in a dozen refugee tongues— Russian, Finnish, Polish. When they saw that she didn't under-stand—her translator-earpiece hung detached—they switched to waving their hands and arms, drawing attention to patches of open space.

One used a theatrical flourish, like a stage magician materializing bouquets of imaginary flowers, all in a showy attempt to draw her glance to the awning above his stall. Tor wasn't shopping, though.

She had her specs tuned to omit adverts, so the merchant's virtual come-on remained invisible.

Well, she thought, shrugging at his disappointment. *The real world has always been crueler than our hopeful imaginings.*

The shopkeepers' own specs must have tattled, revealing her selective blindness. Still, even knowing it was futile, the tradesmen kept on smiling and waving as she passed. Several of them murmured compliments in broken English, that Tor took as sincere.

Well, it's nice to be noticed, in a friendly way.

Would she have chosen to be in news, if it didn't involve admiration?

Even nowadays, when a person's looks were largely a matter of taste, augmentation and budget, it felt good to make heads turn. Anyway Sandiego never lacked for pretty people. More flocked in all the time, undeterred by the prim legal admonitions and health warnings. She was depriving no one by moving away.

Out of habit, she tooth-clicked commands that tapped into other eyes, other cams. First a satellite view of this area, with the *Spirit* standing out most prominently, bobbing gently but hugely against her mooring mast at the nearby Zep-Port. In contrast, a little farther away, arsenal ships anchored by the new Shelter Island Naval Base appeared fuzzy, as demanded by security protocols. Silly. You could zoom in on them from three million, four hundred and seventy thousand, five hundred and twelve other points of view that Homeland Security did not control.

One of those POVs—a penny cam somebody had stuck on a lamp post, just above the chewing gum—won a brief auto-bid auction to sell her a closer view of the marketplace. A good panorama for half a mil. Not that Tor cared about that. Omnipresence

spread and prices fell as the cams bred and proliferated like in-
sects.

It sure was changing the news biz, at least in urban areas. Wherever cam overlap grew beyond seven layers deep, lying became
damn near impossible. Any kind of lying at all.

I guess the next generation will take that for granted, Tor thought.
But at twenty-six, she was old enough to remember when people
tried all sorts of tricks to fabricate images and fancy POV-deceits,
using tech wizardry to fake events, alibis and attempt blackmail.
Till the age old solution of *more witnesses* made that kind of scam
increasingly impossible. *With enough savvy eyes at work, consensus-
reality must come closer to reality itself.*

Or so went the latest truism. Tor distrusted all truisms.

We'll see if it still holds next year.

The quay was already getting crowded. S-trolling sailors haggled
with a street artist whose super-delicate portraits—molded out
of gel-smoke—could not be reproduced by fax or shipped by
omail, the very trait that made this medium valuable. That left
the boys—(few married men were stationed in Sandiego)—
without leverage to negotiate. No way to bid out the same service
elsewhere—at least not right away. Accepting the artist's price,
they forked over hard cash and she set to work, puffing from a
hookah pipe, adding clots of fast-congealing haze to a cloudy
caricature that grew texture and shape while onlookers sighed
approvingly.

Tor recalled a story she had been pondering, about how the
Navy assigned mostly young males to Big S. Supposedly to protect
the more radiation-sensitive fertility of female sailors. But one of
her leads had grumbled about old-fashioned sexism, a desire by
codgers at the upper ranks to preserve one base where macho elan
could still prevail in its full, grunting, TwenCen flavor.

Look into it later, Tor thought, subvocalizing a note to her specs, putting the topic on action list for when she had the full resources of MCX at hand.

Nearby, a tourist haggled with the proprietor of a craft shop selling hand-made canes and walking sticks. Using latest software and flex-fibers, the sticks could apparently perform a variety of strides and even break into a jog. The visitor—you could tell an out-of-towner because they always wore lead-lined underwear— agreed to a price, then asked about delivery.

"They're for my sister's store in Duluth," said the man, who perhaps did not realize that his metal briefs were causing telltale ripples in the display patterns of his vis-fiber jump suit. The effect made him look like a pot-bellied satire of Superman. Underpants on the outside. "Can she get them in a week?"

Waggling fingers and tapping his own specs, the shopkeeper quickly knew everything about the customer, his sister, the Duluth store and their ability to pay. Holding out a hand, he said—"Make it ten days. I'll have a batch mature by then. Deal?"

The two men shook. Their specs recorded. So did several on-lookers' including Tor's. No contract needed. As in villages of old, your reputation mattered more than any legal document. And now the "village" was worldwide.

Tor walked on.

Although her specs were tuned to omit adverts, virtual salesmen, and come-in lures, other kinds of enfo could penetrate, according to her private formula, laying over her viewfield a spiderweb of traces, links, cues and gloss commentaries. Faint nametags appeared under every passerby, for example, provided by automatic face recognition. Data that was dim enough to ignore, unless she decided to look. If her iris dynamics showed actual interest in a passing face, there might suddenly flow text and animation from that person's preening personal profile . . . or else dissenting opinions from an ex-spouse. Well, old-time villages were gossipy too.

For now though, Tor kept the virt overlays to a minimum. No kid stuff—fairy castles or leering caricatures, designed to make every passerby look silly. That was for preteens who quickly learned to squelch their derisive sniggers. A little imaginative dissing was all right. Freedom of Thought. But anything too overt or rude might draw unwelcome notice. The strolling grownup who looked the most clueless might be a member of a liaison-club that wasn't.

These days, when anyone could fight back, you learned courtesy early.

Anyway, who had time for kid stuff? Tor's ersatz world was pragmatic. The world's second stratum of texture, as important to any modern citizen as the scent of food and water might have seemed to a distant ancestor. The modern equivalents to a twig cracking. Hints of predator and prey.

She had assigned one color—a prickly shade of mauve—to glitter near any person or object on a public safety watch list. Everyone did that, adjusting sensitivities to their level of risk aversion. If your virtual view warned that a puddle held suspicious residue, you might step around . . . or else slosh on through, because this was, after all, Sandiego. Anyway, most cancers vanish with a weekly drop-in at the clinic.

Likewise, if a well-dressed man in a crowd wore an overlay-aura of misgiven reputation—on probation for a crime, perhaps, or maybe just a bad credit rating—people in most cities might edge away, made wary almost without thinking. But not here.

You grew a thicker skin in Big S. Some said *callousness*. She preferred calling it tolerance. The kind you found in any frontier town filled with refugees.

Hell, everybody had a past. And very few secrets. So you forgave most closeted skeletons, as others forgave yours.

*Still, mom will be glad to see me move somewhere civilized. Away
from the residuals.*

All the better to nag me for grandchildren.

But Tor knew she would miss the S.

Ever since the Bomb, low property values had pulled in a rich
mix of immigrants—both legal and quasi—mostly escapees from
frozen Europe. Exiles who didn't mind radioactivity levels a tad
above background. Not when compensated by sun, surf and exciting weather that sometimes dropped fish out of the sky. It beat
shivering, watching snowdrifts turn into glaciers outside Helsinki,
Warsaw and Stockholm. The Arctic's revenge, while most of the
planet baked.

Immigrants always stirred things. The music scene was way-*raki*.
The linguistic brew exciting. Manic-experimental arts flourished,
perhaps encouraged by a faint glow that seemed to surround the
buildings of old downtown at night. If you set your specs to notice
beta rays. Or even if you just squinted, bare-eyed, and let your
imagination go.

Tor shook herself and blinked. This wasn't like her. Quietly
strolling instead of S-trolling. Contemplating, not templating.
Musing, instead of sifting the scan spectra for stories to amuse
her fans. Every cubic centimeter above these sidewalks swarmed
with position-tagged information, notifications, e-comments
and post-its that existed only on the high-overlaid planes of IP6
cyberspace. Most of them were supposedly encrypted and per-
son-specific, but accessible to her sophisticated specs, if she used
cracker programs.

She could have been wading through all that, unleashing a pack
of snoop-agents and probing for a story, instead of wandering along

in almost-real mode, maundering nostalgically. What nonsense.

Lifting one hand, she prepared to correct the lapse, twiddling fingers to command . . . .

Too late, she realized, as a low, groaning whistle seemed to permeate, making the very air quiver, beckoning from the Lindbergh-Rutan Skydock. *Boarding call.*

Tor sighed, then turned to go.

But her reaction to the whistle did not go unnoticed. One near-by vendor tapped his specs while looking at her, then smiled and bowed.

"Bon voyage, Miss Tor," he said, with a thick Byelorussian accent.

Of course, he must have scan-correlated, found her on the *Spirit* passenger list and then noted her modest local fame. Another shopkeeper, grinning, pressed a cluster of fresh flowers into her hand as she passed.

A ripple of e-lerts flowed just ahead of Tor and suddenly she found herself walking along a corridor of evanescent goodwill, her arms filling with small, impulsive gifts and her ears with benedictions in a dozen languages.

Half-buoyed by a wave of sentiment for the town she was leaving behind, she made her way toward the terminal where mighty *Spirit of Chula Vista* bobbed ponderously at its moorings, straining for the sky.

Tor—despite the perceptiveness of all her surrogate guardians—never realized that she was being followed all that time. Indeed, there was no reason that she should. For it was a *ghost* that made its way close behind, stalking her through familiar, neighborly paths of a global village.

Beyond the pathways . . . outside the village . . . lay a jungle that her eyes could never see.

Washington was like a geezer—overweight and sagging, but with attitude. Most of its gutty heft lay below the beltway, in waistlands that had been downwind on Awfulday.

Downwind, but not out.

When droves of upper-class child-bearers fled the invisible plumes enveloping Fairfax and Alexandria, those briefly-empty ghost towns quickly refilled with immigrants—the latest mass of *teemers*, yearning to be free and willing to endure a little radiation in exchange for a pleasant five-bedroom that could be subdivided into nearly as many apartments. Spacious living rooms began a second life as store fronts. Workshops took over four-car garages and lawns turned into produce gardens. Swimming pools made excellent refuse bins—until government recovered enough to start cracking down.

Passing overhead, Tor could track signs of suburban renewal from her first class seat aboard the *Spirit of Chula Vista*. Take those swimming pools. A majority of the kidney-shaped ponds now gleamed with clear liquid—mostly water (as testified by the spectral scanning feature of her TruVu spectacles)—welcoming throngs of children who splashed under summertime heat, sufficiently dark-skinned to bear the bare sun unflinching.

So much for the notion that dirty bombs automatically make a place unfit for breeders, she thought. Let yuppies abandon perfectly good mansions because of a little strontium dust. People from Java and Celebes were happy to insource.

Wasn't this America? Call it resolution—or obstinacy—but after three rebuilds, the Statue of Liberty still beckoned.

The latest immigrants, those who filled Washington's waistland vacuum, weren't ignorant. They could read warning labels and health stats, posted on every lamp post and VR level. *So?* More people died in Jakarta from traffic or stray bullets. Anyway, mutation rates quickly dropped to levels no worse than Kiev, a few years after Awfulday. And Washington had more civic amenities.

Waistlanders also griped a lot less about minor matters like zoning. That made it easier to acquire rights-of-way, re-pioneering new paths back into those unlucky cities that had been dusted. Innovations soon turned those transportation hubs into boom towns. An ironic twist to emerge from terror/sabotage, especially when *sky trains* began crisscrossing North America.

Through her broad window aboard the *Spirit of Chula Vista,* Tor gazed across a ten mile separation to the West-Bound Corridor, where long columns of cargo zeppelins lumbered, ponderous as whales and a hundred times larger. Chained single-file and heavily laden, the dirigibles floated barely two hundred meters above the ground, obediently trailing teams of heavy-duty locomotives. Each towing cable looked impossibly slender for hauling fifty behemoths across a continent. But while sky trains weren't fast, or suited for raw materials, they beat any other method for transporting medium-value goods.

And passengers. Those who were willing to trade a little time for inexpensive luxury.

Tor moved her attention much closer, watching the *Spirit*'s majestic shadow flow like an eclipse over rolling suburban countryside, so long and dark that flowers would start to close and birds might be fooled to roost, pondering nightfall. Free from any need for engines of her own, the skyliner glided almost silently over hill and dale. Not as quick as a jet, but more scenic—free of ozone tax—and far cheaper, she followed her own tow cable along the East-Bound Express Rail, pulled relentlessly by twelve thousand horses, courtesy of the deluxe maglev tug, *Warren G. Harding.*

"Will you be wanting anything else before we arrive in the Federal District, Madam?" asked a voice from above.

She glanced up at a *servitor*—little more than a boxy delivery receptacle—that clung to its own slim rail on a nearby wall, leaving the walkway free for passengers.

"No, thanks," Tor murmured automatically, a polite habit of her generation. Younger folk had already learned to snub machinery slaves, except when making clipped demands.

"Can you tell me when we're due?"

"Certainly, Madam. There is a slowdown in progress due to heightened security. Hence, we may experience some delay crossing the Beltway. But there is no cause for alarm. And we remain ahead of schedule because of that tailwind across the plains."

"Hmm. Heightened security?"

"For the Artifact Conference, Madam."

"But—" Tor frowned. "That was already scheduled. Taken into account. So it shouldn't affect our timetable."

"There is no cause for alarm," the servitor repeated. "We just got word, two minutes ago. An order to reduce speed, that's all."

Glancing outside, Tor could see the effects of slowing, in a gradual change of altitude. The *Spirit*'s tow cable slanted a little steeper, catching up to the ground-hugging locomotive tug.

ALTITUDE: 359 METERS said a telltale in the corner of her left TruVu lens.

"Will you be wanting to change seats for our approach to the nation's capital?" the servitor continued. "An announcement will be made when we come within sight of the Mall, though you may want to claim a prime viewing spot earlier. Children and first-time visitors get priority, of course."

"Of course."

A trickle of tourists had already begun streaming forward to the main Observation Lounge. Parents, dressed in bright-colored sarongs and Patagonian slacks, herded kids who sported the latest youth fashion—fake antennae and ersatz scales—imitating some of the alien personalities that had been discovered aboard the *Dean Artifact*. A grand conference may have been called to declare whether it was a genuine case of First Contact, or just another hoax. But popular culture had already cast judgment. The Artifact was cool.

"You say an alert came through two minutes ago?" Tor wondered. Nothing had flashed yet in her peripherals. But maybe the vigilance thresholds were set too high. With a rapid series of clicks on her tooth implants, she adjusted them downward.

Immediately, crimson tones began creeping in from the edges of her specs, offering links that whiffed and throbbed unpleasantly.

Uh-oh.

"Not an *alert*, Madam. No, no. Just preliminary, precautionary—"

But Tor's attention had already veered. Using both clicks and subvocal commands, she sent her TruVus swooping through the data overlays of virtual reality, following threads of a *security situation*. Sensors tracked every twitch of the iris, following and often anticipating her choices while colored data-cues jostled and flashed.

"May I take away any rubbish or recycling?" asked the boxy tray on the wall. It dropped open a receptacle, like a hungry jaw, eager to be fed. The servitor waited in vain for a few moments. Then, noting that her focus lay far away, it silently folded and departed.

"No cause for alarm," Tor muttered sardonically as she probed and sifted the dataways. Someone should have banished that cliche from the repertoire for all AI devices. No human over the age of thirty would ever hear the phrase without wincing. Of all the lies that accompanied Awfulday, it had been the worst.

Some of Tor's favorite agents were already reporting back from the Grid.

KOPPEL—the summarizer—zoomed toward public, corporate and government feeds, collating official pronouncements. Most of them were repeating the worrisome cliche.

GALLUP—her pollster program—sifted for opinion. People weren't buying it, apparently. On a scale of one thousand, *no cause for alarm* had a credibility rating of eighteen, and dropping. Tor felt a wrench in the pit of her stomach.

BERNSTEIN leaped into the whistle-blower circuits, hunting down gossip and hearsay. As usual, there were far too many rumors for any person—or personal ai—to trawl. Only this time, the flood was overwhelming even the sophisticated filters at the Skeptic Society. MediaCorp seemed no better; her status as a member of the Journalistic Staff only won her a queue number from the Research Division and a promise of response "in minutes."

Minutes?

It was beginning to look like a deliberate disinformation flood, time-unleashed in order to drown out any genuine tattles. Gangsters, terrorists and reffers had learned the hard way that careful plans can be upset by some soft-hearted henchman, wrenched by remorseful second thoughts about innocent bystanders. Many a scheme had been spoiled by some lowly underling, who posted an anonymous squeal at the last minute. To prevent this, masterminds and ringleaders now routinely unleashed cascades of ersatz confessions, just as soon as an operation was underway—a spamming of faux regret, artificially generated, ranging across the whole spectrum of plausible sabotage and man-made disasters.

Staring at a flood of warnings, Tor knew that one or more of the rumors *had* to be true. But which?

Washington area beltway defenses have already been breached by machoist suiciders infected with pulmonella plague, heading for the Capitol . . . .

A coalition of humanist cults have decided to put an end to all this nonsense about a so-called "alien artifact" from interstellar space . . . .

The U.S. President, seeking to reclaim traditional authority, is about to nationalize the DC-area civil militia on a pretext . . . .

Exceptional numbers of toy airplanes were purchased in the Carolinas, this month, suggesting that a swarm attack may be in the making, just like the O'Hare Incident . . . .

A method has been found to convert zeppelins into flying bombs . . . .

Among the international dignitaries who were invited to Washington to view the Dean Artifact, there may be a few who plan to . . . .

There are times when human/neuronal paranoia can react faster than mere digital simulacra. Tor's old fashioned cortex snapped to attention a full five seconds before her ais, BERNSTEIN and COLUMBO, made the same connection.

Zeppelins . . . flying bombs . . . .

It sounded unlikely . . . probably distraction-spam.

But *I* happen to be *on* a zeppelin.

That wasn't just a realization. The words formed a message. With subvocal grunts and tooth-click punctuations, Tor broadcast it far and wide. Not just to her favorite correlation and stringer groups, but to several hundred Citizen Action Networks. Her terse missive zoomed across the Net indiscriminately, calling to every CAN that had expressed interest in the zep rumor.

This is Tor Pleiades, investigative reporter for MediaCorp—credibility rating seven hundred and fifty-two—aboard the passenger zep *Spirit of Chula Vista*. We are approaching the DC Beltway defense zone. That may put me at a right place-time to examine one of the reffer rumors.

I request a smart mob coalescence. Feed me!

Disinformation, a curse with ancient roots, had been updated with ultra-modern ways of lying. Machoists and other bastards might plant sleeper-ais in a million virtual locales, programmed to pop out at a pre-set time and spam every network with auto-generated "plausibles"—randomly generated combinations of word and tone that were drawn from recent news, each variant sure to rouse the paranoiac fears of *someone*.

Mutate this ten million times (easy enough to do in virtual space) and you'll find a nerve to tweak in *anyone*.

Citizens could fight back, combatting lies with light. Sophisticated programs compared eyewitness accounts from many sources, weighted by credibility, offering average folk tools to re-forge Consensus Reality, while discarding the dross. Only that took *time*. And during an emergency, time was the scarcest commodity of all.

Public avowal worked more quickly. Calling attention to your own person. Saying: "look, I'm right here, real, credible and accountable—*I* not *ai*—so take me seriously."

Of course that required guts, especially since Awfulday. In the face of danger, ancient human instinct cried out; *Duck and cover. Don't draw attention to yourself.*

Tor considered that natural impulse for maybe two seconds, then blared on all levels. Dropping privacy cryption, she confirmed her ticketed billet and physical presence aboard the *Spirit of Chula*

Vista, with real-time biometrics and a dozen in-cabin camera views.

"I'm here," she murmured, breathlessly, toward any fellow citizen whose correlation-attention ais would listen.

"Rally and feed me. Tell me what to do."

Calling up a smart mob was tricky. People might already be too scattered and distracted by the rumor storm. The number to respond might not reach critical mass—in which case all you'd get is a smattering of critics, kibitzers and loudmouths, doing more harm than good. A negative-sum rabble, its collective IQ *dropping,* rather than climbing, with every new volunteer to join. Above all, you needed to attract a core group—the seed cell—of online know-it-alls, constructive cranks and correlation junkies, armed with the latest coalescence software, who were smart and savvy enough to serve as *prefrontals* . . . coordinating a smart mob without dominating. Providing focus without quashing the creativity of a group mind.

We recognize you, Tor Pleiades, intoned a low voice, conducting through her jawbone receiver. Direct sonic induction made it safe from most eavesdropping, even if someone had a parabolic dish aimed at her ear.

Can you help us check out one of these rumors? One that might possibly be a whistle-blow?

The conjoined mob-voice sounded strong, authoritative. Tor's personal interface found good credibility scores as it coalesced. An index-marker in her left peripheral showed two-hundred and thirty members and climbing—generally sufficient to wash out individual ego.

"First tell me," she answered, subvocalizing. Sensors in her shirt collar picked up tiny flexings in her throat, tongue and larynx, without any need to make actual sound. "Tell me, has anyone sniffed something unusual about the *Spirit?* I don't see or hear anything strange. But some of you out there may be in a better position to snoop company status reports or ship-board operational parameters."

There was a pause. Followed by an apologetic tone.

Nothing seems abnormal at the public level. Company web-traffic has gone up sixfold in the last ten minutes . . . but the same is true all over, from government agencies to networks of amateur scientists.

As for the zeppelin you happen to be aboard, we're naturally interested because of its present course, scheduled shortly to moor in Washington, about the same time that delegates are arriving for the Artifact Conference.

Tor nodded grimly, a nuance that her interface conveyed to the group mind.

"And those operational readouts?"

We can try for access by applying for a Freedom of Information writ. That will take some minutes, though. So we may have to supplement the FOIA with a little hacking and bribery. The usual.

Leave that to us.

Meanwhile, there's a little on-site checking you can do.

Be our hands and eyes, will you, Tor?

She was already on her feet.

"Tell me where to go . . . ."

Head aft, past the unisex toilet.

". . . but let's have a consensus agreement, okay?" she added while moving. "I get an exclusive on any interviews that follow. In case this turns out to be more than . . . ."

There is a security hatch, next to the crew closet, the voice interrupted. Adjust your specs for full mob access please.

"Done," she said, feeling a little sheepish over the request for a group exclusive. But after all, she was supposed to be a pro. MediaCorp might be tuning in soon, examining transcripts. They would expect a professional's attention to the niceties.

That's better. Now zoom close on the control pad. We've been joined by an off-duty zep mechanic who worked on this ship last week.

"Look, maybe I can just call a crew member. Invoke FOIA and open it legally—"

No time. We've filed for immunity as an ad hoc posse. Under crisis rules.

"Oh sure. With me standing here to take the physical rap if it's refused . . . ."

Your choice, Tor. If you're in, press buttons in this order.

A virtual image of the keypad appeared in front of Tor, overlaying the real one.

"No cause for alarm," she muttered.

Feeling somewhat detached, as if under remote control, her hand reached out to tap the proposed sequence.

Nothing happened.

No good. They must've rotated sequences.

At that moment, the voice sounded a bit less cool, more individualized. Then a telltale indicator in her TruVu showed that some high-credibility member of the mob was stepping up with an assertive suggestion.

But you can tell it isn't randomized. I bet it's still a company-standard maintenance code. Here, try this instead.

Coalescence levels seemed to waver only a little, so the mob trusted this component member. Tor went along, punching the pad again with the new pattern.

"Any luck getting that FOIA writ? You said it would take just few minutes. Maybe it would be better to wait . . . ."

Procrastination met its rebuttal with a simple a click, as the access panel slid aside, revealing a slim, tubelike ladder.

Up.

No hesitation in the mob voice. Five hundred and twelve fellow citizens wanted her to do this. Five hundred and sixteen . . . .

Tor swallowed. Then complied.

The ladderway exposed a truth that was hidden from most passengers, cruising in cushioned comfort within the neatly paneled main compartment. Physics—especially gravity—had not changed appreciably in the century that separated the first great zeppelin era from this one. Designers still had to strive for lightness, everywhere they could.

Stepping from spindly rungs onto the cargo deck, Tor found herself amid a maze of spiderlike webbery, instead of walls and partitions. Her feet made gingerly impressions in foamy mesh that seemed to be mostly air. Stacks of luggage—all strictly weighed back in Diegotown—formed bundles that resembled monstrous eggs, bound together by air-gel foam. Hardly any metal could be seen. Not even aluminum or titanium struts.

"Shall I look at the bags?" she asked while reaching into her purse. "I have an omnisniffer."

What model? inquired the voice in her jaw, before it changed tone by abrupt consensus. More authoritatively, it said: **Never mind. The bags were all scanned in Diego. We doubt anything could be smuggled aboard.**

But a rumor-tattle points to possible danger higher up. We're betting on that one.

"Higher?" She frowned. "There's nothing up there except . . . ."

Tor's voice trailed off as a schematic played within her TruVus, pointing aft to another ladder, this one made of ropey fibers.

Arrows shimmered in VR yellow, for emphasis.

We finally succeeded in getting a partial feed from the *Spirit's* **operational parameters. And yes, there's something odd going on.**

They are using onboard water to make lift gas, at an unusual rate.

"Is that dangerous?"

It shouldn't be.

But we may be able to find out more, if you hurry.

She sighed, stepping warily across the spongy surface. Tor hadn't yet spotted a crew member. They were probably also busy chasing rumors, different ones, chosen by the company's prioritization subroutines. Anyway, a modern towed-zep was mostly automatic, requiring no pilot or navigator. A century ago, the *Hindenberg* carried forty officers, stewards and burly riggers, just to keep the ornate apparatus running and to deliver the same number of passengers from Europe to the U.S. At twice the length, *Spirit* carried several times as many people, served by fewer than a dozen attendants.

Below her feet, passengers would be jostling for a better view of the Langley Crater, or maybe Arlington Cemetery, while peering ahead for the enduring spire of the Washington Monument. Or did some of those people already sniff an alert coming on? Were families starting to cluster near the emergency chutes? Tor wondered if she should be doing the same.

This new ladder was something else. It felt almost alive and responded to her footstep by *contracting* . . . carrying her upward in a smooth-but-sudden jerk. Smart elastics, she realized. Fine for professionals. But the public had never taken a liking to ladders that twitch. The good news: it would take just a few actual footsteps at this rate, concentrating to slip her soles carefully onto one rung after the next . . . and worrying about what would happen when she reached the unpleasant-looking "hatch" that lay just overhead.

Meanwhile, the voice in her jaw took on a strange, lilting quality. The next contribution must have come from an individual member. Someone generally appreciated.

Come with me, higher than high,
  Dropping burdensome things.
Lighter than clouds, we can fly,
  Thoughts spread wider than wings.

Be like the whale, behemoth,
  Enormous, yet weightless beings,
Soundlessly floating, the sky
  Beckons a mammal that sings.

Tor liked the offering. You almost wanted to earn it, by coming up with a tune . . .

. . . only the "hatch" was now just ahead, or above, almost pressing against her face. A throbbing iris of polyorganic membranes, much like the quasi-living external skin of the *Spirit*. Coming this close, inhaling the exudate aromas, made Tor feel queasy.

Relax. The voice was back to business. Probably led by the zep mechanic. **You'll need a command word. Touch that nub in the middle to get attention and say** *cinnamon*.

"Cinnamon?"

It was only a query, but the barrier reacted instantly. With a faintly squishy sound, the door dilated. The stringy stepladder resumed its programmed journey, carrying her upward.

Aboard old-time zeps like the *Hindenberg*, the underslung gondola had been devoted mainly to engines and crew, while paying passengers occupied two broad decks at the base of the giant dirigible's main body. The *Spirit of Chula Vista* had a similar layout, except that the gondola was mainly for show. Having climbed above all the sections designed for people and cargo, Tor now rode the throbbing ladder into a cathedral of lifter cells, each of them a vast chamber filled with gas that was much lighter than air.

Hundreds of transparent, filmy balloons—cylindrical and tall like Sequoia trunks—crowded and pressed together, stretching from the web-floor where she stood all the way up to the arching ceiling of the *Spirit*'s rounded skin. Tor could only move among these towering columns along four narrow paths leading port or starboard . . . fore or aft. The arrow in her TruVu suggested **port**, without pulsing insistence. Most members of the smart mob had never been in a place like this. Curiosity—the strongest modern craving—formed more of these ad hoc groups than any other passion.

Heading in the suggested direction, Tor could not resist reaching out, touching some of the tall cells, their polymer surfaces quivering like the giant bubbles that she used to create with toy wands at birthday parties. They appeared so light, so delicate . . . .

Half of the cells contain helium, explained the voice, now so individualized that it had to be a specific person—perhaps the zep mechanic or a dirigible aficionado. **See how those membranes are made with a faintly greenish tint? They surround the larger hydrogen cells.**

Tor blinked.

"Hydrogen. Isn't that dangerous?"

She pictured the *Hindenberg*—or *LZ-129*—that greatest and most ill-fated zeppelin, whose fiery end at Lakehurst, New Jersey, marked the sudden end of the First Zep Era, in May of 1937. Once ignited—*how* remained a topic of fierce debate—flames had engulfed the mighty airship from mooring-tip to gondola, to its swastika-emblazoned rudder in little more than a minute. To this day, journalists envied the news crew that had been on-hand that day with primitive movie cameras, capturing onto acetate some of the most stunning footage and memorable imagery that ever accompanied a technological disaster.

Nowadays, what reff or terror group wouldn't just love to claim credit for an event so vivid? So attention-grabbing?

As if reading her mind, the voice lectured.

Hydrogen is much lighter and more buoyant than helium. Using it improves the economics of zep travel. Hydrogen is also cheap and readily available. Though of course, care must be taken . . . .

Tor was approaching the end of her narrow corridor. For the first time, she encountered the trusswork that kept *Spirit* rigid—a dirigible—instead of a floppy, balloonlike blimp. A girder made of carbon tubes, woven into an open latticework of triangles, stretched and curved both forward and aft. Nearby, it joined another tensegrity girder at right angles. That one would form a girdle, encircling the *Spirit*'s widest girth.

Tracking Tor's interest, her TruVu spun out statistics and schematics. At 800 feet in length, the *Hindenberg* had been just ten percent shorter then the *Titanic*. In contrast, the *Spirit of Chula Vista* stretched more than twice that length. And yet, its shell and trussworks weighed less than half as much.

Naturally, there are precautions, the voice continued. *Take the shape of the gas cells. They are vertical columns. Any failure in a hydrogen cell triggers a pulse, bursting open the top, pushing the contents up and out of the ship, skyward, away from passengers, cargo or people below. It's been extensively tested.*

Also, the surrounding helium cells provide a buffer, keeping oxygen-rich air away from those containing hydrogen. Passenger ships like this

one carry double the ratio of helium to hydrogen that you'll find on
cargo zeps.

"They can replenish hydrogen en route if they have to, right? By
cracking water from onboard stores?"

Or even from humidity in the air, using solar power.

And yes, the readouts show unusual levels of hydrogen production,
in order to keep several cells filled aboard the *Spirit*. That's why we
asked you to come up here. There must be some leakage. One scenario suggested that it might be accumulating in here, between the
cells.

She pulled the omnisniffer from her purse and began scanning. Chemical sensors were all over the place, nowadays, getting cheaper and more acute all the time—just when the public
seemed to need them. For reassurance, if nothing else.

"I'm not detecting very much," she said. Tor wasn't sure how
to feel—relieved or disappointed—upon reading that hydrogen
levels were only slightly elevated in the companionway.

That confirms what the onboard monitors have already shown.
Hardly any hydrogen buildup in the cabins or walkways. It must be
leaking into the sky—

"Even so—" Tor began, envisioning gouts of flame erupting toward the heavens from atop the great airship.

—at rates that offer no danger of ignition. The stuff dissipates very
fast, Tor, and the *Spirit* is moving, on a windy day. Anyway, hydrogen isn't dangerous—or even toxic—unless it's held within a confined
space.

Tor kept scanning while moving along the spongy path. But
hydrogen readings never spiked enough to cause concern, let
alone alarm. The smart mob had wanted her to come up here for
this purpose—to verify that the onboard detectors hadn't been
tampered with by clever saboteurs. Now that her independent

readings confirmed the company's, some people were already starting to lose interest. Ad hoc membership totals began to fall.

Any leakage must be into the air, continued the voice of the group mind, still authoritative. *We've put out a notice for amateur scientists, asking for volunteers to aim spectranalysis equipment along the Spirit's route. They'll measure parts-per-million, so we can get a handle on leakage rates. But it's mathematically impossible for the amounts to be dangerous. Humidity may go up a percent or two in neighborhoods that lie directly below Spirit's shadow. That's about it.*

Tor had reached the end of the walkway. Her hand pressed against the outer envelope—the quasi-living skin that enclosed everything, from gas cells and trusses to the passenger cabin below. Up close, it was nearly transparent, offering a breathtaking view outside.

"We passed the Beltway," she murmured, a little surprised that the diligent guardians of Washington's defensive grid would have allowed the *Spirit* to pass through that wall of sensors and rays without delay or scrutiny. Below and ahead, she could make out the *Warren G. Harding,* tugging hard at the tow cable, puffing along the Glebe Road Bypass. Fort Meyers stood to the left. The zeppelin's shadow rippled over a vast garden of gravestones—Arlington National Cemetery.

The powers-that-be have downgraded our rumor, said the voice in her jaw. *The nation's professional protectors are chasing down other, more plausible threats . . . none of which have been deemed likely enough to merit an alert. Malevolent zeps don't even make it onto the Threat Chart.*

Tor clicked and flicked the attention-gaze of her TruVu, glancing through the journalist feeds at MediaCorp, which were now—belatedly—accessible to a reporter of her level. Seven minutes after the rise in tension caused by that spam flood of rumors, a consensus was already forming. The spam flood had *not* been intended to distract attention *from* a terror attack, concluded mass-wisdom. It *was* the attack. And not a very effective one, at that. National productivity had dropped by a brief diversion factor of one part in twenty-three thousands. Hardly enough damage to be worth risking prosecution or retaliation. But then, hackers seldom cared about consequences.

Speaking of consequences; they were already pouring in from her little snooping expedition. The mavens of propriety at MediaCorp, for example, must be catching up on recent events. A work-related memorandum flashed in Tor's agenda box, revising tomorrow's schedule for her first day of work. During lunch—right after basic orientation—she was now required to attend counseling on *Exercising Good Judgment In Impromptu Field Situations.*

"Oh great," she muttered, noticing also that the zeppelin company had applied a five hundred dollar fine against her account for Unjustified Entry Into Restricted Areas.

PLEASE REMAIN WHERE YOU ARE, MS. PLEIADES, said an override message. **AN ATTENDANT WILL ARRIVE AT YOUR POSITION SHORTLY IN ORDER TO HELP YOU RETURN TO YOUR SEAT FOR LANDING.**

"Double great."

Ahead, beyond the curve of the dirigible's skin, she spotted the massive, squat bulk of the Pentagon, bristling with missiles, antennae and other security measures … still a highly-protected enclave, even ten years after the Department of Defense moved its headquarters to "an undisclosed location in Texas."

Soon, the mooring towers and docking ports of Reagan-Clinton National Skydrome would appear, signalling the end of her cross-continental voyage. And of any chance for a blemish-free start to her new career in the Big Time.

"I don't suppose any of you have bright ideas?" She addressed the group mind.

But it had already started to unravel. Membership numbers were falling fast, like rats deserting a sinking ship, Or—more accurately—monkeys. Moving on to the next shiny thing.

Sorry, Tor. People are distracted. They've been dropping out to watch the opening of the Artifact Conference. You may even glimpse some limos arriving at the Naval Research Center, just across the Potomac. Take a look as the *Spirit* starts turning for final approach . . . .

Blasted fickle amateurs! Tor had made good use of smart mobs on several occasions. But this time was likely to prove an embarrassment. None of *them* would have to pay fines or face disapproval in a new job.

Still, a few of us remain worried, the voice continued.

That rumor had something about it.

I can't put my finger on it.

The "voice" was starting to sound individualized and had even used the first person "I." And yet, Tor drew some strength from the support. Before an attendant arrived to escort her below, there was still time for a little last minute tenacity.

"Can I assume we still have some zep aficionados in attendance?"

Hardly anyone else, Tor.

Some of us are fanatics.

"Good, then let's apply fanatical expertise. Think about that *leakage* we discussed a while ago. We've been assuming that this zeppelin is making hydrogen to make up for a major seep. Have any of those amateur scientists studied the air near *Spirit*'s flight path?"

A pause.

Yes, several have reported. They found no dangerous levels of hydrogen in the vicinity of the ship, or in its wake. The seep is probably dissipating so fast . . . .

"Please clarify. No dangerous levels? Is it possible they found no sign of a hydrogen leak *at all?*"

The pause extended several seconds longer, this time. Suddenly the number of participants in the group stopped falling. In the corner of Tor's TruVu, she saw membership levels start to rise again.

Now that's interesting, throbbed the voice in her jaw.

Several of those AmScis have joined us now.

They report seeing no appreciable leakage. Zero extra hydrogen along the flight path. How did you know?

"I didn't. Call it a hunch."

But at the rate that *Spirit* has been replacing hydrogen . . . .

"There has to be some kind of leak. Right. It must be going somewhere."

Tor frowned. She could see a shadow moving beyond the grove of tall, cylindrical gas-cells. A figure approaching. A crewman or attendant, coming to take her, firmly, gently, insistently, back to her seat. The shape wavered and warped as seen through the mostly transparent polymer tubes—slightly pinkish for hydrogen and then greenish-tinted for *helium.*

Tor blinked. Suddenly feeling so dry-mouthed that she could not speak aloud, only subvocalize.

"Ask the AmScis to take more spectral scans along the path of this zeppelin. Only this time look for helium."

The inner surfaces of her TruVus showed a flurry of indicators. Amateur scientific instruments, computer-controlled from private backyards or rooftops, could zoom quickly toward any patch of sky. There were thousands of such pocket observatories, in and around any urban center. Dotted lines appeared. Each showed the viewing angle of some amateur astronomer, ecologist or meteorologist, turning a home-made or kit-made instrument toward the majestic cigar shape of the *Spirit of Chula Vista* . . .

. . . which had passed Arlington and Pentagon City, following its faithful tug into a final tracked loop, approaching the dedicated zeppelin port that served Washington DC.

Yes, Tor. There is helium.

Quite a lot of it, in fact.

A plume that stretches at least a hundred klicks behind the *Spirit*.

The voice was grim. Much less individualized. With ad hoc membership levels suddenly skyrocketing, summaries and updates must be spewing at incredible pace.

Your suspicion appears to be well-based.

Extrapolating the rate of helium loss backward in time, half of that gas may have been lost by now . . .

" . . .replaced in these green cells by another gas." Tor nodded. "I think we've found the missing hydrogen, people."

It all made sense, now. Smart polymers were programmable—all the way down to the permeability of any patch of these gas-containing cells. If you did it very cleverly, you might insert a timed instruction where two gas cells touched, commanding one cell to leak into another. Create a daisy chain. Helium vented into the sky. Hydrogen transferred into the helium cells to maintain pressure. Trigger automatic systems to crack onboard water and "replace" the hydrogen, replenishing the main cells. Continue.

Continue until you have replaced the helium in enough of the green cells to turn the *Spirit* into a flying bomb.

"The process must be almost complete by now," she murmured, peering ahead toward the great zep port, where dozens of mighty dirigibles could already be seen, some of them vastly larger than this passenger liner, bobbing gently at their moorings. Spindly fly-cranes went swooping back and forth as they plucked shipping containers from ocean freighters at the nearby Potomac Docks, gracefully transferring the air-gel crates to waiting cargo-zeppelins. A deceptively graceful, swaying dance that propelled the engines of commerce.

The passenger terminal—dwarfed by comparison to those giants—seemed to beckon with a promise of safety. But indicators showed that it still lay as much as ten minutes away.

We have issued a clamor, Tor, assured the voice in her jaw. Every channel. Every agency.

A glance at telltales showed Tor that, indeed, the group mind was doing its best. Shouting alarm toward every official protective service, from Defense to Homeland Security. Individual members were lapel-grabbing friends and acquaintances while smart mob attendance levels climbed into five figures, and more. At this rate, surely the professionals would be taking heed. Any minute now.

"Too slow," she said, watching the figures with a sinking heart. With each second that it took to get action from the Protector Caste, the perpetrators of this scheme would also grow aware that *the jig is up*. Their plan was discovered.

Speaking of the perps, Tor wondered aloud:

"What can they be hoping to accomplish?"

We're pondering that, Tor. Timing suggests that they aim to disrupt the Artifact Conference. Delegates arriving at the Naval Research Center are having a cocktail reception on the embankment right now, offering a fine view toward the zep port, across the river.

Of course it is possible that the reffers plan to do more than just put on a show, while murdering three hundred passengers. We are checking to see if the *Warren G. Harding* has been meddled with. Perhaps the plan is to hop rails and collide with a large cargo zep, before detonation. Such a fireball might be seen all the way from the Capitol, and disrupt the port for months.

One problem with a smart mob. The very same traits that multiplied intelligence could also make it seem dispassionate. Insensitive. Individual members surely felt anguish and concern over Tor's plight. She might even access their messages, if she had time for commiseration.

But pragmatic help was preferable. She kept to the group mind level.

One (anonymous) member (a whistle-blower?) has suggested a bizarre plan using a flying-crane at the zep port to grab the *Spirit of Chula Vista* when it passes near. The crane would then hurl the *Spirit* across the river, to explode right at the Naval Research Center! In theory, it might just barely be possible to incinerate—

"Enough!" Tor cut in.

Almost a minute had passed since realization of danger and the issuance of a clamor. And so far, nobody had offered anything like a practical suggestion.

"Don't forget that I'm here, now. We have to do something."

Yes, the voice replied, eagerly and without the usual hesitation. There is sufficient probable cause to get a posse writ. Especially with your credibility scores. We can act, with you performing the hands-on role.

Operational ideas follow:

Cut the towing cable. (Emergency release is in the gondola. Reachable in four minutes. Risk factor: possible interference from staff. Ineffective at saving the zeppelin/passengers.)

Persuade zep company to commence emergency venting procedures. (Communication in progress. Response so far: obstinate refusal . . . .)

Persuade onboard staff to commence emergency venting procedures. (Attempting communication despite company interference . . . .)

Persuade company to order passenger evacuation. (Communication in progress. Response so far: obstinate refusal . . . .)

Upgrade clamor. Independently contact passengers urging them to evacuate. (Dangers: delay, disbelief, panic, injuries, fatalities, lawsuits . . . .)

The list of suggestions seemed to scroll on and on. Rank-ordered by plausibility-evaluation algorithms, slanted by urgency, and scored by likelihood of successful outcome. Individuals and sub-groups within the smart mob split apart to urge different options with frantic vehemence. The inner face of her TruVu flared, threatening overload.

"Oh, screw this," Tor muttered, reaching up and tearing off the specs.

The real world—unfiltered. For all of its paucity of layering and data-supported detail, it had one special trait.

It's where I am about to die.

Unless I do something fast.

At that moment, the zep-crew attendant arrived. He rounded the final corner of a towering gas cell, coming into direct view— no longer a shadowy authority figure, warped and refracted by the tinted polymer membranes. Up close, it turned out to be a small man, middle-aged and clearly frightened by what his own TruVus had started telling him. All intention to arrest or detain Tor had already evaporated during the last minute. She could see this in his face, as clearly as if she had been monitoring vital signs.

WARREN, said a company name tag.

"Wha—what can I do to help?" he asked in a hoarse whisper.

Though hired for gracile weight and people skills, the fellow clearly possessed some courage. By now he knew what filled many of the slim membranes surrounding them both. And it didn't take a genius to realize the zep company was unlikely to be helpful during the time they had left.

"Tool kit!" Tor held out her hand.

Warren fumbled at his waist pouch. Precious seconds passed as he unfolded a slim implement case. Tor found one promising item—a vibrocutter.

"Keyed to your biometrics?"

He nodded. Passengers weren't allowed to bring anything aboard that might become a weapon. This cutter would only respond to his personal touch. It required not only a fingerprint, but volition—physiological signs of the owner's will.

"You must do the cutting, then."

"C-cutting . . . ?"

Tor explained quickly.

"We've got to vent this ship. Empty the gas *upward*. That'll happen to a main cell if it is ruptured *anywhere* along its length, right? Automatically?"

A shaky nod. She could tell Warren was getting online advice, perhaps from the Zep Company. More likely from the same smart mob that she had called into being. She felt strong temptation to put her own specs back on—to link-in once more. But she resisted. Kibitzers would only slow her down right now.

"It might work . . . ," said the attendant in a frightened whisper. "But the reffers will realize, as soon as we start—"

"They realize *now!*" She tried not to shout. "We may have only moments to act."

Another nod. This time a bit stronger, though Warren was shaking so badly that Tor had to help him draw the cutter from its sleeve. She steadied his hand.

"We have to slice through a helium bag in order to reach the big hydro cell," he said, pressing the biometric-sensitive stud. Reacting to his individual touch, a knife edge of acoustic waves began to flicker at the cutter tip, sharper than steel. A soft tone filled the air.

Tor swallowed hard. That flicker resembled a hot flame.

"Pick one."

They had no way to tell which of the greenish helium cells had been refilled, or what would happen when the cutter helped unite gas from neighboring compartments. Perhaps the only thing accomplished would be an early detonation. But even that had advantages, if it messed up the timing of this scheme. One lesson you learned early nowadays: any citizen can wind up being a front-line soldier for civilization, at any time.

"That one." Warren moved toward the nearest.

Though she had doffed her TruVu specs, there was still a link. The smart mob's Voice retained access to the conduction channel in her jaw.

Tor, said the group mind. **We're getting feed through Warren's goggles. Are you listening? There is a third possibility. In addition to helium and hydrogen. Some of the cells may have been packed with—**

She bit down twice on her left canine tooth, cutting off the distraction in order to monitor her omnisniffer. She inhaled deeply, with her eye on the indicator as Warren made a gliding, slicing motion with his cutter.

The greenish envelope opened, as if along a seam. Edges rippled apart as invisible gas—appreciably cooler—swept over them both.

HELIUM, said the readout. Tor sighed relief.

"This one's not poisonous."

Warren nodded. "But no oxygen. You can smother." He ducked his head aside and took another deep breath. The next words had a squeaky, high-pitched quality. "Gotta move fast."

Through the vent he slipped, hurrying quickly to the other side of the green cell, where it touched one of the great chambers of hydrogen.

Warren made a rapid slash.

Klaxons bellowed, responding to the damage automatically. (Or else, had the company chosen that moment, after several criminally-negligent minutes, to finally admit the inevitable?) A voice boomed insistently, ordering passengers to move—calmly and carefully—to their escape stations.

That same instant, the giant hydrogen gas cell convulsed, twitching like a giant bowel caught in a spasm. The entire pinkish tube—bigger than a jumbo jet—*contracted*, starting at the bottom and squeezing toward a sudden opening at the very top, spewing its contents skyward.

Backwash hurled Warren across the green tube. Tor managed to grab his collar, dragging him out to the walkway. There seemed to be nothing satisfying about the 'air' that she sucked into her lungs, and she started seeing spots before her eyes. The little man was in worse shape, gasping wildly in high-pitched squeaks.

Somehow, Tor hauled him a dozen meters along the gangway, barely escaping descending folds of the deflated cell, arriving at last where breathing felt better. *Did we make any difference?* She wondered, wildly.

Instinctively, Tor slipped back on her TruVu specs. Immersed again in the info-maelstrom, it took moments to focus.

One image showed gouts of flame pouring from a hole in the roof of a majestic sky-ship. Another revealed the zeppelin's nose starting to slant steeply as the tug-locomotive began pulling frantically on its tow cable, reeling the behemoth toward the ground. *Spirit* resisted, like a stallion, bucking and clinging to altitude.

Tor briefly quailed. *Oh Lord, what have we done?*

A thought suddenly occurred to Tor. She and Warren had done this entirely based on information that had come to them from *outside*. From a group mind of zeppelin aficionados and amateur scientists who claimed that a lot of extra hydrogen had to be going somewhere, and it must be stored in some of the former helium cells. But *that* helium cell had been okay. And now, amid all the commotion, she wondered. What about the smart mob? Could that group be a front for clever reffers, who were using *her* to do their dirty work? Feeding false information, in order to get precisely this effect?

The doubt passed through her mind in seconds. And back out again.

This smart mob was open and public. If something smelled about it, *another* mob would have formed by now, clamoring like mad and exposing the lies. Anyway, if no helium cells had been tampered with, the worst that she and Warren could do was bring a temporarily disabled *Spirit of Chula Vista* down to a bumpy but safe landing atop its tug.

Newsworthy. But not very. And that realization firmed her resolve.

Tor yanked the attendant onto his feet and urged him to move uphill, toward the stern, along a narrow path that now inclined the other way. "Come on!" She called to Warren, her voice still squeaky from helium. "We've got to do more!"

Warren tried gamely. But she had to steady him as the path gradually steepened. When he prepared to slash at another green cell, farther aft, Tor braced his elbow.

Before he struck, through the omniscient gaze of her TruVu, Tor abruptly saw three more holes appear in the zep's broad roof, spewing clouds of gas, transparent but highly-refracting, resembling billowy ripples in space.

Was the zep company finally taking action? Had the reffers made their move? Or had the first expulsion triggered some kind of compensating release from automatic valves, elsewhere on the ship?

As if pondering the same questions, the Voice in her jaw mused.

Too little has been released to save the *Spirit* from the worst-case scenario. But maybe enough to limit the tragedy and mess up their scheme.

It depends on whether some of the helium cells have been refilled with oxygen. After experimenting with the programmably permeable polymer, one of us found that the fuel replenishment process could be jiggered to do that. If so, the compressed combination—

Tor shouted "Wait!" as Warren made a hard stab at one of the green cells, slicing a long vent that suddenly blurped at them.

This wave of gas wasn't as cool as the helium had been. It smelled terrific, though. One slight inhale filled Tor with sudden and suspicious exhilaration.

Uh oh, she thought.

At that moment, her TruVu display offered a bird's eye view as one of the new clouds of vented hydrogen contacted dying embers, atop the tormented *Spirit of Chula Vista*.

Like a brief sun, each of the refracting bubbles ignited in rapid succession. Thunderclaps shook the dirigible from stem to stern, knocking Tor and Warren off their feet.

Is this it? Her own particular and special End of the World. Strangely, Tor's clearest thought was one of professional jealousy.

Someone down below ought to be getting truly memorable and historic footage. Maybe on a par with the Hindenberg Disaster.

While the violent tossing drove Tor into fatalism, all that invigorating oxygen seemed to have an opposite effect upon Warren, who surged to his feet, then charged across the green cell, preparing to attack the giant hydrogen compartment beyond, heedless of the smart-mob, clamoring at him to stop.

Tor tried to add her own plea, but found that her throat would not function.

Some reporter, she thought, taking ironic solace in one fact— that her TruVu was still beaming to the Net.

Live images of a desperately unlikely hero.

Warren looked positively giddy—on a high of oxygen and adrenaline, but not too drugged to realize the implications. He grimaced with an evident combination of fear and exaltation, while bringing his cutter-tool slashing down upon the polymer membrane—a slim barrier separating two gases that wanted, notoriously, to unite.

✪

Sensory recovery came in scattered bits.

First, a smattering of dream images. Nightmare-flashes about being chased, or else giving chase to something dangerous, across a landscape of burning glass. At least, that was how her mind pictured a piling-on of agonies. Regret. Physical anguish. Failure. More anguish. Shame. And more agony, still.

When the murk finally began to clear, consciousness only made matters worse. Everything was black, except for occasional crimson flashes. And those had to be erupting directly out of pain— the random firings of an abused nervous system.

Her ears also appeared to be useless. There was no real sound, other than a low, irritating humming that would not go away.

Only one conduit to the external world still appeared to be functioning.

The Voice in her jaw. It had been hectoring her dreams, she recalled. A nag that could not be answered and would not go away. Only now, at least, she understood the words.

Tor? Are you awake? We're getting no signal from your specs. But there's a carrier wave from your tooth-implants. Can you give us a tap?

After a pause, the message repeated.

And then again.

So, it was playing on automatic. She must have been unconscious—out of it—for a long time.

Tor? Are you awake? We're getting no signal from your specs. But there's a carrier wave from your tooth-implants. Can you give us a tap?

There was an almost overwhelming temptation to do nothing. Every signal that she sent to muscles, commanding them to move, only increased the grinding, searing pain. *Passivity* seemed to be the lesson being taught right now. Just lie there, or else suffer even more. Lie and wait. Maybe die.

Also, Tor wasn't sure she liked the group mind anymore.

Tor? Are you awake? We're getting no signal from your specs. But there's a carrier wave from your tooth-implants. Can you give us a tap?

On the other hand, passivity seemed to have one major drawback. It gave pain an ally.

Boredom. Yet another way to torment her. Especially her.

To hell with that.

With an effort that grated, she managed to slide her jaw enough to bring the two left canine teeth together in a tap, and then two more.

The recording continued a few moments—long enough for Tor to fear that it hadn't worked. She was cut off, isolated, alone in darkness. But the group participants must have been away, doing their own things. Jobs, families, watching the news. After about twenty seconds, though, the Voice returned, eager and live.

Tor!

We are so glad you're awake.

Muddled by dull agony, she found it hard at first to focus. But she managed to drag one canine in a circle around the other. Universal symbolic code for QUESTION MARK.

«?»

The message got through.

Tor, you are inside a life-sustainment tube. The rescue service found you in the wreckage about twelve minutes ago, but it's taking some time to haul you out. They should have you aboard a medi-chopper in another three minutes, maybe four.

We'll inform the docs that you are conscious. They'll probably insert a communications shunt when you reach hospital.

Three rapid taps.

«NO»

The Voice had a bedside manner.

Now Tor, be good and let the pros do their jobs. The emergency is over and we amateurs have to step back, right?

Anyway, you'll get the very best of care. You're a hero! Spoiled a reffer plot and saved a couple of hundred passengers. You should hear what MediaCorp is crowing about their "ace field correspondent." They even back-dated your promotion a few days.

Everybody wants you now, Tor, the Voice finished, resonating in her jaw without any sign of double entendre. But surely individual members felt what she did right then.

Irony—the *other* bright compensation that Pandora found at the bottom of her infamous Box. At times, irony could be more comforting than hope.

Tor was unable to chuckle, so her tooth did a half circle and then back.

«!»

The Voice seemed to understand and agree.

Yeah.

Anyway, we figure you'd like an update.

Tap inside if you want details about your condition. Outside for a summary of external events.

Tor bit down emphatically on the outer surface of her lower canine.

Gotcha. Here goes.

It turns out that the scheme was to create a garish zep disaster. But they chiefly aimed to achieve a distraction.

By colliding the *Spirit* with a cargo freighter in a huge explosion, they hoped not only to close down the zep port for months, but also to create a sudden fireball that would draw attention from the protective and emergency services. All eyes and sensors would shift for a brief time. Wariness would steeply decline in other directions.

They thereupon planned to swoop into the Naval Research Center with a swarm attack by hyper-light flyers. Like the O'Hare Incident but with some nasty twists. We don't have details yet. Some of them are still under wraps. But it looks pretty awful, at first sight.

Anyway, as it turned out, our ad hoc efforts aboard the *Spirit* managed to expel some of the stockpiled gases early and in an uncoordinated fashion. Several of the biggest cells got emptied, creating gaps. So there was never a single, unified fire when the Enemy finally pulled their trigger. That kept the dirigible frame intact, enabling the tug to reel it down to less than a hundred meters.

Where the escape chutes mostly worked. Two out of three passengers got away without injury, Tor. And the zep port was untouched.

Trying to picture it in her mind's eye—perhaps the only eye
she had left—took some effort. She was used to so many modern visualization aides that mere words and imagination seemed
rather crude. A cartoony image of the *Spirit*, her vast upper bulge
aflame, slanted steeply downward as the doughty *Harding* desperately pulled the airship toward relative safety. And then, slender
tubes of active plastic snaking down, offering slide-paths for the
tourist families and other civilians.

The real event must have been quite a sight.

Her mind roiled with questions. What about the rest of the
passengers?

What fraction were injured, or died?

How about people down below, on the nearby highway?

Was there an attack on the Artifact Conference, after all?

So many questions. But until doctors installed a shunt, there
would be no way to send anything more sophisticated than these
awful yes-no clicks. And some punctuation marks. Normally,
equipped with a TruVu, a pair of touch-tooth implants would
let her scroll rapidly through menu choices, or type on a virtual
screen. Now, she could neither see nor subvocalize.

So, she thought about the problem. Information could inload
at the rate of spoken speech. Outloading was a matter of clicking
two teeth together.

Perhaps it was the effect of drugs, injected by the paramed-
ics. But Tor found herself thinking with increasing detachment, as if viewing her situation through a distant lens. Abstract
appraisal suggested a solution, reverting to much older tradition
of communication.

She clicked the inside of her lower left canine three times. Then the *outer* surface three times. And finally the inner side three more times.

What's that, Tor? Are you trying to say something?

She waited a decent interval, then repeated exactly the same series of taps. Three inside, three outside, and three more inside. It took one more repetition before the Voice hazarded a guess.

Tor, a few members and ais suggest that you're trying to send a message in old-fashioned Morse Code.

Three dots, three dashes, then three dots. S.O.S.

Is that it, Tor?

She quickly assented with a *yes* tap. Thank heavens for the diversity of a group mind.

But we already know you are in pain. Rescuers have arrived. There's nothing else to accomplish by calling for help . . . except . . . .

The Voice paused again. **Wait a minute.**

There is a minority theory floating up. A guess-hypothesis.

Very few modern people bother to learn Morse Code anymore. But most of us have heard of it. Especially that one message you were using.

S.O.S. Three dots, three dashes, three dots.

Is that what you're telling us, Tor?

Would you like us to teach you Morse Code?

Although she could sense nothing external, not even the rocking of her life-support canister as it was being hauled by evacuation workers out of the smoldering *Spirit of Chula Vista*, Tor did feel a wash of relief.

«YES», she tapped.

Most definitely yes.

Very well.

Now listen carefully. We'll start with the letter A . . . .

It helped to distract her from worry, at least, concentrating to learn something without all the tech-crutches relied upon by today's college graduates. Struggling to absorb a simple alphabet code that every smart kid used to memorize, way back in that first era of zeppelins and telegraphs and crystal radios.

Back when the uncrowded sky had seemed so wide open and filled with innocent possibilities. When the smartest mob around was a rigidly marching army. When a journalist would chase stories with notepad, flashbulbs, and intuition. When the main concern of a citizen was earning enough to put bread on the table.

Way back, one human lifespan ago, when heroes were tall and square-jawed, in both fiction and real life.

Times had changed. Now, destiny could tap anybody on the shoulder, even the shy or unassuming. You, me, the next guy. Suddenly, everybody counts on just one. And that one depends on everybody.

Tor concentrated on her lesson, only dimly aware of the vibrations conveyed by a throbbing helicopter, carrying her (presumably) to a place where modern miracle workers would strive to save—or rebuild—what they could.

Professionals still had their uses, even in the rising Age of Amateurs. Bless their skill. Perhaps—with luck and technology—they might even give Tor back her life.

Right now, though, one concern was paramount. It took a while to ask the one question that burned foremost in her mind, since she needed a letter near the end of the alphabet. But as soon as they reached it, she tapped out a Morse Code message that consisted of one word.

«WARREN»

She did not expect anything other than the answer that her fellow citizens gave.

Even with the hydrogen cell contracting at full force to expel most of its contents skyward, there would have been more than enough right there, at the oxygen-rich interface, to incinerate one little man. One volunteer. A hero, leaving nothing to bury, but scattering microscopic ashes all the way across his nation's capital.

Lucky guy, she thought, feeling a little envy for his rapid exit and inevitable fame.

Tor recognized what the envy meant, of course. She was ready to enter the inevitable phase of self-pity. A necessary stage.

But not for long. Only till they installed the shunt.

After that, it would be back to work. Lying immersed in sustainer-jelly and breathing through a tube? That wouldn't stop a real journalist. The web was a beat rich with stories, and Tor had a feeling she was going to get to know the neighborhood a whole lot better.

And we'll be here, assured the smart mob. **If not us, then others like us.**

You can count on it, Tor.

We sure as heck do.

We all depend on it. ✪

NEGATION ELIMINATION

BY ROBERT BURKE RICHARDSON

$$\frac{\neg \neg A}{\therefore A}$$

NEGATION ELIMINATION: *In logic and the propositional calculus, a rule stating that double negatives can be eliminated without changing the content of the proposition.*

PROFESSOR THOMPSON TANG GAO developed strange habits during his weeks in the airborne prison. View impeded only by the rows of golden, birdlike flying machines trailing the *Vimana*, Gao rose each morning before dawn to watch the stars slowly wink out. He would read or write, not certain whether sun or moon illuminated his page, until suddenly the day gained undisputed dominance over the shifting cloudscape. It was during such a moment that Captain Visvajit summoned him for the first time.

Gao's guardsman escort closed the door to the captain's cabin, stifling the wind of the exposed walkway (an addition that, like the air-chariot docks, Visvajit had made after stealing the *Vimana* from the Tsar's Imperial Air-Fleet) and leaving only the hum of the zeppelin's engine. Judging from his possessions, Visvajit was part military commander, part holy pilgrim. Sandalwood incense floated over a map-covered war table and a statue of Shiva stood opposite a wall decorated with sabers. Visvajit wore a white *shalwar khameez* with a plain soldier's sword at his hip. He knelt on an ornate rug, head bent in prayer.

"Have you reconsidered using the Leibniz Machine to aid our conquest?"

Gao frowned. "You did not ask me to—"

Visvajit laughed, an easy, powerful sound. He stood from his prayer and, for a moment, Gao thought the captain's head would hit the ceiling. It fell quite short, and Gao chided himself. Visvajit's charismatic presence made him seem taller than he actually was.

"I did not need to ask, Professor. Your position is well known." Visvajit poured two cups of tea. The scent of cardamom tantalized Gao's taste buds. "But the world looks different from up here. I wanted to share my perspective with you."

Gao took the double meaning. Visvajit had arranged the view from Gao's cell to take in both the fantastic sunrises and the fleet of ancient air-chariots. Gao accepted a cup and drank deeply, enjoying the hint of adventure the exotic flavors evoked.

"I'm afraid my position remains unchanged," said Gao. "I will neither sanction nor aid your invasion of Kamchatka."

"But you came here to tell me something." Visvajit placed his empty cup on the table, shifted the sword in his belt and sat in a high-backed chair. He gestured for Gao to sit as well. "You allowed yourself to be captured, Professor. Your Martian friends would not allow your imprisonment unless you wished it."

A thinker as well as a military leader, Visvajit impressed the professor. Gao decided to trust him with the truth. "This world is counterfeit," Gao said without preamble. "The Leibniz Machine predicts an 1884 completely unlike the one we are living."

Visvajit steepled his long fingers. "My people have known for millennia that the world is Maya. Illusion. Still, what *is* matters. If you hoped to upset me—"

"That wasn't my intent," said Gao. "Our universe is faulty. Absurd. I've witnessed it first hand."

"How so?"

"No doubt you are familiar with the lasting peace I secured for our planet several years ago by solving the murder of the Martian ambassador. What is less well known is that the ambassador had killed himself—at my bidding."

Visvajit frowned and sat up straighter. "At your bidding?"

"So it seemed," Gao continued. "The ambassador's death was designed to lead me to Planet X, the then-hypothetical ninth planet of our solar system, where I encountered an impossible mystery." Gao set his cup carefully on the table. "I met an old man on that icy world, Captain—a Thompson Tang Gao a quarter century older than I am now. I—*he*—had lured me there to impart a heavy burden: our universe, he explained, is dying."

"This too my people have always known," Visvajit said. "Mother Kali will devour the universe at the end of all days. But I wouldn't expect you to simply accept a statement like that."

"I didn't," said Gao. "I've spent the last two years tracking down and investigating every inconsistency and contradiction the Leibniz Machine could identify."

Visvajit leaned forward and nodded. "It was your investigation into seeming historical inaccuracies that resulted in my people finding their way back to the surface world. I have not forgotten that. If not for you, we would be little more than fanciful stories in the *Rig Veda*—"

Gao punched his palm for emphasis. "A great absurdity rests within the very fabric of our universe, Captain, spawning all manner of conundrums. I have learned that new realities are created and destroyed regularly, as part of a cosmic growth process. Unfortunately, because of its inherent irrationality, our reality will soon be erased from existence."

Visvajit remained silent for a long moment. "An interesting hypothesis, Professor, but I do not see why it should affect my immediate plans."

"We must use the time left to us wisely," said Gao. "Military conquest is futile. All we have is the meaning we make." He could tell by Visvajit's expression that he had failed to completely convince the captain. Gao sighed. Not only had the Leibniz Machine indicated that the professor's presence here could stop Visvajit from starting a war, it had further suggested that Visvajit could help Gao come to terms with the fact that the universe they inhabited would one day cease to be. Unfortunately, Gao had been unable to coax any clearer derivations from the complicated reasoning machine.

Visvajit stood. "A battle has been joined," he said. "One that will be fought here, in this room, between you and I, with words instead of swords or stolen airships."

Gao nodded and moved with Visvajit to the door. He had not convinced the captain outright, but he had planted a few seeds. Wind roared as the door opened and the guardsman led Gao away.

Now to wait, thought Gao, *and see what springs forth.*

An area of high cirrus tapered like gossamer wings in the distance. Nearer the *Vimana*, clouds bunched like fields of white mushrooms. Sunlight glared from a chromium-gold hull as one of the chariots dipped momentarily into view. The *Vimana* shuddered and Gao decided the chariot must have docked with the great zeppelin.

Symbols swirled in Gao's mind as he assembled and reassembled the last sets of derivations created before he set off to stop the war. The answer continued to elude him, so he crossed his legs on the thin mat and opened his notebook. "Perhaps I've made an error with the existential quantifier," he muttered, reaching for the bottle of India ink he had smuggled aboard.

Raised voices drew Gao's attention. He moved to the window, but could not see what had caused the commotion. Cocking an ear, Gao focused his hearing beyond the steady drone of the *Vimana's* engines. He could just make out a series of high-pitched *tings*, like the workings of some strange machine—or the clash of blades.

A voice rang out in pain and anger. Gao gasped as a man fell past his window, silver turban unraveling as he plummeted through the sky. His white uniform flashed red where he had been impaled on a sword.

"Barbaric," Gao whispered. It had been a leadership challenge, he realized. Someone had questioned Visvajit's orders, and this is how the captain had responded. It was a different take than Gao had encountered during his last trip to the Hindustani empires, but then Visvajit practiced an older, more savage form of the culture, evolved during the centuries spent underground.

Keys jingled and the heavy door to Gao's cell opened. Visvajit walked in carrying a length of bandage. His forearm had been cut, staining his *khameez*, but he appeared otherwise intact. "The war cannot be stopped," he said. "The merest hint that my faith in the campaign had wavered provoked a leadership challenge." He shrugged and, for the first time since Gao had met him, Visvajit seemed the size of a normal man. "My men are committed. They are loyal to me, but their hearts are set on battle. It would be unwise for us to try to convince them to abandon the glory." He shook his head. "It is imperative that we move forward with the attack."

"War," Gao said, "is never imperative."

Visvajit wrapped the bandage around his bloody arm. "Damn you, Gao. This should be a glorious moment. A man must make bold moves and sacrifices in order to inspire other men to follow him into battle."

"I didn't say anything about it."

Visvajit glared. "Your meek presence says enough. You play at tranquility because of what you've learned about the universe, but it is obvious that the knowledge has broken you."

Gao staggered as if Visvajit had struck him a physical blow. He had struggled for two years to reconcile himself with the fate of the universe. It was only in the past month that Gao felt he had really started gaining acceptance—and now Visvajit had knocked him from his calm center by characterizing him as "broken." Looking up at Visvajit's anguished features, Gao realized his own arguments had had a similar effect on the captain.

"I am the commander of the greatest military force this planet has ever seen," Visvajit continued. "Yesterday, I knew my place. And my purpose." He shook his head and turned back to the door. "I must continue with the invasion. Nothing short of the Tsar surrendering can stop the war now—and we both know that's not going to happen." He stopped half-way out the door and looked significantly at Gao. "I am open to other options, however."

The door closed and Gao listened to Visvajit's footsteps creak on the wooden staircase above his cell. Gao nodded, taking the captain's message: Visvajit had neglected to lock the door.

Habit woke Gao just before dawn. That, and the creaking steps of the soldier who slid hot tea and a breakfast of dosas with peach chutney through the feeding slot. Gao had gleaned very little about the movement of personnel aboard the *Vimana*, but he knew traffic in his section of the hull wouldn't pick up until the sun emerged sometime in the next half hour or so. He went to his cell door, but turned back to his breakfast instead of leaving. "It would be illogical to try to escape on a completely empty stomach," he reasoned, stuffing a dosa into his mouth.

Finding no one outside his cell, Gao ascended the creaking staircase. He had to find some way to reach the Tsar and, once he did, find some way of convincing the Tsar to surrender. Gao sighed at the near impossibility of his task. If only he'd been able to bring the Leibniz Machine along . . . .

The staircase led to a trapdoor, which opened onto the section of the deck exposed to the sky. As he had hoped, wind-roar hid the noise of his movements. Two soldiers stood nearby, checking a net that secured several large barrels. Gao ducked behind a support beam, reasonably sure he had escaped detection.

Wondering how he might gain control of one of the air-chariots, Gao turned his gaze to the wooden rail, a section of which had been broken and not yet mended. *That must be where Visvajit's opponent fell*, Gao realized with a shiver. Visvajit strode out of his cabin at that very moment, and Gao jumped involuntarily. The captain and the two soldiers laid eyes on him.

Visvajit squinted, mastering what Gao believed was a look of dread, and his hand moved to the pommel of the sword at his belt. He turned to his men and squared his shoulders, and suddenly Gao knew what the captain intended to do. Like Gao, Visvajit had been wrestling with the changes that knowledge of the universe's impending doom had wrought in his heart. Unlike Gao, however, Visvajit was a man of action, and he meant to make a last stand.

"I know what you're planning," Gao said just above the wind.

A half-smile curled Visvajit's lip. "I'm not like you, Gao. I cannot simply submit to the inevitable. I love my people, and hate to hurt even one of them, but—"

"But nothing," said Gao, noting the confused expressions on the faces of the soldiers. He stepped from behind the pillar. "Who knows how many you'll kill before you're finally defeated?"

Visvajit's eyes were hard, but lucid. "I don't like that things have turned out this way. Most of all, I regret the changes you have wrought in me. Yet I must remain true to myself."

"This is stupid," Gao said. One of the soldiers went into the main hull, presumably for reinforcements. "You're not barbarians."

Visvajit's fingers curled tighter around the pommel of his sword. "Then give me another option, Thompson."

Gao cursed himself. For all his reputation, he had been completely unable to formulate a solution to the problem at hand. Adding insult to injury, the Leibniz Machine had indicated that a solution did exist—one that would help both Gao and Visvajit—but Gao was simply too blind to see it.

Star after star in the twilight sky snuffed out as night gave way to day. Gao had come to think of this event as symbolic of the order of things but, as the sunlight lit Visvajit's defiant features, Gao's metaphor flip-flopped. The sunlight, he realized, was a mad challenger, fighting and winning an impossible battle against the darkness every morning. His subconscious had been trying to tell him, via the dawn, that it was possible to fight the inevitable.

"We will not go to war with the Tsar," Visvajit announced as the open deck began to fill with his men. "Let any who—"

"There is a bigger enemy!" Gao blurted, piecing a plan together as he spoke. "An enemy lurking at the very heart of our universe!"

Visvajit turned concerned eyes on Gao, clearly worried for his sanity. Gao stepped between Visvajit and his men. "This fleet is the most powerful force in the world. That's why I came here. Or why I was sent!" Gao cursed his lack of dramatic ability. Rather than inspiring the soldiers, his impromptu oratory seemed only to further confuse them. "That's why I freed you from your underground prison!"

Visvajit must have caught on, for he clasped Gao's shoulder and strode forward. "The Tsar is no match for us. Our savior, Professor Gao, traveled here to make us aware of the greatest enemy there is: the universe itself! He has challenged fate, and in this venture I have pledged our support."

A lieutenant with a forked-beard took a tentative step forward. "With respect, Sir, what are you talking about?"

"I have learned," Gao said, "that our universe is to be destroyed."

The lieutenant turned worried eyes on Visvajit. He seemed to want to believe, but his hand moved to the pommel of his sword. He probably feared Gao had infected Visvajit with some sort of madness. "Go against the universe?" he asked. "What would that mean?"

Gao looked up to see Visvajit smile. "Glory the like of which has never before been known," said the captain. "Glory enough to sate Kali-Ma herself."

Visvajit's people had lived in isolation so long, had believed themselves the only sentient beings in existence, and had now been reacquainted with a world that had passed them by. They were looking for a way to distinguish themselves, seeking a greater destiny of which they could be a part. It was that fact, Gao reasoned, that would sway them. It didn't matter how many pretty speeches Visvajit made, or how many clever rationales Gao concocted: the people would side with them only if it was their destiny to do so.

The lieutenant drew his sword, and offered it to Visvajit. A cheer went up from the gathered officers.

"You cut it a little close," Visvajit said.

Gao snorted. "I only—"

The sound of cannon-fire stopped Gao short. Shouts of alarm went up from the soldiers as the Tsar's fleet came into view, dark dirigible stars against a white-gray sky.

"All hands to battle-stations!" Visvajit bellowed. He dragged Gao across the deck. "Come on, Professor."

"Where am I going?" Gao asked, running to keep from falling. Visvajit nodded to the section of railing broken during his duel. He whistled loudly and an air-chariot—the *Shakuna*, if Gao read the characters correctly—moved into position beneath them. Gao's stomach twisted as he realized how Visvajit intended for him to board the vessel.

"You're going to talk to the Tsar," said Visvajit. He exchanged a complex series of hand-gestures with the *Shakuna*'s pilots, nodded curtly, and pushed Gao off of the *Vimana*.

The world blurred as Gao's stomach leapt into his mouth. The golden air-chariot grew huge beneath his kicking feet, and a shrill scream filled his ears. Some detached corner of Gao's mind noted that the scream was his.

Gao banged his knee on the chrome hull, but fell into the leather seat relatively unhurt. Golden wings stretched behind the craft, clicking as their gears worked against each other. Gao's eyes widened as the *Shakuna* dropped below the clouds, revealing an endless view of Siberian taiga. Trying to stave off the fear of falling, Gao focused his attention on what he could possibly tell the Tsar to convince him not to respond to the staggering force invading his country.

"Just focus on the Tsar," he muttered as the *Shakuna* skittered on some turbulence.

"Normally that would be a good idea," one of the pilots said over a chubby shoulder. He looked pointedly at a brass handle built into the hull beside Gao. "But you might want to hang on to something for this part."

Gao clenched his fingers around the handle. The *Shakuna* skidded on air, then headed straight up and into the clouds. They came up in the middle of the Tsar's fleet, directly under a twilight-gray zeppelin nearly twice the size of the *Vimana*: the Tsar's flagship, the *Kamchatka*.

Gao's wrist twisted and his legs left the seat. He realized with a shock that he was falling. Pulling with all his might, Gao threw himself back into the seat, knocking the wind from his lungs. The *Shakuna* leveled out and Gao fought nausea.

"You might want to hold on again," the other pilot warned.

Gao looked up. The *Kamchatka* filled the entire sky. A bay window rushed toward them and the *Shakuna* flew straight into it. They hit the deck, sliding through tables and chairs on a wave of broken glass. Gao caught glimpses of knives, forks, and a frightened chef, then went flying from the chariot as the *Shakuna* bumped to a stop.

The pilots picked Gao up and his world turned. He did a quick inventory: "I have no broken bones," he said.

"Good," said the chubby pilot. "Can you walk?"

Gao stepped onto the leg he had banged when he boarded the chariot. It hurt, but held. "Yes," Gao said.

"Then walk this way," said the other pilot, drawing his sword as he moved through an open doorway.

An astonished look on his lined face, the Tsar waited beyond the doorway, standing over a table overturned during the *Shakuna*'s unorthodox entry. He moved his head, and it seemed to Gao that the Tsar's red whiskers pointed out each of the fur-clad soldiers arrayed about him. Visvajit's pilots dropped their weapons and knelt before the Tsar. Gao did the same.

A soldier leveled a musket at Gao's head. "We come in peace," Gao said. "I request an audience with Tsar Ruslan Rustam."

"Who sent you?" asked Rustam, his voice deep and gravelly.

Gao looked up into the Tsar's pragmatic eyes. He seemed an eminently serious man, not given to abstract or metaphorical thinking, but Gao had to be honest with him. "The sunrise sent me," he answered.

One of the soldiers cupped a hand and whispered in the Tsar's ear. Recognition glinted in Rustam's eyes.

"Professor Gao," he said. "Or should I call you Doom-Bringer? It pains me to see you've fallen in with my enemies. You once had a reputation as a man of reason."

Annoyed with the Tsar's tone, Gao sat up. The soldier shook the musket pointed at his head.

"Go ahead and shoot me," said Gao, rising to his feet. "We'll all be dead soon if you don't listen to what I have to say."

Rustam gestured for his soldier to remove the musket, but his wary eyes narrowed. "*You'll* be dead soon," he said, "if I don't like what you have to say. I'll stand for none of your doom-peddling."

"Well, I'm selling a new idea now: survival."

Rustam snorted. "The only way for me to ensure survival for my people is to deal with Visvajit and his fleet."

Gao felt a swell of pity for the Tsar and did not attempt to hide it. "If what I have discovered is true, you'll soon have much bigger problems to deal with. We all will."

A smirk settled on Rustam's stately face. "It doesn't speak well for your cause that you are resorting to vague threats."

"Then I'll make it more concrete," said Gao. "I have traced the source of the universe's irrationality—the doom to which you've chosen to close your ears—to the planet Earth." He paused a moment, giving the Tsar a moment to grasp the significance of his statement. "There are some who would rather see the Earth destroyed than preside over the end of reality itself."

Rustam swallowed. "The Martians wouldn't . . . . Who's to say destroying the Earth would eliminate this irrationality?"

Gao shrugged. "I have no idea if destroying the Earth would save the universe, but I have no doubt the Martians would try." He raised his eyebrows. "What would you do, in their place?"

The Tsar turned to his advisor, seemingly at a loss as to what course of action to take. Gao turned his focus inward, summoning again the complicated series of unresolved derivations. The solution eluded him still, but he sensed it just beyond the reach of his conscious mind.

"Whatever the future holds," said Rustam, "we must protect ourselves now in order to—"

The *Kamchatka* shook and cannon-fire echoed. Visvajit's fleet had reached them. The Tsar bellowed an order, but the sound was lost as wood splintered and the deck lurched. Gao fell into the soldier who had placed the musket to his head and they went down in a tangle of limbs.

Muskets fired and steel sounded against steel. Gao regained his feet just in time to dodge left as a wounded soldier flew through the open doorway. Visvajit entered a moment later, gleaming armor covering him from head-to-toe.

One soldier helped the Tsar to his feet. All others trained their weapons on Visvajit. The captain glanced at Gao, then raised his bloody sword . . . and placed it at Rustam's feet. He creaked to a kneeling position. "I place my life in the hands of the Tsar."

"And why," Rustam asked, "has the mighty Visvajit surrendered himself thus?"

Visvajit looked up. "You and I control the most powerful military forces on the planet. I've come to propose an alliance."

"An alliance?" the Tsar asked. "Against who?"

"Against the universe," said Visvajit. "I don't like Gao's doom any more than you do. Together, with the professor's aid, we might be able to stop it."

Gao gasped as the last element of his derivations snapped into place. He had traced the source of the universe's irrationality to the Earth—perhaps he could pinpoint it further.

Gao punched his palm. "We'll find it, and eliminate it."

Rustam shook his head. "That's absurd. How could I justify military spending on such an . . . ethereal venture?"

Gao laughed. "How much will a war with Visvajit cost you?"

The Tsar considered Gao's words for a full minute, but Gao knew he had convinced him.

"You two will travel aboard the *Kamchatka*," said Rustam, "until the invading fleet has left my country."

Seeing Visvajit about to protest, Gao said, "A sensible precaution."

Visvajit shifted, trying to find a comfortable way to kneel in armor. "I left your kitchen relatively intact," he said. "Since returning to the surface, I have heard a lot about one of your treasures. I think it is pronounced, *baklava*."

Rustam smiled. Gao nodded, wondering at the diplomatic powers of desserts.

Wrapped in furs from the Tsar's supply ship, Gao stood upon the *Vimana*'s deck, watching the sun set. "I'll miss this ship," Visvajit said, coming up beside him. "Unfortunately, the Tsar wants it back."

"I think Rustam could be persuaded to let you continue to command her."

Visvajit made a non-committal grunt. He was not used to having a co-ruler. "The stars are out," he said.

Gao nodded at the still dully-twinkling lights, knowing they would get much stronger as the night fell. He turned his attention to the combined air-fleet that filled the skies beside and behind them. Zeppelin engines broke the daunting silence, running lights pushing back the darkness, and Gao felt a swell of sympathy for the forces of nature marshaled against them. It was a silly feeling, born of the giddiness of his victory with the Tsar, but at that moment, with the cold wind in his hair and the deck thrumming beneath his feet, Gao felt the impossible within his grasp. ✪

WHY A DUCK

BY LESLIE WHAT

ANTHONY, DEAD FOR A MONTH, LIVED, as it were, for flying. He had taken to the sport rather late in life, never managing enough air time to suit him. Now he was riding in a hot air balloon that cruised above three thousand feet. He felt deliriously joyful. Technically, it wasn't his balloon, but technicalities seemed beyond the point.

The pilot went about his duties, unaware that in his gondola he carried Anthony and his wife Beatrice, two ghostly stowaways. Anthony stood at the edge of the basket and looked out. All around him, hot-air balloons hissed like unruly geese competing for the forward point in the formation. The only barriers between here and eternity were the fog-shrouded mountains, the colorful balloons being blown across the sky like a spray of opaque bubbles, and a gently waving banner of pastel clouds. The view was spectacular: CircleRama theater without the nausea.

The balloon passed through a pocket of dead air, hovering momentarily. Anthony watched as a swirl of leaves stopped moving through the sky and was held in one place like pressed flowers between two planes of wind. "Beautiful," he whispered to Beatrice.

"Yes, dear," Beatrice answered. She would have been happier flipping through a *Reader's Digest*.

It might have been his imagination but he could smell the earthy odor of the potato fields below, a pleasant scent, like clean dirt and sun-warmed wings of ladybugs. An eddy of wind forced them downward and for a moment the peppermint pink-striped envelope went slack before it straightened out and lifted the balloon back into position.

"Whee!" cried Anthony. Uncertainty was all part of the fun.

Beatrice shivered. She squeezed in front of Anthony to stand beneath the burner.

"I'm cold," she said as she thrust her translucent hands into the flames. Her skin took on the elegant appearance of candied orange peel. She stared into the mouth of the balloon and stuck out her tongue.

Though Anthony had nothing to compare her to, he thought she made a most attractive dead lady. She was still wearing her red jogging suit with a white stripe down the pants, and clean white sneakers. Too bad she had not died in something lacy and crotchless, but oh well, she complemented this particular balloon rather nicely. She was a lovely woman, even in polyester, even dead.

He did his best to puff out his chest and hoped he still looked good to her. He was not terribly vain, a good thing, as vanity was something of a wasted conceit on a ghost.

The balloon dipped again, and the pilot, a man wearing a funny little engineer's cap the same pink shade as the balloon silk panels, dumped some ballast and moved in from the edge to check his cables. The pilot tightened a screw on the load rings and gave a couple of twists to the nozzle to release more hot air into the envelope. He said, "That ought to do it," without an indication that he believed anyone was there to hear him. When most people talked, they were only talking to themselves anyway. This man was no different.

Anthony was dressed in the same hospital gown he had died in. Barefoot, except the toe tag. Bare-bummed, not by choice. The nurses had found it necessary to cut off his briefs in the emergency room. A cool gust of wind parted his gown and smacked his ghostly butt cheeks. He found the sensation refreshing.

The pilot wanted to break away from the middle of the pack and fly out front, where he could lay claim upon the sky. Crossing the sky in a hot air balloon could make a man do crazy things, as Anthony knew too well. After all, it had been his idea to let Beatrice pilot the craft the day they'd crashed.

Beatrice seemed to think he'd been crazy for a long time; she had never shared his passion for ballooning. Anthony sighed. This was more than a hobby: it had given him a reason to go on in his golden years. He had been so very bored since his retirement. Once you've seen the world, what was left? Only seeing it from above, a desire that Beatrice refused to understand. They didn't really have much in common. Especially if you didn't count those fifty years and seven children.

And now, of course, this.

"I'm cold," Beatrice said.

She was always cold. Anthony suspected some problem with her metabolism. There had to be an explanation for why she still felt cold even in sweat pants, while he was practically naked and yet cozy as ever.

"Do you want my," he started, before remembering he had no coat. It wouldn't do to give her his gown, not that he would mind the sacrifice. He wasn't so sure he could manage undoing the straps in any event. He was clumsier here than in life, while Beatrice was as composed and meticulously calm as ever. He and Beatrice were mirror opposites in so many ways; for one thing, Beatrice would not want to spend eternity seeing him naked.

She was hugging herself and he moved close to wrap his arms around her. She was difficult to hold onto and his hands passed right through her. "We need more mass," he said.

She gave him a funny look. "Like that would help any," she said.

"It couldn't hurt," he said.

"You and your harebrained schemes," she said. "Why do you think we're here in the first place?"

"Don't start," he warned. There was only so much blame that a man could accept. Whenever you took chances, unintended consequences happened. Even when you stood in one place, you couldn't be so sure that you would be safe. That was the nature of reality. So what if ballooning had become a late obsession? It had given him something to live for. Too bad he had died, but the point still stood.

Who would want to take root in the middle of a potato farm when he could soar above eagles? Who would want to mow the lawn if he could be in the hangar stuffing sandbags?

"If you think back, you'll remember that I warned you there was a cold front coming!" she said. "I told you we shouldn't go up in those conditions."

"If you think back," he said, "you'll remember that you doused the flames when I told you to stoke the fire."

"Did not," she said.

He was about to rehash their argument when he grew dizzy and the colors inside the basket began to swirl like colorful clay atop a potter's wheel being shaped into a bowl. He could no longer hold himself upright. He pitched backward.

"Not again," he said. This was the down side of the death

experience. They faded in and out of scenes as their balloon drifted out of range of their haunt zone. This scene was almost over.

"Shit!" Beatrice screamed. It was so unlike her to curse. "Here
it comes! I hate this part. How could you do this to me?" She may
have continued on with her complaint, but he did not hear her.

When he recovered consciousness, they were in another balloon; this one checkered and brown. This pilot was dressed in
army fatigues and wore thick black boots. Anthony gazed over at
the compass and noted that they were in the same starting place
as before. Below them, the potato fields resembled a spotted green
and brown blanket that had gone through the wash a few too
many times to look pristine.

A feeling of emptiness overwhelmed him. Anthony whipped
around and felt a sense of relief course through him when he
spotted Beatrice hugging the burners. Not that Beatrice could
have gone anywhere without him, but it was reassuring to see she
was still there.

"You okay?" he asked.

"It's cold," she said. She squinted. "Why couldn't we be planted
in a field like normal people? Why couldn't we be out haunt-
ing a house and scaring the cats and saying normal things, like,
'Boo!'?"

"I don't know," he said. He was happy they hadn't settled down,
taken root like old potatoes. If only she were happy, eternity would
be so much more fun! It must have been difficult, being a woman
of her time. After the children left home, Beatrice had never really
found herself. If anyone had ever needed a hobby, it was her.

The pilot opened a hinged box and got out his oxygen mask.
He was about the age that Anthony had been, before the accident.
Old. Ancient. Wrinkled. The age at which, when you smiled at
a young lady, she mistakenly assumed that you were only being

polite instead of horny. The pilot took a hit off his oxygen mask and smiled at the expanse of sky.

"Lightweight," said Anthony. They weren't even at four thousand feet. He beat his chest and pretended to gulp in the air. Plenty of oxygen here, he thought. Lightweight!

"Eternity is so, well, so boring," Beatrice said. "Look at this!" She pointed down to the potato fields and at a couple of turkey vultures circling to the north in preparation for descent. "I deserve more. I want angels! I want heavenly harps!"

"I'm sorry," Anthony said. "If I knew how, I'd find you harps and angels." After all this time, he didn't understand his wife. Why did she always want more than he offered? What was it with women, anyway?

"I'm cold," Beatrice said. "I don't like being surrounded by so much air. I want to be wrapped up, buried under ground where the wind won't touch me."

That sounded horrible; coffins were so confining. He refused to feel guilty for making her miserable. Besides, if she'd listened to him, they would have risen above the bad air and died in a home, like normal people. It was all her fault and he was tired of taking the blame. He hoped the fade would come quickly and they could get out of this scene. Maybe in the next one, they wouldn't fight. Unfortunately, they were caught in a headwind and the balloon drifted back the way it had come.

The pilot took another hit of oxygen and flashed a stoner smile at the sky. Anthony tried to will him to dump ballast or steer them out of here, but his ethereal presence didn't register a blip on the pilot's radar. This pilot didn't care about winning this race. Anthony disliked the man. They weren't going anywhere, and the pilot was taking them there.

"Why do men want balloons, anyway?" Beatrice asked.

He shrugged. It seemed too obvious to explain.

"Weren't the children enough? What about your job? And me? Why did you need more than that?"

"Look around you," he said. "Isn't this glorious?"

"Glory, schmory," she said. "If I wanted glory I would have died at the Macy's after-Christmas sale."

"I hardly think you can compare the experience of mark-down linens with this," Anthony said.

"Shopping has a point! A beginning and an end! With balloons, you just float around and never go anywhere."

"You do too."

"Do not! When you land, a crew hauls you back to your car. How is that going anywhere?"

"The point is that you're already there. Think of it this way. We're having an adventure."

"This isn't an adventure!" she said. "It's play-acting adventure. In real adventure you get sharks!"

He was tired of fighting with her and wanted it to end. "That's it!" he said. "The last straw. You want real adventure? I'll give you something to remember!" He felt emboldened and floated up to the basket rim. There, he teetered on the edge. He held out his hands in Superman position. "I'll jump!" he said. "If you say another word, that's what I'll do!"

"Oh, please," said Beatrice. Her teeth were chattering without making any noise. "You're not the jumping type."

"I'll jump! I really will!" he said. He leaned into the wind and let the currents hold him aloft. "Here I go!"

"You're afraid," she said. "You won't really do it."

That's where she was wrong. He pushed off, arching his back in his best approximation of a swan dive. But he didn't fall very far. To fall, you had to weigh more than the air inside of a cookie cutter.

"I told you that you couldn't do it!" Beatrice said. She made a tsk-tsking sound. "Now get back in this balloon before the scene fades!"

"I don't think so," Anthony told her. He still wanted to jump.

She frowned. Wrinkles formed and made her face look like a balloon before it was fully inflated. "Anthony, please," she said. She wrung her hands. "What will happen when we fade if you're out there and I'm in here? What if we get separated?" Her voice was a worried warble.

He held his moral ground. "You'll have to stop blaming me for everything that's wrong," he said, and risked a look into her eyes to see if she were the slightest bit amenable.

She grimaced. "You're just as bad," she said. "If I say I'm sorry, will you stop blaming me?"

"I don't know," he said. "We're going to be together an awfully long time. But I'm willing to try. Are you?"

"Maybe," she said. "Get back in here and we'll talk about it."

"I don't think so," he said. He wanted to test their relationship and now was just a good a time as forever. "Come out here and be with me," he said.

She shook her head and did not look convinced. "I should have married Burt Pinkerton," she said. "He was a banker, had his feet on the ground."

"I remember Burt," Anthony said. "He had dandruff and a black mole on his upper lip."

"Well, besides that," she said, as she moved toward the edge of the balloon. She reached for him.

Out of habit, he grasped her hand to help her out of the gondola. Now, for the first time, he could feel her. "Oh wow," he said, her small ghostly hand fitting snugly in his slightly larger one. "You don't know how nice this feels."

She smiled with coyness he still found charming. "I know," she said. "I know."

A flock of wood ducks approached in classic "V" formation, their feathers iridescent as green balloon skins. "I have an idea," Anthony said. He let go of her hand and turned away from her. "Quick! Wrap your legs around my waist; I'll give you a piggy-back ride."

"Anthony Wilson, are you crazy?"

"No. As sane as I ever was! Trust me. This will work."

"Oh, for heaven's sake," she said. She climbed atop his back as he suggested.

He could feel her light-as-air, cool body pressed against him. Her arms snuggled kudzu-like around his neck. If he had been alive, she would have choked him. Being dead, he rather enjoyed the extra stimulation. With Beatrice hugging him, he felt almost whole. "Here's what to do: the second the ducks fly by, grab them. Use their mass to carry us away."

"This is ridiculous," she said.

"I don't think so. It's science."

"What kind of science uses ducks?" she asked.

"There's no time to argue," he insisted.

As the ducks passed over them, he reached up toward the forest of scaly feet and managed to snag two ducks. He gripped one twig-like leg in each hand and felt the webbed feet tense beneath his palms. It was working! Alone, each ghost was nothing; together they were something. The ducks could not ignore them.

His fingers curling around the duck feet must have felt like spider webs; the ducks tried to shake him off in order to rejoin their group.

"Boo," Anthony said as the ducks quacked and complained.

That shut them up. He turned his chin toward Beatrice, "See! It works."

Beatrice seemed afraid to lessen her hold and grab a duck of her own. "Sorry," she said. "They're too fast for me."

"It will be okay," he said. "We'll share. Take one of my ducks."

"I'm afraid," she said. "I don't want to let go."

"Squeeze me tighter with your legs," he said. "You won't fall."

"Oh, Anthony!" she said.

"It's okay," he said. "We'll make it work with only the two ducks between us. I've done the calculations."

"Well," she said, "you were always good at math."

"Go ahead and grab one of mine," Anthony said. "Take hold of one foot in each hand and let it carry your weight, not that you have much."

"I'm not sure about this," she said. He could feel the pressure of her elbow squeezing his temple as she reached up to grip the duck by its leg. She was terrified but knew how to be brave.

"Perfect," he said. "Now the other hand."

"I'm afraid."

"It will be all right," he said. "Trust me."

"I do trust you," she said. She let go of Anthony's neck and blindly grabbed for the duck's other leg. Anthony could tell that she was scared by the way her feet dug into his belly.

Her grip was insecure so he did not let go of her duck, but concentrated on steering his. Her duck was uncooperative. It twisted its neck and wiggled its tail as it tried to shake them off. Her leg hold around his waist tightened. "I'm afraid," she said, and he tired to reassure her.

They dipped, sped up, ascended, then plummeted, and having no ballast, could not control their rapid descent. Wind whipped up his hospital gown like a flag at half-mast in the middle of a hurricane.

Beatrice screamed. So did the ducks. In her disorientation, Beatrice let go of her duck and it slipped away, squawking.

He couldn't blame her. It was her first skydive. His too, without a parachute. She grabbed his neck. "Oh, Anthony," she said. "I've lost a duck. I'm so sorry!"

"Not a problem. Whee! This is great!" Anthony said. He had never felt such exhilaration. They continued to accelerate as his duck approached the ground. "Isn't this wonderful?" he asked.

She was screaming too hard to answer.

"I'm sorry for everything!" Beatrice screamed. "I'm so sorry. Say you forgive me."

"Of course I forgive you," he said. "I'm sorry, too."

He felt her relax into him. "I love you," she said, but he didn't know if that meant she'd forgiven him or just temporarily lost the need to assign blame.

His duck tried a new tactic to be rid of them and flew around in circles.

"This feels so wrong," Beatrice said. "I don't think one duck will be enough to get us very far."

"We'll make do," Anthony told her. "One duck is more than most people get. We might as well make the best of things or eternity won't be very much fun."

"I want to kiss you," she said, and she carefully climbed around to face him, never quite letting go. She wrapped her legs around his hips and pressed her cold chest against his to snuggle. One arm gripped his neck as the other encircled his shoulders. She brought her icy lips to his and said, "I love you."

Then, surprising him, she started to let go, one hand reaching up to grab his duck's left leg, just above the foot joint. Her hand brushed his; there was something equally disgusting and erotic about the way they both gripped the duck's bare leg. She brought her other hand up to the other leg and grabbed hold. She said, "Here goes nothing," and dropped both her legs from his waist. The two of them dangled, facing each other, while the duck carried them through the sky.

"Whee," Beatrice said.

Anthony felt the tickle from the duck's webbed foot as it struggled to escape. "Are you still cold?" he asked.

"Who cares about the weather?" she said. Her voice was more animated than usual.

They were off-balance and started to spin. With her facing him, Anthony could not control his duck with any degree of precision. The duck, being a duck, did as it wanted, which was try to shake them off. Soon, they were tumbling and falling through the air as both duck and human pilots struggled to steer the craft. The potato fields were below them while at the same time above them or beside them. Thrill and terror coursed through him.

"Whee!" Anthony said.

He felt lightheaded as he watched a world pass by him in fast-forward. "Hold me!" he shrieked. "Don't ever let me go!"

"Okay," she whispered in his ear. He felt the warmth and moisture of her breath and a comforting pressure as she again slid her legs around his waist.

"I must confess I rather like that," he said. This was how things were supposed to work in a successful marriage; when things didn't go your way, you figured out another plan.

"Screw the duck," she said, letting go so she could wrap her arms around his neck and smother his lips with hers. "I just want you to know I forgive everything."

Distracted, he forgot what he was doing and in that split-second when his mind was elsewhere, the duck slipped away.

"I love you," he said.

"Me too," she answered.

Without warning, the scene faded. When Anthony came to, Beatrice was still humping him but they were in a new gondola piloted by a man who was having some trouble lighting his pipe. He pulled on the pipe until at last, a small ember glowed.

Anthony sighed. "Thank God, we didn't end up in a potato field," he said, hoping it wasn't the wrong thing to say after their adventure, that it wouldn't get her started again.

Beatrice smiled up at him. "It's not what I expected, but I'll try to adjust," she said. "I'm just glad we died together. I'd hate to be alone."

He was quieted by the somber thought that dying alone might mean you spent eternity alone. "Oh, Beatrice," he said. "I never thought I'd say this, but thank you for killing us."

"I love you," she said.

"Me too," he answered. "I still think you're hot."

She winked. "We'll just have to make the best of it. Like we always did."

"What do you suggest?" he asked.

Beatrice pointed upward. A lone duck flew way behind his flock as it tried to catch up. "Look, Anthony! There goes one. Can we do it again?"

"I think so," he said, feeling clam-happy. This was everything he'd ever wanted. Maybe more. Too bad it hadn't all happened earlier; thank goodness, it wasn't too late now.

"I have another idea," Anthony said.

"Tell me," said Beatrice.

"We're ghosts," he said. "Let's take ourselves seriously." Anthony gulped in air, then shouted in the scariest voice he could muster, "Boo!" He managed to keep from laughing.

The pilot looked around, but seemed to convince himself that it was just the wind.

Beatrice understood what Anthony was up to at once. "Oh! That was a good one. Boo!" she screamed in the most maniacal voice he had ever heard her use. She reached out with one hand to extinguish the tobacco. When the pilot didn't flinch, she stomped her foot and thrust two fingers up the pilot's nose.

At last, the pilot flinched.

"That's the spirit," Anthony said. "Boo!" he shouted again. He tickled the pilot's ears from the inside. With a great sense of glee, Anthony noted that the pilot's expression had melted from the scowling look that signaled irritation, to the wrinkle-free open-mouthed tension of alarm.

"You're the best spook in the world," Beatrice said, and Anthony beamed with pride. ✪

MATRIARCH

BY FORREST AGUIRRE

THERE SITS THE MATRIARCH, naked, piloting the zeppelin. An anachronistic blob, a Willendorf Venus save for the sniper rifle (Mauser 7mm) in one hand, a plate of Twinkies (flour, sugar, FD&C yellow, etc) in the other. Smoke chokes the behemothic hag, particulate remains of the Krupp-gunned city below. Her two cronies, LeBlanc and LeFevre, push bodies over the sides of the cabin.

Twenty carcasses dangle from ropes. From a distance the dirigible is a Portuguese Man o'War, tentacles thrust into the blackened urban jungle. Most of the corpses are uniformed, all hail from the city in ruins. The mayor, his cabinet and a dozen war heroes twist and bump, medals and ribbons and golden keys-to-the-city snagging on the wreckage of the metropolis.

LeFevre is caught off-guard when the tugging begins and goes vaulting over the edge into the crowds of famished children waiting beneath. LeBlanc watches as his comrade disappears beneath the mass then resurfaces a clean skeleton moments later. Blood covers the children's lips as they pass the bones hand-over-hand to a hill of gleaming fossils. LeFevre's remains become a part of the mound, as do the hanging heroes and cabinet—stripped to the bone by the starving youth.

Engines strain, fizzle, pop and the zeppelin sags toward the city's blasted spires in a shower of sparks, a cloud of hazy diesel. A slow rumbling sun setting among brick towers. The fireball fades to soot and LeBlanc looks down blister-burned at the approaching arterial streets. A surge in the crowd and atop the wave crest a tall, gaunt figure in gray, medallioned and decorated through a hundred wars—the militia general, the last adult leader of the cannibal child-army, leads his crawling troops toward the dilapidated craft.

The Matriarch stands and waddles to the side overlooking the mob, cradling her rifle like a baby. The Twinkies are all gone. She flips up the man-sight, adjusts for distance and brings the gun to her shoulder. CRACK! and the smell of gunpowder stings LeBlanc's nostrils as the general falls stiff back into the churning mass. A bustle and a shiver and his bones are body-surfed onto the fossil pile.

LeBlanc rises from his crisped hands and knees.

"You have despatched the enemy, my queen, but your defeat is sure. A pyrrhic victory, after the mob throws you to the bone hill."

She turns, the leviathan turns and, tossing the gun to the city, caresses LeBlanc's face and hair. A thick-lipped smile creases her face as her minion tastes electric fear on the roof of his mouth. Sweat courses down over her fat folds.

"My wayward child—you forgot—I am the Matriarch."

And she consumes his head.

The children shout: "HUZZAH!" as she steps down from the dirigible's wreckage.

Mommy's home.

Victory is achieved. ✪

AEROPHILIA

BY TOBIAS S. BUCKELL

"You know, the thing about zeppelins is that they got a bad rap," Vince says. He's actually twirling a virtual mustache. Nutjob. "I mean, in the famous 'Oh, the humanity' accident only thirty-five passengers died. Out of ninety-seven!"

He steps forward and looks at me critically.

"Ever heard of a sixty-four percent survival rate in *any* crash? Space or air?" He doesn't wait for an answer, but turns around. "No!"

I can't answer him anyway. My mouth is gagged with a rubber ball and strap, and my hands are cuffed in front of me. My lips are starting to dry out and stick to the black rubber ball.

The key to the handcuffs has been flushed out of the airship through the toilet. It's probably still falling, and will fall for a few hours more until crushed into liquid metal by the deadly atmosphere far below us. It would continue falling, being crushed ever smaller, until it joined the great diamond core of the gas giant that was Riley.

Or so some physicists I once saw quoted in a touristy introduction to Riley had said.

Four passengers sitting on the side of the gondola stare at me with wide eyes. They're local colonists. Three guys in tuxedos on their way to a party and a lady in a hoop skirt and purple plastic corset. Probably lived all of their lives in any one of the aerostat cities in Riley's upper atmosphere. They've certainly never seen a down-on-his-luck spacer like me, likely because there has never been such a thing as a down-on-his-luck spacer. It's almost oxymoronic.

"On a planet like this," Vince continues, "zeppelins are too useful to ignore. But I think the colonists are missing something."

The colonists: they look at me as if am crazy. And from their perspective it can't be too far off, right? What they've seen with their normal, unaugmented, fleshy eyeballs has been me, and only me, boarding their dirigible for a regular flight from one city to another. Routine for them, until I knocked out their pilot, took over the airship, and reprogrammed the ship's destination to somewhere deep into the atmosphere of Riley .

"Nobody try to fly this ship, or call for help, or you'll all regret it," I'd announced. Then I'd stuffed a ball gag in my mouth, handcuffed myself, and slumped into the corner of the gondola.

The problem being, from my side, is that my Id is a total asshole. He hates my guts. We split up yesterday and he hijacks my skull today in retaliation.

So I'm not really me right now. And no one else can see Vince. He's just a computer-induced hallucination inside my own skull.

I work up some spit to try and moisten the ball gag a bit. Drool runs down my lips, and one of the men across from me shakes his head in disgust.

Even though Vince is using my own body-wide neural network against me to induce hallucinations and control my motor movement, I can still access some basic functions. I dial out of the airship and make a call. As a spacer I'm totally cyborged, constantly seeing and interacting with information laid over everything I see.

I manage to contact my ex-girlfriend's secretary persona. A virtual image pastes itself in the left corner of the inside of my artificial eyes.

The persona looks just like Suzie as I remember her sixty years ago: blond, brown eyes, but more digitized. It laughs when it sees me.

"You look exactly as we remember you," it says.

My hopes lift.

"I need help," I subvocalize. "Can I talk to Suzie?"

The secretary mimics sitting back and folding her arms. Lifts an eyebrow.

"Why in hell would we want to talk to you?"

"I'm in trouble." My subvocal throat grunts get another disgusted look from the colonists in the actual gondola. In the picture in my head the secretary leans forward.

Somewhere between the two I can see Vince flickering as he paces around the edge of the gondola, muttering to himself. He passes through one of the colonists, like a ghost.

"You're always in trouble, Vincent," the secretary says.

"Yeah, but now I'm in really deep. I need Suzie's help."

A click.

Then it's Suzie. The real Suzie.

"Hello?"

The secretary fades away. I try to clear my throat, gag, and close my eyes. The insides of the gondola disappear, but Suzie remains, still staring at me.

"Suzie," I subvocalize. "My god, you look . . . great." She doesn't.

She looks really old. Even with aging treatments, she's been sitting in real time for sixty or so years while I skipped out a relativistic few months near the speed of light to try and build up my financial empire.

Compound interest is every light hugger's friend. You leave a bank account behind for a couple months in your time reference and come back to your original departure planet rich.

I'm hoping those decades softened the memory of my departure.

"Son of a bitch," Suzie says, realizing who I am.

"I need help, Suzie. Please. Do you still work for the Air Guard?"

She shakes her head.

"Sixty freaking years, Vincent. Sixty."

"I'm so sorry, I can explain, but right now I'm handcuffed in the gondola of an airship and I need your help."

"Do you realize I've had a whole life since then? A marriage? Kids? Grandkids?"

I pause.

"We could talk about this over coffee, or something. After you help me?"

"If you can call me you should have called the Guard yourself," Suzie says, and hangs up.

I mouth the ballgag for several seconds, then redial.

It's the secretary.

"She doesn't want to talk to you," the younger image of Suzie says. "She's really pretty ticked that you even dredged all those old memories back up for her. You left her after taking all her money, and even worse, you didn't even tell her you were leaving. You know she would have given you the money if you had asked."

"I'm so sorry to be doing this." I sigh around the edges the rubber ball. "I don't know what else to do. My Id became a persona inside of my own neural network, and now it's taken me over."

"Well you really messed her up. She lied, you know, she never actually had a husband or grandkids, she just threw herself into work. For a while she became part of an anti-Spacer activist group," the secretary leans forward. "Look, you could just turn off all your neural devices and go totally normal, just regular wetware."

"That's a bit drastic, isn't it?" I've been wired since, well, as long as I can remember. I wouldn't be able to make calls, check up on info, see floating data tips around me, if I shut it all down. I'd be just like the colonists staring at me.

"People on Riley manage it all that time. Not everyone is a high-rolling spacer."

The secretary smiles. Funny tickly feelings are running up and down my chip-packed spine. I ignore them.

"And if you buy yourself some time, I imagine I could work the old lady over, if you know what I mean." She winks. "There are, after all, some very good memories we're dredging up as well."

She's gone.

It's a bit of a flimsy plan, but it beats calling the Air Guard directly and guaranteeing arrest. Susie might still fly out and rescue us.

Vince sits next to me.

"I think that's a bad idea," he says. "I've been trying to keep you occupied and distracted. Which is easy, by the way. I didn't want you to think of doing that."

Hah.

I start getting the codes ready.

"Just ponder this," Vince says, leaning closer to me. "I'm always the one that comes up with the good plans. I always get us out of the bad scrapes on instinct. I always get the girl when you stop over-thinking things. You have to trust me."

Good plans my ass. I'd been unaware of my Id until he'd started giving me anonymous messages, leaving links to stories about a lost aerostat city that had kept actual gold bars in its bank, now abandoned and waiting for someone to plunder it. My Id has gone insane. He splintered off into his own personality when I started resisting his plan to go down searching the lower atmosphere for this mythical lost city.

"I'm taking good care of us right now. This is all part of a plan."

I initiate a shut down.

Vince finally flickers away.

It's different going a hundred percent wetware. When I look out the observation windows I can't see little weather tags telling me where the thermals around us are. People's public ID info sheets don't hover over their heads.

But I can wiggle my fingers and move my still-cuffed hands.

I rip off the ball gag and take a deep breath, then stand up.

The colonists flinch.

"It's okay," I reassure them. "I'm okay now."

They don't believe it.

"I had a software problem," I explain, wiping my cracked lips with the sleeve of my dress shirt. "My personality kinda got messed up and split, then the splinter tried to take me over. Bit of a glitch in the programming allows that."

One of them raises his hand.

"So which one is in charge now?"

"I am," I say brightly. "I'm Vincent."

They all chorus: "Hi Vincent."

I nod.

"Vince is gone now, so we're all okay. He was the one that knocked out the pilot and reprogrammed the airship. I'm more normal."

One of the colonists leans over to the purple corseted lady and stage whispers, "Does this happen to off-worlders often?"

She shakes her head.

"So . . . ," I say. "Can we wake the pilot up now?"

They enthusiastically approve of this course of action.

We trudge over to the front of the gondola where the bank of displays and switches gleam. The pilot is an elderly man with brown hair, slumped in the well-padded pilot's seat. A heads up display flickers green figures over the roiling red clouds of Riley on the windowscreen in front of him. This is how the colonists access the layers of information around them.

I shake the pilot's shoulders, but his head lolls. Other than that, he looks okay. I don't have the ability anymore to ping his health icon, but the lady colonist leans over and pulls her hoop skirt off. She's wearing an elaborate set of lacy knee-length pants underneath. She squeezes in between me and the captain to check his pulse.

"He's dead," she says.

Everyone is looking at me.

I've become a murderer, though I doubt even my Id was crazy enough to kill the pilot.

"Heart attack, probably," the lady says, pushing past me and pulling her hoop skirt back on.

"How can you tell?"

"I'm a doctor." She sits back down, smoothes the skirt out over her legs.

It's a small relief.

"Does anyone here know how to fly this thing?" I ask.

They all shake their heads.

I slump to the floor.

I could fly it. But I'd have to reboot my neural network to get that kind of information. And then Vince would return.

The airship shakes, and several motors whirr.

"What's that?" I ask.

The doctor looks out the observation windows.

"The bag is venting," she says. "We're dropping."

"Do you know how to use these manual controls to call the Air Guard?" I ask, pointing at the scary rows of controls in front of the dead pilot. If the alternative is plummeting down into the depths of a gas giant, arrest is starting to look good.

The doctor looks at me as if I'm stupid. "Yes."

"Then do it!"

The doctor sits up front speaking into the arm of the seat near the dead pilot. She's talking to the Air Guard.

"How far do you think this ship can fall?" I ask the men around me, trying to keep myself from focusing on the sinking feeling in my stomach that tells me we are still descending.

"This particular ship," says the doctor from up front, "comes from a line of what used to be tourist ships. They would follow the generator cables of the cities way down into the clouds." She throws a paper brochure at us. It lands on the floor. "Didn't any of you read the booklets on each of your seats?"

I feel around the cushions and find a crumpled-up ball of paper.

"Spacers." She stares at me with menace. "They loved riding these things down into the clouds. Until the depression hit. Now they're used for more practical things. We don't get many spacers on vacation here on Riley anymore."

"How long before the Air Guard gets to us?" I ask, trying to deflect the cloud of animosity in the air. My stomach begins to settle.

"They said an hour."

"And how long before we would get crushed?"

The doctor shrugs.

"Your programmed autopilot seems to be leveling us off," she says.

Ah. So maybe we would live. Relieving. I get up and walk forward, peering out of the windows. We're in what looks like a red fog now, the light inside tinted with the color. Everyone looks angry in this kind of lighting, or at least out of breath.

Nothing to do but wait for the Air Guard.

The prospect of being arrested doesn't do much for me. I sit down in a funk and continue staring at the shifting hues outside.

"What are you even doing down here?" the doctor asks. "Spacers don't even come down to the cities anymore."

I turn back to look at her.

"I'm bankrupt."

"I thought all spacers were rich," one of the men says.

"Well I'm not," I snap. "There are costs, right? You have to fuel the ship. Make repairs. Hire crew. Find cargo. And most importantly, invest intelligently." I look around at them. "I left here sixty years ago with a couple thousand in a bank account and some various investments. It was everything I had left after paying for my ship's needs." I had taken the money from Suzy, planning to pay her back in spades when I returned. "The depression wiped it all out by the time I came back." Though if I had come back twenty years earlier I would have been a multi-billionare.

"You're not a very lucky spacer," the doctor observes.

I shake my head.

"No, I'm not." But at least the doctor sounds sympathetic, unlike Vince, who ridiculed me for days straight about it. "I left people behind when I skipped out because I was close to broke sixty of your years ago as well. Now I don't even have them."

Vince led me down to the floating cities of Riley as a last-ditch effort to save ourselves.

Floating ghost cities. He'd been nuts in the end.

"I'm really sorry for doing this to you guys," I say. The men all nod.

"It's okay, man."

The doctor stands up.

"Don't you dare sympathize with him like that. When the Air Guard rescues us we're booking charges. *All* of us."

"I . . . ."

"Look, does he even know any of our names? Did he even bother to check our names before he took us all hostage on his crazy last spacer joyride?"

I try to recall if I checked their names. I don't think I did.

"That's right," she says. "Didn't even bother, did you?"

I have nothing to say to that.

The man closest to me speaks up. "Well, my name is . . . ."

"Don't do that," she yells. "Don't give him your name. You don't want him showing up on your doorstep one day, do you? Don't forget, he's probably unstable. He's got some sort of implant problem. Just wait until the Air Guard gets here. Don't talk to him anymore."

She sweeps past us all, hoop skirt bouncing, to go use the bathroom. The men look anywhere in the gondola but at me or at the door to the head.

I distract myself similarly by wondering if her waste will suffer the same fate as the keys to my handcuffs. I imagine the carbon-based remains will be compressed into the form of diamonds by the time they reach the core of Riley.

Back when Riley was colonized, scientists tried to study what the pressure did to things dropped in Riley's lower atmospheres, but apparently the depression killed the more speculative kinds of exploration like that. And any diamond prospectors formed up during the first years of colonizing Riley had quickly turned to finding other ways to make a living.

Like making airships to trade between the great floating cities.

It's a long, quiet hour before the Air Guard ship snares us. The gondola shakes a bit, and then a long snaking tube attaches itself to the airlock. My cuffs are still on, so I'm sure that will just make their job easier.

Someone knocks on the door to the airlock. The doctor opens it, and Suzie walks in. She's frail, but wearing her old blue and red Air Guard uniform and projecting authority.

"Get up the chute," she orders the colonists.

The men grab the pilot's body and scramble up awkwardly through the tube with it. I watch as the doctor pulls off her hoop-skirt.

She looks back at me.

I start to ask her name, but Suzie steps between us and the doctor starts scrambling away.

"Hi, Suzie."

"You wouldn't believe the strings I had to pull to get here this quick. I had to get back aboard one of my old ships just to come after you." She shakes her head.

"But thank you so much," I say. I reach out to hug her. She pulls out a stun gun, fires it at my chest, and I drop to the floor of the gondola, convulsing.

"You self-involved asshole." She grabs the ball gag from the corner of the cabin and ties it back on me.

"Mfff?"

"I've had sixty years to despise you. My secretary program, on the other hand, based on a younger version of me, is quite infatuated with you. Well, at least my memories of you." Suzie is quite strong for a ninety year old. She's hogtied me with a piece of rope around my ankles and the handcuffs, and dragged me to the back of the gondola. "But she came up with quite a compromise. We come get your Id, which is the real you that we always loved anyway. I always sensed he was in charge when we were together back then. And then *I* get to kill *you*." She points the stun gun right at my temple. "I'll turn you into a vegetable right now unless you boot your neural network up and give us Vince."

I need little convincing. She can have him. I hold up my cuffed hands. Suzie grabs them. A data link opens, using the very conductivity of our skin to transmit all the necessary information, and I reboot my entire neural net. All those chips in my spine warm up.

Vince appears, looks around, and swears as I allow the data transmit. He dissolves, fading away in the air in front of my eyes. Suzie's body network has him now.

He's gone, and Suzie has a big grin on her face as she lets go of my hands. She headbutts the wall, giving herself a bad bruise on the cheek. "I'm going to tell them you resisted my attempt to save you," she says, walking over to the airship controls. She kills all the communications, then takes out her stun gun and fires it into the control panel. Sparks fly. I check. I'm unable to piggyback a signal out of the gondola. "That you were crazy right there at the end. They'll believe me, too. You're suicidal, and dangerous, and there is no reason for anyone to attempt to come back in here."

A trickle of blood runs down the side of her nose as she walks over to the airlock door.

"You should have told me you were going to leave, sixty years ago, Vincent. Or at least invited me aboard your damn ship."

"Uhmfff mfffmfff," I say, and meaning it.

"It's too late for sorry," Suzie says. "I've let some of the gas out of your airbag. You won't be able to rise, but you might be able to float around on the level you're until you starve or die of dehydration. Good bye, Vincent; it was so nice to see you again."

She gets in the airlock. The tube pulls away and she's gone. The Air Guard is gone. They're not coming back.

It takes the better part of an hour to free myself and stand up. Again I rip off the gag.

I have my advanced senses, though. I can see thermals outside. I can find out how to fly this airship. Each instrument has a tiny instruction manual icon floating over it.

As I sit in the pilot's chair, trying not to freak myself out because he'd only been in it just an hour earlier, Vince appears next to me.

"Shit!" I scream.

"Relax, I'm not going to hijack you again," he says.

"You didn't get . . . ."

"I really didn't want to end up with those two psychos. Gave them a copy of myself that will self-destruct in a few hours. Wouldn't want to miss out on all the fun here."

"Me dying?"

"Well," Vince says, "the airbag thing is a problem of course. But remember when I said you should trust me?"

"You always say that," I sigh.

"Who decided to make a run for it sixty years ago when we

realized we were almost bankrupt?"

"Me."

"Right. Now what you should have done was listen to me then." Vince walks around behind me. "I told you it was a bad idea. It felt wrong, didn't it?"

"You wanted to buy an airship," I say. "But wouldn't tell me why."

"I told you to research what happens at the heart of a gas giant," Vince admonishes me from the other side of the chair.

"You moron," I snap. "Most theories propose a giant diamond at the center of the giant, squashed into being by all those pressures at that depth. Which, if you're thinking of trying to get at it, means we get crushed too. You know what else? Diamonds really aren't worth all that much these days."

Vince pretends hurt. He claps a virtual hand over his chest.

"Why are you focused on one big diamond?"

I frown.

"Every day these aerostat cities are dumping carbon-based trash that falls downward," Vince says. "Where it gets crushed. But look around you," he points at the roiling cloud we're in, and at the massive upwelling thermals.

Deep down at their hearts they're strong enough to throw almost anything up. And no tourist ship has gone this near. Civilized cities and easy tourist jaunts avoid that kind of turbulence.

"No diamond prospector ever found anything when they first came to Riley, even in the upwells," I say.

"Yes," Vince says. "But that was before almost seventy years of dumping trash into the atmosphere, right? It was virgin then. Humans hadn't been dumping shit into the lower atmospheres yet."

I'm dumbfounded. He's got a point.

"Do you trust me?" he asks again.

This time it is from somewhere inside me. Looking down into the depths of Riley, I've managed to reclaim my Id.

"I want to see this," I whisper, as we begin to slide downwards.

"Better buckle in, then," Vince says in a last fading whisper.

There are journeys, and then there are rides, and this was a ride to hell and back. Or at least Riley's version of hell. I slipped ever downward to the thermal my former Id had identified as the prime upwell spot, trusting my instincts to bring the airship as far down into the depths as had ever been done.

We floated through a sea of diamond specks before we smacked the heart of the upwell and rode the thermal. It was like straddling a rocket straight back up. It spit us out high enough that we coasted into the nearest aerostat city with several hundred feet of altitude to spare.

We landed covered in diamond dust.

Several weeks later I'm standing near the great foam pillars of the courthouse. Suzie spots me waiting for her to come out, stops, then walks over. A green and red police droid follows two steps behind her.

"Hello, Vincent."

She doesn't seem too surprised to see me. We've faced each other in court for the past week . But all that's over. The best psychiatrists, lawyers, journalists, and judges have all pored over our plights. I'm acquitted of murder, but my implants have been torn from me so that there is no danger of my Id getting free again.

And I had to cover court costs. My starship was confiscated and auctioned off. The Riley government took its share of the court costs, Air Guard rescue fee, taxes, and handed me the rest.

"I never felt like I got to finish things," I say. "Or properly apologize."

She shakes her head sadly.

"And even if you do, so what? You're going to leave on your spaceship for any number of years while I wither away here again? You're wasting your time if you think there's anything to rescue with us."

"I sold it," I tell her. "I don't have a ship anymore."

She starts walking away from the courthouse. The droid and I follow her.

"I would like to give you the money back, with interest." It's almost everything I have left.

"And then what are you going to do here, on Riley?"

"Buy an airship, offer some very hair-raising tours of this world. Famous tours that spacers will come to try from all over." It feels like something I'll be good at, the pit of my stomach agrees with this. Deep down, I've always liked airships.

We walk together a little further before she stops.

"You don't just get forgiveness like that," she says. "It just doesn't happen like that."

Her sentence for marooning me involved guided therapy and personality adjustment. That and a twenty-four-hour police droid for a year, until the therapy kicked in fully.

I reach over and grab her hand, softly, and place a diamond in it.

"A memento," I explain. "It was lodged in one of the spars when I got back."

She pockets it and suddenly laughs. It is a symbolic thing for me. Important. I want to try and undo some of the damage. I'm not sure how to take the laughter.

"Okay Vincent. I'm drugged up out of my mind right now, and

it makes some sort of warped sense. At the very least," she smiles, "I'm no longer interested in killing you."

"Thank you," I say. It's a start.

We part.

I walk down a plastic city street, looking up at the great city guywires that lead to the superstructures of pressurized gas that hold us up.

I wonder how hard it would be to get an entire city down to the diamond sea far below my feet? ✪

THE JEWELS OF LEMURIA

BY RICHARD A. LUPOFF

THE CENTRAL RAILROAD TOWER in the very heart of the world's greatest city rises forty-two stories into the air. It houses the offices of more than three thousand companies, lawyers, dentists, and physicians. And one mysterious organization, the frosted glass of whose doorway is marked, simply, *C. W. Enterprises—by Appointment Only.*

The Seacoast City telephone directory contains no entry for C. W. Enterprises, and a call to the information operator elicits only a terse, "I am *sor*-ree, I have no *lis*-ting for that *par*-tee."

Any curiosity seeker who knocks at the door of C. W. Enterprises will be met only by silence; if he tries the knob, he will find the door securely locked.

And yet, were it not for C. W. Enterprises, Seacoast City, the world's hub of commerce, culture, and transportation, would lie helpless before the marauding forces of crime and corruption.

The lobby level of the Central Railroad Tower plays host to an oyster bar, a cigar and news stand, a dry cleaning establishment, a newsreel theater, and the Central Barber Shop.

It is in the last named establishment that our story begins.

Two men sat in adjacent barber chairs. The nearly identical jackets of their fine hundred-dollar suits hung on the establishment's brass coat rack. Their nearly identical fedoras, blocked and brushed, awaited them on the hat stand. Despite their careful grooming there was something vaguely disquieting about these men. Perhaps it was the cold expression in their eyes. Perhaps it was the abnormally wide, flat appearance of their mouths.

The co-proprietors of the Central Barber Shop, twin brothers Alberto and Roberto Morelli, danced around their customers, snipping here, powdering there. The brothers' hair was wavy, graying; each wore a neatly-trimmed moustache.

Each customer had already been carefully shaved with an imported straight razor of finest Toledo steel and the precious faces of both customers were covered with lightly scented, damp towels. Unlike most men in their position, for whom the towels were heated before application, these two insisted upon theirs being chilled. The Morellis thought this odd, but their business ethic required them to provide the service that their customers demanded.

Kneeling before one customer, Clarence Willis, the Morelli brothers' faithful employee, worked his shoeshine magic on a pair of handmade cordovan bluchers. In Clarence's hands shoe wax coated leather like honey on a clabbered milk muffin, brushes danced like Bojangles' feet, and a soft flannel cloth popped and rang like a bullwhip.

A battered Emerson radio stood on the shelf between rows of potions and elixirs, the voices of the greatest tenor and soprano in the world emerging in a live broadcast from the great Metropolitan Opera Palace. A copy of the Seacoast City *Daily Reporter* lay beside the radio. The Morelli brothers had been reading the paper when their customers arrived, Roberto scanning the main headlines while Alberto studied the box-score of yesterday's game between the Seacoast City Superbas and the Jenkintown Yellow Sox.

The front page story, copied from a wire service, told of the mysterious disappearance in California of sultry movie vamp Isabella del Sueño. The reporter hinted slyly that Señorita del Sueño was sharing a tryst with Roland Ramirez, her costar in the recent romantic western, *Ride, Vaquero*. The sports section's ace scrivener, one Billy Trout, mourned at length over the Superbas' fourth loss in their past six games, 5 to 3 in eleven innings.

The glorious music that had filled the barbershop was suddenly cut off, replaced by the breathless voice of an announcer.

This is Joseph van Horn in the WSCR newsroom. We interrupt this broadcast to bring you news of a daring robbery. Thieves have made off with the newest and most precious exhibit at the Municipal Museum of Art and History. As has been previously reported, the precious gems and golden scepter recently discovered by the Hopkinson Expedition and believed to be the legendary crown jewels of the Lost Continent of Lemuria, were to go on display to the public at a grand ceremony scheduled for six o'clock this evening.

As the display was being set up a mysterious gas was released in the museum, which was closed in preparation for the gala event. Curators, guards and workers alike were rendered unconscious. When they recovered, the jewels were missing.

Police have no clues as to the identity or location of the criminals involved, but the public is urged to be on the lookout for suspicious characters.

The Emerson switched back to the opera.

The customer in one barber chair removed the cold towel from his freshly shaven face. "Well, waddaya think of that?" he inquired.

The customer in the other chair removed his towel as well. "It's a cryin' shame, a cryin' shame. A honest citizen can't do nothin' nowadays without runnin' into criminals and crooks, can he?"

The two men burst into raucous laughter.

"Hey, barber," one of them growled, "you and your partner there, you seen us here, right? Lookit the clock, you better notice what time it is."

Alberto Morelli blinked. "But—why?"

"Never you mind why," the customer growled. "Just remember. You get me? We're Mr. Smith and Mr. Brown. We been here for the past hour."

He climbed out of the chair. "Here," he snarled. He reached into his pocket and pulled out a roll of bills held in place by a gleaming money clip. "This should help you remember us!"

He peeled a large-denomination bill off the roll and handed it to Alberto.

"And you, too!" The customer peeled a second bill of the same denomination from the roll and handed it to Roberto.

"Now, where's that shoe-shine boy?" He reached into his pocket and extracted a silver dollar. A deep crease appeared between his eyes. "Where'd he go?"

But Clarence Willis was nowhere to be seen. The only clue to his whereabouts was a tattered comic book left open on his shoe-shine stool, and the door of the closet where he stored his push-broom, his shoeshine kit, and the instruments and tools of his humble profession when not in use. The door stood slightly ajar.

Alberto Morelli took the few steps required to reach that door and carefully closed it.

"That Clarence, he just disappears sometimes," Alberto explained. "He's not too bright, you know. He's a good boy, we try and take care of him, but sometimes he just disappears."

At this very moment, forty-two stories above ground in the topmost suite of the Central Railroad Tower, a shadowy figure was moving among an array of instruments and tools of a very different sort. Electrical devices hummed and cast an orange radiance that gave the room an eerie glow, for opaque steel shutters were drawn across the windows. By coincidence the sounds of WSCR gave warmth and presence to the otherwise scientific surroundings. At this moment the station was broadcasting Emile Waldteufel's *Les Patineurs*.

A woman sat on a tall stool. Her fingers were long and graceful. As the hands of a great cellist draw music from the bow and strings of her musical instrument, hers sped with unerring accuracy and ultimate sensitivity across a panel of knobs and switches. Needles flickered and dials glowed before her sharp eyes.

Behind her a pair of doors slid back, their sound a soft hiss that most would have missed, but the woman perched atop the tall stool whirled. The figure she beheld was a humble one. A man with stooped shoulders and downcast eyes, his clothing clean but plain, clearly the veteran of countless washings and numerous patchings, his feet encased in shoes that were scuffed and worn.

As the doors hissed shut behind him the man concealed himself behind a screen. Moments later there emerged a figure who would hardly have been taken for the same individual, yet it was he.

"Wizard," the woman perched atop the stool whispered in greeting. She nodded her head. Her blue-black hair was braided in an exotic fashion, her features astonishingly like those of the famed bust of Cleopatra, her skin the color of ebony.

"Nzambi."

The speaker was tall. One might even think that he was the same person as the humble figure who had disappeared behind the screen, drawn to his full height, his muscular shoulders and slim waist merely suggested by the shimmering red material of his costume. By some oddity of the lighting in the room, perhaps, or perhaps by some clever device of the weaver's art, the eye could hardly focus on his closely-cut tunic and trousers.

Strange as was the effect of his costume, even stranger was that of an attempt to focus on his face. He wore no mask, nor would an observer say that his features were invisible, yet the eye would fix itself involuntarily to the left or to the right of his face. A group of observers attempting to agree upon a description of him would discover to their embarrassment that they were uncertain as to the length of his hair, the slope of his nose, the height of his forehead or the color of his eyes.

"Are you aware of today's events at the Municipal Museum of Art and History, Nzambi?"

"The Jewels of Lemuria were stolen. Our agent at police head-quarters notified me, Wizard."

"This is a serious matter."

"Cannot the police handle it?"

"If it were a simple jewel robbery I would leave it in their hands. They bumble but they are no less competent than most official-dom. But I am concerned that this matter goes far deeper than the theft of a crown and a scepter. What do gold and emeralds and sapphires mean? Very little, my dear, very little."

"Why, then? Why does this matter warrant the attention of the Crimson Wizard?"

"Have you heard of the Society of the Deep Ones?"

"Vaguely. There is a lodge with a similar name, I've heard men-tion of them on a radio show. They are the butt of humor."

The Wizard laughed without mirth. His was a bitter laugh, the laughter of one who responds to irony rather than humor.

"The Society of Deep Ones is no object for amusement. Their tentacles reach high and low, they reach deep into society. That radio show you mention—I know it well, everyone knows it well—it is part of their campaign of disinformation, designed to fool us into thinking that they are not serious. But they are. They are very serious. And very dangerous."

The lovely Nzambi slid from her perch atop the tall stool. "Their reputation is that of a silly group of people who get together and play-act. They wear vainglorious costumes and give themselves titles like 'Lord High Octopus' and 'Mistress of the Mystic Seabed.' They exchange secret passwords and practice mock-religious rituals, like a group of schoolchildren playing at grown-up ceremonials."

"Indeed." The Wizard brushed past Nzambi and studied an assemblage of complex electrical gear. Hands that were hard for the eye to follow, that seemed strangely out of focus, made delicate adjustments. The Wizard turned away from the instruments and faced his lovely assistant once more.

"That is part of their diabolically clever means of operating. The Society of Deep Ones has deep roots, roots that burrow into the sands of time, Nzambi. They are the inheritors of a religious tradition with its origins among the peoples of the ancient world. They are the heirs of a civilization that was old when our own ancestors were barely emerging from savagery to develop the arts of thought, of mathematics, of astronomy and of writing. Arts which were copied by even more primitive Europeans who turned the fruits of our own civilization against us and laid low the once mighty empires of the Dark Continent."

Perhaps the Wizard gestured, perhaps it was the play of light on the unique material in which he was garbed, but energy appeared to play across his figure.

Once again he spoke, his voice deep yet soft, cultured and marked with precision.

"Were the human race to be called for judgment, Nzambi, there would be much to answer for. The sins of our petty species are many and horrendous, and the greatest of them may be our pride. We think that our vaunted intellect, our skill with tools and with weapons, entitle us to lord it over the rest of Creation. The authors of our holy books place words in the mouth of God, giving Man dominion over all of nature. What a foolish pretense that is!"

Nzambi smiled ruefully. "But Man does rule the planet, does he not, Wizard?"

The laugh that emerged from the weird vision that was the Crimson Wizard was a compound of painfully gotten wisdom and bitter amusement. "Man thinks he rules the planet. Let us hope that he is wrong, for the legacy of our generation will be nothing but misery and pain for our descendents, should we even survive to have any. No, Nzambi."

The Wizard paused. He strode across the room and stood over his assistant. Although her slim, tall figure towered over most women and many men, she was obliged to tilt her head backwards if she hoped to catch even a glimpse of his stern, elusive, ever-shifting features.

"No," he repeated. "There were species before ours whose civilizations would put our own to shame, whose achievements were such that we should be awe-struck and reduced to fear and trembling had we but the remotest inkling of their greatness and their threat. The descendents of those beings dwell to this day midst the distant stars, and their agents walk among us, unknown, unrecognized, as plain before us as the purloined letter before the Parisian *sureté* in M. Poe's brilliant tale."

With a swirl of red, the Crimson Wizard swept from the room.

Fleeting moments passed.

A panel slid back atop the Central Railroad Tower. The hangar that topped the soaring structure was invisible from any other building in Seacoast City. Within the hangar stood an array of the world's most advanced aircraft—a Cierva gyroplane, a Sapphire-MacNeese sm-10 monoplane, and a miniature lighter-than-air craft. The mechanics who maintained the fleet had been vetted for reliability and were as highly skilled as they were highly paid. Any of the Wizard's aircraft was ready for use at any time.

On this occasion the Wizard selected the lighter-than-air craft. It was coated with a special paint developed by the Wizard's scientific aide, Nzambi. It was the world's least reflective pigment, rendering the miniature zeppelin virtually invisible by day or by night.

To the Wizard the craft was almost a person. He had named the airship *Kpalimé* after his ancestral city in Africa, but when he settled behind the controls of the miniature zeppelin and spoke her name, it was if he spoke the name of a beloved woman rather than a machine.

Unlike most zeppelins, *Kpalimé*'s propellers were powered by silent compressed air generators. Thus, the tell-tale buzz of internal combustion or Diesel engines that announced the presence of conventional airships was absent. *Kpalimé* was as silent as she was elusive. In her, the Crimson Wizard could approach his target unseen, unheard, undetected.

He guided the airship out of her berth atop the Central Railroad Tower, pressing a control that caused the hangar door to slide shut behind *Kpalimé*. The airship slipped through the wintry sky above Seacoast City's concrete canyons. The lights of theaters and restaurants, of a hundred thousand apartment dwellings and of as many automobiles clogging the metropolis's thoroughfares, turned the cityscape into a fairyland of glittering jewels.

But these were not the jewels that concerned the Crimson Wizard. His mind was focused on the jewels that had been stolen from the Municipal Museum.

The Wizard tapped out a new series of instructions on the nearly invisible zeppelin's control panel and *Kpalimé* slowed, then halted in midair, hovering more than 200 feet above the gabled roof of the museum. A few night-flying birds and bats were the only company that the silent airship encountered. Even the sharp senses of these aerial creatures would not have detected the sensor rays that emanated from *Kpalimé*.

Inside the airship the Wizard bent and placed his eye to the viewing lens of a special instrument created at his behest by his assistant, Nzambi. The viewer was teamed with the airship's ray emitter. The emanations of the ray emitter made it possible for the Wizard to detect the passage on the ground below of any source of organic chemicals. The trail of each species, he knew, left a chromic signature all its own, and the scent-track of each individual differed as subtly yet as distinctly as did their fingerprints.

With a sardonic grin, the Wizard referred to the device as his spoor detector.

Now he drew his breath sharply, lifted his eye from the viewer and sat silently, contemplating what he had seen. A trail led from the Municipal Museum of Art and History. To the naked eye the trail would have been invisible. To the Wizard it stood out as vividly as a stream of luminous water flowing through a darkened countryside.

The trail led to the curb in front of the museum. There, it disappeared.

The Wizard uttered a low exclamation. He had located the spoor of his prey, only to lose it almost at once at the point where they entered a waiting vehicle and drove away. The Wizard had suffered a setback, but he was not one to accept defeat. He manipulated the controls of the miniature zeppelin and its compressed air engines whispered back to life. *Kpalimé* moved silently through the air above Seacoast City, describing an outward spiral with its center directly above the Municipal Museum of Art and History.

The miniature airship whispered its way over Seacoast City's theater district, over the avenues of expensive shops and great department stores, over the luxurious apartment buildings that housed the city's wealthy and powerful and over the noisome tenements where the poverty-stricken and their outcast brethren huddled in misery. Full dark had long since fallen and from the vantage point of the airship the million lights of the city gleamed like as many luminous gems, but the Crimson Wizard had no time to enjoy the sight that unraveled to his view.

A quarter mile away and a thousand feet above *Kpalimé*, the transoceanic night-flier, a Langley-Hawker trimotored biplane, carried its capacity load of sixteen passengers toward their destination, the Seacoast City Municipal Aerodrome.

Soon *Kpalimé* whispered through a bank of mist that had risen from the Saturn River on whose banks Seacoast City had been built. The rays of the emitter penetrated the mist effortlessly. The Wizard uttered an exclamation of pleasure. The trail that had disappeared in front of the museum had reappeared in this district of warehouses and piers.

Guided by the skilled hands of the Wizard, the airship slipped lower and lower. At last it came to hover above a darkened warehouse that clearly had seen better days. The luminous trail led from a dark Packard sedan and into a passageway toward the rear of the building. From this noisome alley the trail led up a short flight of wooden stairs and onto a rickety-looking loading dock. There, at the rolling door, the path disappeared.

No one thought to watch the sky here at the riverside, but had an observer been present he would have been astonished at what he beheld. A hatch opened in the seeming nothingness above. A figure whose shimmering scarlet garments were barely visible in the Seacoast City night appeared in the opening. The figure—a man—stepped from nowhere into nothingness. As he fell he arched forward, spreading his arms and legs. The thin but incredibly strong cloth of his costume stretched to form a kind of parachute or glider like that of a flying squirrel.

A moment later the Wizard landed with a muffled thump on the loading dock. He looked up at his airship and touched a control on the belt of his costume. The door in the side of the airship slid closed. *Kpalimé* remained on station, utterly silent, virtually invisible.

The Wizard studied the lock on the rolling door. He smiled contemptuously and extended his hand. Were those tools that flashed almost invisibly at the Wizard's fingertips, or were his fingers themselves the only tools he needed?

No matter. In seconds the tumblers of the lock snicked into place. The Crimson Wizard flattened himself on the loading platform. He slid the door upward quietly. He slipped beneath the bottom roller, then lowered the door silently behind himself.

Rising to his feet, the Wizard strained to take in his surroundings. His eyes adjusted, gradually, to the miniscule level of illumination that crept through tiny openings in the structure. Clearly, it had been designed to keep prying eyes out, but by like means it was almost impossible for anyone in the building to see without the aid of artificial illumination.

Almost, but not impossible.

The Wizard found himself standing in a gloom-shrouded chamber. So huge was the structure that its farther wall disappeared into the shadows. The Wizard reached into his belt and removed a pellet hardly larger than a common BB. For so tiny an object, the pellet was strangely heavy. The Wizard drew back his scarlet-covered arm and hurled the pellet into the air. When it reached the apex of its path it burst into brilliant illumination, its color the Wizard's trademark shimmering red.

There was no sign of the thieves who had made off with the Crown Jewels of Lemuria. But there was something else. The Wizard dropped to the concrete floor, sniffing for spoor as would a lion in the African veldt. The thieves had been here, and not long before. But the Wizard had learned more than that from the thin traces of their presence they had left behind. There was something about these thieves, something abnormal. They were human, after a fashion, but they were not entirely so. There was something wrong here, something inhuman.

And there was something else. More precisely, there was someone else. There was someone with the thieves but not one of them. And that someone was a woman.

The Wizard rose to his feet.

She was lovely. Her features were regular, her skin a rich olive color, her hair a gleaming jet black. Her costume was minimal, a single white garment that did little to conceal her magnificent figure. A broad belt of gold encrusted with gems glittered in the ruddy illumination of the Wizard's arcing flare.

She sat upon a throne, a magnificent tiara of precious stones resting upon her brow.

And surrounding the goddess-like figure, a retinue of half-human servitors. The leader of these beings held before the woman a weirdly carven bowl from which rose thick fumes.

All of this the Wizard observed in the few seconds that his flare illuminated the great room. The flare dimmed as it arced downward, leaving a trail of swiftly dissipating fumes behind it.

In that same moment, the creatures surrounding the throne whirled toward the source of the rosy illumination. In a deep recess of his lightning-fast brain, the Wizard concluded that these creatures had the ability to see in near-total darkness. Their huge, bulging eyes, visible in the seconds before the flare faded to extinction, bespoke as much. In the darkness that followed, the Wizard could hear their slithering progress as they advanced toward him.

He withdrew several more of the miniature flares from their hiding place and hurled them toward the creatures, but this time instead of sending the flares in an arc that approached the dark ceiling overhead, the Wizard pitched them onto the concrete floor between himself and the semi-human creatures. Again rose-colored light flared, but this time it was many times as brilliant as it had been before.

The creatures halted in their advance toward the Wizard. He saw them throw their arms before their eyes, blocking the bright illumination from their abnormally sensitive retinas. With a shock, the Wizard realized that the creatures had no hands in the human sense. Each of their limbs, instead, terminated in a writhing cluster of pallid tentacles. Their faces were a mockery of human features. The eyes were huge and bulging, the noses flattened and almost nonexistent, the mouths broad and lipless.

When one of the creatures, clearly the leader, opened its broad mouth to issue commands to its followers, rows of razor-sharp triangular teeth glinted red. Unlike the other creatures in the band, this one appeared to be older and stronger. Where the heads of the others were smooth and rounded, the crown of the leader's head was surrounded by a hideous ring of writhing tentacles the color of freshly-spilled blood.

The sound that emerged from the creature's mouth was a terrible batrachian hiss.

In response to their leader's command the creatures swarmed toward the Wizard. But the Wizard was ready for them. Already the flares were fading and he replenished the vital illumination by hurling a handful of the BB-sized pellets against the concrete. In a maneuver that no eye, human or batrachian, could have followed, the Wizard whirled, his shimmering cape spreading around him in a brilliant, blinding, sparkling disk.

The monsters halted, confused, until their leader urged them onward with another of its hideous hissing commands. But before the monsters, where the Crimson Wizard had stood mere moments before, there now appeared a pair, then a quartet, of scarlet-clad, shimmering figures. Then these divided again, and there were eight, sixteen, then thirty-two muscular, defiant Crimson Wizards.

Had the marvel-man truly summoned multiple duplicates of himself? Had he a method of dividing his physical substance to create a brigade of sleek warriors?

Or had he merely cast a glamour over his attackers, seizing control of their amphibious brains, creating the illusion that a single man had become an imposing throng of fierce opponents?

At their leader's hissing command, a contingent of the pallid monsters leaped forward, each of them engaging one of the multiple Crimson Wizards in mortal combat. Battles ensued in parallel, monster against hero, tentacle against fist, blow exchanged for blow and grasp for grasp. In each case it was the Wizard who triumphed. One by one the white creatures backed away, yielding to the combative superiority of their scarlet-clad foes.

Next the monsters formed a phalanx, rhythmically pounding slimy tentacles against their own bare, pallid bodies. A booming cadence like that of a hundred drummers filled the warehouse. At a signal the monsters began a steady, disciplined advance against the ranks of crimson-clad heroes.

One of the Crimson Wizards moved his hands in a baffling gesture. There was a flash of lurid energy in the cavernous room and the ranks of red-costumed men doubled still again.

Was this a real phenomenon or a mere illusion?

The batrachians did not wait to learn the truth. They halted in their tracks. Even their leader, for all the bravado he had shown a moment earlier, drew back. Before the multiple ranks of Crimson Wizards they scattered to the walls of the room. They seemed to lose definition, to melt like gelatinous sculptures left to stand in a withering sun, then to slither snakelike along the base of the walls. An opening existed between the wooden walls and the concrete floor of the old building. Before the Crimson Wizard's eyes the creatures disappeared into the blackness of the opening.

They left behind the noxious stench of their kind.

In the last fading illumination of dying flares the Wizard made a lightning-fast examination of the room. Grotesque candelabra rose to either side of the throne where the goddess-like figure still remained in majestic silence. The Wizard reached into his waist-band and drew out a small metallic device that had been created for him by Nzambi. He held it to each candle, and the wick of each taper in turn burst into flame.

He stood before the throne where the lovely woman awaited. The throne stood upon a dais approachable by a series of low steps. The Wizard advanced toward the woman, climbing step by step. As he did so she kept her eyes fixed on him. Her beauty was marvelous to behold, but it was her eyes that most arrested the

observer. They were filled both with an intelligence seldom encountered and with the lingering terror of one who has recently
undergone an experience that would reduce a lesser person to gib-
bering madness.

Two steps from the top of the staircase the Wizard halted. Here
he stood eye-to-eye with the woman.

"They're gone," he intoned. "You are safe now. Come with me."

The woman shook her head, a forbidding expression on her
face.

"What's wrong?" the Wizard asked. "Don't you see—those
creatures are gone. There is nothing further to fear."

Still the woman neither spoke nor moved. Was she in the grasp
of a hypnotic spell? Or was she, perhaps, still paralyzed with
fear?

"Can you speak?" the Wizard demanded.

The woman nodded. With one graceful, jewel-encrusted hand
she grasped the weirdly formed scepter. Her other hand, each
finger decorated with a magnificent ring, rested upon one of the
ornate arms of the throne.

"Come closer." She did not quite whisper, but rather spoke in
a voice so low that it barely carried to the Crimson Wizard's ears,
yet was so clear and well controlled that every syllable rang with
crystal clarity.

"I dare not move," the woman said. "This throne is connected
to an explosive device planted beneath the floor. They used that
means to keep me from struggling during their horrid ceremonies.
They intended to take me with them when they were finished. I'm
sure they would have set the device to explode once they were
gone. They don't care about this building, they don't care about
the world of humankind at all. The only reason they didn't set it
off is that you surprised them and frightened them away. But if I

try to leave the building will be destroyed and you and I will both be killed."

The Wizard nodded his understanding. "Very well," he instructed the woman. "Don't move."

She breathed a single syllable of assent.

The Wizard climbed the remaining steps to the dais, circling the throne in search of a tell-tale connection that ran to the explosives beneath the aged structure. With an exclamation he dropped to his knees, tracing with sensitive fingertips a slim, sinuous wire that ran from the base of the throne to a tiny opening in the floor behind the dais.

A new tool appeared in his hand and he worked carefully over the wire until the connection was safely removed. He rose to his feet and returned to his position confronting the woman. "I've taken care of that as best I could, but those creatures are devilishly clever. By disconnecting the primary fuse I was forced to set a secondary timer in motion. I have no way of telling how long it is set to run. My guess would be five minutes at most. We had best get out of here and put as much distance as possible between ourselves and this place, as quickly as we can."

With his enemies at least temporarily vanquished and the immediate danger of explosion removed, the Wizard's manner changed dramatically. The taciturn, commanding man of action was replaced by a gentler presence, one nonetheless commanding, but kindly and sympathetic.

"Will you tell me your name?" he asked.

The woman said, "I am Isabella Alejandra Orquidia Paloma del Sueño y Montalvo, *señor*. I thank you for rescuing me from those—" she hesitated, then concluded, "—from those creatures."

"Isabella del Sueño, the star of *Ride, Vaquero*," the Wizard responded.

"That is I, yes."

"You were reported missing from your Hollywood home and from the studio, *señorita*."

She smiled at the courtesy. "I was lured to a supposed charitable event for the relief of suffering in my homeland. I felt it my duty to attend and offer my support. When I arrived I was seized and drugged. I awakened here. I do not even know where I am, *señor*. I am indebted to you for driving those monsters away and freeing me from them, but I need to learn more of what happened. And then, of course, to return to the studio. They will have halted production of my new film, *The Caballero from Monterrey*."

The Wizard nodded. "Of course. But first we must make sure your needs are met. I'll bring you to my headquarters. My assistant Nzambi will care for you. Do you require medical attention?"

"No." Isabella del Sueño pressed her hands to her temples. "My mind is clear now. For a while it was terrible, while I was drugged I seemed trapped in a nightmare from which there was no escape. But I feel now that I am myself once again."

The Wizard led her to the doorway of the aged building, onto the loading dock. He bent to his waist to tap a series of commands into a tiny panel concealed there. In the sky above the building a door opened on nothingness. An automatic reel began to revolve above them, and a ladder of metallic links gradually unwound and descended.

It halted not far above the wooden dock.

The Wizard helped Isabella del Sueño to place her foot on the bottom rung. She was wearing golden sandals. Her toenails were painted a smooth, shining shade of scarlet. Soon the glamorous olive-skinned actress was aboard *Kpalimé*. The Wizard followed her, then drew up the ladder and shut the miniature airship's door behind them.

Kpalimé rose silently into the chilly air of the Seacoast City night. The airship's gas-bag was compact. The amazing lifting power of its content, an element drawn from secret mines in an African valley unknown to the outer world, was the key to its remarkable performance. The gondola slung beneath the gas-bag was similarly compact, its efficient design such as to pack a wealth of controls and comfortable quarters into a small space.

The Wizard engaged the compressed-air engines of the zeppelin and guided it away from the riverfront, toward the tallest building in Seacoast City, the Central Railroad Tower. The airship had covered perhaps half the distance from the river to its hangar when the sky behind it was brightened by a single monumental flash. "Hang on!" After an interval that could not have been as long as it seemed the little airship was rocked by a violent shock-wave. The Wizard nodded. He had expected as much.

Minutes later the door atop the Central Railroad Tower slid back to admit *Kpalimé*. The Wizard guided the airship to her cradle. A crewman locked the ship down. More crewmen swarmed to service the little zeppelin.

Inside the Wizard's headquarters Nzambi awaited. When the Wizard and Isabella del Sueño entered the room, Nzambi took the other woman's hands in hers. The actress introduced herself. Nzambi nodded, unsurprised, and gave her own name. The two women shook hands. "You need clothing," Nzambi said. "I'll lend you some things."

Isabella del Sueño thanked the other woman. "I want to get rid of everything they gave me. This garment. It stinks of those creatures. And these jewels." She ripped a bracelet from her arm. It appeared to be purest gold, studded with emeralds and diamonds. She laid it on a tabletop.

Soon the three of them sat at a low table sharing hot cocoa

and sandwiches. Isabella del Sueño had told her story again, this time going into greater detail than before. The Crimson Wizard had examined the jewelry that the beautiful actress removed. He placed a coded call to a certain telephone number and described the gems and ornaments with which Isabella del Sueño had been bedecked. He listened in silence, then said, "They shall be returned in the morning."

He rose from his place and crossed the room. He twirled the tumblers on a heavy safe and locked the jewels in it. He rose to his full height and said, "*Señorita*, as much as it would please me to entertain you, I'm sure you wish to return to your home and resume your career. You can board a train in the morning and be home in a few days. I advise you to telephone ahead and arrange for protection. We are dealing with evil forces here and they seem to have chosen you for a special role. Do you recall, despite your drugged state, anything that they said to you? Either before you were taken to the riverfront building or while you were there."

The lovely actress frowned. "They didn't really mistreat me. They seemed in awe. They seemed to know that my family were from Spain. That we are of royal Bourbon blood."

"They treated you, then, with the deference due to royalty?"

"Yes, but—something more than that. They seemed almost to worship me. And yet I felt that they intended me no good."

"You are a most perceptive woman, *señorita*. There have been tribes who make gods and goddesses of mortals. They generally favor handsome youths and beautiful maidens. They dress them in finest raiment and shower them with luxuries. But then, when their calendar so dictates, 'when the stars are right,' as they sometimes express it, they slay their deities. I'm afraid, if I hadn't intervened, you were doomed."

"And you saved my life."

"For the time being. But those monsters made good their escape. I blame myself. I should have brought assistance and laid a trap for them, but I didn't realize how serious the menace was. I thought at first that we were dealing with ordinary jewel thieves. Such was not the case. The gems and trinkets that they placed upon you, *señorita*, are unimaginably old and incalculably valuable, but the gems are the least of our concern. These beings are not human, not part of the natural order of our world at all. Their ancestors came from some malign locale beneath the sea. They owe allegiance to no wholesome or decent god or nation but to the foul world from which they came."

The Crimson Wizard paced back and forth, halting at last before a tall window facing toward the Saturn River. A glow illuminated the night sky where flames leaped upward from the now-demolished, abandoned warehouse.

"Someday," the Wizard intoned, "someday I will penetrate to the heart of this foul spew. Someday they will be destroyed. They must be. The only alternative would be too horrible to contemplate. But the time is not yet." With a bitter grin he quoted, 'the stars are not yet right.'

"Still," and behind the shimmering scarlet swirls that hid his features he raised his eyes to the heavens, "still, they must not escape unscathed. They must be pursued and punished for what they have attempted and for what they have done."

The Wizard summoned a trusted female aide from the aircraft hangar. He instructed her to accompany Señorita del Sueño to an exclusive but inconspicuous inn where she would spend the night under an assumed name and under the watchful eye of the Wizard's employee. In the morning they would proceed by luxury rail-liner to the West Coast. The Wizard would see to the return of the jewels to the Municipal Museum of Art and History.

The actress departed, first expressing her gratitude to the Wizard and inviting him to attend the premiere of her next picture. She would, in all likelihood, be in attendance herself. Such was a premise of the Hollywood studio structure and its system of stardom. She would, she stated, take pride in entertaining the Wizard at her table at the celebratory banquet which she expected to precede the showing of the film.

The Wizard's expression, had Señorita del Sueño been able to see it through the swirling crimsons and scarlets that concealed his identity from the world, would have been one of wry amusement. "I should be delighted," he told her as he bent over her hand, "but of course I cannot make a promise, as my obligations are many and often unforeseen."

As soon as the actress was gone the Wizard whirled to engage his assistant in conversation. "If you please, Nzambi, our task is far from complete."

"Of course." With amazing rapidity and precision she shut down Bunsen burners, sealed retorts, and closed notebooks in which were recorded the endless experiments of the Crimson Wizard's laboratory. Moving with a grace that masked her speed she disappeared behind a concealing screen.

When she reappeared she was garbed in a costume similar to that of her employer save for its color. Where the Wizard's outfit was of shimmering scarlet, Nzambi's was of a rich, brilliant yellow. To the Wizard she was Nzambi but to the world she was known only as the Golden Saint.

Together they moved to the elevator that mere hours earlier had brought one Clarence Willis, a humble shiner of shoes and brusher of shoulders from the Central Barber Shop many stories below. For the world had no inkling that the wielder of polishing cloths and whisk brooms was also the famous mystery man whose exploits thrilled multitudes.

The elevator plunged silently toward the lobby of the Central Railroad Tower, but it did not stop in that marble-floored sanctuary of Mammon. One story below the lobby was conducted a great enterprise that connected Seacoast City's pulsing multitudes with the rest of a great nation. Here steam-muscled leviathans loaded and unloaded their precious freight of passengers arriving in the great metropolis to conduct business transactions, to seek fame and glory on the electric-lighted stage, or merely to spend a few days gaping at the incredible skyscrapers of the city. These last would then return to village or farm, filled with tales to brighten their evenings for years to come.

But even now the elevator plummeted past the level where glistening rails led from Seacoast City to the rest of the continent. There was still another level, a level known to none but an inner circle of important and trustworthy men. For beneath the boulevards and the skyscrapers of Seacoast City there still flowed an underground waterway that fed the Saturn River.

The waterway had followed its ancient course for thousands of years before the coming of the settlers who pioneered Seacoast City. The pioneers and city-builders had covered over this tributary, leaving only the Saturn River itself to carry commerce to and from the metropolis. By now, most of the great city's denizens had forgotten all about this stream, or had never heard of its existence. But the Crimson Wizard made use of it.

Now two figures, one garbed in shimmering scarlet and the other brilliant gold, stood on a deserted riverbank. Above their heads a stone ceiling arched away, and above it the bustling railroad station, and above this the towering office building where throngs of workers plied their craft and earned the bread that fed their families.

A few dim lights provided what little illumination there was in the cavern. The only sounds were the gentle lapping of water and the soft footsteps of the man and the woman.

A narrow quay extended into the dark stream. The Crimson Wizard and the Golden Saint strode to the end of the pier. The Wizard knelt and undogged the hatch of a metal-skinned, football-shaped craft. The craft's name was graven in inconspicuous relief on her hull: *Mulungu*. The Wizard and the Golden Saint climbed into the small water-vehicle. Without exchanging a word the two figures proceeded silently to switch on previously quiescent systems, check levels of fuel and oxygen and weaponry, and settle themselves before the panel that held the craft's instruments and controls.

"It's been a while, hasn't it, Nzambi?" the Wizard commented.

The Golden Saint agreed. "Not since the time we took on that supposed ghost of a German U-boat, Wizard."

The Wizard nodded his head. "That was a glorious adventure, wasn't it?"

"If you consider coming within a hair's breadth of a hideous demise, I suppose it was," the golden-clad woman replied,

"But of course. Without peril, what is life?" The Wizard chuckled sardonically.

"There are other things."

By now the Wizard had piloted *Mulungu* beneath the city's teeming streets and buildings and guided it, along the swift-flowing stream, into the Saturn River. The river, in turn, fed Seacoast Harbor. From the harbor it was a short journey into the ocean itself.

Nzambi's graceful fingers flew over the submersible's control panel. *Mulungu* was invisible to the ships that plied lanes of commerce to and from Seacoast City. The submersible's windows showed nothing save the occasional luminous fish that plied the waters off the coast. At this hour of the night, even with a full moon casting its rays onto the city and its adjacent waters, utter darkness surrounded the craft.

The Crimson Wizard switched on a detector similar to that which he had utilized aboard the zeppelin *Kpalimé*. Here on board *Mulungu* the eyepiece served as a sort of reverse periscope, permitting the Wizard to scan the sea-bed as *Mulungu* skimmed along, propelled by silent blades powered by an advanced motor similar to that which propelled *Kpalimé* through the air.

"I see it!" the Wizard exclaimed.

"They leave their spoor even in the sea?" the Golden Saint exclaimed.

"Everywhere they go, yes." The Wizard's voice was grim. "It's fortunate that we came upon their path as quickly as we did. Water is not as stable an element as earth. The constant flow of currents would surely have carried away every trace of them had we not found their trail soon after they laid it down."

The Wizard lifted his eye from the viewer. To Nzambi he said, "Here, have a look at this."

The yellow-clad woman bent over the viewer. After a moment she lifted her head. "Their trail wavers through the water like the body of a giant serpent."

"So it does."

"And—look!" She had stooped and taken one more sighting through the device, then straightened and pointed through the window of *Mulungu*. "I think I can see them."

The Wizard followed his assistant's pointing finger. "Yes. But so many!"

Ahead of them, swimming in almost military formation and with more than military precision, a squadron of figures could be seen. They were vaguely human-like in shape, but none could mistake them for humans. They were bereft of clothing, their bodies the albino-white of creatures who avoided the healthful influence of the sun as scurrying vermin avoid the light of farmers' torches.

Some of them appeared to be carrying weapons.

Healthier denizens of the sea circled, their own teeth exposed in hungry grins as if yearning to pounce upon the white creatures, yet held at bay by the monsters' unity and their deadly weapons.

"They're bound for home," the Wizard ground out. "My guess is they're headed for a marshalling point where they will be picked up by their companions. They'll be in a craft that makes *Mulungu* look as primitive as *Kpalimé* would make a Lilienthal kite. I'd love to get a look at their vehicle, but I'm afraid *Mulungu* would be no match for it. So we've got to act before they reach their rendezvous point."

"But I don't understand," Nzambi complained. "Are they fish? Do they have a civilization?"

The Wizard made a gesture with both hands, as if he were summoning up an image from a distant land and time. "Our people, Nzambi, worshipped gods of the sea. So did the Greeks, the Phoenicians, all the ancient peoples who lived near water. Each race had legends of lost cities and continents, the flood of Noah, the sinking of Atlantis, the lost continent of Mu. The jewels that these monsters stole from the museum and with which they bedecked their erstwhile queen, Isabella del Sueño, may or may not have come from Lemuria. That puzzle remains to be solved. But there is no doubt that the sea contains wonders and terrors far beyond any imagined by mere men."

"Then you're saying that they have a city."

"They have a civilization—if you wish to call it that. And we must stop this band of monsters from getting back there. A great and final Armageddon will someday be fought between the beings of the sea and those of the land, but the time is not yet right for that battle. What we engage in this night is a mere skirmish on the outskirts of a war."

By now the submersible was cruising above the white monstrosities. The Wizard leaned forward, straining for a better view of the beings. They did not swim like any normal aquatic creatures so much as they writhed and squirmed, their progress suggesting the motion of leeches across the flesh of their hapless victims.

At the head of the band of monstrosities the Wizard observed one larger than the others, its head surrounded by a ring of writhing tentacles the color of freshly spilled blood. The leader, seemingly sensing the presence of *Mulungu*, turned its hideous face and bulbous eyes toward the submersible. Its tentacles waved, its hideous broad mouth gaped.

The armed monstrosities turned their weapons toward *Mulungu*.

Without command from the Wizard, Nzambi pressed a stud on the control panel of the submersible. With a hiss and a stream of bubbles, a sleek pressure bomb issued from *Mulungu* and sped through the water toward the white creatures. As it approached them it exploded in a burst of gold and scarlet flame. The shock wave rocked *Mulungu* but the sturdy little craft righted itself without apparent damage.

Such was not the case with the white creatures. Some dead, some injured, some merely dazed, they floated helplessly and harmlessly. From the dark waters surrounding the scene of the brief but violent encounter, marine predators swooped upon the pallid flesh, devouring the beings one after another.

Only, as the Wizard and Nzambi watched, the tentacle-crowned leader of the band proved itself capable of rapidly recovering from its shock. With a furious rippling of its tentacles it dived to the muddy sea-bottom. A cloud of particles rose, obscuring the scene. By the time it had settled there remained no evidence of the white creatures or of their leader.

"It has escaped," Nzambi intoned.

"Just so." The Crimson Wizard relieved his assistant at the controls of *Mulungu*. He turned the little craft back toward Seacoast City and her berth in the dimly-lit, echoing cavern deep beneath the Central Railroad Tower.

The next morning the Morelli brothers, Alberto and Roberto, arrived at their tonsorial establishment on the ground floor of the Central Railroad Tower. To their surprise their floor-sweeper, shoe-shiner and general man-of-all-tasks, Clarence Willis, was already present, assiduously preparing the shop for its day's trade.

To the even greater surprise of the Morellis, Willis was accompanied by a honey-complected, raven-haired, sloe-eyed vamp clad entirely in white. When the brothers stood staring at this startling beauty, Clarence Willis spoke in his slow drawl.

"This is my cousin, Ruby Mae Jones. She just arrived from Savannah. I was thinkin', bosses, we could use a manicurist here. And Ruby Mae, she do needs a job."

Roberto Morelli looked at Alberto Morelli. Alberto Morelli looked at Roberto Morelli. The brothers offered identical shrugs.

Alberto said, "Sure, we give her a try."

Roberto said, "We got Mr. Smith and Mr. Brown comin' in today for manicures. We try you out on them, Ruby Mae."

Clarence Willis and his "cousin," Ruby Mae Jones, exchanged a knowing glance. ◉

COUNTING ZEPPELINS

BY ERIC MARIN

SOME PEOPLE COUNT SHEEP. I count zeppelins. Most nights, when I lie awake, clutchin' for the sleep I never get enough of, I see zeppelins floatin' outside my window. Not them old-style *Hindenburg* types, or even Goodyear's tame version, but smooth and silver-skinned giants slippin' through the darkened clouds, as many as ten at once, waltzin' through the night sky like air-swimmin' whales.

I know, I know. There ain't no zeppelins like that left, or even ever built, but I still see them travel-dancin' across the Texas sky. I see a lot of things other people don't see, but that's my gift and my curse; why I've spent time "gettin' help" at the Big Spring State Hospital, why I can read tarot cards in ways that leave my customers wide-eyed and tremblin', and why no woman can live with me for more than a few months before runnin' off, freaked out of her mind by what I see.

Still, I see those zeppelins, and I don't rightly know what they signify, if anythin' at all. I can see the future sometimes, muddy and fractured, flickin' across my inner eye, but I see them zeppelins clear as a bottle of that French water folks pay too much for at fillin' stations. So, they ain't the future, least not in the way that I see it. Maybe they're symbols of somethin' else, but I sure can't read them like I can read cards.

Maybe I just see zeppelins. If that's so, I sure don't mind. There's a lot of things I see and have seen that I don't want to see again.

So, if I get to count zeppelins instead of sheep most nights, that's just fine by me. Lord knows, I need all the peace I can get. God help me, I do. ✪

LOVE IN THE BALANCE

BY DAVID D. LEVINE

THEOPHILE NUNDAEMON CLOSED THE BOOK, shaking his head over the images he'd found therein. So sad, so mad ... He closed his eyes and set the volume aside, a few maroon particles of the decaying cover dusting the ormolu surface of the table.

Unobserved, a cleaner descended silently and snuffled the debris away. It sniffed at the book as well, but Theo's scent on the cover indicated this was no discard. The little creature puffed itself up to grapefruit size and drifted off to its nest in the corner of the room. Immature cleaners peeped supersonically and opened wide their jaws.

Theo opened his eyes and stared out the window. Beyond the glass loomed the fog of endless night, and bulbous shapes drifting. Here and there a spotlight picked out the sigil of one or another House on a pennant or tail fin. The red bat of the Unknown Regalia ... the silver spoon-and-circle of Theo's own Guided Musings ... and there, the gilded fish of the Pulp Revenants. Angrily Theo twisted the brass and crystal handle beneath the worn sill, and wooden slats snapped shut over the view.

How *dare* Kyrie summon the zombies again—on this day, of all days, and upon the Musings, of all Houses? How *dare* she?

Theo picked up the book and shoved it back on the shelf. That compendium of ancient lore and legends was nearly as useless as the endless mutterings of the House Fathers. He paced before the shuttered window, heedless of the books' shuffling and murmuring as they rearranged themselves alphabetically, and lit his pipe. Then a low familiar foghorn sounded outside the window, and Theo sighed and opened the shutters.

Looming from the dark and fog came the nose of the *Grand Edison III*—the personal airship of Kyrie Strommond, the flagship of the Revenants, and the long-estranged lover of Theophile Nundaemon.

Theo still felt fondly toward the *Edison*, and he knew that, despite everything, she still held some warmth in her engines for him. But those cooling ashes of love would be no protection at all from the zombie warriors the *Edison* now bore within her gravid silver hull. For fluttering from the foremast was Kyrie's own sigil—Capricorn on a field of stars.

That damnable goat.

A tear gathered in the corner of Theo's eye. "Zenobia," he called to his personal servant. "Prepare my zeppelin gun."

Not waiting for a response, Theo strode from the library and descended the brass-railed oak spiral stair to his quarters. There he shrugged on his black wool overcoat, with the high, stiff collar and gold-braided epaulets of a Commander of the Musings. He descended two more flights, then took a long corridor—his thudding boots raising dust from the worn carpet below portraits of long-dead zeppelin captains—to the reception bay, where the house slaves had already opened the doors and extended the boarding ramp to meet the descending *Edison*. A cold, damp breeze blew in from the endless night. Theo fastened his top coat button.

He stood silent, marinating in memory and regret, as shouting slaves tossed lines to the *Edison* and made her fast. Then her hatch opened, the boarding stair unrolling itself like a great slatted tongue, and Kyrie Strommond descended to the ramp, majestic in the green uniform of a Commander of the Revenants.

Though the threads of gray in her hair now outnumbered the black, Kyrie was still a handsome woman, with keen, intelligent green eyes and clear, pale skin. But the mouth tightened in a hard line as she saw who had come to meet her. "Honor to you, Theophile," she said, "and honor to your House."

"Honor to you, Kyrie," he replied, "and honor to your airship."

It was a calculated insult, barely within the bounds of protocol, but his only reward was a single blink. Despite himself, Theo had to admire her steel. It was a shame they could never be friends.

"I require quarters for my troops," she said, "as stipulated by the Compact."

"That may be . . . difficult. At this time of year. How many?"

"Three hundred." At that, Theo blinked. So large a contingent had not been seen in centuries. What could the Revenants be planning? "But they require no food or water, and only the minimum of space."

"Of course." He escorted her to an alcove in the wall, where a wooden model of the House of the Guided Musings floated in the air. He touched one of the brass knobs that studded its surface, and the model obediently split open, revealing the warren of rooms and corridors within. Thousands of tiny wooden pegs populated the spaces—mahogany for men, maple for women, fir for slaves—their fitful motion reminding Theo of a disturbed anthill. "As you see," he said, "the Reunion Day crowds have already arrived."

Naturally, since this model was in a public space, much of the information was lies. But Theo's lip quirked in amusement at the two pegs, maple and mahogany, that stood by the alcove in the model's reception bay.

Theo turned the model this way and that, opening and closing its various sections. "Ah, I believe the children's squander-ball games can be moved from the lesser gymnasium. Would that do?"

Kyrie pondered the model gymnasium, as though trying to discern its size. The model did not show the steel doors and man-traps that surrounded it, of course, but Kyrie would be looking for tell-tale voids and discontinuities. Theo sweated under his heavy coat. He had supervised the reconstruction of the Red Diamond section himself, and the model's complex of feints and deceptions was superb, but Kyrie was a formidable strategist.

"Yes," she said at last, "that will suffice."

Theo pointed out the route from the reception bay to the gymnasium. "Your troops will be escorted, to prevent them losing their way."

"Thank you." She gave a smile that appeared nearly genuine.

As Kyrie returned to the *Edison*, Theo climbed an aluminum ladder to the glass-enclosed mezzanine. There he stepped to a brass trumpet set in the wall and pulled the chain for privacy. Immediately the reception bay's clatter and banging were stifled to a dull mutter, accompanied by a feeling of pressure in Theo's ears.

The grating voices of the House Fathers emerged from the trumpet. "What does Kyrie plan?" they demanded without preamble.

"There can be little doubt she will attempt to take the House, most likely tonight," he replied. "I have quartered her troops in the lesser gymnasium."

"Excellent. We will transfer Cherub and Centaur divisions to that section immediately."

"You must also prepare to cut the section loose, if necessary. Even with all our preparations, three hundred zombies are a formidable force."

The Fathers muttered in consternation, but finally replied "We will begin the calculations. We hope it will not come to that."

"As do I." Theo hesitated. The final element of his defense plan would be highly controversial, and he considered keeping it to himself until the thing was done. But the long habit of duty compelled him to speak. "There is one other thing."

"What?"

"Kyrie's airship. The *Grand Edison*."

"What about it?"

Theo swallowed. "I intend to kill her."

At that the Fathers' chorus fragmented into a confused babble. "... impossible ... unprecedented ... against the Compact ..."

"Hear me out!" Theo shouted into the trumpet, his throat tight with rage and anguish. "Even if we prevail in this battle, the Revenants have made it clear that they will not hesitate to summon the zombies again and again until they achieve complete domination. They have bent the Compact nearly to the breaking point already. Killing the *Edison* will only complete a process that the Revenants began. And without her, their strength will be reduced to the point that the other Houses can once again balance them. We can restore the spirit of the Compact only by breaking its letter."

Theo's outburst silenced the Fathers for a long moment. "We cannot officially sanction such an action," they replied at last.

"I understand." The privacy field pressed in on Theo's head like a vise. "Any action I take will be my responsibility alone."

Theo took a moment to compose himself before returning to the floor of the bay, where the zombies were already lining up. The smallest of them was over six feet tall and heavily muscled, and their dead gray skin and lifeless eyes hinted at their incapacity for pain and fatigue while belying the speed of which they were capable. Each wore a poison-green uniform, with Kyrie's Capricorn sigil at the shoulder, and carried a heavy spider-rifle. Theo noted that the rifles' bores and magazines were exactly at the limit prescribed by the Compact.

A company of Musings troops, uniformed in black with Theo's personal trident-and-anvil on their shoulders, confronted the zombies with razor-whips at the ready. Theo nodded in approval; standard-issue confusers would be of no use whatsoever against zombies.

The last zombie marched off of the *Edison* and lined up with its fellows. "This is Sergeant Shrive," Theo said to Kyrie. "He and his men will conduct your troops to the gymnasium. Once they are settled, would you do me the honor of joining me for dinner?"

"The honor would be mine," she replied.

"It will be a formal occasion, of course."

They leveled stares at each other like lances at a joust. Under the Compact, a formal dinner was a web of obligations and prescribed courtesies, offering many opportunities for insult. The Revenants' last three battles had all begun over protocol violations at formal dinners—one of them might even have been justified.

As the invited party, Kyrie had the choice of wine. "I have an Upwelling Iris '623 in my cellars. Would that be appropriate?"

"Delightful," Theo replied. The Revenants always used poisons from the cadenine family with that vintage; he made a mental note to issue the appropriate antidote to his steward. "One of my men will bring you to my quarters at seven bells."

They bowed stiffly to each other, sealing the invitation. But with the formalities concluded, Theo had one more request. "As

you may know, I once served aboard the *Edison*. While you are
seeing to your troops' comfort, may I come aboard for a visit? An
informal visit."

Kyrie hesitated. Theo knew she was torn between denying him
the intelligence he would gain and granting him the pain and
distraction the visit would cause. "Certainly," she said at last. "My
captain will escort you."

Theo smiled a grim little smile. As he had expected, Kyrie's sa-
dism had won out over her strategic judgment. His stratagem had
succeeded, but now he would have to live with the consequences.

The captain was a lean, cadaverous man who seemed half zombie
himself. He conducted Theo across the creaking boarding ramp,
stretched across infinite blackness from the House of the Guided Musings, and up the *Edison*'s warm and faintly pulsing steps.
Once inside, Theo was assaulted by an appalled nostalgia—his old
lover's familiar halls, railings, and wainscotings were now covered
with a gray coat of fireproof military paint, and oak sideboards
had been replaced by racks of laser-guided scramblers.

Theo was led on a circuitous route to the airship's audience
chamber. The route itself told him much—clearly something major had been installed on deck three between the fore and mizzen
engines, and the captain didn't want him to see it. He thought it
might be a bay for boarding-craft, but then the scent of hydrazine
in section twenty-five told him it was even worse: guided missiles.
Inwardly he trembled, even as he continued counting men at duty
stations and analyzing the upgraded fire-fighting systems.

"This is the audience chamber," the captain said unnecessarily.
"You may have ten minutes."

"Thank you," Theo said, and slipped down through the opened
hatch.

Unlike the rest of the ship, here nothing had changed. It was still close and moist and warm, echoing with the thrum and gurgle of the great zeppelin's life fluids.

"Hello, Theo." The airship's voice was warm and maternal, but still gave Theo an erotic tingle.

"Hello, Edie."

"I'm surprised you came. I thought you wouldn't want to see me."

Tears pinched at the back of Theo's throat, but he refused them. "I . . . it was a hard choice, Edie. But, the way things have been going lately, I thought it might be my last chance for a while." Maybe forever, he thought.

"I'm sorry, Theo." Warm pseudopods extended from the wall and rubbed his shoulders, and Theo relaxed for a moment into the familiar touch. "Kyrie is keeping me so busy these days."

Theo sat up and brushed the pseudopods away. "Yes, I know. That's what I'm here to talk with you about."

The seat of Theo's chair stiffened and grew cool. "The answer is still no."

"Damn it, Edie!" Now the tears did come, though he sniffed them back. "How could you abandon the Musings—how could you abandon *me*? I loved you!"

"And I loved you too. But the Revenants are the future, Theo. Why can't you see that? The Musings, the Regalia, the Apocrypha . . . they're trying to hold on to the sky by their fingernails. How many Houses have gone down in the past year?"

"Eight," he replied automatically.

"Eight," she repeated, "and madly flapping the Compact isn't going to keep the rest in the air forever. As long as each House holds its thaumaturgies and technologies close to its vest, each will float or fall on its own . . . and each one that falls takes all its secrets with it. Only by pooling our best ideas do we have a chance to keep what remains of humanity aloft."

"The Compact has provisions for information sharing."

"The system isn't working, Theo. The lesser Houses—the ones that float lowest and are closest to losing buoyancy—are naturally the most driven to create new techniques. But because of their reduced status, none will trade with them, and so they fail, and so their learnings are lost to us."

"And the Revenants' forced labor and torture are better?"

"We've already learned so much, by combining the work of the Whistlers and the Philosophers and the Radiant Ones. Once all the Houses are united under Revenant guidance, we will surely find the final solution. And then these unfortunate practices can be brought to an end."

"'Unfortunate practices'? 'Final solution'? Edie, what's become of you?"

"Nothing's changed, Theo. I'm still trying to do what I was built to do—keep you all alive, in the best way I know how." The sounds behind the walls changed, as though the great airship's heart were beating more slowly. "Whether you understand it or not."

The hatch opened, sending the harsh military light of the cabin above into Theo's stinging eyes. "Time's up," said the captain, and without a word Theo climbed out of the audience chamber.

He thought he heard *I love you, Theo,* as the hatch closed. Perhaps it was only his imagination. But as the captain walked him back to the boarding ramp, he pushed the question out of his mind and focused on the enemy airship's defenses.

Seven bells. Theo paced his dining room, sweating in his dress uniform. Five companies of the Musings' best troops were hidden in the walls around the lesser gymnasium. Tanks of acid were pressurized and ready to spew, frenzied eagle-cats snarled and battered great wings against the walls of their cages, and trans-dimensional fields strained the vertices of their dark crystals. All was in readiness, but the forms of the Compact must be observed.

As the sound of the seventh bell echoed away down the oak-walled corridor, the door opened and two men in radiation armor escorted Kyrie in. A tiny constellation of five pea-sized diamonds orbited above each of the epaulets of her dress uniform.

"So pleased you could join me, Kyrie." He proffered his arm. "May I show you to your seat?"

"Why, thank you." Her uniform sleeve was lined with ceramic plates, which struck rigidly against the defensive field grid sewn into his own.

He pulled out her chair—the one facing the door, as required—and brushed off the seat with his handkerchief. She sat, and he helped her to push in her chair.

Kyrie peered at the table. All the cutlery was in the proper positions. The napkins were folded appropriately for the time of day and the season. The number and size of servants were within prescribed limits. Theo was certain there was nothing Kyrie could use to provoke an incident. "What a charming table."

Theo bowed, and called for the first course. A serving cart rolled out on silent rubber wheels, parked obediently by the table, and raised its silver dome, revealing fairy shrimp steaming in a glistening brown sauce. The steward carefully ladled out a precise portion on each plate.

Kyrie took a bite . . . and immediately spat it out. "This tastes like shit!" she said.

"Yes," Theo said, and smiled. "My own, to be precise."

Kyrie sat, mouth open, too stunned to say anything.

"I decided to cut short the agony of waiting and give you your opportunity to attack in the first course."

"You . . . ." Then she snapped her mouth shut and gave him a brief bow of acknowledgement, not taking her eyes off him. "Very well. I, Kyrie Destinia Strommond of the Pulp Revenants, do take the gravest offense at this violation of protocol, and under Article XVII, Section 7 of the Grand Compact of Humanity, I invoke my right to restitution." And then she clapped her hands together and vanished with a blue flash, leaving behind the tingle of thauma-turgical energies and the smell of ozone.

Theo bent down and spoke to the brass trumpet fastened to the arm of his chair. "We are at war."

"Acknowledged," came the voices of the Fathers, and alarms sounded throughout the House.

Throwing his napkin on the floor, Theo hurried up the spiral stair to the library. The bookshelves had already been cleared away, replaced by screens and crystals showing views from throughout the House and the air nearby. On one screen, zombies in pale shimmering armor waded through hip-deep acid, their spider-ri-fles spitting poisonous metal spiders at the defenders. On another, an enormous zombie, stripped to the waist, mowed down Theo's black-uniformed troops with a broadsword in each hand.

But Theo's attention was riveted to the three-dimensional dis-play in the center of the room, a rotating web of crystal threads that depicted the House and the nearest airships. With the excep-tion of the *Edison*, they were all Musings ships; on Reunion Day, all members of each House would be with their loved ones. And the Musings' best zeppelins were no match even for the *Edison* in which Theo had served, never mind her new configuration.

Nonetheless, Theo ordered his zeppelins into combat. *Tarantella* and *Eagle Scout* immediately slipped their moorings and drove ponderously toward the *Edison*, followed shortly by *Razor* and

Wedgwood. Edison responded smartly, whipping out of her berth
with the full power of her seven enormous engines. She began
hammering the Musings' airships with missiles, lasers, and black
coruscating webs of arcane energy; soon *Razor* and *Eagle Scout*
had been reduced to embers, fluttering down into the endless
dark, and *Tarantella* was listing badly.

Theo cursed the loss of life, but the attack had achieved the
desired effect: it had brought *Edison* out into the range of his
zeppelin gun. He ordered his first subcommander to take charge
of the aerial defense and clambered up the ladder to the highest
point in the House.

Zenobia had done well. The zeppelin gun gleamed, its long
brass barrel polished to perfection, its sights precisely aligned, its
every nickel-plated wheel and lever gleaming bright. The harpoon
was loaded and charged, humming with electricity and shimmering with thaumaturgical energies.

This one harpoon had cost nearly half of Theo's defense budget
five years ago. The arguments had gone on for months. Now he was
vindicated, and nothing could have made him more miserable.

Theo stepped into the zeppelin gun's shoulder braces and placed
his hands on the grips. The dome overhead divided smoothly, letting in a wedge of night and fog. He peered through the gunsight
at the *Edison*, heeling hard to the right as she unleashed a flight
of missiles at *Wedgwood*. With only the one harpoon, he had to be
certain of his aim.

"Commander!" cried his second subcommander from the room
below. "The zombies are breaking through into the Blue Star section!"

Theo spat out a curse, then spoke into the trumpet to the House
Fathers. "Cut loose the Red Diamond section immediately."

"Acknowledged." A new set of alarms sounded, ear-shattering

and urgent. On the displays, those Musings troops not directly engaged with the enemy dropped their weapons and ran; in the library, subcommanders and lieutenants began securing equipment.

The voices of the House Fathers sounded over the public address system. "The Red Diamond sector will be separated in sixty seconds." It was the first time Theo could recall the Fathers speaking to the entire House at once.

"Fifty seconds." In the sight, the *Edison* had finished off the *Wedgwood* and was turning to strafe the House. She would be inside the gun's minimum range in less than a minute. He engaged the harpoon's tracking, evasion, and anti-thaumaturgical systems.

"Forty seconds." Theo breathed a prayer and pressed the firing stud. The floor shuddered and, with a scream of superheated steam, the harpoon flung itself out of the gun, trailing its cable behind.

"Thirty seconds." Steam obscured Theo's view. The floor thrummed as the cable paid out. Theo cursed, over and over.

"Twenty seconds." The view in the gunsight cleared just as the harpoon pierced *Edison*'s silvery envelope. The great zeppelin twitched all over at the impact, then convulsed as a mighty charge flowed into the harpoon from the alchemical batteries beneath Theo's feet. He could almost hear her scream through the gunsight.

"Ten seconds." *Edison* continued to quiver and shake as though with fever, jerking and twisting, but the harpoon held firm in her envelope. Reluctantly Theo stepped back from the gun and slid down the ladder.

"Five. Four. Three. Two. One." Theo held onto the ladder as though it were his long-lost sister.

A rumble as though the whole House had indigestion vibrated

through the floor, the wall, and the ladder, as chemical and magical explosions severed the structural connections between the Red
Diamond section and the rest of the House. Half the displays
went black; most of the rest showed pandemonium.

In the center of the room, displayed in a tracery of crystalline
filaments, a large lobe fell slowly away from the House, while three
huge gasbags detached from the top of the structure to compensate for the lost weight.

Meanwhile, *Edison* thrashed at the end of her line. Then, suddenly, she reversed herself and dove toward the House. "No!"
someone shouted—Theo realized it was himself.

The ghostly, crystalline *Edison* smashed into the top of the
ghostly, crystalline House. The impact drove the House sideways,
knocking everyone in the library except Theo, who still clung to
the ladder, off their feet. The lights flickered, along with the technological displays; when they cleared, it was plain that two of the
House's gasbags had been destroyed by the collision. Above them
the *Edison* floated free, still connected by the slack cable but no
longer twitching. It was unclear whether she was dead or alive.

Theo dragged himself to the nearest trumpet, as the floor shivered and tilted and a queasy feeling of uncontrolled descent flowed
through his stomach. "Deploy emergency lift!" he shouted to the
House Fathers.

"We have already done so," came the reply. "It is not sufficient.
Too much reserve gas was lost in the detachment of the three
gasbags that supported the Red Diamond section."

Theo sagged against the wall. The House of the Guided Musings was doomed. Helpless, he watched the altimeter drop. The
room tilted slowly to one side as the crystalline model of the
House fell away from the model of the *Edison*.

And then the *Edison* came to the end of the cable. Or perhaps the House did. In either case, there was a sickening jerk and the floor suddenly tilted fifteen further degrees. Theo's head slammed against the wall and he lost consciousness.

When he recovered, probably only a few seconds later, the three-dimensional display showed the *Edison* floating at the top of the cable, docile as a child's balloon. The altimeter was nearly stable; the great zeppelin had just enough lift to compensate for the two destroyed gasbags.

Theo stumbled across the tilted, debris-littered floor to the ladder, then clambered up to the gun room. The cable stretched through a gash in the dome, thrumming like a guitar string, and the whole room groaned with structural stress; there was no telling how long the cable, or the drum to which it was attached, or the structure to which the drum was in turn secured, would hold out.

He climbed up on the zeppelin gun, now bent nearly in half, and put his head next to the cable. Peering along its length, through the broken dome, he saw the *Edison* rotating slowly high above. Gas leaked from the rent where the harpoon pierced her skin.

And he heard his own name.

He looked around, but he was alone in the gun room, and the voice was so soft it could not have come from very far away.

Then he heard his name again, and this time he felt it as well— felt it thrumming under his fingers in the cable that held the House to the *Edison*.

He pressed his ear to the cable.

Theo, came Edie's voice, vibrating down the cable to his ear. Or perhaps it was just his imagination. *Theo, Theo, Theo . . . I still love you, Theo, though you have killed me.*

"I still love you, too, Edie," he whispered to the cable.

All around him the shadows deepened, as the House's lighting failed and the endless night crept in. ✪

WHERE AND WHEN

BY JAMES VAN PELT

THE TWO SCIENTISTS SURVEYED THE CABIN'S INTERIOR from their positions behind the crowd at the windows. Jake flicked the command that turned his recorders on, his eyes and ears sending the signal to the computer buried in his jawbone, while Martin stepped to a table and retrieved what turned out to be a menu. He held the pages like they were holy script.

"After all these years," Jake exulted, while turning slowly for the recorder's sake. A silk wallpaper imprinted with a map of the world covered the bulkhead beside him. Rich contrasting carpet. Recessed ceiling lights. The transition had been without effect. No sound or dizziness. No flash of light or sensation of falling. Just a blink. "What did we do differently?"

"The math never came out even, but it should have always worked. Maybe there are more opportune moments." Martin carefully opened the thin document. "A thousand failed attempts. Wouldn't Brownson be proud?"

Jake grimaced. "If he had survived." For an instant, he thought he saw Brownson among the people at the window. Broad shoulders. One arm. Gray hair. But the light shifted, and Jake could see he was wrong. Two arms. Blond hair. A stranger.

The project had been Brownson's from the beginning. All the theoretical work, most of the construction, only letting them help when he needed two hands. Spending long nights bouncing his ideas off them. Arguing with them about paradoxes. His faith buoyed them when they were ready to quit. His determination to succeed drove them on. His obsession. He should be here, Jake thought. This day belongs to him.

A soft thrumming filled the air, and both men compensated slightly as the floor moved beneath their feet.

Jake's breathing came hard. It *had* been a thousand attempts. They'd pored over Brownson's papers until their vision had blurred. Constructed and reconstructed the device dozens of times. Was it a math problem? Was there a flaw in the underlying theories? Were the old saws about paradox and the impossibilities true, the ones that had worried Brownson incessantly? "We must be able to get around it," he'd said. If only the old man had confided in them more before he'd died in the explosion, alone in the lab. "I'm going to try something," he'd said. The investigators concluded later that a bomb destroyed the building. They found chemical traces and a melted timing mechanism. Rival government? Terrorists? Jake and Martin had labored from then on in paranoid secrecy.

"Where and when are we?" Jake said to himself. We're here! he thought, wherever here is. And we're now, whenever that is. He panned around the long room, across the backs of the people at the windows, and over metal-framed chairs pushed up to the tables. He lingered his focus on a yellow piano in the room's center. A wine glass and crystal carafe poised above the keyboard tossed bright glisters from the ceiling lights. The room smelled of cologne and perfume and roast beef. His fingers glided coolly on the silk wall. Jake smiled. What style were the clothes the people wore? 1920s? 1930s? If he queried the computer, it might tell him, but it was more fun to guess. None turned to look at them.

At the window, a middle-aged woman with a cane hooked over her arm said, "Finally. The family has been waiting for hours." Reading glasses hung from a silver cord around her neck.

Ahh, English, thought Jake. He spoke French, High German, Italian, Spanish and a smattering of Mandarin. Martin knew Portuguese, Russian and Swiss German. If needed, their computer implanted in his jaw could translate, but that was an awkward way to talk. Jake hoped the recorder caught what the people said. Voices from the past. Real ones. The linguists would salivate over the subtleties of vowel shifts, the nuances and shading of pronunciations from hundreds of years in the past. Not radio recordings or movie voices, but real people talking among themselves. The social historians would write treatises on the ways of the era based on his recordings. Whole new areas of study would be opened up.

They'd succeeded! They'd jumped the unjumpable chasm.

"The Germans build a marvelous ship, but they can't control the rain and wind," an older man with dark muttonchops and a gray smoking jacket replied. "Not yet, anyway." From the way the woman with the cane and the mutton-chopped man stood together, their arms almost touching, their chins at the same angle as they looked out the window, Jake guessed they were husband and wife.

Jake moved to an unoccupied length of window. By putting his face next to the glass that leaned out from the top, he could see that, three hundred feet below, a grassy airfield waited. He strained to see what was to the right and left beyond the cabin:

long stretches of silver-gray fabric, and above them a bulging gray fabric shelf that blocked part of the sky. No wings, he thought. We're in a blimp.

Cars the size of matchboxes covered the ground on one side of a long wooden building. People ran beneath the ship, looking up. He hoped the glass wouldn't mess up the recorder's images.

The mutton-chopped man said, "We're tail heavy. If those folks don't watch out below, they'll get a good soaking."

"How so, dear?" asked his wife. She smiled at him, a brief look, then she gazed out again.

"Water ballast."

A nearly subsonic, mechanical thump bumped the room, then the people who'd been running scattered, their hands covering their heads as water streamed down from somewhere aft of the cabin. The mutton-chopped man laughed.

Martin sidled up beside Jake. "Look at this," Martin whispered, holding the menu he'd retrieved from the table.

Jake scanned the German text. "Nice wine list. Do you want the beef broth with marrow dumplings or the cold Rhine salmon with spiced sauce and potato salad?" He could barely keep from giggling. They had done it!

"No, not the food. Look at the name." He stabbed a finger at the top of the page.

Trying to settle his heart, trying to keep the grin off his face, Jake read the heading.

"We're going to Hindenburg? Is that where this airfield is?" Were the people he'd listened to American or English tourists on holiday in Germany?

Martin shook his head. "No, no. We're *on* the *Hindenburg*. The zeppelin. *The Hindenburg*."

Jake's computer squeaked for attention with a bone-induction message only he could hear: *The* Hindenburg, *first commercial flights in 1936. Final flight, May 6, 1937. Gas volume of 7,062,000 cubic feet. Gross lift of 242.2 tons. Originally designed for helium, the ship . . . ."* Jake flicked the voice off.

Ahead and to the left of the ship, a solidly-built tower of cross-beams and heavy struts awaited them. The zeppelin turned ponderously toward it.

The tower slid slowly toward the front of the ship. The grass below had given way to cement and tarmac, dark with long puddles of standing water. Fragments of the ship's reflection shown back at them.

"*When* are we on the *Hindenburg*?" said Jake. A crew member opened one of the windows so the passengers could see better. A refreshing, rain-scented breeze filled the cabin.

Martin tapped his finger against the top of the menu impatiently. "What does it matter? We're on the *Hindenburg*. The go-down-in-flames-oh-the-humanity *Hindenburg*."

"It *does* matter. The *Hindenburg* flew for a year before it blew up. If it's 1936, we're in great shape. Can you imagine? 1936! Franklin Roosevelt is president. The Berlin Olympics. The Spanish Civil War. Picasso is alive, and so is Errol Flynn and Ginger Rogers. We can go to Hollywood! What are the odds of all the places and times in the world that we'd end up on the *Hindenburg* in 1937 when it goes down?"

"Why are we in an airship at all?" Martin looked out the window at the ground. "Brownson said temporal and physical destinations were random. No guessing where we'd end up. The math said we wouldn't end up *in* anything, like a mountain, but he didn't say anything about landing *on* something. If we'd arrived ten feet that way," he waved beyond the cabin, "our visit here would have been short."

Long cables dropped from the front of the ship. Men on the ground ran to catch them. The hum that pervaded the background shifted, and the cabin shuddered. Jake braced a hand against the slick metal windowsill to compensate for the change in speed.

Martin shook his head. He stepped around Jake. "Excuse me, sir," he said to the man with muttonchops. "My friend here is a little confused. Would you tell him what year it is?"

Before the man could answer, Jake heard a soft pop from outside the window, like a gas burner being turned on. The woman with the cane over her arm leaned out the open window, looking up. "What is that, dear?" She reached behind her without turning her head and grabbed the mutton-chopped man's wrist. "It's like a sunrise."

A pink and yellow glow brightened the zeppelin's fabric toward the tail. Jake leaned out too to record the image, but the soft glimmer turned into flames racing toward them, furiously fast.

Jake pushed away from the window.

"It's on fire!" someone screamed. The floor began to sink beneath their feet.

His face calm, voice measured, the mutton-chopped man said to his wife, "We have to disembark."

"Of course," she said.

Martin faced Jake, his expression serious. "Nineteen thirty-seven."

They reached for the panic switches under their shirts at the same time. Before the world blinked away, the mutton-chopped man and the woman with the cane dropped themselves out the window.

Jake thought before the world flickered and they were back in the laboratory: We're still 300 feet above the ground!

*   *   *

Collapsed in a chair, Jake still breathed in interrupted hitches, his heart pounding in his throat. His hand fluttered as he reached for the coffee cup. Martin, though, bustled from his workbook full of figures, to the computer, and back again.

"*Nothing* in Brownson's notes said we could end up in a zeppelin."

Jake closed his hand on the cup. Gripped hard to stop the shaking. "Not *any* zeppelin. The *Hindenburg*." He shut his eyes for a second, but he could see the mooring mast looming in front of him, beams and struts reflecting a hard, blazing light. In his vision, the woman, her cane still carefully tucked over her arm, tumbled out the window after her husband.

Martin ran his finger down a line of notes, turned the page, kept reading. "A hundred to four hundred years in the past, Brownson said. Location variable. But I thought the math kept us on the ground. Of course, the damn math never made any sense in the first place. Equations never balanced equally. Nothing reduced perfectly. Nothing was absolute."

Jake shivered as he pushed away from the chair, glad for the coffee's heat. From their lab's single window, he could see the tarpaper and gravel roof running to a low, brick border. Beyond that, a few clouds rested on the horizon. Their lab perched on the roof of the industrial park's highest building. If he opened the door and walked to the edge, a handful of equally nondescript structures with equally bland roofs would lay out before him, like a bleak checkerboard. They were far from Brownson's destroyed lab and whoever bombed it. He remembered the last time they'd seen Brownson, his only hand protectively over the top of the device, the place for the sleeve for his other arm sewn shut at the shoulder. No sleeve dangled. "Don't want it catching in the equipment," he'd said. Brownson, now, was gone, in explosion and fire, like the passengers on The *Hindenburg*.

"Those people are all dead."

Martin looked up from the notebook. "You're being sentimental. They've been dead for two hundred and fifty years. Their children are dead too, and *their* children. But if you're talking about the people on the *Hindenburg* we saw, that's not true. Only thirty-three died because of the crash. Sixty-two lived."

The flames had come down so fast. "Only thirty-three?" Jake's mouth was dry. Every swallow hurt.

After a moment, Martin, his voice distracted and preoccupied, said, "Yes, and two dogs. The rest got out when the ship was low enough. Didn't your computer tell you all this?"

"I turned it off."

Jake could still feel the radiant heat. The people screaming, all of them at once. The floor slipping away toward the ship's tail. Glassware tumbling from the tables, and chairs falling toward the back wall. He had kept pressing the panic switch. How long would the device take to snatch them back? What if it wouldn't?

"I behaved badly," said Jake. "I . . . ." His gaze roamed the room. Electronic equipment piled on the work table. Security video displayed on four monitors. No one would plant a bomb in their lab! The table, the monitors, the lab on a building's roof were so far away from the collapsing ship, from old people jumping from windows. "I didn't help anyone."

Martin turned the computer off. He shut the notebook. "Jake, those people were dead before we got there. They'd been dead for a quarter of a millennium. You couldn't help them. You couldn't harm them. You couldn't change their fate." He sat on the table's edge and smiled. "I know it's a shock. I'm still quivering myself."

He held his hand out, but if it was trembling, Jake couldn't see it. "We traveled in time, Jake, and we returned. All that nonsense about causality loops and killing your grandfather so you won't be born, and a dead butterfly changing human history, it's wrong. Brownson's fears were wrong. We can travel in time. Think about how wonderful you felt when you realized what we'd done."

Surprisingly, the coffee tasted good. Jake took another sip. "That's true. When we arrived. Yes, it was great." He brightened. "We've made history."

Martin laughed. "That's the spirit." He checked the clock on the wall. "It's early, still. You know what we need to do, don't you?"

Jake sat up, put the coffee cup on the table, straightened his shoulders, ran a quick diagnostic on his implanted computer. "Yes, I do."

"That's right," said Martin. "We have to go again."

He pressed the button that activated their synchronized devices.

"See, we're on the ground," said Martin.

They stood on a narrow brick-paved road between a line of two-story shops, neatly-swept concrete stairways leading to their doors, arched stone lintels over the windows. The signs were in French. *Tobacco and Supplies. Fresh bread every morning at 10:00.* Overhead, low, dark clouds grayed the sky, but the sun on the horizon, cut under them, casting shadows on the buildings across the street.

A newspaper hung inside the bakery's window. "*Les Colonies,* 'Voice of the French Peoples Everywhere,'" said Jake. His computer said, *There are 785 unique matches to newspapers entitled* Les Colonies. Then it pinged off. Jake needed more information for it to give him a useful analysis. He wiped a thin layer of dust from the glass, then read from the top story. "It says the governor and his wife are in town and not to worry." He struggled with the translation. "The commission, it says, declares that the crisis is past. It doesn't say what the crisis is. Lots of news about an upcoming election."

"So, where and when in the French speaking countries are we?" Martin walked part way down the street, peering into the windows. "Everything seems closed."

Jake scanned the rest of the paper he could see. "Religious holiday. Ascension Day. Early morning services at *Nôtre-Dame de l' Assomption.*" The computer chirped to define Ascension Day.

Martin looked back at him, eyebrows raised.

"Catholic holy day in May. Everyone goes to mass. No date on the paper, though. No city name."

Ladies' hats rested on red velvet stands at the next shop. Martin sniffed. "Do you smell that? It's the ocean."

Jake joined Martin walking up the street which curved slowly to the left. Their shoes kicked up puffs of dust, and when Jake turned, he saw their footprints buffed the bricks clean as if they had just missed a momentary snowstorm, but the air was warm. A pile of wooden baskets were turned upside down beside one shop door, shreds of lettuce still clinging to the slats.

"Ah, there you go," said Martin. A gap between two buildings revealed a bay to their left only a couple blocks away. A handful of single and double-masted boats, their sails furled, rested quietly on the smooth water, where sea gulls perched on the docks' pilings or skimmed the surface between the ships.

Appearing from around the street's curve, a family walked toward them. The man wore a jacket with wide lapels, and he carried a walking stick. Beside him, the woman held the front of her long dress up to keep the hem from trailing in the dust. A pair of ten-year-old boys walked primly behind them, both hugging a book to their chest. When they passed, Jake offered a *"Bonjour."*

The man stopped, tipped his hat, revealing dark hair slicked to his skull and parted in the middle. *"Bonjour.* You are scientists?" the man said in a French Jake barely understood. Some kind of creole? The woman stood beside him, and the children hid behind, but they peeked around her skirt.

"We are visitors," Jake said, confused. Why would the man call them scientists? It would only be more startling if he'd called them time travelers. "Yes, scientists, I suppose. Why do you ask?"

"Your clothes, monsieur. The fashion on the continent, I suppose. We don't get important visitors on the island often."

"We are safe?" said the woman. Her voice was surprisingly deep. "There is noise at night, and the dust. The children worry." She waved her hand at the air.

One of the children shook his head. Jake put his hand to his mouth to hide a smile.

"Of course we're safe," said the man. "The governor's family, after all. Would they be within a hundred miles of here if we were not? Come, we will be late. *Au revoir."*

The man set off at a brisk pace. The woman gathered a child's hand in each hand, and followed.

"What did you find out?" said Martin. "Did you get a date?"

"No. We're on an island, though. Not France. And he said something about the continent. A French colony then. And they're worried about something. He thought we were scientists."

Martin looked at the road. "There's no room for an automobile here. No radio or television antennas. Sailing ships in the harbor. We could be in the 1800s." He laughed. "It worked again, Jake. We've slipped time's surly bonds."

Unease kept Jake from joining Martin's joy. The memory lingered too strongly of the growing roar, the flames reaching around the zeppelin's side. How could they have arrived then and there? A change in the light caught Jake's attention. Where the sun cut a sharp shadow on the buildings now all was a uniform shade, as if dusk was falling. Rolling like a slow ocean at storm, the clouds squirmed overhead. The two-story buildings standing so close together under a ceiling of black clouds suddenly seemed imprisoning. Jake ran ahead. What hid on the other side? Why were the clouds so strange? He passed an old man in his Sunday best, walking with a heavy limp. A young girl, leading a dog on leash, watched wide-eyed as Jake dashed by.

"What are you doing?" yelled Martin.

Jake reached a junction. Across the street, a small park held cast-iron benches with brightly painted red seats. In a small white gazebo, surrounded by yellow flower beds, a man in military uniform leaned on the railing, smoking a pipe. He tipped his hat at Jake, but Jake's attention was beyond the gazebo, up and up. Martin joined him. "We should stay together. This is an unfamiliar time, and . . . ."

Beyond the park, beyond and above the rows of houses that made the rest of the city, a mountain rose against the sky, pouring black clouds from its peak. No gentle oozing of clouds either. They catapulted from the shrouded mountain, ascended, caught in a high wind that didn't reach the ground, and flattened over the town.

Jake strode across the street, into the park, his gaze trapped by the silent display. The mountain was close, no more than five miles. Houses in rows lapped against the sloping flank of it. How quiet the town was. None of the seabirds called out. Water in the bay made no sound under the docks. Only his muffled footfalls in the dusty grass. His own breathing.

On the gazebo, the soldier watched Jake's approach.

"Where are we?" Jake demanded. He gripped the gazebo's railing as if to vault himself beside the soldier, a teenager, by his unlined face, so new to his uniform that he looked uncomfortable in it.

"Martinique," said the man with a rise in his voice, like he had asked a question.

Nervelessly, Jake's hand fell away from the painted wood. All the horizon held was the mountain and its billowing performance. "What town is this?" he nearly whispered. Martin walked to the gazebo's side, staring at the volcano.

Puzzled, the young man said, "It is St. Pierre. My company is here to proctor the election."

"Oh, no," said Jake. "We've done it again."

Martin turned back to him. "What?"

"I know the mountain."

From somewhere in the town behind them, a church bell rang out, breaking the silence with its somber tolling.

The soldier laughed nervously. "The Angelus bells. I must be going, monsieur."

"That's Mount Pelée, isn't it?" said Jake in English. "*C'est Mont Pelée?*" He grabbed the soldier's arm as he went down the steps. Under the heavy flannel uniform, the man's arm felt slender. He's just a boy, thought Jake.

"Yes, Pelée. I must go to the cathedral," said the young man. "I'm already late."

Jake's computer said, *Mt. Pelée exploded in* . . . . A thunderous clap of sound overwhelmed the rest of the message.

On the mountain, a cloud wall boiled down the slope, its folds and wrinkles glowing like veins on fire. Trees vanished behind it. Within seconds, the upper half of the prominence became all cloud, rolling down, swallowing land, obscuring what before had been clear.

Martin said, "Should we be worried about that? What is it?"

The soldier wrenched free from Jake's grasp, glanced over his shoulder at the mountain, then ran down the street, away from the engulfing cloud. In its squeaky voice, the computer recited a litany of facts.

Jake didn't move. Didn't even twitch. His thoughts slowed down and felt cold to him. Emotionless. "Pyroclastic flow." Another explosion ripped the hidden mountaintop.

Martin took a step back. "Will it reach us?"

"In about two minutes." Near the peak, the smoke radiated an incandescent orange, and a series of smaller detonations like cannon fire rattled the park. Jake's insides had emptied. Had the family with the two little boys reached the church yet? If they were lucky, they had time for a short prayer. The computer talked to him. Twenty-nine thousand people would die in the next few minutes: the governor and his wife, in town to calm the population, the scientists who pronounced the volcano safe, the farmers who had fled fields where crops had died in the weeks of ash fall, the people who'd abandoned villages close to the mountain for the safety of St. Pierre, all of them would be gone. Only a prisoner in a basement cell would survive. Rescuers would find him days later, horribly burned, crying weakly from beneath the jail's rubble. "Geologists call it *nuée ardente*, the glowing cloud. Super-heated air and volcanic ash traveling a hundred miles an hour. Strong enough to knock down buildings. So hot that breathing it boils the lungs."

"How did we get here?" shouted Martin above the growing roar. Furious, he glared at the cloud that reached the town's edge, hiding homes and shops and factories. "This is not random at all!" He touched the button inside his shirt, vanished.

Jake could feel the fear around him. If he turned, citizens would be on the street, drawn by the noise. The cathedral would empty. Hymn books in hand, they'd be waiting. Children, grandparents, craftsmen, soldiers, wives. Trash in the street beyond the park stirred. Now, all was dark. As if it contained a thousand freight trains rumbling headlong down their doomed tracks, the mountain bellowed.

Before the heat. Before the flesh-stripping wind. Jake pressed the button within his shirt.

Without taking his hand off the monitor input, Jake flicked from one image to the next, grainy black and white photographs of buildings without roofs, all the windows gone, bricks scattered in the street, and everywhere, bodies burned black. "They had plenty of warning, you know," he said. "The mountain had been misbehaving for weeks. People had already died. There were mud avalanches and a tidal wave and ash falls, but they didn't leave. How can you keep your children with you when there are ... signs ... portents?" He sighed and turned off the monitor. "When there are evil omens in the sky?"

"Damn it, Jake. What's important here is the impossibility of us showing up at two disasters. History is mostly boring, repetitious, day after day existence where people go about their ordinary lives. Historic events are rare. How could we possibly be present for two of them in a row?"

"I don't know what the science is, here. Brownson's math looks more like chants and incantations to me than physics anyway. We built a machine that we don't understand. I wonder if Brownson even knew. If only we could ask him."

Martin swore and slapped his notebook closed. "The one-armed bastard. Maybe if he hadn't been so cryptic with us, we'd have a better chance of figuring it out." He paced around the lab, head down. "We've been time travelers for all of what, ten minutes total? Both times we've been scared. We're not thinking straight." He paused, looked at Jake. "We need rationality. *We* were never in danger. We could come back to the lab anytime." He paced again, circling their work table, passing behind Jake at the monitor. "Here's the problem: we only have two points on the graph. We can't reach a conclusion without more information. I say we try again."

The blank screen looked back at Jake, but he could still picture the old images from centuries past. He'd never thought of the people who'd lived before as people, really. Those lives were abstractions. Nothing to do with him. But he could see them now, the living, beating, desperately intense faces from the past, trying to avoid their fates, staring down the rushing pyroclastic cloud burning toward them at a hundred miles an hour, or on the *Hindenburg*, waiting for the ground to come close enough so they could jump, not knowing if the raging hydrogen and diesel-fueled fire would reach them first.

"I don't want to visit the dead anymore," he said.

Martin put his hands on the back of Jake's chair. He could see Martin's reflection in the monitor overlaying the ghost images of a destroyed town. "I told you already, they were dead before we started. *We're* dead, Jake, to someone in our future, but you're thinking about it all wrong. They're alive too. Everything they've ever done is still being done. Nothing is in the past now. It's all redoable. Replayable."

He checked the equipment strapped across his chest under his shirt. "We have to go again, and we need to do it now. I can't tell

from Brownson's figures why it's working. So much of his calculations are about the paradoxes, and they're a waste. 'Solve the
paradox!' he said. 'Solve the paradox!' There's no paradox. We've
traveled, but we can't guarantee we can keep doing it. Maybe the
Earth has to be in the right place in its orbit. Maybe the atmospheric conditions have to be just perfect. If we don't go now, we
might not be able to go again."

For a moment, Jake didn't stir. It was like the weight of Mount
Pelée coming toward him and nothing mattered. He pushed away
from the monitor and faced Martin. Finally, he nodded. Martin
was right, he was dead anyway he figured it.

At first Jake thought he'd gone blind until he saw the nearly full
moon through thin clouds. A cold wind pushed against his face.
He took a step, kicked something yielding, and a sleepy voice said,
"Watch it, goll darn ya'. Can't a soldier get a decent sleep anywhere on this boat?"

Standing still, Jake listened until his eyes adapted to the pale
light. Water sloshed heavily to both sides. A substantial pounding
vibrated the floor beneath his feet, and before the first faint lights
grew visible on the shore a couple hundred yards away, he'd already
decided they were on a steamboat, near the bow. He turned his back
to the wind. Moonlight revealed twin gray smokestacks belching
smoke and sparks above a pilot's cabin, and dark forms that covered
the deck like a lumpy landscape. He looked down. The man he'd
kicked had rolled onto his side, pulling a thin blanket over him.
The bundles were men sleeping on nearly every inch of exposed
surface. Walking without stepping on someone would be hard.

"When and where are we?" said Martin.

"Someplace that's going to sink soon, or catch fire, or be at-
tacked." Jake said.

Martin grunted. "I should have brought a coat."

"Go back and get one." On the shore, ghostly trees touched their branches to the water. A lone cabin, a dim light flickering in its window, peeked out from the woods. On the boat's other side, the river reflected the moon like a long, undulating silver plate until it vanished in a low fog that hovered just off the surface. The air smelled cool, wet and muddy.

"Big river. Steamboat. English spoken here. The Mississippi." Martin strode over a silent shape, careful not to step on it. Jake followed. Gingerly they moved toward the shore-side railing. Men sat up there, some leaning their heads on the shoulders of others. Some talked among themselves.

"He's dead, the bastards," said one. No one replied. "A coward's shot, I tell 'ya. A yella' deed, it was."

Jake took a place at the rail. Below, the river flowed past slowly. The ship's headway was gradual. The cabin on shore crept astern.

"You'll feel better when we hit Cairo and head home," said another voice.

"Vicksburg, Memphis, Cairo, Evansville. What's it matter? Dead is dead."

Farther down the boat, the paddle wheel churned, digging into the water with quick, ponderous movement.

"You didn't even vote for him."

"I would've."

Dampness on the rail chilled Jake's arms. The only warmth was Martin standing beside him, blocking the wind.

"Who is dead?" said Martin.

A log with one crooked branch sticking out like a bony, broken bone drifted by only thirty feet away. At the end opposite the branch, a pair of birds, their beaks tucked under wing, huddled side by side.

"The president, ya' cracker. Ain't ya' talked to no-one? Some southern dog of an actor they say done it."

Jake leaned back, but the men were swathed in shadow. He couldn't see who spoke.

"Lincoln?" said Martin. "Are you talking about the assassination of Lincoln?"

Someone snorted in disbelief. "Twarn't Jefferson Davis."

Jake's computer squeaked to life. Before he muted the citation, it said, *Abraham Lincoln died on April 14, 1865. John Wilkes Booth fired on the president during a performance . . . .*

"How long ago?" said Jake. He couldn't remember much about the Civil War beyond the obvious. If Lincoln was already dead, then the war was over. Antietam and Gettysburg and Chancellorsville were in the past. Certainly nothing to fear, like the destruction of the Hindenburg or Mt. Pelée erupting. The shooting had ended.

"Don't know what today is," said the voice. "Ten days, maybe. Two weeks."

Jake activated a search for the dates with attention on disasters. A second later, the computer said, *At approximately 2:00 a.m., April 27, 1865, the massively overloaded steamboat,* Sultana, *exploded. At the time it carried approximately 2,100 repatriated Yankee soldiers, most from the Andersonville prison camp. Between 1,700 and 1,900 men died.* The voice carried on. Facts, figures.

Jake swallowed hard. "This is the *Sultana*, isn't it?"

"Yep."

"Would you know what time it is?"

"Don't know that neither."

Jake whispered to Martin. "The boat is going to blow up."

Martin's head dropped to his arms. "That doesn't make sense. The figures . . . the math . . . random times, Brownson said."

Closer to the pilot's cabin, another man slouched on the rail. Jake's gaze lingered on him. The moon's light burnished him like a bleached shadow. Was this also a soldier who would never make it home? His posture seemed familiar and out of place.

"We should leave, Jake. An explosion won't give us time to escape. I need to get to the lab and redo the calculations. I've missed something."

Jake straightened, moved toward the pilothouse. A rift in the cloud cover brightened the light for a moment, showing the man's shirt sewed shut at the shoulder. No arm. Jake thought, these are Civil War veterans; many of them have lost a limb. As he looked at the landscape of sleeping men, he saw a half dozen crutches resting across blankets. Still, Jake's neck tingled. No empty sleeve dangled from the one-armed man. It was gone, sewn up, as if there had never been an arm for that space.

Martin sounded panicked. "I'm going."

Jake's back grew cold. Wind brushed against him, and the air felt empty. Without looking, Jake knew that Martin had gone. He approached the man at the rail, stepping over outstretched legs, until he stood next to him.

"You were fools to come. It's not worth it," said Brownson. The old man stared into the water, the side of his face a chalky reflection of moon and river air. "How much time did you give yourself?"

"I don't know, but it can't be long." Jake imagined the boilers deep in the ship's bowels, leaking steam, over-pressured, fighting the current and the crowded deck, maybe seconds from ripping at the seams. He put his hand next to Brownson's, and behind his eyes he felt a sudden pressure. His voice caught in his throat. "Your lab . . . they've bombed it. You can't go back."

"They?" Brownson sounded tired. His voice was flat.

"Yes. Someone. Maybe another government. They might have found out what we were doing and became scared. Maybe they thought you could solve the paradox. But there was a bomb. You sent us away that day, or we would have gone up too."

"So, how did you get here? How did you arrange it?" said Brownson.

Jake could feel his brow wrinkling. "What do you mean? Your machine, of course. Your design worked. There's no paradox."

Brownson turned to face him. Moon shadows under his eyes made him look a hundred years old. "I didn't solve the paradox—I worked around it, and so did you, or you wouldn't be here."

No answer worked. What did he mean? "We just activated the device. We didn't solve anything."

Closing his eyes, the old man sighed as if he never wanted to breathe again. "The information paradox stops time travel, as I argued. Information that would change people's actions can't go forward or back. The time line is immutable."

If it wasn't for the beating of the paddle wheel and the soaking Mississippi breeze, Jake could almost feel back home in the lab. This was the direction of a hundred arguments. It was where the math piled up, making no sense. "But we're here."

"Yes, we are, and we can go anywhere the information we carry doesn't matter. We go to time's dead ends, like this sad ship."

Jake's thinking felt sluggish. So much had happened in the last hour. Too much to comprehend. "I don't understand."

How close were the boilers to letting go? Jake's hand crept up to the panic button under his shirt.

Brownson said, "We can't bring information from the future to the past, but we can't bring it forward either. Not if we could tell other people what we found. I planted the bomb."

Overhead, the moon vanished within the clouds, and darkness covered the steamboat. Brownson's voice came out of the black. "It was sealed. Undefusable. When I set it, when I couldn't get away, I made the first trip. I've proven that you can travel in time, but no one will ever know."

"How much time?" Jake's hand caressed the switch.

"How much time did you give yourself?"

"We didn't do anything."

"You didn't? Then it must be something else. Something unexpected." Brownson faced away from the river, looking over the sleeping forms. The two soldiers who'd Jake had talked to earlier were still conversing. "Lincoln's dead, the cowards. Lincoln's dead," spoke one, his voice without feeling. Brownson said, "You poor boy. These men didn't do anything either, but their stories are over. The unexpected is on its way for them, the inevitable, as it is for me, here or in my lab or somewhere else." He paused for a raspy breath. "Just as it is for you. Your lab won't be there long."

Before he could hear another word, before the boilers could let loose to fling hundreds of men into the frigid Mississippi, before the bitter soldier talking in the cloud-veiled night could say again that Lincoln was dead, Jake pressed the button and disappeared.

Martin sat at the worktable, his hands wrapped around the back of his head, his forehead pressed against the scarred work surface. He didn't look at Jake when he appeared in the room, but he talked anyway. Perhaps he'd been talking the whole time. "Our destinations weren't random. The physics of the paradox tossed us where we couldn't matter."

"I know."

"The math says that Pelée is here, right here in the room with us, and so is the *Sultana* and the *Hindenburg* and everything else. The end is on its way." He began weeping.

"What did you say about Brownson's math?" said Jake.

"Tornado. Earthquake. Meteor strike. Nuclear bomb. Fire. Flood. Famine . . . quick famine. It's on the way. That's how the equations balance."

Jake ripped open his shirt. Double checked the equipment. Power was good. "You told me something about the math once, about the equations." He looked out the window. Was the sky turning dark? Was there a rumble in the building's basement. The unexpected was surely on its way. "Brownson told us that information couldn't travel in time. That's the paradox at work, but you said the math never solved perfectly. The numbers were always a little unbalanced."

"I don't get you," said Martin. "The numbers don't matter now."

"Only thirty-three people died on the *Hindenburg*. One man survived Mount Pelée. Five hundred or so lived through the *Sultana*." Jake spoke fast. What had happened began to make sense, if he had enough time. If he could get to where he needed to go before the time ran out. "If information is prevented from traveling backwards and forwards *perfectly*, if the equations add up *perfectly*, then we should only have been able to travel where there were no survivors. There could be no chance for escape, but if I get to the right place I might have a chance."

He pressed the button and found himself on a steel deck, slick with ice. The ship's name, *Halifax*, was printed across a lifeboat.

He pressed the button. Martin flinched when he reappeared.

Jake pressed again. Another mountain rose up before him. Its top too was smoke-covered.

He pressed the button. Martin said, "Where are you going?"

The button gave way. A cityscape. People streamed by, many on bicycles. Street signs were in Japanese. Without looking, he knew a lone bomber flew over the city.

"Tell me where and when!" shouted Martin.

Jake paused, ready to go again. How much time did he have? None to be wasted, for sure, but the numbers didn't lie. Their imperfections held all the hope he needed. Maybe *most* information could not go from the future to the past. All he could believe was that in the fractions that didn't add up, he could slip away.

"The *Hindenburg*," he said. "If I wait long enough. If I jump from the window not so high that I'll die, not so low that the ship will crush me, then I'll survive. Sixty-two people lived. I can be the uncounted sixty-third."

There's no point in not trying, he thought, and he pressed the button. ✪

SEVEN DRAGONS MOUNTAINS

BY ELIZABETH BEAR

"MING-FENG SAYS SHE SAW A DRAGON over the bay when she went for tea three nights ago."

"Ming-feng." Chueh-hsin pressed fingertips into velvety dough and did not look at his honored customer. Tacky-surfaced circles took shape under his caress; they would soon be stuffed with aromatic ginger, with green onion and tiny shrimp and fat pork. "Your Ming-feng, Mr. Long? Her master sends her all the way around the bay for his special blend?"

"He does." The honored customer sipped his tea and smiled, bending his long neck to watch his lunch prepared. "All the way to the tea-shop by the English Governor's Palace on the other side of the island. Still, the walking keeps her legs pretty."

Chueh-hsin laughed, tasting the scent of peanut and sesame oil and the tang of roasted chilies. He stopped himself from looking into the kitchen to call for a fresh pot of tea. There was no one but himself to serve the customers in the small restaurant now, and so he sighed and patted the last dumpling wrapper flat. He glanced past the honored customer, beyond the row of long-necked ducks hung dried along the edge of the awning. Chueh-hsin squinted into the light as if his gaze might pierce the soaring steel, marble and glass towers and cross the bay to the rolling green backs of the auspicious Seven Dragons Mountains, and he might glimpse a dragon of his own.

The canyon of the street darkened, but it was no sacred animal's passing that he noted: only the shadow of one of the ever-present dirigibles. The fountain in the restaurant behind the honored customer splashed; Chueh-hsin leaned forward, and caught a glimpse of a knobby jade-dark serpentine head slipping back below the surface.

Mr. Long lifted his cup on five knobby fingers and noticed the angle of his gaze. "Are you saving that turtle for soup?"

Chueh-hsin shook his head. "Though a man may consume any beast whose back faces heaven, that turtle is not for eating," he answered, and wiped his hands on his apron before he went to measure the fine curled shapes of *chun mee*, the tea called *precious eyebrows*, into a pot that he then filled with nearly boiling water. When he glanced up again, he looked at the sunlight on the caramelized skins of the ducks, at the passers-by who would soon enter his humbly successful restaurant for a bowl of noodles or a plate of dumplings, at the softly flaking crimson paint on the timbers under the eaves. "Did Ming-feng notice what color the dragon was?"

"Yes," Mr. Long answered. "The dragon was the color of the sun and of golden jade. He had five fingers on each hand."

"An Imperial dragon," Chueh-hsin said. He tilted his head as he poured the fine, pale-green, astringent-smelling tea and noticed the jade-green head had risen above the water once more. "That must be an omen. I wonder what it means, an Imperial dragon?"

The turtle splashed as it submerged. "Perhaps it means the

British will be eradicated soon," Mr. Long said, but he lowered his voice and glanced toward the door before he said it. He rattled five curved fingernails on his eggshell-thin teacup and smiled through long, yellow teeth.

Mr. Long stayed until the lunch crowd had emptied back out again, drinking tea and eating dumplings that seemed to have no effect on his spare frame, but at last Chueh-hsin stood between the doorposts and watched as the white-haired man bicycled away. Mr. Long held himself as erect as one of those doorposts, Chueh-hsin thought, as he turned his plaque to read 'closed', sighing in anticipation of his own much-delayed meal.

A scratching sound made him turn back to the door before he had gone more than a few steps inside. Chueh-hsin squinted into the sunlight to make out the silhouette of a man in a monk's uniform, his feet dragging as he staggered with exhaustion. He found himself halfway back to the door before the name was out of his mouth. "Chueh-min! Chueh-min!"

Chueh-hsin grasped his younger brother by the shoulders, and then almost stepped back as Chueh-min clutched his wrists tight and hissed for silence.

"Not so loud, oldest brother," Chueh-min said, ducking his head under paper streamers as he hurried into the shop. He moved along the front counter, untying the strings on the bamboo shades between the restaurant and the street and letting them fall to hide the interior. Chueh-hsin stepped back against the inside counter and watched, noticing the grey mud caking his brother's sandals, the violet shadows surrounding his eyes.

Chueh-hsin bit his lips on the questions, turning his back on Chueh-min. He leaned over the counter and withdrew a red-veined ivory oval from a silk-lined basket. He knocked the preserved duck egg—from which he had already peeled the clay and ash coating—on the counter and began to lift the stained shell from the gelatinous white with the tip of his fingernail.

"Thousand-year-old eggs?" Chueh-min had come up alongside him. He smelled as if he'd been traveling, his hair falling in greasy tangles across his forehead.

"It's for the turtle," Chueh-hsin answered, and picked up his cleaver to cut the egg into bits.

"Have you one for your first younger brother as well, after so long away?"

Chueh-hsin turned, the cleaver in his hand, and caught Chueh-min's subtle half-smile. "Welcome home," he said, and swept the gluey egg into a bowl. "Help yourself. I will make tea soon: are we not brothers? Is not my wealth your wealth, and my duty your duty?"

"It is," Chueh-min said, as if the subtle reprimand had not affected him, and reached into the basket as Chueh-hsin brought the bowl to the edge of the fountain.

He picked up a bit of greenish yolk between his fingers and sank down on lip of the fountain, letting his hand hang down so that the edge of his palm brushed the water. He waited, perfectly still, breath held, while Chueh-min rolled the second egg against the countertop. The sound of the shell cracking was like crazing glass; he turned his head to watch, and almost shivered when the turtle took advantage of his distraction to lift the bit of yolk from his fingertips. The green beak nibbled and withdrew, five tiny claws brushing his skin as the reptile trod water. Chueh-hsin lifted his hand and retrieved another fragment of egg without looking away from Chueh-min. "I notice you waited until the customers had left to approach my restaurant, first younger brother."

Chueh-min turned toward him, sucking delicately at the quivering surface of the egg. "Can you hide me until I can make it to the Governor's palace unobserved?" he asked plainly, and Chueh-hsin smiled.

"It would appear, younger brother, that I already am."

Red lanterns lit the warm night; Chueh-min finally awakened from a long, hard sleep in the room behind the restaurant, after the dinner hour had passed. Chueh-hsin served noodles and tea and sat beside his brother on the floor mat while they ate, shoulder to shoulder in silence as if five years had not passed.

"Where is Xiumei?" Chueh-min asked when he had finished drinking his broth. He laid his chopsticks parallel across his bowl and poured himself another cup of tea, which he held elevated on long fingers, his palms cupped face to face as if enjoying the warmth.

"She wished to return to her family," Chueh-hsin answered, which was not exactly a lie. "Where have you been for half ten years, first younger brother?"

"Japan," Chueh-min answered, and Chueh-hsin started to his feet, upsetting the empty bowls. His teacup sprayed steaming liquid across the mat; it flowed close to Chueh-min, but Chueh-min did not rise.

"How can you say that so calmly?" And then Chueh-hsin blinked, and laced his fingers together before himself. "How did you manage to come back to the island, from Japan?"

"I took a dirigible into Russia," Chueh-min answered. "From there to Korea, and from Korea to Taiwan."

"And thence home again? Here, and not to the Emperor?"

"Sit, eldest brother," Chueh-min admonished. "I am not a spy."

He sipped his tea and rolled his shoulders in a shrug. "Or if I am, I am a loyal spy, let us rather say."

"Then why have you not been spying on the British rather than on their behalf? We have argued about this before, first younger brother."

"Because the British are the lesser evil," Chueh-min answered, and tipped his head to indicate that Chueh-hsin should sit.

And Chueh-hsin did, reaching for a cloth to dab at the spilled tea before he remembered that it was his mat, his tea, and his sleeping room. *Chueh-min should have been the eldest son,* he thought—not for the first time. The fountain in the restaurant splashed softly, filling the silence that lingered between them. Chueh-hsin shook his head surreptitiously: no. Chueh-min would have chafed under the responsibilities of an eldest son, and Chueh-hsin was not cut out for adventure.

A man's place in the world truly was predetermined for the best, by his duty to his ancestors and his family.

"I must report to the Governor by morning," Chueh-min said, breaking Chueh-hsin from his study. "Will you help me get there?"

"It's a long way to his palace," Chueh-hsin said doubtfully. He reached out to right the eggshell-fine teacup, and noticed that it had cracked when he overturned it. It looked as if it would still hold tea, however, and he poured himself another cup. "We should leave immediately, if we must be there by dawn."

"Put your boots on," Chueh-min said, and set his cup aside before he stood. Chueh-hsin drank his tea in haste and followed.

A half-moon gleamed in the sky like a baroque pearl tumbled on a bed of tangled silk, and the air was as cool as silk as well. Chueh-hsin pressed his fists into his sides through the quilted cotton of his jacket, breathing deeply to ease the stitch under his ribs. He was not accustomed to climbing, and his calves trembled with the effort of the road through the passes of the Seven Dragons. The wealthy suburb where stood the Governor's palace—and several expensive tea shops—was at the very tip of the peninsula that half-encircled the bay, directly across from the city. It was usually reached by private motor ferry, by those with means to take one.

The ferries did not run so late. Nor were they particularly discreet. Chueh-hsin and his brother walked.

Chueh-min was fitter, but limping in his sandals, and Chueh-hsin found himself taking his brother's elbow to help him over the steeper parts of the road. The motion made the front of Chueh-hsin's jacket swing against his breast. He felt the hard, retracted shape of the turtle in his breast pocket when it did so. He should have left her in the fountain, he knew, but it seemed somehow safer to keep her close. Two thousand-year eggs lay in his sleeve pocket, smooth and warm as beach pebbles.

He'd never been able to bear letting the turtle out of his sight for long, and now that Chueh-min had returned, the urge to keep her close was that much stronger.

"Come this way," Chueh-min said, tugging his sleeve.

"That's away from the road."

"It's faster."

"It's steeper," Chueh-hsin argued, but he turned to follow.

"If I can do it, you can do it—"

"You are the one who's limping."

"Exactly."

Chueh-hsin leaned forward, digging his toes into the soft green earth of the mountain's flank. He released Chueh-min's arm and steadied himself, one hand on the slope before him as they climbed. The turtle never moved, still as a stone. Probably frightened to be taken from the fountain where she had spent the last five years, Chueh-hsin thought—and silently reprimanded himself for pitying her.

Chueh-min paused at the top of a dragon-backed ridge, belly down so he would not be silhouetted against the ragged, moonlit sky. Chueh-hsin crouched low beside him. They remained for a moment, panting, and Chueh-hsin put his hand on his first younger brother's shoulder.

"You are not a monk," he said.

"I am a monk," Chueh-min replied. "I also am in the service of the Governor."

"The British Governor."

Chueh-min shrugged. "They are our allies against the Japanese," he answered. "Politics are eternal. China has been conquered before and will be conquered again: always she rises, China still. Like the Phoenix. Look, do you see the dirigible?" He raised an arm and pointed.

Chueh-hsin turned his head to follow the cascade of teal and emerald and golden electric lights across the sky. The dirigible's side was picked out in a pattern of a phoenix and a dragon-turtle, and Chueh-hsin sighed at its loveliness. His preoccupation was interrupted by Chueh-min's voice, hesitant and almost reverential as he dropped his gaze from the dirigible to its lights, reflected in the broken surface of the bay.

"Did Xiumei really go back to her family?"

Chueh-hsin did not answer directly. He pressed his fist against the center of his breast, easing his breathing. "She was unhappy after you left, first younger brother."

Chueh-min lifted one hand and pointed out over the bay. "Then she's out *there* now?"

"No," Chueh-hsin said, unwillingly. "I said she wanted to go home. I did not say she did."

"Then where is she?" Chueh-min glanced over, his voice too carefully casual.

Chueh-hsin smiled to himself, knowing that even the bright moonlight was not enough to reveal so slight an expression to Chueh-min. Something must have showed, however, because Chueh-min glanced quickly away. "Where I can keep her," Chueh-hsin said. "Hurry. The moon will set soon, and we are only halfway there."

Chueh-min's shortcut led them unerringly toward the winking lights of the little town at the end of the peninsula. Chueh-hsin followed in his brother's footsteps. They did not speak of Xiumei again.

Chueh-hsin could not say when he first became aware that something was wrong among the mountains. Perhaps it was the faint sallow light that did not fade as the moon set, but seemed to rise from behind the hill to the left, as if starlight soaked the earth of its far flank. He laid his hand on Chueh-min's sleeve and turned him toward the light. "Do you see it?"

"Yes," Chueh-min said, and set off in that direction without hesitation, the exhaustion gone from his step as he scrambled toward the spiked crest of the ridge.

Chueh-hsin had no choice but to follow until Chueh-min halted at the lip of a staggering cliff.

There was a valley below, a narrow steep-sided niche between mountains that would be almost completely inaccessible to a man on foot. Gullies and treeless cuts, furred green in verdant grass, sloped down to a ravine that seemed to have only two exits. A worn switchbacked trail ran up a steep incline on the far side of the valley, toward the road which they had abandoned for this more direct route, and from which the valley was shielded by an even higher ridge. On the near side, a rope ladder dangled the height of the cliff face.

Electric torches lit the scene below. Men in dark uniforms hurried—efficient, purposeful as ants—around the site in utter silence. Chueh-hsin caught his breath as if the heavy rasp of it in his throat could carry far enough to give them away.

In the center of the activity, at the bottom of the valley, gilded red and crimson in the light of the torches, slumbered a dragon. Chueh-hsin could see the stout black cables twined across its back, pinning each five-toed extremity to the ground. Chueh-hsin glanced at his brother, but Chueh-min had eyes only for the scene below. "The Governor must know of this," Chueh-min said.

"As he must know of the other news you carry?" Chueh-hsin could not keep the bitterness out of his voice. In all the truth of it, he did not even try.

"This is the other news I carry," Chueh-min said. "I didn't know it was here already, elder brother."

"The dragon? But he must know, if he's sent all those men—"

"That's not a dragon," Chueh-min said patiently. "It is an airship. And those men are Japanese." This time he did meet Chueh-hsin's eyes. And then cursed softly under his breath and yanked Chueh-hsin away from the edge of the cliff, as the bustle below increased. The men threw the dragon's tethers free, and slowly—majestically—the amazing animal rose.

It writhed in the sky like a serpent, its thousand-yard length glittering. Its throat glowed blue with flame, jaws working like the mouth of a horse champing the bit, and Chueh-hsin could see that it was lit like a paper lantern from within.

"No airship could look so real," he murmured.

He might have stood hopelessly and watched its gold, five-toed claws clench and twist on air, but Chueh-min clutched his wrist and dragged him into a staggering run.

"They'll bomb the Palace from the air."

"Worse," Chueh-min called over the thud of their feet on the grass, the sporadic rattle of gunfire behind them. They must have been seen when they started to run. "It breathes fire. It's here to destroy the Governor's Palace. The people will see the Imperial Dragon rise from the mountain to destroy the British overlords. There will be an uprising—"

And worse still, Chueh-hsin thought, hearing the amplified cries of pursuit above and behind them as the grass lit sharp-edged and white beneath their feet, the dragon-ship's searchlights coming to bear. *The Japanese will walk into a China already softened by war.* Chueh-min stumbled, his sandaled feet sliding on the grass, pulling Chueh-hsin into the orbit of his arms and rolling with him as they fell. Bullets sang around them: Chueh-min shielded Chueh-hsin in the curve of his arms. And Chueh-hsin curled himself taut around the hard-shelled object that jabbed his bosom as they rolled.

Chueh-hsin could never have described what happened after. He lost one sandal as they tumbled down the long green slope, suffering bruising collisions with rocks and earth. Chueh-hsin gagged at the sound of green twigs snapping, not knowing at first if his own bones had broken or Chueh-min's. The eggs in his sleeve pocket crushed like teacups under a big man's boot. Chueh-hsin fell atop his brother and heard a bubbling groan, spread himself wide across Chueh-min's body to absorb the expected impact of bullets.

The airship slid overhead, gleaming like the moon it eclipsed, silent except for the tremble of wind against its taut, scaled skin, and nothing touched Chueh-hsin at all.

He pulled back and rolled over, amazed, watching that long sinuous body glide by like a living river of gold. And then he heard Chueh-min cough wetly, and heard his brother's slick, soft hiss of pain. "Chueh-hsin." Not so much speech as the bubble of a voice from a great deep.

"Don't talk," Chueh-hsin said. "You're hurt."

"I'm dying. At least one bullet has entered my back," his brother answered, matter-of-factly, and black shining blood dripped from the corner of his mouth. He gasped between each word. "Run to the Governor. Can you run, elder brother?"

"It's no use," Chueh-hsin said. "I can't outrun an airship. And we have no duty here—"

"You owe me this."

"I owe you nothing."

"Your duty as my elder brother."

"As you fulfilled your duty as my younger brother when you went into the pay of the British? Or as you fulfilled it when you fucked my wife?" He stopped, appalled at his own bright-edged words, and pressed his hand against his bosom. The turtle— if the turtle had been crushed—

He pulled her out, a hard dome of jade no larger than his palm, and tried to see her in the moonlight. He smelled his own sweat, the fermented reek of the thousand-year eggs, the hot red iron of Chueh-min's blood. He held her cupped in his palms, close to his face, turning to the copper moonlight and tilting his head as if, through the darkness, there were any chance at all that he could see a jagged crack marring the green of her shell.

Huddled close within her carapace, she didn't stir, even when Chueh-hsin blew across the opening for her head to let her taste his breath.

"Xiumei?" Chueh-min said, or tried to say. Chueh-hsin cupped his fingers carefully around the turtle in his palm, and reached out with his other hand to take Chueh-min's.

He looked down, surprised. Chueh-min's fingers lay slack and boneless between his own, and his eyes reflected the moonlight dully, slitted open beneath clotted lashes.

"Xiumei," he said in answer, as if Chueh-min could hear him, and turned his head to follow the inner-lit silhouette of the dragon against the star-scattered darkness above. Fire wreathed its mouth, the mechanical jaw working through what must be some fantastic contrivance. Chueh-hsin dropped his brother's hand and stood, the contracted turtle held up before him like an offering, and imagined he could hear the shouts of terror as the puppet-dragon came down on the Governor's Palace.

The turtle lifted her head and watched with her husband as the dragon fell. She blinked tiny, rice-paper lidded eyes in the moonlight, and turned her gaze to Chueh-hsin. "Free me, honored husband," she said, "and I will call my father to put an end to that paper dragon."

Chueh-hsin bit his lip. "Obedience is a wife's duty," he said.

"It is," she answered. "As loyalty is a brother's. Chueh-min saved your life, my husband—"

He watched the incandescent gold ribbon of the dragon turn against the night sky, watched it begin to descend, still dripping fire, upon the tea-shops and the houses near the Palace. "Call your father," he said.

"Will you free me, Chueh-hsin?"

"Call your father," he said, and the turtle closed her eyes and withdrew her head into her shell.

"Promise—"

"Call your father." A third time. "I will promise no such thing."

Her sigh was as faint and brief as Chueh-min's passing breath. "Honored husband. It is done."

Chueh-hsin tucked his wife into his breast pocket, and lifted his brother's body over his shoulder, and carried them both up the ridge to watch as a knobby, jade-dark shape as vast as the island under their feet rose above the gleaming ocean beyond the bay. Its bulk against the greying horizon was nothing but a shadow, the rough shape of a turtle, domed shell and lamp-lit golden eyes. One of its hands broke the surface, five grasping moon-white talons reflecting starlight like ship's masts carved of ivory. Tendrils streamered from its head and back.

Chueh-hsin held his breath as the dragon-turtle cast a searching glance across the island and rose into the air, its dark knobby outline silhouetted against the stars, as unlike the shining fantasy of the puppet airship as a mossy shrine is unlike a paper lantern. Ineffectual flashes of light sparked off its shell, glittered around the puppet airship like fireflies. Their report reached Chueh-hsin seconds later, and he realized he heard gunfire.

His brother's weight hung against his side like a sack of meat and sticky wetness plastered his robes to his body, but he would not put his burden down. He stood on the ridgeline and watched the airship make a grand slow turn and bear down on the mansion and the town, the dragon-turtle sliding across the sky toward it, just perhaps in time.

In time. After all, in time. There was no contest when they met. The dragon-turtle moved through the airship like a stone through a paper fan, and tore it into burning, drifting shreds, which settled over the town as the dragon-turtle settled back into the sea: in abject silence, once the screams of falling men came to their end.

*   *   *

Chueh-hsin cupped his hands under the turtle's belly and crouched where the waves lapped most gently. He knelt, feeling the sand sucked from under his quilted trousers, the wet cloth salting his skin, and lowered the turtle into the ocean, ignoring the dry, possessive prickle of thwarted ownership against the back of his throat.

"A turtle that size will never survive in the bay," Mr. Long commented, leaning forward over the basket of his bicycle. "Something bigger will eat her, don't you think?"

"She'll be fine," Chueh-hsin said, watching the jade-green serpentine head emerge for a moment from the foam-honeycombed waves. "She has many friends. They will take care of her." *And she will grow as big as they are, one of these centuries.*

Mr. Long scratched his cheek with his knobby five-fingered hands. "If you had one wish," he said, "one wish in all the world. What would it be, Chueh-hsin?"

"What have I done to deserve a wish, Mr. Long?"

The tall man's skinny throat bobbed as he swallowed, tilting his head and opening his hands, a disarming, half-embarrassed gesture. "Call it a family obligation. A debt for a debt repaid."

Chueh-hsin knuckled his chest below the collarbone and thought, watching a dirigible drift out over the bay. There were things he desired: Wealth. Fortune. Love. A restaurant where the walls were lacquered red and gilded gold, rather than hung with paper streamers and peeling paint.

He thought of the Governor gone, of the Japanese contained. *Politics and conquest are eternal,* he thought. *China is the Phoenix. China consumes whatever is given her, no matter how bitter, no matter how foul, and rises from the ashes whole.*

There were things he wanted. Like Xiumei. And there were things he was required to do, and a death to which he owed his life. "My brother back," he said, hating to say it, as the sea wind lifted his hair.

"Done," said the dragon beside him. "He will be waiting when you go home."

Chueh-hsin scowled; Mr. Long dipped his head in benediction and slipped like a turtle into the sea, where he belonged. ✪

SILK

BY LEE BATTERSBY

THE WORST HOUSE IN THE BEST STREET, that's what Dad always told me. You can renovate a house, but you can't improve a neighbourhood unless you leave it, he'd say, signalling my step-mum for another beer. The house we bought was a rundown afterthought, planted firmly at the end of the street like a gatecrasher who can't quite believe his luck. Dad walked in, nodded his approval, and put his arm around Susan with a familial warmth neither of us were ever entirely comfortable with.

"You'll be all right here," he said with an undercurrent of envy. "You'd be surprised what these old houses can do, once you start digging away. I was born in one just like this, a couple of months after the War started. Bomb-proof, they are." He punched a wall with an affectionate fist. "You'll be surprised."

And surprised we were. I've never been one for hard graft, but once we got stuck in to the task it became addictive. The joy of finding just that right tint of paint, or the perfect paper, to recreate the feeling of the house's original days was like the thrill of the hunt. We became a dog pack of two, patiently running down wrought iron railings and shellac, lead-free fillers and wood stains, until we could separate our chosen prey from the herd and bring it down with a howl, credit cards raised in feral triumph. The day we found a working radio from the '40s I was like an ancestor who'd single-handedly brought down a mastodon. Only the veneer of civilisation stopped me from pulling Susan to the ground and having her right there in the carpark.

We worked our way from back to front, starting with those rooms we could not live without and leaving the casual rooms until last. The kitchen and bathroom were early successes, as was the master bedroom, where pride of place was accorded the ceiling rose Dad had gifted us once he'd seen the job we were doing. By the time we were ready to tackle the living room the house was almost complete. Only this last room and the patio area remained to be conquered. Susan and I stood at the door and surveyed our objectives.

"I call the floor," she shouted, an all-important half second before me.

"You did the last one."

"Quick or dead, my friend," she laughed, striding into the room and picking up the crowbar. "You should know by now."

I snorted in return and made my way to where the paper stripper leaned against the wall, waiting. "You won't be so quick when you're looking at the bricks outside."

She raised her eyebrows in amusement, grabbed the metal bar, and began quartering the floor, tapping and poking at the floorboards. Every now and again she would bend down and make a mark with a stick of carpenter's chalk, delineating spots where timber putty, or outright replacement, was merited. I watched her, my own task forgotten, lost in the movement of her lithe body and the childlike frown that always adorned her face whenever she was deep in concentration. She was halfway across the room when the crowbar thunked down on a board and went through without pausing.

"Crap!" Susan jumped back in shock, then pulled the jemmy out. "Oh hell, that whole section's going to need ... hey, what's that?"

She knelt, and peered into the opening the accident had created. "David, check this out."

"What?" I dropped down next to her. "I can't see. Where did we put the torch?"

"Watch yourself." The crowbar slid past my face and back into the hole. Susan grunted. A six-inch section of floorboard whipped up and spun away.

"Shit!"

"Told you to watch yourself." She bent her head once more. "Now, what is this?"

Before I could warn her about holes and the things that live in them, she reached in and pulled something out, looking at it in wonderment.

"It's silk."

"What?"

"It's silk. Loads of it. It's crammed in there, David. I can see tonnes of the stuff." She started pulling at the material, dragging it from its confinement. "Help me."

I grabbed the crowbar and used it to lever up the surrounding floorboards. Soon we had a gap large enough to pull up armfuls of the grubby fabric. It lay heaped around us, filling the living room in drifts almost to our knees. We looked at each other across a snowfield of dirty grey material.

"Well," I said eventually. "What now?"

"Let's get it outside. I think this is all one piece. If we spread it out on the lawn we might be able to see what it is."

We managed to drag the massive pile of silk out into the front yard, then around to the back where we could open it out without attracting the attention of neighbours and passers by. Our backyard is huge, nearly 20 metres to a side. It was one of the reasons we bought the house: room to grow, room for a garden, room for children to play, one day. We covered almost every inch of it. The more we grabbed handfuls and walked in opposite directions, the more of the stuff there seemed to be. Finally, after nearly an hour of sweating and straining, we stood hand in hand on the patio and surveyed our handiwork.

"It's a balloon," I said in bemusement, finally seeing the full shape of the thing for the first time.

"It's a barrage balloon."

"How did you work that out?"

She smiled. "They're called books, David. You really should try them sometimes."

"Oh, ha ha. So what the hell is it doing under my floor?"

She frowned. "I don't know. The house was built in the '30s, but I don't think there were any balloons in Perth during the War. Maybe some Londoner owned the house and brought it with them, used it as insulation under *our* floor."

"Insulation? We should put it back then."

"Are you kidding?" She put her hand on my arm to stop me from gathering up the material, and looked at me with that look which says she's working through an opportunity and needs just one minute more to figure out how to start making it pay.

"Uh oh. What are you thinking?"

"Do you know how much this stuff is worth? That's parachute-grade silk, not the flimsy Chinese stuff. Dressmakers will pay a bundle for it. We've got to have, what, seven or eight hundred square metres?"

"It's filthy." I indicated the grey-brown surface. "Who's going to clean that up? Not me."

Susan shrugged. "We're not using the yard at the moment. Leave it out here. It's going to rain tonight. We can just hose off whatever's left in the morning, see how it looks."

That's my Susan. Always has a plan, even if the rest of us can't see it. She turned and went back inside, the problem solved in her mind, no longer miraculous or even terribly interesting. I stayed outside a few minutes longer, eyeing the lake of silk, until the smell of burnt toast and Susan's cry of "Lunch!" drew me back inside.

It did rain that night, a vicious attack of heavy drops that had us lying under the covers, giggling and listening to the thunderclaps overhead like little children. I drifted off to sleep late, finally lulled by the warmth of Susan's body against mine and the smell of our lovemaking.

When I woke I was alone, and the house was silent. I found Susan out on the back patio, standing stiff and cold in the early morning light. She jumped when I came up behind her and put my arms about her waist.

"Someone's been fucking about," she said in a tight, frightened little voice.

"What?"

I looked past her into the garden. Empty grass stared back. The silk was gone. Someone had stolen our balloon! To make it worse, they had dumped a monstrous concrete block in its place, an ugly grey edifice the height of my shoulder, sitting squarely in the middle of our lawn, like a gravestone marking the death of our avaricious dreams. I walked out toward it on unsteady legs.

"How the hell . . . ?"

"No way," I heard Susan behind me. "No way could they have got it in here without us hearing."

I paused, remembering the sounds of the storm, and of Susan screaming my name and urging me along. Then something about the block caught my notice. A cable rose from the far side, disappearing tautly into the sky. I rounded the mass, and saw the winch attached to its far side. I tilted my head, following the cable's ascent. A black shape hung far above me, as if weightless. I shaded my eyes with my hands, and squinted. It was our balloon, no longer flat and lifeless but bulbous and pregnant, straining against its tether as if seeking escape beyond horizons only it could see.

"Susan . . . ."

"I see it." Her voice came from just behind my shoulder, where she had come while I stood staring. "But how?"

"I don't know. What do we do now?"

She looked up, her hands raised in imitation of my own. "I've no idea."

"We can't just leave it there."

"No, I know." She lowered her hands. "Let's go inside. I'm hungry, and maybe you'd better put something on before the police get here and tell us to stop blocking the flight path."

She looked me up and down, and I realised I was still naked. I smiled sheepishly, and we turned back into the house. I went into the bedroom to get dressed, and open the curtains upon the day. What I saw made me swear an unconscious oath.

"What's the matter?" Susan called from the kitchen.

"The trees! Some bastard's painted the trees!"

"What?" She came into the bedroom, two plates of toast in her hands.

"Look." I pointed outside. "Some bastard's painted the trees in the front yard black."

"Son of a bitch." She placed the plates onto the bed and pressed up against our window. "It's not just us, look. Across the road's is the same, and Mrs. Henderson's. Unbelievable."

"This is too much. First our balloon and now this. I thought this was supposed to be a good neighbourhood?"

"It is."

"Prove it."

Munching our breakfast, we headed onto the front patio and scanned the street. Blacked-up trees ran its full length. Susan saw Mrs. Henderson in her front yard, so we headed over to say hello.

"Terrible, isn't it?" Susan said to her, nodding toward a formerly-beautiful jacaranda which dominated the old lady's garden. "Have you ever seen such a thing?"

"What's that, dear?" Mrs. Henderson replied, squinting through brick-thick glasses in the direction of Susan's pointing finger.

"The trees. To paint them like that. It's such a blatant act of vandalism."

"Really? Oh dear, that would be awful. Just like the War."

Susan and I looked at each other.

"Why do you say that, Mrs. H?"

"They used to paint trees during the Blitz, you know," our neighbour replied, peering up at us through thick glasses. My Susan is a petite girl, barely five foot three in her stilettos, but next to the old lady even she stood tall. "Helped with the blackout or something, I suppose. I was only a young girl then, up in Coventry."

"The Blitz? Hey, you wouldn't know anything about barrage balloons, would you?" I asked. "You don't know how anyone could have brought one here with them?"

She blinked at me in surprise. "That's an odd question. Why do you ask?"

"Well," I said, gesturing to where our dressmaking fortune

floated five thousand feet above us. "Look what we found."

Mrs. Henderson peered into the sky. "I'm sorry, dear. What is it you wanted me to see?"

I followed her gaze. The balloon hung heavy and obvious before us, its comic-cigar shape bright against the blue sky. Even with her myopia, our old neighbour couldn't have missed it. It would be like failing to see the full moon on a clear night.

"There, Mrs. H. Right there."

She favoured me with the patronising smile I have never liked from teachers and parents, never mind casual acquaintances.

"Yes, dear. I'm sure there's something very nice there. Must be my eyes. Will you excuse me? I think I hear the kettle whistling."

She shuffled away from us, retreating into the dim recesses of her house.

"Humph. Typical. Can't see a giant balloon, but the old biddy's got the hearing of a bat if she can hear a kettle from this distance."

Susan smiled. "Poor baby. Still don't recognise an excuse when you hear one."

"Very funny." We walked back toward our house. "Still, you'd think she'd see it. It's hardly unnoticeable."

"No, no it isn't." We reached the front door and Susan preceded me inside. "Still, she is old, and . . . ."

She stopped so suddenly I banged into her.

"What's the . . . ."

"The living room. David . . . ."

I looked into a place I had never seen. Before we had left the house, it was an empty space with a broken hole in the floor. Now it was . . . well, it was a living room. A wallpapered, painted, furnished living room. Our newly-bought radio, the one in need of sanding back and varnishing and with two knobs missing, dominated the view. It stood between two armchairs—near the fireplace we didn't have twenty minutes ago—dark wood shining, knobs gleaming. There was the sound of static, and then it burst into life.

"This is the BBC Home Service . . . ."

"That's John Snagge." I spoke in quiet shock, recognising his voice from numerous guest spots on my collection of Goon Show LPs. "But he died in the mid-nineties . . . ."

"Maybe it's a tape recording." Susan sounded dreamy, disconnected. I felt the same. This wasn't real, couldn't be real. Weeks of work confronted us, possibly months. There was no way someone could sneak into our house and do it while we chatted to our neighbour in full view of our entrance. Not to mention there was absolutely no reason *why*.

"But . . . but he stopped reading the news . . . just after the War . . . ."

"David, this is getting freaky." Susan was frightened. I did my best to hold down my own rising fear.

"I think we should go outside. Now."

We back-pedalled out of the front door, our eyes fixed on the alien room. When we reached the patio we stopped, and turned around.

"David?"

"I see them."

A cable rose from beyond a house at the other end of the street, a barrage balloon floating serenely at its upper reach. Beyond that hung another, and another, the sky a dark backdrop to a legion of globular white shapes, spread out to the horizon. Through the black painted trees I saw cars in the driveways around us, upright shapes I'd only ever seen in movies, with running boards and external headlights like bug eyes. Directly across from us, three houses had disappeared, including Mrs. Henderson's. In their place lay a wasteland of rubble and ruin. I stared at it in horror. I suddenly wished very much to see the enormous jacaranda I had stood beneath less than half an hour ago.

Susan's hand flitted against mine. I opened my clenched fingers to grasp it, reassuring each other that we stood as real and solid as always. People passed in the street, their hairstyles and dress relics of a time our parents were only just able to remember. One doffed his hat to a lady in a W.A.C. uniform, then looked over in our direction.

"Hey! Turn that bloody light out!" he yelled. Reflexively I reached behind me to the door and pulled it shut, blocking the early evening gloom from the hallway's glare. I had not even noticed the changing of time, nor wondered why the day had so suddenly disappeared before us. We had just finished breakfast, yet we now stood at the beginning of night. The light failed before our eyes. The foreign world slipped into darkness while we watched, our hands entwined, too afraid to look at each other lest the illusion be complete. I didn't want to see the paint-stained and tattered t-shirts and jeans we loved so much replaced by garb indistinguishable from that of the passers-by who glanced up at the sky and hurried away.

When the light deserted us completely, and we stood engulfed in shadows, Susan slipped her hand from mine.

"What now?" she whispered.

"I'm afraid."

"Me too."

I turned my head then, and regarded the front door. "We can't stay out here."

"I know."

"We have to go in."

"I know."

"Maybe we'll wake up in the morning and this will all have been an hallucination. A dream."

"Yes. Too much paint stripper, or something."

"Yes."

"Yes."

I reached out and pushed the door open. Our hallway stretched out before us, resplendent in the old-time fashions we had taken so much pride in recreating. Our bedroom stood shut to our left, and to our right, the terrible and awful living room mocked our gaze. We stepped inside, and shut the door behind us.

"You still have your clothes on."

I looked at her.

"So do you."

She smiled at me then, a small and brave thing that crept uncertainly onto her face and disappeared just as quickly.

"I'm not hungry."

"Neither am I."

I opened the bedroom door and made to reach for the light switch.

"Don't."

I stopped my hand. Susan moved tentatively past me and into the room.

"I don't want to see. I don't want to find the room changed. Not our bedroom. Not here."

I left the light off. We undressed in the dark, on opposite sides of the bed, then climbed under the thin, scratchy blankets that lay in place of our soft duvet. We made no mention of it to each other, simply drew the harsh fabric around ourselves and reached shivering arms out. Her head found the crook of my arm, and we turned toward each other.

"An hallucination."

"A bad dream."

We lay awake in the dark, listening to the wind through black-painted trees, and the distant drone of engines.

I began crying when the first bombs fell. ✪

BIOGRAPHICAL NOTES TO "A DISCOURSE ON THE NATURE OF CAUSALITY, WITH AIR-PLANES" BY BENJAMIN ROSENBAUM

BY BENJAMIN ROSENBAUM

ON MY RETURN from PlausFab-Wisconsin (a delightful festival of art and inquiry, which styles itself "the World's Only Gynarchist Plausible-Fable Assembly") aboard the *P.R.G.B. Śri George Bernard Shaw*, I happened to share a compartment with Prem Ramasson, Raja of Outermost Thule, and his consort, a dour but beautiful woman whose name I did not know.

Two great blond barbarians bearing the livery of Outermost Thule (an elephant astride an iceberg and a volcano) stood in the hallway outside, armed with sabres and needlethrowers. Politely they asked if they might frisk me, then allowed me in. They ignored the short dagger at my belt—presumably accounting their liege's skill at arms more than sufficient to equal mine.

I took my place on the embroidered divan. "Good evening," I said.

The Raja flashed me a white-toothed smile and inclined his head. His consort pulled a wisp of blue veil across her lips, and looked out the porthole.

I took my notebook, pen, and inkwell from my valise, set the inkwell into the port provided in the white pine table set in the wall, and slid aside the strings that bound the notebook. The inkwell lit with a faint blue glow.

The Raja was shuffling through a Wisdom Deck, pausing to look at the incandescent faces of the cards, then up at me. "You are the plausible-fabulist, Benjamin Rosenbaum," he said at length.

I bowed stiffly. "A pen name, of course," I said.

"Taken from *The Scarlet Pimpernel?*" he asked, cocking one eyebrow curiously.

"My lord is very quick," I said mildly.

The Raja laughed, indicating the Wisdom Deck with a wave. "He isn't the most heroic or sympathetic character in that book, however."

"Indeed not, my lord," I said with polite restraint. "The name is chosen ironically. As a sort of challenge to myself, if you will. Bearing the name of a notorious anti-Hebraic caricature, I must needs be all the prouder and more subtle in my own literary endeavors."

"You are a Karaite, then?" he asked.

"I am an Israelite, at any rate," I said. "If not an orthodox follower of my people's traditional religion of despair."

The prince's eyes glittered with interest, so—despite my reservations—I explained my researches into the Rabbinical Heresy which had briefly flourished in Palestine and Babylon at the time of Ashoka, and its lost Talmud.

"Fascinating," said the Raja. "Do you return now to your family?"

"I am altogether without attachments, my liege," I said, my face darkening with shame.

Excusing myself, I delved once again into my writing, pausing now and then to let my Wisdom Ants scurry from the inkwell to taste the ink with their antennae, committing it to memory for later editing. At PlausFab-Wisconsin, I had received an assignment—to construct a plausible-fable of a world without zeppelins—and I was trying to imagine some alternative air conveyance for my characters when the Prince spoke again.

"I am an enthusiast for plausible-fables myself," he said. "I enjoyed your 'Droplet' greatly."

"Thank you, Your Highness."

"Are you writing such a grand extrapolation now?"

"I am trying my hand at a shadow history," I said.

The prince laughed gleefully. His consort had nestled herself against the bulkhead and fallen asleep, the blue gauze of her veil obscuring her features. "I adore shadow history," he said.

"Most shadow history proceeds with the logic of dream, full of odd echoes and distorted resonances of our world," I said. "I am experimenting with a new form, in which a single point of divergence in history leads to a new causal chain of events, and thus a different present."

"But the world *is* a dream," he said excitedly. "Your idea smacks of Democritan materialism—as if the events of the world were produced purely by linear cause and effect, the simplest of the Five Forms of causality."

"Indeed," I said.

"How fanciful!" he cried.

I was about to turn again to my work, but the prince clapped his hands thrice. From his baggage, a birdlike Wisdom Servant unfolded itself and stepped agilely onto the floor. Fully unfolded, it was three cubits tall, with a trapezoidal head and incandescent blue eyes. It took a silver tea service from an alcove in the wall, set the tray on the table between us, and began to pour.

"Wake up, Sarasvati Sitasdottir," the prince said to his consort, stroking her shoulder. "We are celebrating."

The servitor placed a steaming teacup before me. I capped my pen and shooed my Ants back into their inkwell, though one crawled stubbornly towards the tea. "What are we celebrating?" I asked.

"You shall come with me to Outermost Thule," he said. "It is a magical place—all fire and ice, except where it is greensward and sheep. Home once of epic heroes, Rama's cousins." His consort took a sleepy sip of her tea. "I have need of a plausible-fabulist. You can write the history of the Thule that might have been, to inspire and quell my restive subjects."

"Why me, Your Highness? I am hardly a fabulist of great renown. Perhaps I could help you contact someone more suit-able—Karen Despair Robinson, say, or Howi Qomr Faukota."

"Nonsense," laughed the Raja, "for I have met none of them by chance in an airship compartment."

"But yet . . . ," I said, discomfited.

"You speak again like a materialist! This is why the East, once it was awakened, was able to conquer the West—we understand how to read the dream that the world is. Come, no more fuss."

I lifted my teacup. The stray Wisdom Ant was crawling along its rim; I positioned my forefinger before her, that she might climb onto it.

Just then there was a scuffle at the door, and Prem Ramas-son set his teacup down and rose. He said something admonitory in the harsh Nordic tongue of his adopted country, something I imagined to mean "come now, boys, let the conductor through." The scuffle ceased, and the Raja slid the door of the compartment open, one hand on the hilt of his sword. There was the sharp hiss of a needlethrower, and he staggered backward, collapsing into the arms of his consort, who cried out.

The thin and angular Wisdom Servant plucked the dart from its master's neck. "Poison," it said, its voice a tangle of flutelike harmonics. "The assassin will possess its antidote."

Sarasvati Sitasdottir began to scream.

It is true that I had not accepted Prem Ramasson's offer of employment—indeed, that he had not seemed to find it necessary to actually ask. It is true also that I am a man of letters, neither spy nor bodyguard. It is furthermore true that I was unarmed, save for the ceremonial dagger at my belt, which had thus far seen employment only in the slicing of bread, cheese, and tomatoes.

Thus, the fact that I leapt through the doorway, over the fallen bodies of the prince's bodyguard, and pursued the fleeting form of the assassin down the long and curving corridor, cannot be reckoned as a habitual or forthright action. Nor, in truth, was it a considered one. In Śri Grigory Guptanovich Karthaganov's typology of action and motive, it must be accounted an impulsive-transformative action: the unreflective moment which changes forever the path of events.

Causes buzz around any such moment like bees around a hive, returning with pollen and information, exiting with hunger and ambition. The assassin's strike was the proximate cause. The prince's kind manner, his enthusiasm for plausible-fables (and my work in particular), his apparent sympathy for my people, the dark eyes of his consort—all these were inciting causes.

The psychological cause, surely, can be found in this name that I have chosen—"Benjamin Rosenbaum"—the fat and cowardly merchant of *The Scarlet Pimpernel* who is beaten and raises no hand to defend himself; just as we, deprived of our Temple, found refuge in endless, beautiful elegies of despair, turning our backs on the Rabbis and their dreams of a new beginning. I have always seethed against this passivity. Perhaps, then, I was waiting—my whole life—for such a chance at rash and violent action.

The figure—clothed head to toe in a dull gray that matched the airship's hull—raced ahead of me down the deserted corridor, and descended through a maintenance hatch set in the floor. I reached it, and paused for breath, thankful my enthusiasm for the favorite sport of my continent—the exalted Lacrosse—had prepared me somewhat for the chase. I did not imagine, though, that I could overpower an armed and trained assassin. Yet, the weave of the world had brought me here—surely to some purpose. How could I do aught but follow?

Beyond the proximate, inciting, and psychological causes, there are the more fundamental causes of an action. These address how the action embeds itself into the weave of the world, like a nettle in cloth. They rely on cosmology and epistemology. If the world is a dream, what caused the dreamer to dream that I chased the assassin? If the world is a lesson, what should this action teach? If the world is a gift, a wild and mindless rush of beauty, riven of logic or purpose—as it sometimes seems—still, seen from above, it must possess its own aesthetic harmony. The spectacle, then, of a ludicrously named practitioner of a half-despised art (bastard child of literature and philosophy), clumsily attempting the role of hero on the middledeck of the *P.R.G.B. Śri George Bernard Shaw*, must surely have some part in the pattern—chord or discord, tragic or comic.

Hesitantly, I poked my head down through the hatch. Beneath, a spiral staircase descended through a workroom cluttered with tools. I could hear the faint hum of engines nearby. There, in the canvas of the outer hull, between the *Shaw*'s great aluminum ribs, a door to the sky was open.

From a workbench, I took and donned an airman's vest, supple leather gloves, and a visored mask, to shield me somewhat from the assassin's needle. I leaned my head out the door.

A brisk wind whipped across the skin of the ship. I took a tether from a nearby anchor and hooked it to my vest. The assassin was untethered. He crawled along a line of handholds and footholds set in the airship's gently curving surface. Many cubits beyond him, a small and brightly colored glider clung to the *Shaw*—like a dragonfly splayed upon a watermelon.

It was the first time I had seen a glider put to any utilitarian purpose—espionage rather than sport—and immediately I was seized by the longing to return to my notebook. Gliders! In a world without dirigibles, my heroes could travel in some kind of immense, powered gliders! Of course, they would be forced to land whenever winds were unfavorable.

Or would they? I recalled that my purpose was not to repaint our world anew, but to speculate rigorously according to Democritan logic. Each new cause could lead to some wholly new effect, causing in turn some unimagined consequence. Given different economic incentives, then, and with no overriding, higher pattern to dictate the results, who knew what advances a glider-based science of aeronautics might achieve? Exhilarating speculation!

I glanced down, and the sight below wrenched me from my reverie:

The immense panoply of the Great Lakes—

—their dark green wave-wrinkled water—

—the paler green and tawny yellow fingers of land reaching in among them—

—puffs of cloud gamboling in the bulk of air between—

—and beyond, the vault of sky presiding over the Frankish and Athapascan Moeity.

It was a long way down.

"*Malkat Ha-Shamayim*," I murmured aloud. "What am I doing?"

"I was wondering that myself," said a high and glittering timbrel of chords and discords by my ear. It was the recalcitrant, tea-seeking Wisdom Ant, now perched on my shoulder.

"Well," I said crossly, "do you have any suggestions?"

"My sisters have tasted the neurotoxin coursing the through the prince's blood," the Ant said. "We do not recognize it. His servant has kept him alive so far, but an antidote is beyond us." She gestured towards the fleeing villain with one delicate antenna. "The assassin will likely carry an antidote to his venom. If you can place me on his body, I can find it. I will then transmit the recipe to my sisters through the Brahmanic field. Perhaps they can formulate a close analogue in our inkwell."

"It is a chance," I agreed. "But the assassin is half-way to his craft."

"True," said the Ant pensively.

"I have an idea for getting there," I said. "But you will have to do the math."

The tether which bound me to the *Shaw* was fastened high above us. I crawled upwards and away from the glider, to a point the Ant calculated. The handholds ceased, but I improvised with the letters of the airship's name, raised in decoration from its side.

From the top of an *R*, I leapt into the air—struck with my heels against the resilient canvas—and rebounded, sailing outwards, snapping the tether taut.

The Ant took shelter in my collar as the air roared around us. We described a long arc, swinging past the surprised assassin to the brightly colored glider; I was able to seize its aluminum frame.

I hooked my feet onto its seat, and hung there, my heart racing. The glider creaked, but held.

"Disembark," I panted to the Ant. "When the assassin gains the craft, you can search him."

"Her," said the Ant, crawling down my shoulder. "She has removed her mask, and in our passing I was able to observe her striking resemblance to Sarasvati Sitasdottir, the prince's consort. She is clearly her sister."

I glanced at the assassin. Her long black hair now whipped in the wind. She was braced against the airship's hull with one hand and one foot; with the other hand she had drawn her needle-thrower.

"That is interesting information," I said as the Ant crawled off my hand and onto the glider. "Good luck."

"Good-bye," said the Ant.

A needle whizzed by my cheek. I released the glider and swung once more into the cerulean sphere.

Once again I passed the killer, covering my face with my leather gloves—a dart glanced off my visor. Once again I swung beyond the door to the maintenance room and towards the hull.

Predictably, however, my momentum was insufficient to attain it. I described a few more dizzying swings of decreasing arc-length until I hung, nauseous, terrified, and gently swaying, at the end of the tether, amidst the sky.

To discourage further needles, I protected the back of my head with my arms, and faced downwards. That is when I noticed the pirate ship.

It was sleek and narrow and black, designed for maneuverability. Like the *Shaw*, it had a battery of sails for fair winds, and propellers in an aft assemblage. But the *Shaw* traveled in a predictable course and carried a fixed set of coiled tensors, whose millions of microsprings gradually relaxed to produce its motive force. The new craft spouted clouds of white steam; carrying its own generatory, it could rewind its tensor batteries while underway. And, unlike the *Shaw*, it was armed—a cruel array of arbalest-harpoons was mounted at either side. It carried its sails below, sporting at its top two razor-sharp saw-ridges with which it could gut recalcitrant prey.

All this would have been enough to recognize the craft as a pirate—but it displayed the universal device of pirates as well, that parody of the Yin-Yang: all Yang, declaring allegiance to imbalance. In a yellow circle, two round black dots stared like unblinking demonic eyes; beneath, a black semicircle leered with empty, ravenous bonhomie.

I dared a glance upward in time to see the glider launch from the *Shaw*'s side. Whoever the mysterious assassin-sister was, whatever her purpose (political symbolism? personal revenge? dynastic ambition? anarchic mania?), she was a fantastic glider pilot. She gained the air with a single, supple back-flip, twirled the glider once, then hung deftly in the sky, considering.

Most people, surely, would have wondered at the *meaning* of a pirate and an assassin showing up together—what resonance, what symbolism, what hortatory or aesthetic purpose did the world intend thereby? But my mind was still with my thought-experiment.

Imagine there are no causes but mechanical ones—that the world is nothing but a chain of dominoes! Every plausible-fabulist spends long hours teasing apart fictional plots, imagining consequences, conjuring and discarding the antecedents of desired events. We dirty our hands daily with the simplest and grubbiest of the Five Forms. Now I tried to reason thus about life.

Were the pirate and the assassin in league? It seemed unlikely. If the assassin intended to trigger political upheaval and turmoil, pirates surely spoiled the attempt. A death at the hands of pirates while traveling in a foreign land is not the stuff of which revolutions are made. If the intent was merely to kill Ramasson, surely one or the other would suffice.

Yet was I to credit chance, then, with the intrusion of two violent enemies, in the same hour, into my hitherto tranquil existence?

Absurd! Yet the idea had an odd attractiveness. If the world was a blind machine, surely such clumsy coincidences would be common!

The assassin saw the pirate ship; yet, with an admirable consistency, she seemed resolved to finish what she had started. She came for me.

I drew my dagger from its sheath. Perhaps, at first, I had some wild idea of throwing it, or parrying her needles, though I had the skill for neither.

She advanced to a point some fifteen cubits away; from there, her spring-fired darts had more than enough power to pierce my clothing. I could see her face now, a choleric, wild-eyed homunculus of her phlegmatic sister's.

The smooth black canvas of the pirate ship was now thirty cubits below me.

The assassin banked her glider's wings against the wind, hanging like a kite. She let go its aluminum frame with her right hand, and drew her needlethrower.

Summoning all my strength, I struck the tether that held me with my dagger's blade.

My strength, as it happened, was extremely insufficient. The tether twanged like a harp-string, but was otherwise unharmed, and the dagger was knocked from my grasp by the recoil.

The assassin burst out laughing, and covered her eyes. Feeling foolish, I seized the tether in one hand and unhooked it from my vest with the other.

Then I let go.

Since that time, I have on various occasions enumerated to myself, with a mixture of wonder and chagrin, the various ways I might have died. I might have snapped my neck, or, landing on my stomach, folded in a V and broken my spine like a twig. If I had struck one of the craft's aluminum ribs, I should certainly have shattered bones.

What is chance? Is it best to liken it to the whim of some being of another scale or scope, the dreamer of our dream? Or to regard the world as having an inherent pattern, mirroring itself at every stage and scale?

Or *could* our world arise, as Democritus held, willy-nilly, of the couplings and patternings of endless dumb particulates?

While hanging from the *Shaw*, I had decided that the protagonist of my Democritan shadow-history (should I live to write it) would be a man of letters, a dabbler in philosophy like myself, who lived in an advanced society committed to philosophical materialism. I relished the apparent paradox—an intelligent man, in a sophisticated nation, forced to account for all events purely within the rubric of overt mechanical causation!

Yet those who today, complacently, regard the materialist hypothesis as dead—pointing to the Brahmanic field and its

Wisdom Creatures, to the predictive successes, from weather to history, of the Theory of Five Causal Forms—forget that the question is, at bottom, axiomatic. The materialist hypothesis—the primacy of Matter over Mind—is undisprovable. What successes might some other science, in another history, have built, upon its bulwark?

So I cannot say—I cannot say!—if it is meaningful or meaningless, the fact that I struck the pirate vessel's resilient canvas with my legs and buttocks, was flung upwards again, to bounce and roll until I fetched up against the wall of the airship's dorsal razor-weapon. I cannot say if some Preserver spared my life through will, if some Pattern needed me for the skein it wove—or if a patternless and unforetellable Chance spared me all unknowing.

There was a small closed hatchway in the razor-spine nearby, whose overhanging ridge provided some protection against my adversary. Bruised and weary, groping inchoately among theories of chance and purpose, I scrambled for it as the boarding gongs and klaxons began.

The *Shaw* knew it could neither outrun nor outfight the swift and dangerous corsair—it idled above me, awaiting rapine. The brigand's longboats launched—lean and maneuverable black dirigibles the size of killer whales, with parties of armed sky-bandits clinging to their sides.

The glider turned and dove, a blur of gold and crimson and verdant blue disappearing over the pirate zeppelin's side—abandoning our duel, I imagined, for some redoubt many leagues below us.

Oddly, I was sad to see her go. True, I had known from her only wanton violence; she had almost killed me; I crouched battered, terrified, and nauseous on the summit of a pirate corsair on her account; and the kind Raja, my almost-employer, might be dead. Yet I felt our relations had reached as yet no satisfactory conclusion.

It is said that we fabulists live two lives at once. First we live as others do: seeking to feed and clothe ourselves, earn the respect and affection of our fellows, fly from danger, entertain and satiate ourselves on the things of this world. But then, too, we live a second life, pawing through the moments of the first, even as they happen, like a market-woman of the bazaar sifting trash for treasures. Every agony we endure, we also hold up to the light with great excitement, expecting it will be of use; every simple joy, we regard with a critical eye, wondering how it could be changed, honed, tightened, to fit inside a fable's walls.

The hatch was locked. I removed my mask and visor and lay on the canvas, basking in the afternoon sun, hoping my Ants had met success in their apothecary and saved the Prince; watching the pirate longboats sack the unresisting *P.R.G.B. Śri George Bernard Shaw* and return laden with valuables and—perhaps—hostages.

I was beginning to wonder if they would ever notice me—if, perhaps, I should signal them—when the cacophony of gongs and klaxons resumed—louder, insistent, angry—and the longboats raced back down to anchor beneath the pirate ship.

Curious, I found a ladder set in the razor-ridge's metal wall that led to a lookout platform.

A war-city was emerging from a cloudbank some leagues away.

I had never seen any work of man so vast. Fully twelve great dirigible hulls, each dwarfing the *Shaw*, were bound together in a constellation of outbuildings and propeller assemblies. Near the center, a great plume of white steam rose from a pillar; a Heart-of-the-Sun reactor, where the dull yellow ore called Yama's-flesh is driven to realize enlightenment through the ministrations of Wisdom-Sadhus.

There was a spyglass set in the railing by my side; I peered through, scanning the features of this new apparition.

None of the squabbling statelets of my continent could muster such a vessel, certainly; and only the Powers—Cathay, Gabon, the Aryan Raj—could afford to fly one so far afield, though the Khmer and Malay might have the capacity to build them.

There is little enough to choose between the meddling Powers, though Gabon makes the most pretense of investing in its colonies and believing in its supposed civilizing mission. This craft, though, was clearly Hindu. Every cubit of its surface was bedecked with a façade of cytoceramic statuary—couples coupling in five thousand erotic poses; theromorphic gods gesturing to soothe or menace; Rama in his chariot; heroes riddled with arrows and fighting on; saints undergoing martyrdom. In one corner, I spotted the Israelite avatar of Vishnu, hanging on his cross between Shiva and Ganesh.

Then I felt rough hands on my shoulders.

Five pirates had emerged from the hatch, cutlasses drawn. Their dress was motley and ragged, their features varied—Sikh, Xhosan, Baltic, Frankish, and Aztec, I surmised. None of us spoke as they led me through the rat's maze of catwalks and ladders set between the ship's inner and outer hulls.

I was queasy and light-headed with bruises, hunger, and the aftermath of rash and strenuous action; it seemed odd indeed that the day before, I had been celebrating and debating with the plausible-fabulists gathered at Wisconsin. I recalled that there had been a fancy-dress ball there, with a pirate theme; and the images of yesterday's festive, well-groomed pirates of fancy interleaved with those of today's grim and unwashed captors on the long climb down to the bridge.

The bridge was in the gondola that hung beneath the pirate airship's bulk, forwards of the rigging. It was crowded with lean and dangerous men in pantaloons, sarongs and leather trousers. They consulted paper charts and the liquid, glowing forms swimming in Wisdom Tanks, spoke through bronze tubes set in the walls, barked orders to cabin boys who raced away across the airship's webwork of spars.

At the great window that occupied the whole of the forward wall, watching the clouds part as we plunged into them, stood the captain.

I had suspected whose ship this might be upon seeing it; now I was sure. A giant of a man, dressed in buckskin and adorned with feathers, his braided red hair and bristling beard proclaimed him the scion of those who had fled the destruction of Viking Eire to settle on the banks of the Father-of-Waters.

This ship, then, was the *Hiawatha MacCool*, and this the man who terrorized commerce from the shores of Lake Erie to the border of Texas.

"Chippewa Melko," I said.

He turned, raising an eyebrow.

"Found him sightseeing on the starboard spine," one of my captors said.

"Indeed?" said Melko. "Did you fall off the *Shaw*?"

"I jumped, after a fashion," I said. "The reason thereof is a tale that strains my own credibility, although I lived it."

Sadly, this quip was lost on Melko, as he was distracted by some pressing bit of martial business.

We were descending at a precipitous rate; the water of Lake

Erie loomed before us, filling the window. Individual whitecaps were discernable upon its surface.

When I glanced away from the window, the bridge had darkened—every Wisdom Tank was gray and lifeless.

"You there! Spy!" Melko barked. I noted with discomfiture that he addressed me. "Why would they disrupt our communications?"

"What?" I said.

The pirate captain gestured at the muddy tanks. "The Aryan war-city—they've disrupted the Brahmanic field with some damned device. They mean to cripple us, I suppose—ships like theirs are dependent on it. Won't work. But how do they expect to get their hostages back alive if they refuse to parley?"

"Perhaps they mean to board and take them," I offered.

"We'll see about that," he said grimly. "Listen up, boys—we hauled ass to avoid a trap, but the trap found us anyway. But we can outrun this bastard in the high airstreams if we lose all extra weight. Dinky—run and tell Max to drop the steamer. Red, Ali—mark the aft, fore, and starboard harpoons with buoys and let 'em go. Grig, Ngube—same with the spent tensors. Fast!"

He turned to me as his minions scurried to their tasks. "We're throwing all dead weight over the side. That includes you, unless I'm swiftly convinced otherwise. Who are you?"

"Gabriel Goodman," I said truthfully, "but better known by my quill-name—'Benjamin Rosenbaum'."

"Benjamin Rosenbaum?" the pirate cried. "The great Iowa poet, author of 'Green Nakedness' and 'Broken Lines'? You are a hero of our land, sir! Fear not, I shall—"

"No," I interrupted crossly. "Not that Benjamin Rosenbaum."

The pirate reddened, and tapped his teeth, frowning. "Aha, hold then, I have heard of you—the children's tale-scribe, I take it?

'Legs the Caterpillar'? I'll spare you, then, for the sake of my son
Timmy, who—"

"No," I said again, through gritted teeth. "I am an author of
plausible-fables, sir, not picture-books."

"Never read the stuff," said Melko. There was a great shudder,
and the steel bulk of the steam generatory, billowing white clouds,
fell past us. It struck the lake, raising a plume of spray that spotted
the window with droplets. The forward harpoon assembly followed, trailing a red buoy on a line.

"Right then," said Melko. "Over you go."

"You spoke of Aryan hostages," I said hastily, thinking it wise
now to mention the position I seemed to have accepted *de facto*, if
not yet *de jure*. "Do you by any chance refer to my employer, Prem
Ramasson, and his consort?"

Melko spat on the floor, causing a cabin boy to rush forward
with a mop. "So you're one of those quislings who serves Hindoo
royalty even as they divide up the land of your fathers, are you?"
He advanced towards me menacingly.

"Outer Thule is a minor province of the Raj, sir," I said. "It is
absurd to blame Ramasson for the war in Texas."

"Ready to rise, sir," came the cry.

"Rise then!" Melko ordered. "And throw this dog in the brig
with its master. If we can't ransom them, we'll throw them off at
the top." He glowered at me. "That will give you a nice long while
to salve your conscience with making fine distinctions among
Hindoos. What do you think he's doing here in our lands, if not
plotting with his brothers to steal more of our gold and helium?"

I was unable to further pursue my political debate with Chippewa Melko, as his henchmen dragged me at once to cramped
quarters between the inner and outer hulls. The prince lay on the
single bunk, ashen and unmoving. His consort knelt at his side,

weeping silently. The Wisdom Servant, deprived of its animating field, had collapsed into a tangle of reedlike protuberances.

My valise was there; I opened it and took out my inkwell. The Wisdom Ants lay within, tiny crumpled blobs of brassy metal. I put the inkwell in my pocket.

"Thank you for trying," Sarasvati Sitasdottir said hoarsely. "Alas, luck has turned against us."

"All may not be lost," I said. "An Aryan war-city pursues the pirates, and may yet buy our ransom; although, strangely, they have damped the Brahmanic field and so cannot hear the pirates' offer of parley."

"If they were going to parley, they would have done so by now," she said dully. "They will burn the pirate from the sky. They do not know we are aboard."

"Then our bad luck comes in threes." It is an old rule of thumb, derided as superstition by professional causalists. But they, like all professionals, like to obfuscate their science, rendering it inaccessible to the layman; in truth, the old rule holds a glimmer of the workings of the third form of causality.

"A swift death is no bad luck for me," Sarasvati Sitasdottir said. "Not when he is gone." She choked a sob, and turned away.

I felt for the Raja's pulse; his blood was still beneath his amber skin. His face was turned towards the metal bulkhead; droplets of moisture there told of his last breath, not long ago. I wiped them away, and closed his eyes.

We waited, for one doom or another. I could feel the zeppelin rising swiftly; the *Hiawatha* was unheated, and the air turned cold. The princess did not speak.

My mind turned again to the fable I had been commissioned to write, the materialist shadow-history of a world without zeppelins.

If by some unlikely chance I should live to finish it, I resolved to make do without the extravagant perils, ironic coincidences, sudden bursts of insight, death-defying escapades and beautiful villainesses that litter our genre and cheapen its high philosophical concerns. Why must every protagonist be doomed, daring, lonely, and overly proud? No, my philosopher-hero would enjoy precisely those goods of which I was deprived—a happy family, a secure situation, a prosperous and powerful nation, a conciliatory nature; above all, an absence of immediate physical peril. Of course, there must be conflict, worry, sorrow—but, I vowed, of a rich and subtle kind!

I wondered how my hero would view the chain of events in which I was embroiled. With derision? With compassion? I loved him, after a fashion, for he was my creation. How would he regard me?

If only the first and simplest form of causality had earned his allegiance, he would not be placated by such easy saws as "bad things come in threes." An assassin, *and* a pirate, *and* an uncommunicative war-city, he would ask? All within the space of an hour?

Would he simply accept the absurd and improbable results of living within a blind and random machine? Yet his society could not have advanced far, mired in such fatalism!

Would he not doggedly seek meaning, despite the limitations of his framework?

What if our bad luck were no coincidence at all, he would ask. What if all three misfortunes had a single, linear, proximate cause, intelligible to reason?

"My lady," I said, "I do not wish to cause you further pain. Yet I find I must speak. I saw the face of the prince's killer—it was a young woman's face, in lineament much like your own."

"Shakuntala!" the princess cried. "My sister! No! It cannot be! She would never do this—" she curled her hands into fists. "No!"

"And yet," I said gently, "it seems you regard the assertion as not utterly implausible."

"She is banished," Sarasvati Sitasdottir said. "She has gone over to the Thanes—the Nordic Liberation Army—the anarcho-gynarchist insurgents in our land. It is like her to seek danger and glory. But she would not kill Prem! She loved him before I!"

To that, I could find no response. The *Hiawatha* shuddered around us—some battle had been joined. We heard shouts and running footsteps.

Sarasvati, the prince, the pirates—any of them would have had a thousand gods to pray to, convenient gods for any occasion. Such solace I could sorely have used. But I was raised a Karaite. We acknowledge only one God, austere and magnificent; the One God of All Things, attended by His angels and His consort, the Queen of Heaven. The only way to speak to Him, we are taught, is in His Holy Temple; and it lies in ruins these two thousand years. In times like these, we are told to meditate on the contrast between His imperturbable magnificence and our own abandoned and abject vulnerability, and to be certain that He watches us with immeasurable compassion, though He will not act. I have never found this much comfort.

Instead, I turned to the prince, curious what in his visage might have inspired the passions of the two sisters.

On the bulkhead just before his lips—where, before, I had wiped away the sign of his last breath—a tracery of condensation stood.

Was this some effluvium issued by the organs of a decaying corpse? I bent, and delicately sniffed—detecting no corruption.

"My lady," I said, indicating the droplets on the cool metal, "he lives."

"What?" the princess cried. "But how?"

"A diguanidinium compound produced by certain marine dinoflagellates," I said, "can induce a deathlike coma, in which the subject breathes but thrice an hour; the heartbeat is similarly undetectable."

Delicately, she felt his face. "Can he hear us?"

"Perhaps."

"Why would she do this?"

"The body would be rushed back to Thule, would it not? Perhaps the revolutionaries meant to steal it and revive him as a hostage?"

A tremendous thunderclap shook the *Hiawatha MacCool*, and I noticed we were listing to one side. There was a commotion in the gangway; then Chippewa Melko entered. Several guards stood behind him.

"Damned tenacious," he spat. "If they want you so badly, why won't they parley? We're still out of range of the war-city itself and its big guns, thank Buddha, Thor, and Darwin. We burned one of their launches, at the cost of many of my men. But the other launch is gaining."

"Perhaps they don't know the hostages are aboard?" I asked.

"Then why pursue me this distance? I'm no fool—I know what it costs them to detour that monster. They don't do it for sport, and I don't flatter myself I'm worth that much to them. No, it's you they want. So they can have you—I've no more stomach for this chase." He gestured at the prince with his chin. "Is he dead?"

"No," I said.

"Doesn't look well. No matter—come along. I'm putting you all in a launch with a flag of parley on it. Their war-boat will have to stop for you, and that will give us the time we need."

So it was that we found ourselves in the freezing, cramped bay of a pirate longboat. Three of Melko's crewmen accompanied us—one at the controls, the other two clinging to the longboat's sides. Sarasvati and I huddled on the aluminum deck beside the pilot, the prince's body held between us. All three of Melko's men had parachutes—they planned to escape as soon as we docked. Our longboat flew the white flag of parley, and—taken from the prince's luggage—the royal standard of Outermost Thule.

All the others were gazing tensely at our target—the war-city's fighter launch, which climbed toward us from below. It was almost as big as Melko's flagship. I, alone, glanced back out the open doorway as we swung away from the *Hiawatha*.

So only I saw a brightly colored glider detach itself from the *Hiawatha*'s side and swoop to follow us.

Why would Shakuntala have lingered with the pirates thus far? Once the rebels' plan to abduct the prince was foiled by Melko's arrival, why not simply abandon it and await a fairer chance?

Unless the intent was not to abduct—but to protect.

"My lady," I said in my halting middle-school Sanskrit, "your sister is here."

Sarasvati gasped, following my gaze.

"Madam—your husband was aiding the rebels."

"How dare you?" she hissed in the same tongue, much more fluently.

"It is the only—" I struggled for the Sanskrit word for 'hypothesis', then abandoned the attempt, leaning over to whisper in English. "Why else did the pirates and the war-city arrive together? Consider: the prince's collusion with the Thanes was discovered by the Aryan Raj. But to try him for treason would provoke great scandal and stir sympathy for the insurgents. Instead, they made sure rumor of a valuable hostage reached Melko. With the prince in the hands of the pirates, his death would simply be a regrettable calamity."

Her eyes widened. "Those monsters!" she hissed.

"Your sister aimed to save him, but Melko arrived too soon—before news of the prince's death could discourage his brigandy. My lady, I fear that if we reach that launch, they will discover that the Prince lives. Then some accident will befall us all."

There were shouts from outside. Melko's crewmen drew their needlethrowers and fired at the advancing glider.

With a shriek, Sarasvati flung herself upon the pilot, knocking the controls from his hands.

The longboat lurched sickeningly.

I gained my feet, then fell against the prince. I saw a flash of orange and gold—the glider, swooping by us.

I struggled to stand. The pilot drew his cutlass. He seized Sarasvati by the hair and spun her away from the controls.

Just then, one of the men clinging to the outside, pricked by Shakuntala's needle, fell. His tether caught him, and the floor jerked beneath us.

The pilot staggered back. Sarasvati Sitasdottir punched him in the throat. They stumbled towards the door.

I started forward. The other pirate on the outside fell, untethered, and the longboat lurched again. Unbalanced, our craft drove in a tight circle, listing dangerously.

Sarasvati fought with uncommon ferocity, forcing the pirate towards the open hatch. Fearing they would both tumble through, I seized the controls.

Regrettably, I knew nothing of flying airship-longboats, whose controls, it happens, are of a remarkably poor design.

One would imagine that the principal steering element could be moved in the direction that one wishes the craft to go; instead, just the opposite is the case. Then, too, one would expect these brawny and unrefined air-men to use controls lending themselves to rough usage; instead, it seems an exceedingly fine hand is required.

Thus, rather than steadying the craft, I achieved the opposite.

Not only were Sarasvati and the pilot flung out the cabin door, but I myself was thrown through it, just managing to catch with both hands a metal protuberance in the hatchway's base. My feet swung freely over the void.

I looked up in time to see the Raja's limp body come sliding towards me like a missile.

I fear that I hesitated too long in deciding whether to dodge or catch my almost-employer. At the last minute courage won out, and I flung one arm around his chest as he struck me.

This dislodged my grip, and the two of us fell from the airship.

In an extremity of terror, I let go the prince, and clawed wildly at nothing.

I slammed into the body of the pirate who hung, poisoned by Shakuntala's needle, from the airship's tether. I slid along him, and finally caught myself at his feet.

As I clung there, shaking miserably, I watched Prem Ramasson tumble through the air, and I cursed myself for having caused the very tragedies I had endeavored to avoid, like a figure in an Athenian tragedy. But such tragedies proceed from some essential flaw in their heroes—some illustrative hubris, some damning vice. Searching my own character and actions, I could find only that I had endeavored to make do, as well as I could, in situations for which I was ill-prepared. Is that not the fate of any of us, confronting life and its vagaries?

Was my tale, then, an absurd and tragic farce? Was its lesson one merely of ignominy and despair?

Or perhaps—as my shadow-protagonist might imagine—there was no tale, no teller—perhaps the dramatic and sensational events I had endured were part of no story at all, but brute and silent facts of Matter.

From above, Shakuntala Sitasdottir dove in her glider. It was folded like a spear, and she swept past the prince in seconds. Nimbly, she flung open the glider's wings, sweeping up to the falling Raja, and rolling the glider, took him into her embrace.

Thus encumbered—she must have secured him somehow—she dove again (chasing her sister, I imagine) and disappeared in a bank of cloud.

A flock of brass-colored Wisdom Gulls, arriving from the Aryan war-city, flew around the pirates' launch. They entered its empty cabin, glanced at me and the poisoned pirate to whom I clung, and departed.

I climbed up the body to sit upon its shoulders, a much more comfortable position. There, clinging to the tether and shivering, I rested.

The *Hiawatha MacCool*, black smoke guttering from one side of her, climbed higher and higher into the sky, pursued by the Aryan war-boat. The sun was setting, limning the clouds with gold and pink and violet. The war-city, terrible and glorious, sailed slowly by, under my feet, its shadow an island of darkness in the sunset's gold-glitter, on the waters of the lake beneath.

Some distance to the east, where the sky was already darkening to a rich cobalt, the Aryan war-boat which Melko had successfully struck was bathed in white fire. After a while, the inner hull must have been breached, for the fire went out, extinguished by escaping helium, and the zeppelin plummeted.

Above me, the propeller hummed, driving my launch in the same small circle again and again.

I hoped that I had saved the prince after all. I hoped Shakuntala had saved her sister, and that the three of them would find refuge with the Thanes.

My shadow-protagonist had given me a gift; it was the logic of his world that had led me to discover the war-city's threat. Did this mean his philosophy was the correct one?

Yet the events that followed were so dramatic and contrived—precisely as if I inhabited a pulp romance. Perhaps he was writing my story, as I wrote his; perhaps, with the comfortable life I had given him, he longed to lose himself in uncomfortable escapades of this sort. In that case, we both of us lived in a world designed, a world of story, full of meaning.

But perhaps I had framed the question wrong. Perhaps the division between Mind and Matter is itself illusory; perhaps Randomness, Pattern, and Plan are all but stories we tell about the inchoate and unknowable world which fills the darkness beyond the thin circle illumed by reason's light. Perhaps it is foolish to ask if I or the protagonist of my world-without-zeppelins story is the more real. Each of us is flesh, a buzzing swarm of atoms; yet each of us also a tale contained in the pages of the other's notebook. We are bodies. But we are also the stories we tell about each other. Perhaps not knowing is enough.

Maybe it is not a matter of discovering the correct philosophy. Maybe the desire that burns behind this question is the desire to be real. And which is more real—a clod of dirt unnoticed at your feet, or a hero in a legend?

And maybe behind the desire to be real is simply wanting to be known.

To be held.

The first stars glittered against the fading blue. I was in the bosom of the Queen of Heaven. My fingers and toes were getting numb—soon frostbite would set in. I recited the prayer the ancient heretical Rabbis would say before death, which begins, "Hear O Israel, the Lord is Our God, the Lord is One."

Then I began to climb the tether. ✪

YOU *COULD* GO HOME AGAIN

BY HOWARD WALDROP

The Joint is Jumpin'

THEY HAD SLIPPED THEIR MOORINGS at Ichinomaya, Japan, in the early evening of September 15, 1940, amid the euphoric shouts of well-wishers, fresh from the Tokyo Olympics that had just ended.

Wolfe hadn't noticed the crowds. He'd arrived late, a couple of new shirts (specially tailored—the Japanese weren't used to six-foot-six men buying off their racks, and he'd had to get the address of a British men's shop from someone at the American Embassy) in one hand, his old suitcase and bulging, torn briefcase in the other. He'd barely made it; the boarding platform was being unbolted at the bottom as he ran up to it.

He'd been shown to his stateroom; felt a lurch as they got under way. Then he'd folded down the couch that made into an upper and lower berth, and had sprawled across the lower one and had slept for a little more than an hour.

He awoke near sunset. The bell in the dining salon was ringing. He was disoriented. Then memories of the last two weeks had come back to him; the Olympics, the crowds, being a giant once more (as he used to feel in America before the operation and the

327

weight loss) in a world of Lilliputian Japanese.

He put on his robe, found the Gentlemen's washroom for his set of cabins, showered, then shaved, something he'd forgotten to do during the last two days of *bon voyage* parties.

He went back to his stateroom, made up the couch and changed for dinner. Then he laid his things out on the desk while sitting on the folding, backless stool which fit under it. (Wolfe was glad of that: he'd usually had to take the backs off chairs in the old days—his body had been so tall and thick, chairs had seemed like toys that cramped him, making him feel like a golliwog in some circus act.)

He went to the reading and writing room just after dinner (he'd had double portions of everything) and dashed off a postcard or two, which he knew he would forget about if he didn't do it then. He could have put them in the pneumatic tube that took them straight to the mailroom, but decided to take them there himself tomorrow. Instead, he read over the passenger list.

It was the usual kind for a trip going back to Europe and America from the Orient the long way, going west. Wolfe had traveled every possible way in his life: luxury liners, tramp steamers, ferries, airplanes, coal barges, buses, a thousand different trains, cars (after that National Parks thing—six thousand miles in twelve days with two guys that led up to the illness that almost killed him two years ago—he'd sworn never to ride in any automobile but a taxi cab again), bicycles, hay wagons, once even roller-skating for two miles with some kids when he lived in Brooklyn.

There were the usual two dozen nationalities on the manifest— lots of Americans, Brits, Frenchmen, Indians, Syrians, Swedes, Germans, a Russian or two (probably White), some Brazilians and Argentines, an Italian count, and several Japanese.

In all, there were 320 passengers and a crew of 142 on the first leg of this trip. Several would be leaving in India, more no doubt getting on there, going on to Egypt, then up to Italy, and the rest of the European stops.

As he read the list, a man with sergeant's chevrons on his R.A.F. uniform came into the writing salon, nodded, sat down and began scribbling on a small pad.

Wolfe heard music in the air. They must have cleared away the last of the dishes from the evening meal, the stewards would have pulled back the tables, and the band begun to play in the main salon. He finished the postcard in his (since the operation) much smaller and more controlled loopy scrawl. He looked at his watch. It had been an hour since he'd eaten. Time had a way of getting away from him lately.

He stood, nodded to the R.A.F. man, who gave him back a strange smile. The man was heavily tanned, though blondish; his eyes stood out like bright blue marbles in a brown statue. It re-minded him of the face of one of the stone angels that used to stand on the porch of his father's shop in Asheville.

Wolfe checked his own reflection in the corridor mirror—brown suit, buff vest, white shirt. Thinning on top (he turned his head far to the left, smoothed the bit of hair that always stood at right angles over the scar from the brain operation), cheeks now a little sunken in a long wide face (three teeth removed, and seventy-five pounds of lost weight), eyes too big and bright. He pulled on the knot of his black tie with its Harvard Club tie tack, grimaced to make sure there was no food on his teeth, and went back to the main salon.

He eased his way through the few couples who stood talking at the doorway of the ballroom. Art Deco metal palms arched to each side of the opening, forming a heart-shaped portal in a glassine wall.

It was smoky inside. Candles were lit on the tables; waiters went back and forth between the chairs and the dimly-lit bar on the right side. Wolfe made his way toward it, where other men traveling alone, and a few women, stood watching the band.

Bars were always something Wolfe had liked in the old days.

The band—clarinet, banjo, violin, cornet, drums, bass and pi-ano—were on a small raised platform. The unused piano looked dull and grey from the bar area. Probably the light, thought Wolfe. The band was in evening wear. They played "Marie" but, as no one was singing, it sounded thin. A spot for dancing had been cleared; no one was taking advantage of that, either.

"Bourbon and Coca-Cola," said Wolfe to the barman. That was one thing about a trip like this. Everyone was first-class: there were no passenger divisions, no one-deck-for-you-Mr.-Average-Guy, the other for the Hoity-Toity. That was one reason Wolfe had chosen to travel this way.

He got his drink, turned, and leaned against the aluminum bar with his right elbow. He saw, with some discomfort, two women looking at him, talking back and forth. He knew, without a second glance, that they were asking each other whether that could be *him*; no, he's tall but too thin-looking, and much older than his photos. (The one on the jacket of his newest book had been taken two years ago, before the operation. Not that he didn't look bad enough then, he just looked differently, and worse, now.) Wolfe fo-cused his attention toward the front of the salon. He'd had plenty of shipboard flings in his time. (The great love of his life, so they told him in those fuzzy first days at Johns Hopkins, had started on the *Berengaria* in 1926. To him it was only a skewed memory. When he had seen the woman, Aline, for the first time during his recovery, he had been puzzled. This woman—twenty years older than me, hard of hearing, hair going grey—was the love of my life?) But in the last two years, some memories had come back. (Wolfe sometimes viewed himself as standing on the far northern shore of Canada, looking out to sea, and occasionally an iceberg, heavy with remembrance and emotion, would drift toward him from the North Pole of Time, crash into him, immersing him in a flood of scents, thoughts, visions, from a past usually as closed off to him as if he were locked in a vault with no key.) He recalled some of the affair with Aline; the memories were fragmentary. He remembered fights as often as lovemaking, jealousy of her theater friends as well as the quiet afternoons in Paris hotels, an attempt of hers at what he first thought of as suicide, which wasn't.

Now, he was on his way to Germany to see another woman.

As he turned toward the band, Wolfe saw a huge light-skinned black man with a pencil-thin mustache sitting at a table near the front, deep in conversation with two other Negroes.

It was then that Wolfe realized how unobservant he had become. The last thing he would have thought was that the T. W. Waller on the passenger list was Fats.

Wolfe had seen him many times before. He dimly remembered trips to Harlem in the late twenties when he had still been an English instructor at Washington Square College. They'd gone to Connie's Club, where Waller was playing to packed houses. He'd had quite a following among the jazz-mad students. One night Wolfe had been surprised to hear Waller on the radio, singing some novelty tune. Then suddenly, he had been everywhere. While Wolfe had been struggling to be a playwright, Waller had three or four revues or musicals running in the late twenties—and unlike other songwriters and composers, Fats had been right there every night playing the piano for the shows.

Wolfe had seen both movies Waller had made in the thirties. He lit another cigarette, signaled for another drink. The band finished its number, "Nagasaki," a corny tribute to the land they'd just left.

The bandleader—surprisingly, the banjo player—stepped up to the star-webbed microphone (there were loudspeaker boxes at the rear of the salon so people there could hear as well as those up front) and said, "Thank you, thank you," to polite applause. "We're the Band in the Stars, and we'll be with you for the whole voyage. But enough about us—" the drummer hit his tom-tom *thump!* "Tonight, we're honored—we really are—gee whiz!—to have a special appearance, a special guest, one of your fellow passengers—I think he'll be with us to France—" There was a yell from the audience, "England!" "—England, but he says he needs some sleep, so, tonight only, he'll be sitting in—er, ladies and gentlemen, the Band in the Stars, and the *Ticonderoga,* are proud—well, here he is, the one, the only, Mister Fats Waller!"

Some people were taken aback—there were gasps and oohs—as the huge man stood up at his table. Waller was dressed in a black pin-striped double-breasted suit with a black vest, white shirt and a flamingo-pink tie, wide as a normal person's leg. He waved to the crowd. He would have seemed incredibly round, except that he was so tall, he seemed only plump. He walked to the grey piano—like all huge men he had a smooth grace about him, not as if he were moving in slow motion, just that thin people moved too fast; his motions reminded Wolfe of Oliver Hardy's.

"Thank you, thank you," he said, pulling out the piano bench. "I never played on an al-loomin-eum piano before. Let's see—" he ran his fingers over the keys, "—my, my, that's sweet. I see it's tuned in the key of R. Well—" *Blang!* he hit the keys. "Here I am, one night only, 'cause gee I'm tired." The man at the table with him brought a full gin bottle and a glass and set them on the piano. "Oh, suddenly I ain't so tired any more!" He took a drink straight from the bottle. "Wow! That's the stuff. Now I feel like I can play till we hit an iceberg!"

The passengers laughed.

"All right. Here I am, Mrs. Waller's Harmful Little Armful, Mr. Fats himself. Let's go. One two three—" he pointed at the band, who had no idea what was coming, so waited. He broke into a medium stride measure, his left hand covering ten keys between notes, his right way down at the other end, and he began "The Joint is Jumpin'," and the Band in the Stars jumped in right behind him.

As he sang, Fats noticed a great big galoot watching him from the bar with his eyes all bugged out.

The audience roared when they finished the song. Fats drank more gin and leaned back, making tiddling noises with his fingers on the keys.

"Ain't this band sharp?" he asked the audience. "Dressed like that, you'd think the only song they knew was 'Penguins on Parade', wouldn't you? And me as the walrus. Haha."

Then he struck up "I Can't Give You Anything But Love," and the bandleader and he did *sotto voce* repartee over it, making fun of the lyrics, themselves, the passengers. It was totally unrehearsed, so it worked.

"Like working with Charlie McCarthy," said Fats, when it was over. "'Cept he always brings that guy Bergen along. I don't know why he don't split up the act. We know who's got all the talent in that team, don't we?

"I worked with everybody," said Fats. "'Bout the only two I ain't performed with is Donald Duck and Goofy, and I hear tell Disney's trying to book me with them three weeks at the Apollo next year!"

There was laughter and more applause.

"Next thing you know, ol' Fats will be selling U.S. shares and singing on the floor of the Stock Exchange with Ferdinand the Bull! That'd be a tough act to follow, wouldn't it?"

He took a drink. "Well, we gonna hafta do it sooner or later before drunks start yelling for it, so we might as well give Hoagy his two cents now."

Then they did "Stardust" and the cornet man took a surprisingly good solo, for someone in a ship's band.

"Most beautiful music *this* side of the Monongahela!" said Waller as they ended the song. "I can say that without fear of obloquy."

They went into a medley of five of Fats' songs, the band shifting tempo and lyrics with him as soon as they heard a few notes; these guys, they shouldn't just be playing here.

When Waller looked up again, wiping the sweat from his mustache, reaching for the bottle, he noticed that the big guy at the bar was gone.

Wolfe crossed the promenade deck and turned starboard. He went out to the observation area, with its open louvered windows and its delicate decorated aluminum railings.

They were steering west-southwest, so there was still the last vestige of a late summer sunset out the windows. A slight breeze blew in, but much less than Wolfe had expected. He barely felt it in his thinning hair. There was also a hum, like the wind, barely noticeable.

The western sky, over the South China Sea, looked like a peeled pink Crayola left forgotten to melt against a dark blue windowpane. There were stars out up from the horizon. Wolfe looked down at the sea. It was like a flat sheet of dark leaded glass full of the dot and wink of stars, merging with pale red where it met the afterglow.

He heard people passing by toward the salon behind him and the subdued music. Part of him wanted to stay here, watching full night come on, the farthest from home he'd ever traveled. The other half wanted to drink in every note from the piano. There would always be beautiful evenings somewhere in the world; there might not always be a Fats Waller.

With a last puff, he took his cigarette from between his lips, gripped it between thumb and back-curled middle finger, and with a former paperboy's sure aim, flipped it far out away from the window railings.

He watched the orange dot blinking in a long arc; leaning closer to the window he saw it part of its way down the three thousand feet where it would land in the dark, star-pinned sea.

Looking up and out, he could see one of the ten Maybach twenty-cylinder engines that pushed the U.S.I.A.S. *Ticonderoga* through the cloudless sky. He imagined, as he looked at the propellers, that the hum in the air was louder, but it wasn't.

He turned and headed back down the promenade.

Ain't Misbehavin'

He finished "Honeysuckle Rose," the fingers of his left hand splayed far across the keys between each bass note. The right hand came down in another triplet, and the salon was still. Then the roar was deafening.

"My, my, yes," he said. He smiled at the crowd. "You better stay awake, because as soon as Fats is through, he's gonna be asleep for the entire rest of this trip. Them Japanese people done partied me for a week.

"What'll we do next, boys?" he asked the band. "Maybe we

could do something I played with the Little Chocolate Dandies? Or McKenzie's Mound City Blue Blowers? How 'bout the 'West India Blues' I did with the Jamaica Jazzers?"

"We don't know that!" the band yelled back.

"Well, I could do something I learned from James P. Johnson. That's how I learned piano, you know, listening to his piano rolls. I used to turn the drum one note at a time, put my hand on the keys when they went down. Seemed like the only way to learn music to me." He grinned at the passengers. "Course I was only about nine years old then.

"I went in and auditioned for Willie 'The Lion' Smith—he needed a piano player for when he was taking a break. I was 'bout twelve years old, corner of Lexington and 114th, went down there and played for him. He pretended he wasn't even listening. I got through and says, 'what you think, Mr. Lion' and he says, 'no pissant gonna play intermission piano for me in *shorts*' and he marched me next door and bought me my first pair of long pants.

"Well, enough of this frothy badinage, let's get busy, boys! Hang on!"

He made a run, the bandleader started snapping along with his fingers, pulled his banjo up, and the band joined in on "(You're Just a) Square from Delaware."

Fats looked up as they played. "Uh. You know that, huh?" he said over the music. "Looka that man with the horn. Blow the end off it, Lips! Oh. Here comes that hard part again. There it comes. Think I got it. Yes, yes! Let's see if we can't get the last eight bars in six!" The music got faster, lost nothing. "O-Kay!" he said, as they slammed to a finish. During the clapping, Fats reached out and shook the bandleader's hand, nodded to the others.

Then they did "Abercrombie had a Zombie," something Waller had recorded a few months before, which had become, for some obscure reason, a dance-band standard the world over.

"You boys can take a little break if you want to," said Fats. "I'll doodle around on this tin box till you get back, and then we'll see if we can't blow all the rubber off this balloon."

The band rushed for the bar.

Fats straightened himself in his suit.

"You probably wonderin' what I was doing in Japan," he said to the audience. "I woke up yesterday wonderin' the same thing. No, no. Don't get me wrong. I been good lately."

Then he did an instrumental version of "Ain't Misbehavin'."

He stood up when he was through. "Y'all mind if Fats takes off his coat?" They yelled approval.

Two huge wet circles plastered his shirt under the arms. "Y'all tell me the second I begin to perspire, will you?" he asked.

He leaned forward, his hands only a fraction of an inch above the keys, and he played a Bach *partita*.

Until the Real Thing Comes Along

It had been the Olympics that brought him back, in many ways.

In those strange first days in Johns Hopkins, when he was meeting his mother and sisters and friends, for the second time, snatches of his former self would come to him unbidden, but isolated, with no indication which memory came first, or how far apart they were.

Then, like Faulkner's Benjy, things had quit spinning around and settled into a smoothness. The chronology sorted itself. First, he must have done this. This before that, this memory goes somewhere between *here* and *there*.

Still, there had been no linchpin holding it together, no relation to the 'me' he was.

It was in November, two months after the operation. He was still in Baltimore, in a hotel-apartment, looked after by his mother and sister.

"Well, Thomas," said his sister. "I'll be expecting you'll be wanting to see that film about the Olympic Games, especially since it's by that German woman."

"Whatever do you mean?" he'd asked from the couch.

"Well, you were *there*. It's all you talked about or wrote home about for six months."

"That's right," said his mother from the kitchen, where she was shelling butterbeans she'd somehow found for supper in November.

He had a dim memory of crowds, moving colors, events of some kind. What he remembered mostly was a pretty woman's face. Who was she?

His mother wiped her hands on her apron, stood in the doorway.

"Don't tell me you forgot that, too? You were over there for two solid months, both sides of the Games. Then you upped over to Austria and back to Holland, and who-knows-where-else you didn't tell us about."

"There are so many things, Mama. So many trips. They all run together. If you hadn't shown me the postcards, I wouldn't even have known I'd ever been in Seattle."

"Well, you went everywhere, and you was at the Olympics two year ago, and now there's a film about it," said his sister.

"I can't believe I did that and can't remember it," said Tom.

So they'd gone to the movie later that week. It was almost a mistake from the start. It was four hours long, and the first part of it was full of naked people throwing things around and running with torches with their willies out. Tom's sister covered her eyes when there were naked people up there. His mother kidded her about it.

Then the film switched to the '36 Olympics: the opening parade, the torch, events with shooting and horses, then the track and field. Lots of it was in slow motion, or from above or under the ground. Tom knew it was a great film, but he still had no sense of being there. Maybe he'd gone to Europe on a two-month bender and made up all the postcards?

Suddenly there was a Negro on the screen, getting down into starting blocks. Then a long shot of the race ready to begin. The camera lingered over the German entrant. You would think they would show more of the Negro man. Tom was irritated. The cameras panned over to the Chancellor's box. There was a shot of a fat man and a small man with a mustache. Get the camera off them, thought Tom, and back on the track. (It's a film, he reminded himself. These things are not happening right *now*.) Then the gun went off, and in slow-and-normal motion, the Negro man flew down the cinders, getting to the tape three steps ahead of the German and the rest.

There was a shot of the small man with the mustache turning his head sharply to the left, as did the others in the box, toward some commotion up and behind them.

Of course, thought Tom, that's when I yelled so loud for Jesse Owens from the American ambassador's box where I was sitting with Martha Dodd, that even Hitler was annoyed. Göring too.

"Why, Tom," asked his mother, "what's the matter?"

He was sitting still, tears running down his cheeks.

"I remember now, Mama," he said. "I *was* there."

And the pretty woman's name had been Thea Voelker.

*   *   *

"Mr. Wolfe?" asked a young male voice at his side.

"Yes?"

"I'm the social director on this trip," said the thin young man with black hair in a blue suit, holding out his hand. "Call me Jerry."

They shook hands.

"I'm not very sociable right now," said Wolfe. "What can I do for you?"

"Well, I have to ask you the usual questions and all. Like what do you like to do on trips like these?"

"Sleep and write. And drink."

"Hmmm. Mostly what I've got here is people who play checkers, chess, bridge, table tennis, the kinds of things young matrons—there are a few on this trip—like to do. There's skeet shooting tomorrow morning on the port side. Of course, you're welcome to come down to the activity room anytime—I see you're with us to Germany—to look over the stuff for the costume ball two nights from now. Lots of masks and things—I doubt we have any whole costumes themselves that will fit, but ... we just might rig up something to make you very *mysterioso* . . . ."

"Who's *not* going to know it's me?" asked Wolfe, quite seriously, then smiled.

The Jerry guy laughed. "I see what you mean. You're even bigger than your pictures make you look. And I saw the one of you with a German policeman under each arm."

"Really?" asked Wolfe. "Did that make the American papers?"

"I don't know. I was the games instructor on the *Bremerhaven* then. '37. When the chance came last year to sign on the *Ti*, I took it. Some way to travel, huh?"

Wolfe looked out over the dark ocean, heard the hum of the ten engines pushing them gently through the night sky at ninety miles per hour.

"It really is," he said. "My first time on an airship."

"We have tours tomorrow, eleven a.m. and three p.m. ship's time."

"I could maybe make the late one." Wolfe nodded toward the ballroom. "I'm going to watch him play till one of us drops."

"He's pretty good, isn't he? I'm not a boogie-woogie man myself," said Jerry, "but he sure beats . . . ," he looked around conspiratorially, ". . . any of those guys in the ship's band."

Wolfe was looking once more at the darkened horizon aft.

"She's a great ship," he said.

"*He's* a great ship. Him," said Jerry. "That's left over from the German zeps. They called them that, for obvious reasons. Half the crew on the *Ti* and his brother ships are old U.S. Navy men. Took them a long time to get used to it; Navy still calls their airships *her.* Most of the new U.S.I. Airship Service people are trained in Germany, so it comes naturally to them. Still, there's just about a fight about it every week. President Scott, or the Congress Committee or somebody's going to have to make an official declaration, once and for all, is it *him* or *her?*"

"I didn't know that," said Wolfe.

Jerry looked around. "I didn't either, till I signed on the *Ti.* You know, Mr. Wolfe, there's one thing—"

Wolfe thought he knew what was coming. He'd heard it a thousand times since the operation, so it must have happened a million before then. There's one thing I always wanted to be—a writer, only I don't use words so good. But I've got this idea worth a million bucks. I'll tell it to you, and you write it up and we'll split the money fifty-fifty, right down the middle. Wolfe steeled himself, ready to make the usual polite denial, explain how with him, anyway, the ideas had to come from within, be driven by his experiences, his need to tell the story.

"—I bet you get tired of," said Jerry, "is people always coming up to you telling you they got an idea that'll make a million bucks, if only you'll write it up, they'll split the money with you."

Wolfe laughed nervously. Was this some new kind of preamble?

"Does that happen a lot, or am I just imagining it?" asked the social director.

"Way too much," said Wolfe, looking down at the official name tag on his blue suit coat. "Aren't you one of those people who wants to be a writer?"

"Me? Heck no!" said Jerry. "Give up a life of adventure and dames, flying all over the world, free drinks in the only official arm of the U.S. where it's legal to serve 'em? Give that up to sit in some crummy dump in the Bronx, collecting the Social, staring at a wall while the rats gnaw your feet, trying to think of something to write for *Swell Stories?* No thanks!"

Wolfe laughed again.

"Not that that's what *you* do, Mr. Wolfe," said Jerry. "I thought *O, Lost* was a really great first novel."

"Why, thank you."

"There's anything I can do for you on this trip, just let me know. Office is always open—I'm not there, just leave a message on the corkboard. It's really very nice to meet you." They shook hands again, and he was gone back toward the salon.

After watching the darkness and the stars a little longer, Wolfe went back that way too.

It's a Sin to Tell a Lie

Fats took another swallow of gin.

He saw that the big guy who'd been watching from the bar was gone again. He'd seemed familiar somehow. But Fats had looked at a million faces in his time.

He ran his fingers over the keys, went *plink-plonk* at the end.

"I don't know about you," he said to the band, "but I ain't making this trip for my health, no, no." He made another rude noise with the keyboard. "I'm on my way to England, Ole Blighty, right now. Gonna make some records over there for Victorola. Only they don't call it that. Over there, it's His Master's Voice. From Nipper. I knew Nipper when he was just a pup. Why, I knew Nipper when he was so little he was listenin' to two tin cans with a string tied between 'em, instead of a phonograph. That's the truth!

"Gonna record with that Frenchman Grapply. Grape-Elly. I seen him bend a fiddle inside out once, had to play the music backwards so it would come out right. He can play better with his feet than Yehudi can with his teeth. I saw them do it myself. I'm also gonna record some music in a cathedral."

He began a slow melodious tinkling on the piano that wouldn't quite become a recognizable tune.

"Then I'll be coming back to good ol' New York City, U.S. of A. Incorporated. Me and my men will be closing out the New York World's Fair this year—well, we'll be closing it down completely, 'cause when we're done, it's through with."

The drummer hit his snare.

"Thank you, thank you. Any of you people out there come to N.Y.C., come on out and give us a listen. We'll be playing at the big Bandhouse there, for your dancing pleasure. To find us, just follow the fire trucks. I might even play the Mighty Wurlitzer organ for the Aquacade. While you're there, you might want to take in the fair, too."

Another drum roll.

"You can watch me on the new tele-vision there. Hey, you

hear they got a robot-man there, the Electro-Man or something like that? He can talk. He can even play little tunes and stuff. I can hear his *repertoire* now: 'Junkyard Blues', 'Will You Love Me When I'm Oiled and Grey?', and 'Nobody Loves You When You're Rusty and Brown'. Maybe I can get him to sit in with the band.

"We could play duets. Can't be any worse than some of the stuff me and Andreamentano Razafinkierfo—or, as he's better known to the American Society of Composers, Artists and Performers—Andy Razaf and me used to do. He used to say his playing was too mechanical, so working with Electro-Man'll be just like playing with Andy!"

Another snare drum shot, ending in a cow bell.

"Thank you. Okay, let's play something. Try to follow along, boys," he said to the Band in the Stars. "It gets too much for you, just lay down and take off your coats."

He counted off slow, then went into an easy melody with his right hand. After a couple of bars the band joined in, one and two at the time. "That's right, that's it," said Fats.

He sang "It's a Sin to Tell a Lie."

As he did so, he watched the big lunk come back in, knock back a drink, order another, pick it up and leave.

Either he don't like me, thought Fats, or the live experience of Victor's Cheerful Little Earful is too much for him.

Hold Tight (Want Some Seafood Mama)

The song, which had once had one powerful effect on Wolfe, now had another.

Intellectually, he remembered what it meant in the old days. Now, it no longer connected emotionally with anything in him, and that realization made him take his drink out of the ballroom, through the companionway, where the promenade, cabin and lower deck corridors met. His first impulse had been to go back to the reading and writing salon, but instead he went down the spiral aluminum staircase to the lower deck lounge area.

Most of the lower deck was the remainder of the cabins, two more observation areas, and farther back, crew's quarters and mess, and the freight and baggage compartments. He would see it all tomorrow; he knew this from the brochure they'd given him when he'd booked on the flight.

It was much quieter here. A few people sat about on the light but comfortably padded chairs and the settees. Most of the passengers were smoking, something impossible on the old dirigibles, before the Panhandle find of helium in Texas, and the other one in South Africa.

Two men sat at one of the only two cocktail tables—the other was occupied by a *pukka-sahib* type, and Wolfe could do without that right now.

One of the men at the table looked up—it was the R.A.F. sergeant he had seen writing earlier, the one with the sandy hair and blue eyes. Now he was in civilian clothing, khaki shirt, light wool pants—no vest, coat or tie. The other was a tall thin man with a large nose, receding hairline, dressed in a grey suit and vest, with a black tie.

The taller man said something to the other, then motioned Wolfe over. He carried his drink over to them.

"H-hello," said Wolfe, sticking out his hand.

"Join us, please?" asked the taller man. "My name's Norway. This is Sergeant Ross."

"Surely," said Wolfe. "Pleased to meet you, Mr. Norway. Sergeant. I'm an American."

"Who doesn't know that, Mr. Wolfe?" asked the sergeant. "How's the music up there?"

"It's great!" said Wolfe, loosening his tie. "Too good. I had to get away for a few minutes, get some air. I—I've seen him before, long time ago. He was great then, too." He came to a stop, aware that he was sounding like a child who'd just seen his first puppet show.

"Perhaps we'll go listen soon, eh Ross?" asked Norway. The sergeant nodded.

"I suppose I'll just have to put on a coat," he said to Norway; then to Wolfe, "Do relax."

"We were just talking about your country, about the Technocrats. Do you have *any* idea what's next?" asked Norway.

Wolfe stammered. "I'm the last person to ask about anything political. For the first four years of the Depression, all I did was write. I came up for a breather around 1935, then got back to writing and traveling around for another three years. Then I got pretty sick, I'm just now getting on my feet again. So, sorry, I can't help you very much that way."

"Well," said Norway, I don't think your case is much different than most other Americans."

Wolfe laughed. "It did seem like it happened overnight, I guess. Sort of like the Magna Carta with you people."

Sergeant Ross laughed. "I suppose so. But that wasn't in a democracy, with a constitution."

"People will do lots of screwy things when they're hungry," said Wolfe. "I try to steer clear of politics with other Americans. Saves a lot of wear and tear on my fists. Like I said, I haven't paid much attention to politics since the '32 elections."

"That was—Long and Scott?—wasn't it? I was over there while that was going on," said Norway. "Seemed like a lot of

consternation after—what's his name, governor with poliomyeli-
tis . . . Roosevelt—choked on that ham sandwich—"

"It was a chicken bone, I think," said Wolfe.

"—chicken bone just before the convention."

"Whoever was nominated was going to beat Hoover," said
Wolfe. "So it was Long, and he chose Scott for veep, not because
he was a technocrat, but because he was a Yankee."

"Then Scott brought in all his technocratic colleagues. I met
most of them back in '33," said Norway. "I never thought it had a
chance of working."

"Well, I don't think it would have, if Long hadn't of been killed,
and Scott took over. And the people hadn't voted for the Twentieth and Twenty-First Amendments."

"Well, you certainly needed the first of those. You got back your
3.2 beer."

"All of America was drunk on 3.2 beer that day," said Wolfe.
"That's one thing I *do* remember. You had to ask *not* to have it if
you went to a restaurant. Scott himself said, 'a little beer is good
for America'."

"He also said, 'a sober America is a working America'," said
Norway.

"Spoken like a true engineer," said Ross.

The tall man looked at him.

Wolfe saw there was an intensity about Ross that he could almost feel, like this conversation was the most important thing
in the world. He'd met people like that before, but usually going along with the intensity was a heaping helping of ego. Wolfe
didn't feel that from this man.

"Uh, what do you do, Mr. Norway, *are* you some kind of engineer?"

Norway laughed. "Well, yes. Aeronautical engineering."

"Why, you must feel right at home!" said Wolfe, pointing all
around them.

Ross laughed very hard.

Wolfe blinked. "Did I say something wrong?"

"No," said Ross. "You said something very funny. Norway built
this airship. And all its sis—" Norway looked at Ross "—brother
ships. Did the designs, top to bottom."

"Really?" asked Wolfe.

"I helped," said the engineer. The U.S. Incorporated Airship
Service called in a very *many* British and German consultants."

"Don't be quite so modest, Neville," said Sergeant Ross.

"You mustn't forget, I also helped with the *101*," said Norway, a
little sourly.

There was a small pause. Wolfe remembered the disaster headlines from many years ago.

"Those were the old days. Things were different then. Hydrogen, for instance," said the sergeant.

"Hydrogen had nothing—"

"Well, Mr. Ross," asked Wolfe, "what brings you halfway around
the world, and on an American airship? If I'm not prying."

"I assure you, I couldn't afford this trip on my non-commis-
sioned officer's pay," he said, smiling. He looked away.

"Since he's too modest to tell you, I will," said Norway. "Sergeant Ross is being flown back to England to be a technical advisor on a motion picture."

"Really? What's it about? Flying? The Great War?"

Ross looked very embarrassed.

"It's about Lawrence," said Norway, looking at Wolfe, who
creased his brow. "T. E.? Of Arabia?"

"Oh!" said Wolfe. "Did you serve with him?"

"I knew Lawrence in Palestine. Before the war. But the man

I knew then was only slightly the one the film is being made about."

"But they still wanted you as technical advisor?"

"Yes. I told them that, but they insisted. I had studied all the man's writings, intimately. I think it was that they wanted." He struck a match against his thumbnail, watched it burn for a few seconds, put it out. "It's going to be a very strange film. Not as strange as it would be if they could find out one-tenth of the truth about him. But still, very strange indeed, if you view his life as a whole." The sergeant looked back down at his drink.

The ghost of a tune came down the stairwell. Wolfe thought at first it was one song, then it sounded like another.

Wolfe finished his bourbon and coke.

"Well," he said, rising, "I'd better get another drink. Can I bring you something? No? This is some spectacular airship, Mr. Norway," he said, stamping his foot against the deck. "And I hope the film goes well for you, Sergeant. I'm sure we'll see each other again—I don't leave till we get to Germany. Come on up and hear the music or you'll be sorry you missed it."

Wolfe went up the circular stairs. As he rose, he looked through the aluminum trusses with the octagons cut out of them that formed the railing, saw that Ross and Norway were talking quietly again, as if he had never been there.

He was at the observation windows again. There was only a night full of stars out there. The interior lights had been dimmed to help the seeing, if there had been anything to watch. They were still running, according to the little ship they moved every hour on the world map beside the bulletin board, down the South China Sea before making the right turn that would take them to Karachi, India, the next stop on the *Ticonderoga*'s around-the-world flight. It had started in New Jersey and would end there. New Jersey—Akron—Ft. Worth (for helium)—San Francisco—Honolulu—Ichinomaya—Karachi—Cairo—Trevino—Friedrichshaffen—Paris—London—New Jersey. Wolfe would be leaving in Germany. He was going to see his German publisher. Now that Germany was back on Zone Time, money, which had been locked up during the years before the Army revolted against Chancellor Hitler after the Sudetenland Debacle, was again flowing in and out of the country. Wolfe was to pick up his royalties from the last two books, and was to meet a translator, Hesse, who had done the last book there, supposedly a very good job indeed. Then he would meet Thea again, and they would have six weeks together in Germany and France, ending up at the Oktoberfest in Munich.

Wolfe lit another cigarette, and as he did so he realized with a start that it was exactly two years to the day since he'd awakened in the bed at Johns Hopkins, after the tubercle had been taken out of his brain. He reached back and rubbed the scarred place on his head.

Two women's voices drifted over from the promenade, then one of them laughed at something.

He felt a small moment of dizziness. It was him, not the airship. He still occasionally had them. He reached his hand out to the aluminum railing past the window louvers, and the world came calm again.

At times like this, Wolfe truly felt something was wrong. Not wrong with him—the doctors reassured him on that—but with everything else. The times. The world. His present life. Like there was something fundamentally wrong with the whole business of living.

He'd felt it that evening two years ago in the hospital, when he'd first come to some of his senses. He'd remembered nothing of the weeks of delirium beforehand. They told him it had been six raving weeks since he had caught the cold that led to the flu that opened the old tubercular lesion. That he had been in Seattle. They might as well have told him that he was from Mars.

He had had the same dislocated feeling many times in the past two years. He talked to the psychiatrist friend of Dr. Dandy, the man who'd operated on him. The psychiatrist told him that it was a fairly common side effect of operations on the brain that entailed any memory loss of one kind or another, and that the feeling should go away with the return of memory. But it hadn't, not yet.

It had been his books and his older manuscripts that reinforced the feeling in him. He had read them all, sometimes again and again, in the past twenty-four months. Most of them were intensely personal writings, books about a writer writing books about a writer. When his memory had begun to return, he recalled some of the true incidents which had been transmogrified into the fiction.

But they no longer connected to the person he was. Phrases, words, sentences, sometimes whole pages spoke out to him; but they did so as to a reader, not as to the man who wrote them. It was like some other guy, with the same name, had written these works, and then taken off on a long vacation while Wolfe was sick, leaving only the words behind, like some jumbled private code. It had been up to Wolfe to discover who this person was, decipher the mystery. He had failed.

He'd gone through the long manuscript he and Perkins had broken off from *Time and the River* in '34, and that he had, evidently, later divided into *The Lost Helen* and *The October Fair*, both of which he had been adding and splicing to just before his illness.

There was an aborted, limited-third-person manuscript Perkins told him was the "Doakesology"—about a guy named Joe Doakes. In other places he was named Paul Spangler. Sometimes they were Eugene Gant, in other places it was "I," in other places George Webber.

Wolfe had read the whole jumble over in two years. They were mostly full of great ringing apostrophes to night and America and food and trains. There was some good writing in them, lots of bad, too much of the mediocre. Mainly, they didn't interest him at all, because he no longer recalled the emotions that had made the Other Wolfe, as he referred to him sometimes, write them.

One chunk of manuscript from the two three-feet-by-four-feet pine packing crates full of them at the Scribner's office did interest him. It was a history, spare, told in the third person about (as Perkins and his mother told him) his North Carolina hill-country ancestors, called here the Pentlands and the Joyners. It was funny. It was exciting. It told a story. It wasn't like any of the other manuscripts that surrounded it.

It was this piece he had taken in the summer of '39, fleshed out and finished, and which Scribner's had published early this year as *The Hills Beyond Pentland*.

The reviewers, most of them, had gone crazy, taking it as a sign that a new, mature Thomas Wolfe was walking the field of letters, a writer more in control, one interested in narrative, who could write about people other than himself. (The entire narrative took place twenty years before he had been born.) That, they said, was worth the price of the book.

Others of course bemoaned the loss of the Wolfe who used to howl at the moon, the ones who wanted him to continue writing stories so that, as one of them said, "you couldn't tell if he was sitting down to a Thanksgiving dinner, or about to have sexual relations." (A line he would cherish forever.)

What neither set of critics knew was that some of the material had been written as far back as 1933. Most of it was in manuscript before the hospital stay. All he'd had to do was finish it just as he had started it; he had been capable of this book seven years before. As to the ones who wanted the Other Wolfe back, he was gone. He had disappeared into a hospital, and another writer, wearing his clothes and face, had come out. That man could no longer churn out dithyrambs at blinding speed, no longer overflowed with words like torrents of hot lava, was not a floodgate waiting to be opened by the business end of a stub pencil.

After the illness Wolfe found that sometimes the writing of a postcard could be an onerous chore. His work, his writing, now came slowly, slower than a mason with his bricks or a cabinet-maker with a piece of cedar. There were times when it did flow—a sentence, paragraphs, two, three: once a whole page. When it happened it left him feeling like he had been touched by the gods. But when it went away, there was nothing to do but go back to words, phrases, a sentence at a time. His manuscripts were now full of crossouts, big and little xxx's, six, seven, eight wrong word choices scratched through.

He asked Maxwell Perkins about it. He paused, in his Connecticut way, and then said:

"You used to write faster than any human being, Tom, but I had to have you take it out by the bucketfuls, whole chapters at a time. The stuff you're doing now is the best you've ever done. Don't worry. Just do it as it comes. You've got all the time in the world now, which you didn't used to think you had, which was what made you write too fast."

It was the longest speech he'd ever heard Perkins make.

There had been the time, just before he'd left on the western trip that made him sick, that he had almost broken with Scribner's. That terrible review by de Voto (rereading it lately, Wolfe could dispassionately see the places where it was right, the places where it was wrong) of the small book he did about the struggle to write *Time and the River*. Something about lawsuits they had settled out of court. Something that had gone on for months about a dentist's bill. (Wolfe had used Scribner's as a bank, drawing off his royalties ten and fifteen dollars at a time.) All those things meant zip now: Wolfe had found nothing as revealing as the ten, twenty, thirty page letters the Other Wolfe had written in the heat of rage, sealed in envelopes, but fortunately never mailed.

The Other Wolfe had been a bitter man in 1937 and '38.

But Maxwell Perkins had stuck with him. His had been the first face he'd seen at Johns Hopkins as he came out from under the sedative; it had been the last in New York when he set out on this journey that led to this dirigible over the South China Sea.

It was very late. Wolfe was tired (he was always tired these days—how had the Other Wolfe denied that body sleep and rest for so long without wearing it completely out?), but he wanted to hear more Fats Waller. If the man were as tired as Wolfe was, he would sleep for the rest of the flight once he quit.

Your Feet's Too Big

The band kept up as best it could.

Fats slammed down on the last notes of "One O'Clock Jump." The sound was still holding in the air when he trilled his way up the scales in the opening to "Christopher Columbus." He sang,

and the band joined in the vocals over the chorus. Waller went
into the falsetto for the crewman's voice, and Columbus' basso,
and then they went into an extended jam in the middle.

The ballroom was still two-thirds full, with other passengers
coming in and going out continually. Crewmen, not allowed there
except on duty, stood in the rear doorway that led to the kitchen;
some danced in there, dimly seen through the cigarette smoke
from the passenger tables.

The song kept growing and expanding; the bandleader took a
kazoo from his breast pocket, blew it into the mike while continuing to slam-pick his banjo. He and Fats put their heads close
together at the microphone, singing in good harmony.

The song rattled to its noisy close.

"Wowee!" said Fats. "Talk about a rumpus! My old heart can't
take much of that. Let's see if we can't slow it down a little bit.
Lessee, maybe I can think of something. Here's a thing we wrote
for a Broadway revue, well, fewer years ago than it seems like.
At least on the law books, this stuff don't cut it in the good old
U.S. of A. any more. Believe me, this song's still true."

The bandleader was looking at him expectantly, as if, for once,
he knew what Waller was going to play. He whispered to the cornet player, who stood up. Fats had just finished speaking when
the horn man blew the two-bar introduction, just like on Fats'
recording, in front of Waller's slow piano notes. Fats smiled for a
second at the horn man, before his face went back thoughtful, and
he began to sing, in the smokiest, slowest voice of the night, his
song "(What Did I Do To Be So) Black and Blue?"

The noise level in the salon dropped, then stopped completely.
There was only Fats' voice, a few piano notes, the quiet accompa-
niment of the band, the muted cornet, slow violin, occasional *tum*
from the banjo.

When he finished, there was no sound at all in the place. Then there was an explosion of applause and yells.

"Thank you, thank you," he said, picking up the gin bottle. He leaned over and said something to the violin player, who put his instrument down on the edge of the aluminum piano.

Then he spun around on the piano bench, propped his immense feet up toward the audience. "You ever tried to buy a pair of Size Fifteen Torpedo Boats in Japan?" he asked. He saw, through the crowd, the big guy who'd been watching him all night from the bar suddenly break into a smile. "You saw these things coming at you on a dark night, you'd run screaming for the police." Then he looked down at himself. "Course, on me, they look positively dainty." He stood and struck a cupid pose. "But they're big, no doubt about it." He sat down and hit the opening *clump-clumps* of "Your Feet's Too Big," the song getting louder and more insistent as he played. Then, on the beginning of the chorus, he hit a note on the piano, stood up, missing two beats, picked up the violin and bow, and continued playing, pulling long vibrating sounds out of the strings, fingering rapidly. The violin looked like a toy in his huge hands, but the music from it filled the ballroom. The passengers yelled. Waller stopped, said: "It's easy, if you just knows how," in a mellifluous voice, finished the chorus on the violin, sat back down, again losing two beats, and ended the song on the piano.

He had been there a long time. Waller had taken off his vest and tie, rolled up his shirtsleeves. Someone brought him a garter, and someone else found a derby hat. He put both on, and posed while the ship's photographer snapped a picture.

"Boy, does this take me back!" he said. "Whoever thought when they was playing this music in the back parlors of sportin'—'scuse my Anglo-Saxonism—houses, we'd end up playin' it in the clouds over China? That's the charm of music, the Hegemony of Harmony, the Triumph of Terpsichore, and other melodious metaphors. Right now, you listen to the Band in the Stars, while ol' Fats has to visit the Necessary Room, or whatever they call the Head on this gasbag. I'll be right back."

"No, no!" yelled the passengers.

"You wanta see a big fat man explode all over a piano, or what?" he asked as he walked out the door, waving the derby.

The Band in the Stars played "Don't Get Around Much Anymore."

In three minutes, Waller was back.

Gonna Sit Right Down and Write Myself a Letter

Try as he would, Wolfe could hardly keep his eyes open, even standing against the bar. The drinks had worked on him, the smoke from the cigarettes and pipes scratched at his eyes. He could no longer drink like the Other Wolfe had. Coffee, which he'd been drinking since he was a child, now made him jumpy; it used to have a wakeful but calming effect on him. He had never really gotten his strength back after the operation.

The two men, Norway and Ross, had come into the ballrooom at some point. They seemed to be enjoying Waller's antics as much as his musicianship, laughing quietly along with the rest of the crowd. At one time or another, every single person on the airship must have watched, crew included. The captain was at a corner table for a while—when he left, the second officer came back. Most of the crew Wolfe saw looked Old Navy, like the social director had said.

Fats and the band plunged ahead on "Darktown Strutters'

Ball," which Wolfe knew had other lyrics than the ones usually sung in public. He was sure Waller knew them; maybe the
violin player too: he had that seedy white musician look of a guy
who spends his off-hours (back on the ground) at places where
liquor (no matter how illegal) and other, stronger things always
flow.

The passengers clapped along, faster on the climbing
notes, slower on the descending ones, joining in on the chorus. Wolfe wished he felt as good as the audience sounded.
He waved away the barman coming toward him, nodded goodnight to Sergeant Ross, who happened to be looking his way,
stepped through the perspex doorway with its stamped aluminum
palm trees, and headed down the corridor.

He thought of looking at the stars one more time, maybe from
the lower deck platform, but decided that if he were too tired for
Waller, he was too tired for the most glorious night that ever was.
There would be nothing to see; the little airship on the big map in
the companionway was still over water.

He turned toward his cabin. Partway down the hall (outside
half the doors people had set pairs of shoes to be shined by the
steward) a woman in evening dress came out into the hall, Jerry
behind her. She was newly-made-up and looked like a million
dollars. The social director was readjusting his tie.

"Ah-mmmm," said Wolfe, pointing his right index finger at
them, rubbing back and forth across it with his left index finger.
The woman stepped back, looking up at him, and blushed. Jerry
turned his head.

"Oh, Mr. Wolfe! Still want the tour tomorrow?"

"The late one, Jerry, please," he said, holding his head, feigning
drunkenness.

"Sure thing! He still playing?"

"They'll have to beat him absolutely to death with a crowbar before he'll quit," said Wolfe.

The social director laughed. "We're on our way there now," he said.

"Have a good time. You won't be able to help yourselves. Good night."

He went to his cabin, opened the door, watched Jerry and the woman turn the corner, the guy slipping his arm around her waist in the instant just before they turned the corner, disappearing toward the far sound of music.

The steward had been in and folded the back of the couch up onto its chains for the upper, and pulled the cushions out on the lower. A two-foot-long ottoman formed an extension of the bottom bunk—one of the things Wolfe had requested when he'd booked the airship. (One thing Aline had done for him was to have him a long bed built for his apartment in those days in Brooklyn—the first he'd ever had in his life that his feet didn't hang off of.)

Wolfe undressed down to his undershirt and pants, took off his shoes (not quite Waller's size fifteens, but big enough) and socks. He hung up his other clothes on the open rack opposite the window. He went to it, and something out toward the horizon caught his eye.

It was a ship. He'd been on many ships before, but none like this one. It was huge, even at this distance, this far up from the ocean. It looked like a floating city, all lights and curves; unlike most steamships it was not open-decked, but streamlined, closed in, like it was a smooth, rounded battleship. There was deck upon deck, row upon row of lighted portholes, all the way down to the waterline. It must have been ten stories tall above the first deck, with five more below that. The funnels looked like double shark fins, silhouetted in their own pools of light.

As he watched, the ship sent a hoot of greeting to the *Ticonderoga*, a long high blast that barely carried across the miles. There was a sudden pale light somewhere beneath Wolfe's vantage point. It revolved, red white blue, red white blue, then went off. One U.S.A. Incorporated vessel greeting another. Then the ship was gone, leaving a line of swirling phosphorescence to each side of the sea to mark where it had been. The *Ticonderoga* was going ninety miles an hour; the other ship must have been making fifty knots.

It had to be the *Columbiad*, bel Geddes-designed, commissioned last year. Like the *Ticonderoga*, it went anywhere it was needed, plied all the lanes, showed the flag in every port; anything from a Caribbean cruise to an around-the-world marathon.

A thin line glowing pale green was the only thing to look at out there on the dark. Wolfe closed his window, cranked it down; the air up here was a little chilly late at night.

His tiredness had lifted for a short while—either seeing Jerry and the woman, or the liner, or both, had taken some of his bone-weariness and drink fumes away.

He sat down at the writing desk, pulled up the folding backless stool, took out a sheet of paper. Of course he could wait to write anything until the night before he got off in Germany—nothing would get to New York faster than the *Ticonderoga* itself; it would drop off its mail sacks in New Jersey nine days from now. But he had many letters to write.

There was a light above the desk but Wolfe kept it off. He reached down inside one of the pockets in his huge traveling briefcase and came up with a box nine inches by four. As he lifted it, one of the flaps on the bottom came open and two C-cell batteries fell out and rolled across the decking.

"Damn!" he said, getting down and crawling after them, bringing them back. Then one of the spare bulbs fell out of the box. He caught it on the first bounce.

From inside its box he pulled a child's nightlight. It was a figure of Mickey Mouse, made out of tin, leaning against a fake red candle at the top of which was a bulb shaped like a flame. Mickey was in his usual shorts with the two big buttons, he wore the shapeless bread-dough shoes, one white-gloved hand was waving, the other cupped around the candle, supporting his weight as he leaned against it like a lamppost. On his face was a confident grin.

Wolfe turned it on, then the light above the desk.

The nightlight had been the second thing he saw in the hospital—first Max's concerned face, then the beaming face of Mickey Mouse.

He'd found that his sister had bought it in those weeks of incoherence out west, before they brought him to Baltimore for the operation. She'd gone down the street from the apartment next to the Seattle hospital and had bought the first battery-powered nightlight she had found, since they knew they would be moving him cross-country on a train soon. She had bought it because Tom had seemed, while irrational, to be afraid of the dark.

He hadn't slept a night in the two years without Mickey being on.

He smiled, took hold of Mickey's outstretched hand.

"Hello, Mickey," he said. Then he answered in a falsetto, as close to Walt Disney's as he could get, "Hello, Tom!"

He laughed in spite of himself. Then he took out his old Parker pen, unscrewed the cap, and got his reading glasses from his jacket pocket.

The stationery was official U.S.A. Incorporated Airship Service letterhead, with the embossed dirigible *Ticonderoga*.

16
September ̶1̶5̶, 1940

Dear Max, (he wrote)

Somewhere way over the South China Sea or the Indian Ocean as I write this. We left six p.m. Tokyo time, it must be four a.m. (that damned Fats Waller has kept everybody up all night with his piano playing!) (just kidding!) The Olympics, as I told you last letter (but this might beat it there), were great. Watched Sunpei Uto set a new 100 meter freestyle record (better than Tarzan's). Since Owens wasn't there, we lost all the dash events in track but won some distance (!) races—an American that can run more than a mile—unheard of in the 1930s! I'm sure you read all this in the papers—will tell you all about them when I get back in November.

Saw Scott F. in L.A. before I came over—has he written you?—he looks bad, Max (don't tell him I said that). He's writing some college movie for Columbia (he wrote a Republic Western under a pen name a few months ago)—when are they going to stop thinking of him as a freshman?—he's in his forties. He tried to get me to stay in Hollywood and write ("just till you get your health back, Tom—lots of money to be made out here"). I told him I wouldn't have any health at all if I had to write for the little tin kings out there. Scott also says, "To hell with Technocracy! I want to go into a bar in broad daylight and get drunk again."

It's not that way on this zep, Max. It flows like water. I'm glad you got me to take it, back in June when I was planning the Olympic trip. Smoother than a liner—we should already have come over 800 miles. Like riding in a fast hotel.

Did I tell you I watched the Olympics some on tele-vision? I know they have it at the World's Fair—but not like Japan. They wanted to keep the locals away from Olympic Stadium, so they broadcast it all over Japan—big department stores, town halls, etc. Saved most of the seats for the tourists. We're way behind them in the field of tele-vision. Tell Howard Scott that I said so next time you see him. Tell him to get his crackedest Technocrats on RCA's butt about it.

By the way, ask the accountant to make sure that if my U.S. Inc. shares get put in with my royalties, to turn them back in to my bank account (cashed!) please. I forgot to leave him a note before I left.

Harry and Caresse Crosby were supposed to be on the trip—but nobody's seen them. They either missed the zep, or maybe even never made it to Japan, or are in their cabin jazzing (Xcuse my French)—they saw Lindbergh land at Le Bourget, remember?—now everybody and his dog are zipping around the world in dirigibles (god, I'm beginning to sound like Fitzgerald!)

I think I saw the Columbiad *below us a while ago. You can check the shipping tables and see if I'm hallucinating, or what, Max. Had to be. Looked like Philadelphia in a canoe. Or have they turned out another once since I left? (There I go again.)*

This letter seemed important when I started it, now it just seems like a letter. Am looking forward to the rest of the trip—tomorrow (today) I get to take the tour. The Other Wolfe would have waxed poetic about it, the grandeur, the size, the mystery of all this, the zep, the people, their baggage, weighing less than this pen I'm writing with. (Somebody told me the pilots like to take off with the whole thing weighing about 200 pounds—something to do with the engines.) Once I would have waxed poetic, now I'm lucky if I can wax my shoes. (Sorry.)

Hear the German guy Hesse did a great job. Did you send Rohwolt the galleys of Child By Tiger *(I'm sure you did) so they can start on that?* O, Lost *and* T. A. T. River *had great translations, everybody tells me H. B. Pentland (called—I forget what—*die Alpen Forever* *or something) is even better than those. In German I mean. Am looking forward to the six weeks with Miss Voelker more than anyone knows. (She said she was writing you, but is ashamed of her English, which is better than mine, Max. Did she?)*

Wolfe sat up and stretched his arms, rubbing his left shoulder. He looked toward the window. He couldn't tell if it was getting light, or what he saw was just the airglow off the ship's silver skin.

Now I'm tired Max, so will write more this afternoon. Will tell you all about the passenger list, starting with Herr Bock, Docteur Canard and Monsieur le Coq, and ascending upward to me. Also various other etceteras.

For now,
Tom

Wolfe lay naked on the bunk, orange in the glow from the night-light. He smoked a last tired cigarette, stubbed it out in the weighted conical ashtray he'd taken off the desk and placed on the floor. There was a dull, not unpleasant throb on the deck. He put his hand up against the wall; it was there too. It must be there all the time, the tension of their passage through the air, the smooth vibrations of the engines against the structure of the ship. It was a calming thing.

He lay with his hands behind his head, staring up at the bottom of the unused bunk above him.

He was more than half a mile in the air, hurtling through the sky at nearly a hundred miles an hour, and he'd been listening to a band playing jazz as if he were in a Manhattan basement. He had never felt safer or more secure in his life.

He turned sideways, to face the dim light. All the familiar

things were around him—his pen on the desk, his battered brief-case, his shoes and socks.

And the nightlight; grinning, confident, like President Scott in a pair of baggy shorts. Wolfe closed his eyes.

Into the future, then, reeking of celluloid and Bakelite though it may be, with Mickey Mouse lighting the way.

Cabin in the Sky

The passengers in the salon felt as if they had been beaten with thousand-pound feathers most of the night. Fats took another drink from his bottle, looked at it, finished it.

He'd taken off the derby hat and the garter. His shirt was trans-parent, wet.

The band had quit two hours before, completely worn out. They'd packed up their instruments, left the stage, now sat at tables, watching, marveling, not believing the man. Not many people noticed they'd gone.

There was a sleeping child at one of the front tables. She began to wake up.

"Here's somethin' I should have played first," said Waller. "Way back when I started tonight."

He ran a bunch of high tinkling trills with his right hand, and in a high voice began singing "Cabin in the Sky."

He finished. The forty or fifty passengers left broke into ap-plause.

He glanced out the door where he could get an angle on a win-dow. The sky seemed paler, the stars beginning to fade.

He looked at the child who'd awakened. Her eyes were puffy as she rubbed them with her sleeve.

"Whose baby child is that?" he asked, pointing. The woman at the next table said "Mine." "Well, Ol' Fats is gonna sing one song, just for her, then he wants you to take her and put her in her little bitty bunk bed, and then come on back. But this one's gonna be for you, darlin'," he said, pointing to the girl. "You can help me sing it if you want to."

A man at another table looked at his Cartier wristwatch as Fats began the bass notes.

"Never mind the hour!" he said to the man, "I got the power!"

He started in, and they all—the little girl, her mother, the passengers, the band members, the crew—all joined in, shaking off their lethargy and sleepiness, as he began singing "Who's Afraid of the Big Bad Wolf?" ✪

AFTERWORD

"Yeah, things are tough all over. Have you heard about Technocracy?"

—Spanky McFarland to "Uncle George"
in *The Kid From Borneo*, 1933

When people ask a writer, "What went into this story?" like as not the answer is "Disconnected reading, a lousy day job, and one bad-emotion night."

I've written plenty like that.

Sometimes, though, the answer is "A whole life."

This was one of those.

There are certain writers that have to be read at a certain age. Too soon, or too late, and they never affect you in the same way.

Burroughs (E. R., not W. S.) you have to hit at twelve or

thirteen so you can go to sleep in trees and imagine a dry creekbed is the dead sea-bottoms of Barsoom. By mistake, the librarian in Arlington, TX gave me my adult library card—which you weren't supposed to get until you turned twelve—on my eleventh birthday. The main benefit was you could check out six books a day, instead of the three *mere children* were allowed. But you could also check out *everything* in the library, even books with words like "damn" and "hell" in them, thought to burn the eyes out of anyone under twelve instantly, in those days. I walked into the room with real novels, and there, all thirty or forty of them, was everything Burroughs had ever written. I went through them six a day for ever-how-many days it took, then went to live in the trees all that fall.

H. P. Lovecraft is for the *summer* between junior and senior years in high school. Cosmic fear hits you about then anyway—you realize you'll soon have to Get a Real Job or Go To College or Both and, in those days, Be Drafted. A dose of Cthulhu helps put those feelings in perspective.

Bradbury's in there, along with what little Robert E. Howard was around before the Lancer paperbacks hit.

If you're going to eventually be a writer like I was there were other, more—literary?—figures. At the age of fourteen, I was going to be Dylan Thomas, the poet. I read all his poems and stories and books. I listened to the Caedmon recordings of him reading, endlessly reread John Malcolm Brinnin's *Dylan Thomas in America* and Rollie McKenna's photobook *The Days of Dylan Thomas*. I wrote horrible Welsh poetry, and worse American. By the time I was sixteen or so, I knew Dylan Thomas had been dead for nine years, and so had my poetry.

But Sidney Michael's play *Dylan* led me to drama, which led to Eugene O'Neill. Between, say, seventeen and twenty, I was going to be Eugene O'Neill. Once again, I read everything by and about him: *Curse of the Misbegotten* by Croswell Bowen, *O'Neill* by Arthur and Barbara Gelb, even *Lost Plays*, a pirated edition of his first horrible attempts at being Strindberg back in 1914. Plays; I wrote plays. The Knights of the Round Table set in the Old West, with Barbed Wire in the place of Modred; the Holy Grail a pass the railroads didn't own—ideas worse than I can even *imagine* now. Plays that were, in the words of Sheldon Leonard in one of his last roles on *Dream On*, "fuckin' allegories." Me imitating O'Neill imitating Strindberg in Little Theater for four years.

Overlaid on that was James Agee, who first came to my dim-bulb attention as a movie critic, then as author of *The Morning Watch* and *A Death in the Family*, but mostly for his unclassifiable *Let Us Now Praise Famous Men*. I remember writing rambling stream-of-consciousness letters to George R. R. Martin so long and heavy it took eight cents to mail them (yes, he and I go back that far), under the influence of Agee's sharecropper book. Yow!

It all fits together, believe it or not, and I'm getting to it. Besides all these (as Ed Sanders says in *The Family*) "sleazo inputs," along with SF books, and plays and history, porn and movies, *Life Magazine* and *Uncle Scrooge Comics*, and television—and overriding most of them—was Thomas Wolfe.

Thomas Wolfe (1900-1938) died eight years to the day before I was born (as I pointed out in "Thirty Minutes Over Broadway" in George's *Wild Cards* anthology). This shambling, stuttering, corn-fed North Carolina giant had four books published while he was alive: *Look Homeward, Angel* (1929), *Of Time and the River* (1935), the short story collection *From Death to Morning* (1935), and his 'how-I-did-it' book, *The Story of a Novel* (1936). After his sudden death, three more books were edited from the literally chest-high pile of manuscript he left: *The Web and the Rock* (1939), *You Can't Go Home Again* (1940), and another collection, *The Hills Beyond* (1941).

Go get a couple of biographies of him to find out about the Real Wolfe. The ones I knew growing up were Andrew Turnbull's *Thomas Wolfe*, Elizabeth Nowell's *Thomas Wolfe* and Richard S. Kennedy's *The Window of Memory: The Literary Career of Thomas Wolfe*. There are tons of newer, more definitive ones, like David Herbert Donald's *Look Homeward: A Biography of Thomas Wolfe*.

Well, such an impact he had you can't imagine. It started the day his first book was published, and it continued well into the '60s. (As Keith Ferrell says, now anyone talking about Tom Wolfe is talking about the mauve-glove guy.) Norman Mailer once wrote an article on the great American writers and said, "Wolfe wrote like the greatest 17-year-old who ever lived." (When he reprinted that article a few years later, he added a footnote to the line: "I should have said, 13-year-old.")

Look Homeward, Angel and its successors are the ultimate *romans-a-clef* (as the critics pointed out loudly), "novels about a novelist writing novels about a novelist." There were several libel suits during his short life, when someone thought he'd cut a little too close to the autobiographical, for-real-and-true, bone. Between 1929 and 1937 he really couldn't, he thought, go home to Asheville, NC again.

Here were books about the long-striding, world-engulfing, book-swallowing, drinking, eating, fighting, fearless and foulmouthed days of a writer too large for any American-made chair. Some of it seems overblown and tortured now (a lot still holds up), but it didn't seem that way in 1929, and it sure as hell didn't to me in 1962.

And, as other people than me have said, Wolfe wasn't at his

best in sprawling novels anyway, where the episodes were attenu-
ated, but in the short novels—say 15-30,000 words—taken out,
tightened up and published in the magazines; like "The Child by
Tiger," "The Web of Earth" and "The Party at Jack's." Don't take
our words for it; read them yourselves.

Along about five years ago I was looking to stretch my (so-called)
literary muscles, and I was thinking and thinking. By and by I fell
asleep. Then I woke up and lay on the couch, terrified because two
ideas had come to me.

Usually ideas coming to me are a Good Thing, but not these.
Because they came in the form of ideas for *novels*.

See, I'm a short-story writer. (Before I go further: a) you can't
make a living writing short stories, and b) you have to write novels
if you want to make money.) So far, I have written two novels—
one of them a collaboration published in 1974, one a real novel
All By Myself published in 1984. Ten Years Apart. There's another
one I've been thinking about for 26 years—I'll get to it Real Soon
Now. Anyway, suddenly, two ideas for novels come to me in the
space of, say, 45 seconds.

I applied the Shiner Method to them. Lewis Shiner says: if you
think you have a novel, think about it real real hard, and it'll turn
into a novella. If you think you have a novella, apply your brain;
it's probably a novelette. If you have a novelette, turn it over and
over, it'll become a short story. If you come up with the idea for a
short story, hey presto! it's a short-short. If you have the idea for a
short-short, forget it and go back to sleep.

Well, try as hard as I could, one of them stayed a novel—someday you'll read it as *The Moone World*. But, lo and behold, the other
turned into a novella, the one you just read.

The image came to me just the way it seems to me it should

have: Thomas Wolfe and Fats Waller returning from the 1940 Tokyo Olympics on a zeppelin.

Do yourself a favor: stop reading here and go listen to some Fats Waller. (There's a list of music I used while writing the story as an appendix to this.) Waller, the most exuberant performer, stride piano player and musician of his time, was the exact person I needed to counterbalance the Wolfe of my story—the one who didn't die at Johns Hopkins in 1938. (In the real 1940, Waller still had three years to go before catching pneumonia on the transcontinental train back east from L.A., and being taken, in a blizzard that stopped all rail traffic in America, to die in the room always kept reserved, until the hotel called and asked, for the then-Senator Harry S. Truman at the Hotel Muehlbach in Kansas City. One piano-player to another, as it were.) If you want to see what the world lost, go rent the videotape of *Stormy Weather* (1943); you can't take your eyes off Waller any time he shows up.

Well, I had Wolfe and Waller, and I knew about dirigibles. That left the Tokyo Olympics of 1940, which is where they *would* have been held. The TV coverage I mention would have happened, too. To leave most of the seats at the new stadium for the *gaijin*, the Japanese were building viewing rooms in department stores, meeting halls and theaters for their *own* Imperial subjects. They would have, essentially, set up live remote coverage for the whole city of Tokyo.

So things had to be different. Like the small matter of there being no WW II.

Which brings us to the question asked by Mr. McFarland to the Wild Man From Borneo in the *Our Gang* short.

Most people remembered it looked like three choices in those
depth-of-the-Depression, do-nothing late Hoover days of 1932:
fascism, communism, anarchy. It takes a heap of depression
to turn Democrats and Republicans into fascists or anarchists,
but things seemed close to that point. Go read about the Bonus
March.

But there weren't just three choices; there were too many, in
fact. (Like in Santa Fe; *everybody* had a theory.) Huey Long had
his Share-the-Wealth Plan ("Every Man A King"). There was the
Townsend Plan: give all the old people in America a hundred
dollars if they *promised* to spend every penny of it before the end
of each month. There was a Single Tax movement: take away all
taxes but one, and redistribute it—locally, statewide, nationally;
everywhere that needs it. Upton Sinclair was running for Governor of California on what can only be described as the Home-
Grown Hot-To-Trotsky Ticket; he even scared off support from
FDR, the Democratic presidential candidate.

And if you were paying attention, even a three-year-old like
Spanky would know the word that kept coming up like a mantra:
Technocracy.

It was the brainchild of a guy named Howard Scott. His idea
was simple: build up a database of all the transportation, industrial, electrical, shipping and social engineers in America. Get them
ready. When Things Went Blooey (sometime in early 1933, after
Hoover was reelected, it looked like from the summer of 1932),
move them in. Get everything back on a supply-need basis; move
goods and services from areas of surplus to scarcity; take over vital
functions; put people to work on the what-we-would-now-call
infrastructure—in some kind of credit arrangement—of all the
things that the Depression had knocked the blocks out from under.

It took hold of the imaginations of all kinds of people, not just the poor. It seemed for the first time someone had pointed out that goods and food were still there, just like in 1929, but what was missing was the capital that moved them from one place to another. Replace the capital with brains; and somewhere in there get the exchange part on some other basis: either work credit, or some other funny-money. (One of their neat proposals was to divide the country into sectors by latitude and longitude, with major centers serving them. I write you from Austin, TX, Sector 9830.)

The Technocrats planned and waited. Scott was everywhere that fall and winter. Then something went terribly, terribly wrong for Technocracy. The wheels didn't come off America. The election came and went. FDR took office. His brain trust did a suck-job on some of the best Technocrat proposals. By early 1933 their time had come, and gone.

There are some still around; they're awfully old, but for a few minutes there they saw, like Wolfe, the shining, golden opportunity.

There was a spate of real interest in Technocracy in 1932: books were published, magazines did feature stories on Scott (Dr. Seuss did a Technocracy cover for the old *Judge* magazine). There was an animated cartoon called *Techno-crazy* and a short called *Techno-cracked.*

I knew from the first time I read about it that I'd someday write a story set in Technocracy World (as surely as I'd known I'd write a story about the 1938 Westinghouse Time Capsule, when I first read about it as a kid: "Heirs of the Perisphere"). So, evidently, did Mack Reynolds, who wrote, as far as I know, the only other Technocracy story, called "Speakeasy." I haven't been able to find it to read it.

What I did was use some of Technocracy's ideas, cross them with some of the half-baked other schemes, and recast the U.S. in the form of a corporation, with dividends (of some kind) for all the shareholder-citizen Technocrats.

I was assuming a dirigible like the projected *Graf Zeppelin II*, a sort of next-step big brother to the *Hindenburg*, filled, of course, with helium from the Texas Panhandle wells (Ft. Worth was a dirigible stop for the *Akron* and *Macon* in the thirties). I'd used the *Ticonderoga* before, in "Hoover's Men," set in yet another alternate past.

I worked hard to get the scene when you realize Wolfe's on a dirigible, not an ocean liner. I'd never done one before; they're hard to pull off without being hokey. There is never any reason to do this *unless* the surprise matters to the story. Nothing is changed to the characters, only the reader. Try it sometime.

I bring in T. E. Lawrence (as Sgt. Ross) for a good reason: after Alexander Korda had to stop filming *I, Claudius* due to Merle Oberon's car wreck, with only 40 minutes of Laughton in the can (there's an image), he immediately wanted to start a bio-pic on Lawrence, who had been a friend of Robert Graves. In my world, Lawrence never took that motorcycle ride that morning in 1935, and was posted to some Far Eastern part of the Empire with the R.A.F.

Same with Norway, who really did help design the *R.101* and all the other British zeps (and a lot of Allied secret weapons of WW II). He was also Nevil Shute, who later wrote *On The Beach* (and an ignored book, now retro-sf, called *In The Wet*).

I also bring J. D. Salinger in for a scratch behind the ears. Hard as it is to believe, the most reclusive writer of the 20th Century *had* once been the social director of an ocean liner as one of his college summer jobs. (He could also have been Eugene O'Neill's son-in-law, instead of Charlie Chaplin. But that's another story . . . .)

I wanted to do a couple of things, and there were a couple I *didn't* want to do.

When most people write about Wolfe, they try to write *like* Wolfe. I wasn't going to do that, except in the letter—and his letters weren't usually like his other writing.

Also, when people write about Wolfe somehow surviving the tuberculosis of the brain (brought on by influenza he probably got by sharing a bottle of whiskey with a seedy individual on the Seattle-Vancouver ferry), they have him continuing to be the free-swinging, logorrheic giant he'd always been.

Operations on the brain take it out of you, folks. I wanted to show a Thomas Wolfe who realistically wasn't the same man. He wouldn't remember some of the things he'd done before. I wanted to show a once-vital, exuberant man struggling to regain (he's not quite sure) what he's lost.

I tried to do that mostly through Waller and his music. Watching him, more than anything else, gives Wolfe some idea of what he, Wolfe, must have once been like, and the long struggle that lies ahead before he even gets close to it again.

Some of this is in the letter Wolfe writes Perkins at the end. He doesn't really know what he's trying to say (any more than he ever did), but he's trying to say *something*.

But with the aid of the Mickey Mouse nightlight, and the letter to Max, through Waller's music, and most of all through the *Ticonderoga*, Wolfe is going home again. ✪

Thanks to George and Jan O'Nale, Charon Wood,
Ms. Deborah Beale, Ellen Datlow and Keith Ferrell
for help in various stages of this project.

APPENDIX: "A MUSICAL INTERLUDE"

This is a list of the music on the tapes I made and listened to while I was writing "You *Could* Go Home Again." You might want to make your own version. This fits on both sides of a 90-minute cassette and half a 60-minute one. You'll notice it's not all contemporary (either the music itself, like the Dylan, or the performer, like '30s music played by '60s neo-jug and jazz bands). What I was aiming at was a mood, something either to get me butt-jumping in my chair, or to calm me down. Besides, there's lots of good music here.

1. "The Joint is Jumpin'"—Fats Waller
2. "Gonna Sit Right Down (and Write Myself a Letter)"—Fats Waller
3. "Mood Indigo"—Jim Kweskin Jug Band
4. "The Sheik of Araby"—Jim Kweskin Jug Band
5. "It's a Sin to Tell a Lie"—Fats Waller
6. "Titanic"—Snaker Dave Ray & Spider John Koerner (*they have it going the wrong way . . . .*)
7. "Ukelele Lady"—Jim Kweskin Jug Band
8. "Christopher Columbus"—Jim Kweskin Jug Band
9. "Your Feet's Too Big"—Fats Waller
10. "My Blue Heaven"—Fats *Domino*
11. "I Can't Give You Anything But Love"—Fats Waller
12. "Mississippi"—Turk Murphy Jazz Band
13. "Shipwreck Blues"—Bessie Smith
14. "Smokey Joe's Cafe"—Stampfel & Weber
15. "Corrina, Corrina"—Bob Dylan
16. "In The Mood"—Henhouse Five Plus Two (*chickens do Miller*)
17. "Aloha ka Manini"—Gabby Pahanui
18. "The Sheik of Araby"—Leon Redbone

19. "Emperor Norton's Hunch"—Queen City Jazz Band
20. "Bethena Waltzes"—Queen City Jazz Band
21. "Shine On Harvest Moon"—Leon Redbone
22. "Phonograph Blues"—Robert Johnson
23. "Willow Weep For Me"—Billy Holiday
24. "Mr. Jelly Roll Baker"—Leon Redbone
25. "Hang Out The Stars in Indiana"—New Mayfair Dance Orchestra
26. "After You've Gone"—Queen City Jazz Band
27. "If We Ever Meet Again This Side of Heaven"—Leon Redbone
28. "Ain't Misbehavin'"—Fats Waller
29. "Black Diamond Bay"—Bob Dylan
30. "Yellow Submarine"—The Beatles
31. "Wear Your Love Like Heaven"—Donovan
32. "Mississippi Rag"—Turk Murphy Jazz Band
33. "Gonna Sit Right Down (and Write Myself a Letter)"—Fats Waller (*again*)
34. "There Goes My Baby"—The Drifters
35. "Sea Cruise"—Frankie Ford
36. "Sincerely"—The Moonglows
37. "Goodnight Sweetheart Goodnight"—The Spaniels

✪   ✪   ✪

DAVID MOLES was born on the anniversary of the *R.101* disaster. He has lived in six time zones on three continents, and hopes some day to collect the entire set. (He is, therefore, grudgingly accepting of the replacement of the zeppelin by the more economical modern jet airliner.) His short stories have appeared in *Polyphony, Say..., Flytrap, Rabid Transit,* and *Asimov's Science Fiction,* as well as on *Strange Horizons;* at least one of those stories has a zeppelin in it. His favorite color is blue and his favorite fictional airship is the pirate vessel *Tiger Moth,* from Hayao Miyazaki's 「天空の城 ラピュタ」 (released in the West as "Laputa: Castle in the Sky"). He currently lives in Seattle. ✪

JAY LAKE was born on the twentieth anniversary of D-Day, in Taiwan, a country that makes up for its lack of zeppelin history by being heir to one of the world's oldest cultural traditions and finest cuisines. He sees David's time zones and raises him by a continent, but shares the same hope of collecting the entire set. Jay's other editing projects include *Polyphony* with Deborah Layne, *44 Clowns* with Mike Brotherton, *Exquisite Corpuscle* with Frank Wu, and *TEL : Stories* solo. His short stories appear in dozens of markets, ranging from *Asimov's* to *Realms of Fantasy,* as well as his collections *American Sorrows, Dogs in the Moonlight,* and *Greetings From Lake Wu.* Jay is the winner of the 2004 John W. Campbell, Jr. Award for Best New Writer. When he's not writing, he lives in Portland, Oregon, within sight of an 11,200-foot volcano, which serves admirably to center his attention. ✪

www.ingramcontent.com/pod-product-compliance
Lightning Source LLC
Chambersburg PA
CBHW020254030726
47499CB00001B/202

* 9 7 8 0 9 7 2 0 5 4 7 7 5 *